A
RELUCTANT
SPY

ROSELYN
TEUKOLSKY

GRAVEYARD

PRESS

Graveyard Press
112 S Orange Grove Blvd
Apt 110
Pasadena, CA 91105

Graveyard Press paperback ISBN-13: 978-1-967036-00-4
Graveyard Press e-book ISBN-13: 978-1-967036-01-1

Visit our website at www.graveyardpress.com

First Graveyard Press Printing: February 2025
Printed in the United States of America
0 9 8 7 6 5 4 3 2 1

DISCLAIMER

The wonderful Department of Computer Science at Cornell University bears no relationship to the den of academic vipers conceived of in *A Reluctant Spy*. Any resemblance to actual people at Cornell is entirely coincidental.

— Roselyn Teukolsky

FOR BRENDA

"You could say that all novels are spy novels and all
novelists are spy masters."
— Ian McEwan

CHAPTER 1

I jumped and I survived; nothing else matters.

Mike and I are decked out in jumpsuits, helmets, and goggles, boarding a tiny Cessna. The day is cloudless, with nothing in the soft blue air but a gentle breeze. The jump is a go.

This is the smallest plane we've ever jumped from. We chose it because it was available on this, my thirtieth birthday, which also happens to be our tenth wedding anniversary. It's been a rocky year, and we're trying to make things right.

Part of the tension is Mike wants me to collaborate on his research, but I'm bored with it, pulling away in another direction. It's tricky, because I'm dependent on his grant. Right now, he's Mr. Professor and I'm Mrs. Research Assistant.

I'm not bitter. I love Mike beyond all reason, more than skydiving and mathematics and even computer programming. He's five foot ten, gorgeous, and all golden ratios, while I'm tall and ungainly. Though we're the same height and weight, my body is all out of whack, with arms too long, knees too knobby, and feet like flippers. In his jumping getup, he's a Greek god, beautiful and remote. My feelings are clear in my mind but dead in my throat because I'm inarticulate and tongue-tied. Always have been.

I blurt out that he looks like skydiving Ken doll, causing him to retort that I look like Barbie, and when I punch him, he says, "Just kidding, darlin'." He's always the joker, revved up, all systems go.

People probably wonder what he sees in me. *Weird, wonderful, and brainy, my Madsy, that's what.*

After a rattling liftoff, our pilot, Todd, deftly takes us on a smooth ride, even though this plane seems flimsy, held together by rubber bands. He's one of the best at handling the rush of air when the door is open, with or without bodies hanging on the edge.

The interior of the plane is a dump, with one fraying seat for the pilot and a dark linoleum floor for everyone else. We'll be jumping from eleven thousand feet, the highest this puddle jumper can go.

Through the window below is the dazzling landscape of the Finger Lakes, Upstate New York.

Mike is okay as a skydiver. I've trained him since our first meeting, and he's earned his licenses fair and square. Certainly, in the first few years, our relationship was symbiotic—I taught him how to fly and he taught me how to be in this world. Socializing is not one of my superpowers.

There's another couple on this load, belted to the floor near the pilot's seat. In theory, all skydivers are my friends; though in practice, my nature gets in the way. Mike does enough chatting for both of us.

Over the PA system, Todd announces we'll be on a jump run in about three minutes—time to ditch our safety belts. I sit like the Buddha, cross-legged and perfectly parallel to the door, gathering my mental energy, but Mike can't sit still for a second, hunched over his knees and rapping his knuckles on the floor. "Blue skies, sweetie," I mouth to him. He grins. It's a running joke between us, his hyperactive personality. It doesn't matter what he's doing—pounding a keyboard or pacing in front of a class.

The door light signals it is time. Our plane-mates will jump first. When they flip the door up, a whoosh of air shudders through our flimsy airplane. The jump light is flashing and out we go: one, two, three, four. Mike has never been a natural jumper, and true to form, he tumbles out inelegantly. Then his training kicks in, and he maneuvers into a stable arch. When I jump, there's a familiar rush of stomach-dropping fear, then...freedom!

The wind roars past—it's cold up here, an icy blast of early June, carrying the faint smell of diesel burning off the Cessna.

The four of us get into a round, grasping hands, legs fanning out behind, floating like Matisse dancers, high above the Earth.

When it's time to separate, we turn—rotating 180 degrees—sweep our arms back, and glide far away.

Soon we are floating free, flying solo. Belly down, I own the sky. There's a tingle in my fingertips, an unbearable lightness that's never with me on Earth.

A glance at my altimeter—six thousand feet, not yet time to deploy my parachute, but close. The friction of the air buoys me up as I gaze down, *far above Cayuga's waters*, Ithaca, and the towers of Cornell University, my academic home.

There are the Finger Lakes vineyards, purple and green, a wine-tasting heaven. And the landing area, a large open space of farmland to the west, where we'll drift as we descend.

It's time. I pull the handle to release my pilot chute and a great orange wing blows out above me. My body jerks out of freefall—*what the hell?*—the lines of the parachute are twisted, pulling the fabric from my control.

Stay calm. Deep breath. I reach up to the bundle of lines and begin to tease them apart, while my canopy twirls madly in the wind. An accelerating spin threatens to sink me if I can't fix the problem. My mind tunes out everything but the job at hand, then, all at once, like the fibers of a rope, the lines untwist and the parachute unfolds. Whew, that was close.

I pull both brakes simultaneously, and my billowing canopy and I surge forward in a rush of relief.

Cool under fire—that's me. My mother once said, "You're a cold fish, Madeline, just like your father." My daddy, who died when I was ten.

"SHIT!!" Mike's shout jolts me out of my reverie. He's way too close to me, which means he didn't track far enough away from our formation. He's already under canopy, but he's out of kilter—his lines uneven—spinning out of control. Why isn't he getting himself out of it? A pulse beats in my neck. "MIKE! RELAX! SHOULDER DOWN!" But in the roar of air, he appears deaf and reels wildly on his axis.

When it seems I've lost him, his shoulder dips low, like it should, and his body slows. Finally...

But the crisis isn't averted. His parachute is a tangle of lines, preventing it from opening properly. How is that possible? I packed it myself.

Now he's flailing about, grabbing at lines, twisting in the wind. It's futile to yell—he won't hear a thing—and yet still I shout, "MIKE! USE THE RESERVE!"

We've never had to use the reserve.

Come on, Mike! Do it, Goddammit!

He is heading toward me in a slow-motion horror show— there's no way to prevent the collision of our parachutes.

Paralysis. Terror on his face. His mouth a frozen scream lost to the wind. The tentacles of his twisted canopy wrap themselves around my lines and I'm sucked into his disaster, my tangled chute going into a slingshot revolution, the world turning upside down. We are lashed together in a twin death spiral, plummeting at 120 miles per hour.

He's frantically yanking his red and silver handles, but his equipment is in catastrophic failure. We're heading for a crash.

In a wild panic, I lunge forward—try to grab onto him— something—help us— futile—

Stop! Think! It's suicide to stay attached. Free yourself! My cold brain clicks in. Just one chance to save us both. Like lightning, I pull my own red cutaway handle and release Mike and the whole damn mess. Then the silver handle—a miracle, it turns—my reserve chute slapping open—too near the ground for good deployment, but maybe I'll get some drag before hitting the ground and perhaps the orange-yellow mass of twisted canvas on Mike will inflate enough to slow him down...

My speed is increasing. *Dear God forgive me...*

Breathe. My reserve is only partially inflated but holding. Any drag is good, and I feel it. A bird flying on damaged wings. Icarus. The sun reflected on the farmland below.

Barreling down too fast to survive.

It all flashes past in a Fibonacci spiral of lake, sky, Mike, Earth, pink, curves, trees, forests, gravity, dragging me down down down into the vortex.

CHAPTER 2

I'm gliding, drifting on the air. Somewhere deep inside is terrible pain. A web of light floats above my eyelids...always there.

The first time I wake the wall is puke gray. I shut my eyes again.

Needles coming out of my arm and wrist. *Ow!* Two wrestlers pin me down. *No!* They're hammering nails in me, and I'm crucified. Can't move. Another needle, another syringe. Then the parachute unfurls and sails into space once more.

My mother is at my bedside, holding my hand. "Oh, Maddie, my poor darling, what have you done?"

"Madeline," my brain says. "Not Maddie. Not Bonnie, not Suzie. Madeline."

She used to tell people I was a difficult child. *On the spectrum.* I remember studying an abacus once, trying to figure out how to get the beads off. The structure was rigid, so the solution was to bang it on the floor until one of the sides broke. Such a moment of triumph—a rainbow of colored beads clattering on the wooden floor.

She was livid. "Why must you break everything I give you?"

I threw a handful of beads at her head. I was three.

One side of my face feels as if it's been pushed into my cranium. A woman clings to my hand, quietly weeping. Mommy?

How she hated the skydiving. "Aren't you afraid you'll damage your eggs?" she once said. *My eggs?* All the eggs must be broken now.

Another day in the hospital, another scene. Rain, thunder, lightning, and sudden darkness. "Backup power," someone yells. The hall lights are extinguished, followed by a red glow. *Am I in hell?*

A long soft dialogue in the background, practically inaudible, sketches out a story, "...cracked pelvis, broken leg, crushed knee...broken ribs." A generic man in a white coat checking my chart and the pulley attached to my leg.

"Are we feeling better today?" he says. There is just one of me, and that person feels like shit. "No."

The doctor sits and makes a steeple with his hands. "Please know, Madeline, you will get better. There's good news, almost miraculous, actually. You landed on a piece of farmland plowed the previous day. It cushioned your fall and probably saved your life. Other than some internal bleeding, your insides are in good shape."

"They hurt...can't breathe..."

"You came down on your side and broke all your ribs on the right. Hurts a lot, I know, but you're young, everything will heal. I'm afraid you'll be in a wheelchair for a while. And no more skydiving for you, young lady."

"I should hope not," my mother says.

My poor suspended leg, disembodied in its big white cast. *It* is *going to skydive again.*

But Mike won't be there. They've already told me. "My husband?" I whisper.

The doctor pats my hand. "I'm afraid he didn't have a chance, Madeline. Death was instantaneous."

Crying hurts—everywhere. Ribs broken. Body broken. Heart broken. We always knew disaster could happen, but in the abstract. You never believe the sky is falling until a chunk of it lands on you.

To my surprise, my mother is crying too. As far as I can tell, she's been living at the hospital for about two weeks, from the day they rushed me in.

Gloria, my favorite nurse, bustles into the room and leans on the railing of my bed. "There's a detective to see ya, Madeline. Says she needs to ask you some questions."

In the movies, when the detective shows up at the hospital and muscles their way into the room where the patient is in no state to talk, the nurses and doctors all shoo them out. In my case, Gloria says,...yes, she's fine...come on in...make yourself comfortable in the chair. That's my mother's chair.

An elegant Black woman in a smart navy pantsuit walks authoritatively into my room and stands at the side of my bed. "Hi, Madeline, I'm Detective Mahoney, New York State Police." She holds a badge in front of my face. Karla Mahoney. "Oh, honey, look at you. Been in the wars, huh?"

No one ever calls me *honey*. It must be the *Zombie Apocalypse* she sees, all bandages and casts with a skeleton head. They had to remove my hair to patch the cuts. A few stitches here and there and some band-aids scattered among pieces of gauze.

Detective Mahoney studies me before sitting, then says, "So sorry about all this, and about Mike."

They're all sorry. I am, too, with zero ability to make small talk. "Why are you here?"

"I'm investigating Mike's death," she says, "trying to understand what happened. May I ask you some questions? Informally, of course—I can see you're sedated."

"Sure." *I don't care.*

Her dark hair is scraped up into a Leaning-Tower-of-Pisa topknot at sixty degrees, an unstable configuration. She's not young. At least twice my age. No wedding ring.

"Did you notice anything out of the ordinary before the jump?" Her voice is like soft gravel.

"Nothing before. Mike was nervous—always is. His parachute opened okay—then he went into a spin—couldn't control it—I packed his rig—" It comes out jumbled because there's a fog in my head. *What does she want?*

"Excuse my ignorance about skydiving, Madeline, but why would he be spinning if his parachute opened okay?"

"His lines were twisted. There's a way to untwist them. But…he panicked…couldn't do it. Then his cutaway handle got stuck…and his reserve parachute wouldn't release." *Death rattle in my voice. Don't want to think about it.*

"How come you packed his gear?" she asks. "Why didn't he pack his own?"

My head lolls off to the side. "He packed mine. It was a romantic thing we did."

"Did you always pack his chute or was it just this one time?"

Her pebbly voice hasn't changed, but it feels like she's dragging some kind of confession from me, like I'm under oath. "One time," I say.

"And your chute was fine?"

"My lines were twisted. It's a…mechanical device. Things can go wrong…we're trained…"

"And then what happened? Did your gear fail too?"

"No—no failure. Mike's chute…collided with mine."

"But you and Mike were not found together." Her eyebrows go up.

"I…cut myself away." My eyes squeeze back the tears. I don't want to see her judging me. "I freed myself…"

She leans over the bed railing and unexpectedly takes my hand, holding it for a beat. *Still Life in Brown and White.* Permission to touch denied. Yellow and orange parachutes, entwined 'til death do us part…

"I'm sorry, Madeline, this is painful, I know." She's invading my airspace, but I get it. There's a half corpse in front of her who didn't save her husband, and she pities it.

She waits a few moments then goes on. "Who had access to the gear before the dive?" *The whole world.*

"The loft is open. Skydivers…trust each other."

"Did people know who owned which kit?"

"No secrets…names on the kits. Why?"

"Well, it could be important if someone fooled around with the chutes before your dive." Her changes in tone…giving me whiplash.

No. "Impossible—"

"So what do you think caused his loss of control?"

"Tension knots in his chute…it sometimes happens. If he'd stayed calm, the lines might have straightened when the canopy blew open."

"So you think his panicking caused the accident?"

"I don't know." It feels like a betrayal.

"What would you say if an FAA safety inspector reported that Mike's rig was tampered with before the dive? That his death was not skydiver's error?"

Trying to decode her through the blur. "Tampered how? I packed it…myself. Checked his lines…"

Detective Mahoney has gold-framed glasses on a chain around her neck. She raises them to her face and refers to her notes. "There were two small knots in the lines of his main parachute. Not tension knots, real knots. The saboteur pulled them tight,"—she tips off the glasses— "which almost certainly led to the spin you described."

"That's crazy!" *Is she accusing me?*

"That's not all," she says, putting on the glasses again. "There were small pieces of wire on his red and silver handles, preventing proper deployment of his reserve parachute."

I stare at her. "No! Not true! Everyone…loved Mike. Who would want to hurt him?"

CHAPTER 3

Gloria appears in the room and says briskly, "You'll need to excuse us, Detective. It's time to check the vitals." Still alive? Heart beating? I've become so docile, it's pathetic. Tongue out, head sideways, arm out for the cuff.

Thankfully, Gloria has my painkiller loaded in the syringe. Shouldn't she be telling the detective it's enough, time to leave the room?

But the leaning tower is back in the chair in her crisp pantsuit, ready to go. "Did Mike have enemies who could profit off his death?" she says.

"Of course he didn't have enemies." Her aggressiveness causes a spurt of adrenaline, a need to push back.

"What about you, Madeline? You and Mike both worked at Cornell. How was that for you?"

Boom. Everything throbbing. "*Work* at Cornell," I say, sharply. "*Work...*"

"Sorry, honey, I know this is hard—but weren't you Mike's assistant?"

"I'm not a *secretary*, Detective." *And I'm not your honey.* I pull myself up in the bed as high as possible, causing the muscles of my broken ribs to spasm. The pain makes me gasp. "I'm a computer scientist." My personhood has been erased by this half-corpse persona.

Not enough strength to explain why Mike was a newly tenured professor, while I'm an untenured research associate, tagging along on his grant.

The detective's eyes are steady, probing. She has a job to do. There's an unemotional vibe to her questioning, matter-of-fact and bloodless, which cuts through the touchy-feely-honey act. She has sharpened her tone.

"Tell me about yourself. You, Mike, your marriage, your job..."

It's so over, my marriage.

If the detective wants details, here they are. Blow by blow.

Maddie is a ne-rd. Maddie is a ne-rd, was the background noise of my school days. I tuned it out and took apart my computer, just for fun, to see what was inside. I was not like the other girls.

MIT accepted me as a math and computer science major, which is where Mike showed up. He told me—much later— he was in all my classes. I was unaware of him, lost in a world of topology, abstract algebra, and computer algorithms.

Two months into my sophomore year, my computer science professor gave the class an assignment that required us to work in pairs. A student in the class appeared out of the blue, stuck out his hand—"Hi, I'm Mike,"—and invited me to be his partner. He'd seen me in front of a computer, typing like lightning.

"No, thanks."

I expected him to push off, but he grinned and said I'd be perfect as a partner. *Symmetrical dimples.* He stood his ground, tall and athletic looking. *Good aerodynamics. Big feet, ideal for landings.* He dropped his backpack onto the floor and said, "C'mon, let's give it a try. I'm smart, I promise. I'll let you choose whatever part of the problem you want."

So sure of himself, he and his Ivy-bound pedigree. Within a minute of my shoulder shrug of assent, he let me know about his 1600 on the SAT and perfect 36 on the ACT. As if it made a difference.

I turn my head toward Karla Mahoney. "Why are men always so comfortable slinging their dicks around?" *Where did that come from?* My meds are providing uplift now, loosening my tongue. Normally, I clam up in the presence of strangers. "Pardon the expression, Detective."

But she laughs and gives an airy wave.

My collaboration with Mike worked well beyond my expectations, which were low. It turned out that Mike Alvarez was a nuts-and-bolts guy, while I was a lightbulb girl, figuring out a solution while he was still reading the specs. But, I had to concede, he was a fabulous programmer. When he'd show me the final version of his program, I'd admire the elegance of his code and ingenuity of his shortcuts, and learn from him. Sometimes, however, I'd expose fallacies in his logic. When he doubted me, I'd devise test data to sink his algorithm. It became a game between us. Could he create code robust enough for me not to break it? The answer was no in the beginning, but eventually, it became mostly yes. We sharpened each other, honing our complementary programming skills.

He was quite smart for someone so good looking, and I began to enjoy working with him. He was easygoing and extravagant in his admiration of me. We got in the habit of putting our heads together after labs. Then bodies, when I taught him how to skydive and we jumped together.

Mike could have had the pick of the student crop, but he stuck with me. He told me I was funny, fierce, and brilliant and he'd rather be with me than anyone else, despite my nerdy personality. Or maybe because of it.

He put his arms around me, pulled me close, and said, "Let's apply to the same grad schools." Simple as that. He was my one and only love.

We got married at Caltech. Of course, my mother didn't like him and thought I could have done better.

Mike and I worked together as grad students and postdocs, honing our research routine. First, we'd solve the problem; then, high on our mutual brilliance, make love. Afterward, more mellow, we tweaked the algorithm. Mike always coded it up, then I tried to break his code.

"I turned him into a brilliant programmer." The detective is listening intently. I sound like a jerk, tooting my horn too much, so I quickly add, "He was very smart. I underestimated him."

Mike, of course, was the one who wrote the papers and presented our work. I had neither patience with the write-ups nor ability in public speaking. The path of least resistance was to let Mike do it. He was a natural, wowing audiences with the brilliance of our work and the force of his charisma.

"So he got a job and you didn't?" the detective says.

"Yes." I bow my head. "It's tough in academia—finding research jobs in the same town. It's called the two-body problem."

It was unthinkable to live apart. We decided to apply to top places in computer science—Carnegie Mellon, Cornell, Urbana-Champaign—as a package deal. There were never two job lines open, however. Just one. Somewhere along the way it became clear that Mike would apply for the "real" job and I'd be the spousal hire. It was a no-brainer. The thought of teaching turned me off, and Mike was a natural. He also had the added advantage of being Hispanic, a minority. We never mentioned my advantage of being a woman in computer science.

It was unspoken at the time, but Mike's ego would never let him play second fiddle.

His trump card in applying for jobs was he'd been promised a generous grant from the McFall Foundation, which would support a full-time research associate, namely me. Cornell would pay my salary the first year, then the grant would kick in. The setup seemed ideal.

We fell in love with Ithaca, especially with Skydive Finger Lakes nearby.

The Computer Science Department embraced Mike, who wouldn't sign on the dotted line until they promised to provide an adjacent office for me. Nonnegotiable. His grant would pay my salary, and Cornell would give me a title—Senior Research Associate.

During the interview, I sat beside Mike without saying boo, while he explained what a great deal it would be for the university. A twofer.

"And this, Detective, is how it worked for seven years. Mike got tenure last year, and, right now, I have the rest of this year, and also next year, left on his grant."

"What was it like for you?" Detective Karla Mahoney asks, softly. "Having to work in a subordinate position? Not having the same prestige as Mike?" She leans toward me in a way that suggests her interest is personal. *What was it like for you, Detective, a Black policewoman rising in the ranks of Upstate New York?*

She must be a very good detective.

"I didn't care. It was a joy to shut the door of my office and disappear into the private universe of our research. No distractions. No interruptions." *No people to deal with.*

My office had a window that looked out onto the campus—the Hotel School and Barton Hall. I watched the seasons change through that window.

In a way, my position was enviable. The Computer Science Department allowed me infinite access to their supercomputer and Cornell's libraries. Plus, my very own front man next door to finish up the coding and present our results to the world. I had no need for accolades.

Mike grew into the job, gaining competence and confidence. The change was so subtle it took me a while to notice. He glowed in the praise of his colleagues. The growth in his self-belief began to cloud his view of his limitations.

"I started resenting him." My voice cracks. "How easily he dealt with success." I'm saying too much, but the words spill out.

The detective's face is impassive, assessing me and my story of heartbreak. "Did Mike give you enough credit for your work?"

"Oh, sure, my name went on all the papers. But I'm not stupid, Detective. Eventually it dawned on me that his colleagues assumed he was being charitable, because I was his wife. They never asked *me* about the work. Everyone went to Mike with their questions."

"And you were okay with that?"

"At first I was."

"And then?"

"After a while, it wasn't okay. But not because I craved glory. I became bored and wanted to branch out. I had some new ideas for decrypting large video files, while Mike wanted to continue our current research on improving encryption. It was—still is—a hot topic."

"Who won?"

"It wasn't a matter of winning or losing. I told Mike I'd be working on decryption and invited him to collaborate with me or not. He went ballistic." I point a finger at my head. "Bang! He swore at me in Spanish—he was fluent—Mexican ancestors—and he punched the wall. He said I was violating our agreement, like I'd signed a legal document to be his research flunky."

"What did you do?" She's on the edge of her seat.

"Kept the peace, Detective Mahoney. His anger frightened me, so I went back to my cave and continued with the encryption series."

Our problems didn't end there. Mike was going through a dry spell and started pumping my brain for new ideas. I resisted. He made a ludicrous suggestion for encrypting small files and I told him he was dumb as a plank. I regretted it straight away, but the damage was done and the shock on his face terrible. For the first time ever, he stormed out of the house and went to work at Cornell for the evening. I'd crossed a line he found hard to forgive.

We got into a cycle of disagreeing about our research. To ease the tension, he went out at night. Our arrangement at work caused me grief. We cooled as a couple. There was no definitive moment; it was more like something inevitable wormed its way into our routine.

The detective inclines her head and watches me. Her face is serious. My brain feels addled. What have I told her? Do I need a lawyer?

"Let me understand something, Madeline. In the middle of all this stress in your marriage, you went skydiving together and packed each other's rigs because it was romantic. Is this what you're telling me?"

"It was a peace offering, on our anniversary," I whisper. "We'd decided to try and move on with our research and make the marriage work. We really were in love, Detective, and wanted to stay together." I jab at my face with a tissue.

"So would you say he was dragging you down in your work?"

"No—never—"

She thinks for a moment and says, "Okay, would you say Mike's death sets you free to move on with your research—your career?"

Even through the morphine, this question pierces me. "Oh, no, God, no..."

I'm drifting off, and she stands to signal the end of the interview. She looks embarrassed. "I know it's weird, honey, but under normal circumstances I'd caution you not to go anywhere." She gestures at my suspended leg and my pathetic, immobilized body. "As I already said—we're treating Mike's death as a homicide."

I manage one more sentence. "I'm a problem solver, Detective...if I wanted to kill him...wouldn't use idiotic knots in his chute lines."

CHAPTER 4

A man I've never seen before stands motionless in the shadows at the back of the funeral parlor. Casually leaning against a pillar, watching me. People come and go, murmuring condolences, gazing into the coffin. But the stranger doesn't approach the front, nor does he look away.

Who is he, and why's he hiding in the back?

Detective Mahoney is in the last row, near an exit. Why does the detective in charge always attend the funeral of the victim?

It's August, two months after the skydive.

The oblivion of endless pain killers has worn off, and now there are sharp edges everywhere.

Aisha Robinson, the computer science administrative assistant, has collaborated with my mother to organize everything, including the storage of Mike's body in a freezer box. They do this in special circumstances. Now Mike has been wheeled out of deep freeze, and the mortician has put him together in a way that makes him presentable. But the apparition in the coffin nauseates me. It's an interloper, a pale wax effigy with too much rouge on its cheeks. It bears no resemblance to my lost husband, the vibrant man in the photo display arranged on a nearby easel.

I lift my face to the gallery of pictures. Mike in his skydiving gear, flashing a victory sign. Mike at the blackboard, arms spread wide. The two of us at our wedding, laughing and immortal.

I make a U-turn in the wheelchair.

The funeral director, a kind man who refers to Mike as "Our Dear, Departed Mike," has placed the coffin on a low cart so I can view him without being lifted. I should be grateful, but I hurt all over and want to punch those who feel free to touch me and squeeze my shoulder. One part of me craves the oblivion of codeine, but my rational inner voice demands cutting down. Those pills turn my brain into scrambled eggs that can't devise a simple algorithm. They dull the danger posed by the Computer Science Department, which has turned up in force on this gray day.

Sitting on the aisle is Judy Holsinger, department chair, dabbing her eyes as if she cared. When she approached me earlier to offer awkward condolences, she said, "Madeline, when you're able to return to work, please do see Aisha to set up an appointment. We need to have a conversation about your options." Which can mean only one thing, despite her pleasant tone—the axe. Judy is a ballbreaker of the first order. Caramel-blonde hair, stylish shoes. Divorced. Beautiful in a vulnerable, bird-like way that belies her toughness. Mike was one of her favorites, but even he steered clear.

When the solemn organ music starts playing, it jolts me from my reverie. A jab at the forward button on my chair causes me to lurch and sideswipe the platform. Damn! Reverse is even worse, but eventually I'm parked next to my mother, whose eyes are red-rimmed.

I'm panic-stricken because Aisha has persuaded me to give a eulogy for Mike, pooh-poohing my fear of public speaking. "I just can't do it," I had said.

She touched my neck with a soft hand. "You knew him best, Madeline. Don't let other speakers hijack your truth."

Everyone listens to Aisha, who is rumored to be descended from Nigerian royalty and runs the Computer Science Department with scary efficiency.

After the mournful organ fugue, the funeral director announces, "We will now have a few words from Madeline Geiger, wife of Our Dear, Departed Mike."

The idea of forming complete sentences in this room of hostile people almost paralyzes me. But of course, I'll drag myself onto the platform and give them their freak show.

There's a rustle in the audience, as heads crane to see me navigate toward the ramp. My hair has grown back in tufts, an unappealing sight. For today, my mother has draped me in something black, dredged out of her wardrobe and discreetly slit open to accommodate my bumps and breakages.

The wheelchair whines as it struggles up the inclined plane. How I loathe being in this chair. It diminishes me. People are embarrassed by it. They must stoop to make eye contact, which I don't always give, because life sucks.

I've become fixated on wheeled things—coffee carts and hospital beds and coffins on wheels rolling into crematoriums. The horror follows me onto the platform now. The musty odor of dead trees and air freshener. A wreath of artificial flowers framing the photo display.

When the chair is parked on the raised platform, the funeral director bumps against a wheel as he tries to lower the mic to accommodate me. No one can get the damn thing to work when it's held at the level of my face. I'll have to shout to be heard. Trouble is, my windpipe is in a knot.

I look up. The stranger in back is still there, arms folded. He's definitely not from the CS Department. Not a skydiver either—too soft and amorphous.

My opening sentence is a stammering disaster. "Mike is...was...the best...person...uh, computer programmer...I know." Sweat runs down my chest.

"Speak up," Mike says. "No one can hear you." His voice, always in my head, trying to train me to speak in public. *No sing-song, Mads—pretend you're talking to me. Plainspoken phrases.*

What I'm expected to say is a mystery. So I talk about skydiving and how game Mike was for new adventures. My stomach churns.

Use your body for emphasis. Choreograph your talk.

I try to sit tall and tell them how he loved Ithaca and Skydive Finger Lakes.

Raise your hand and count the points on your fingers. That forces eye contact with your audience.

But my eyes lock onto the man at the back, who's in my line of sight. He seems riveted by the proceedings, watching me intently. I stare back. He's impeccably dressed, in a dark-blue suit, pale shirt and striped tie. He looks out of place in casual Ithaca, even at a funeral.

Change your pitch and volume. Make them care.

"Mike was my best friend, and I'll miss him." My voice breaks a bit, but I'm a ghost with dry eyes. I won't give them the satisfaction of seeing me cry.

I glance across the room. The mystery man has disappeared.

My eulogy is a struggle to the end. *Rest in peace, Mike.* At last I'm rolling down the ramp. Still alive.

A cousin from California talks about Young Mike, the genius of the family. He was an only child, and his parents are deceased.

One of his skydiving friends tells some unfunny anecdotes about Drunk Mike, the star of the party after a skydive.

The final speaker is David Graham, corralled to speak on behalf of the Computer Science Department. David doesn't have tenure, which makes him vulnerable. He can't say no to any extra shitty thing they ask him to do, like delivering this speech. David looks like a football player, tall and beefy. He doesn't seem like a programmer, which is a stupid thing to say because you could say the same about me.

After a more-than-adequate list of Mike's contributions to the Department, David says, "We'd like to convey our deepest condolences to Maggie, Mike's brave wife. We wish you well and"—he squints at his sheet—"hope you have a speedy recovery."

Poor David. In his six years at Cornell, he's barely spoken two words to me, and doesn't know my name. *Without Mike you're a nobody, so I'll make up a disgusting, belittling name for you, like Maggie.* Mike once said David needed to get going on his research or Judy would get rid of him. His shambling performance stirs some sympathy in me. He's saying nice things. He wants to be here even less than I do.

The ceremony is finally over. The cremation will take place without my presence. Aisha has arranged it down to the last ember. Paid professionals will make the coffin disappear. Someone will deliver the ashes.

The man is sitting on the curb at the side of my car. He's removed his jacket and tie, rolled up his shirt sleeves, and opened some top buttons.

The sight of him startles me. "What do you want?"

His eyes are hiding behind large sunglasses, and he's chewing on a weed.

"Pardon me, ma'am, I need to talk to you privately before you leave. It's in connection with your late husband." His voice has a soft drawl.

"So talk," my mother says. "Madeline is tired. She needs to go home and rest." Mom has moved into my house permanently and become my caregiver. She treats me like she's Mama Bear and I'm her cub.

The thought of Mike going up in flames freaks me out. I need a painkiller. "Call me next week. This isn't a good time."

He stands and removes his glasses, and his eyes are like blue steel. He barely gives my mother a glance. "It must be now. We can have some privacy in that wooded area." He gestures at the trees on the edge of the funeral parlor.

He's pissing me off. "What if I refuse?"

He takes out a badge and holds it at crotch level so I can see it. "FBI, ma'am. Joe Shelmann."

CHAPTER 5

The wheelchair has terrain-friendly wheels that bump along behind him on the grass until we reach a shady alcove behind the trees. It's chilly with the sun gone, and my arms break out in goosebumps.

We're completely hidden from view.

Joe Shelmann lowers himself onto the bulging root of an old tree and dangles his wrists between his knees. "I'm sorry for your loss, Ms. Geiger. I'm not a skydiver, but I sure can imagine the terror you went through."

I don't want to talk about skydiving or shoot the breeze. I want to go home.

"Why am I here?" I say, with no sense of delicacy or restraint.

"Did Mike talk to you about the FBI?" he asks.

"We spoke about lots of things. Can you please get to the point?"

He examines me for a few beats. "So you didn't know he was our paid informant?"

The question is so absurd I can't comprehend it. "What?"

Despite the shade, his sunglasses are back on his unsmiling face.

"We approached him three months ago—someone at Cornell is providing top-of-the-line encryption software to illegal pornographers."

"At *Cornell*? Pornographers?"

"We're not sure. We intercepted a message from an IP address on campus," he says in that soft, unhurried drawl. "Then we couldn't trace the machine, so it may be a bogus address. What we do know is that some programming expert is blocking cops from gaining a backdoor into these terrible online videos."

"What does that have to do with Mike? Or me, for that matter?"

"We suspect there's a rogue programmer in your department, making thousands of dollars on the side—"

"That's ludicrous. This programmer could be anywhere. Everyone and their mother knows how to beef up encryption software."

"We asked Mike to help investigate the Cornell connection—"

"Give me a break. Academics aren't in it for the money."

"With all due respect, ma'am, that's a naïve view. The exploitation porno business has exploded in the last few years—social media, online commerce—there's big money at stake."

"So how did Mike make out in his investigation?" *Mike? Really?*

"Not very well, mainly because it was still early days. Then, out of the blue, he left me a message saying he had a lead. I was supposed to meet him the week before he died. But he didn't show. Nor did he reply when I called his burner phone."

Burner phone?

"Are you suggesting someone from the Computer Science Department tampered with Mike's parachute? Have you spoken to Karla Mahoney—the detective in charge?"

"Detective Mahoney interviewed everyone who worked with Mike. They all told her how much they liked him, and none of them were into parachutes. By the by, ma'am, they all said they didn't know you very well." *True enough.*

The notion of one of those eggheads from Cornell driving out to the skydiving drop zone in the dead of night is beyond surreal.

But Joe Shelmann is serious. There's no humor about him at all. "You're the only person I've told about Mike's undercover work," he says. "We don't know if the encryption expert we're trying to nail is the person who caused Mike's death."

"Shouldn't you be working with Detective Mahoney?"

"No, ma'am, not at this time—my focus is the illegal pornography."

"But surely—"

He raises his hand like he's stopping traffic. "Mike's death is not the point of this meeting. I'd like you to consider taking over from Mike."

I didn't see this coming, not even close. It's so out in left field, I laugh until tears roll down my cheeks and my still-tender rib muscles clench. The laughter morphs into sobbing for real, because the other ache is always right beneath the surface.

"So that's what you want." I dig out a tissue and blow my nose.

His face is impassive.

"Mr. Shelmann, there are so many reasons I can't do what you're asking, I hardly know where to start—"

"When we gave Mike this undercover job, his first response was that we should have asked you. 'She's the real brains of the family,' is what he said. But we told him not to collaborate with you—it was safer to be a lone operator."

I stare at him, trying to deconstruct this conversation and find the underlying algorithm.

He adds, "Mike wasn't a very good hacker. He had both ethical and technical difficulties going into colleagues' computers."

The air is suddenly electric. A rustle of wind through the trees threatens a storm. I should be getting back to my mother, who's waiting at the car. She must be anxious.

Joe Shelmann continues, "We chose Mike because he was an up-and-coming encryption expert in the department, with easy, natural access to the key players. I believe you, too, have the programming skills and connections in the department to assess who might be the source of illegal activity."

"So...what? You're asking me to spy on the Computer Science Department? Break into their offices and computers?"

"If necessary, yes. No one will suspect you."

"Why? Because I'm a woman? A disabled person in a wheelchair?"

Now he's the one who chuckles, and his features soften. Under those sunglasses he has a half-handsome face, which until now I haven't noticed. "No, Madeline—may I call you Madeline?—it's because you're an unlikely spy."

"But I'm *not* a spy. I don't have skills, like breaking and entering. And I can't exactly creep around the building in this Jeep of a wheelchair."

"That's the point," he says. "Conventional policing skills won't do the trick."

"Nonsense! *You're a cop.* Get warrants, go on campus, show your badge, confiscate their computers or whatever it is you do, and find the perp."

"Look, no question I could get one of those newly minted cops with their shiny degree in computer forensics and cybercrime. But what will they do? Ask Mr. Encryption-Expert Professor if they can take a look-see at his computer? That would alert the bad guy straight away, and we'd never find him. We need a *real* programming expert. You could be discreet. Make up believable excuses for being out and about in the department. You belong there. They'll take you at your word. Why shouldn't they?"

"Maybe because Mike was snooping around in the department, and it got him killed?" I say. "So the answer is no. I'm not cut out for cloak and dagger stuff. Just speaking today frightened me. I'm a researcher. I hide in my office. I study the beauty of mathematical systems. And—besides anything else—I'm about to lose my job. I essentially got told that this morning by the department chair."

"Aren't you on a grant? How long do you have left?"

"About fifteen more months of funding for my research position; but I know the department will try and claw the money back for next year, now that Mike's gone. My employment at Cornell was contingent on his being there. I reckon I'll be lucky to keep my position until December."

He stands and brushes leaves off his backside. "Fight for your remaining time. They're probably legally bound to keep you on for those months. Check your contract."

"I'm sorry, Joe, about the abuse and pornography and all—I know about the horrors from the newspapers—but I'm not cut out for...*spying*."

I turn the chair around and start wheeling away. The conversation has energized me—hinting at answers to Mike's death.

"Think about my offer, Madeline. It's an opportunity to move on with your life and get justice for Mike. There are risks involved, but I believe you're ideally positioned to uncover the information we need."

How glib he is. "The main reason I can't do it," I say, "is I'm basically a coward. And as you can see, I'm not in any physical condition to run away from criminals who threaten me."

"But you figured out a way to stay alive in a skydiving accident. I respect that."

"That's got nothing to do with anything. I got lucky and Mike didn't."

"I'm just sayin'."

He places a sleek black phone in the palm of my left hand, then curls my fingers around it. His hand envelops mine like a big warm mitten.

"Keep this well-hidden," he says. "It's prepaid. Use it to call me if you want to talk. Don't under any circumstances use your own phone. Be aware at all times the person we're targeting may be dangerous. No matter what you decide, don't tell anyone about this meeting, not your best friend, not Detective Mahoney, not even your mother."

"What did he want?" my mother asks, helping me slide into the front seat.

"Nothing new. They're still investigating Mike's death."

"Why couldn't he talk in front of me?" She leans across carefully and buckles me in.

"He asked some questions about our family relationships," I say.

When she climbs into the car, I see her mouth quivering. "I hope you told him Mike and I...got along well...that I came around pretty quickly."

I reach across with my left arm and stroke her neck. "Mom, don't worry about a thing. I told the FBI guy that you loved Mike."

I'm struck by how easily the lies slide off my tongue.

CHAPTER 6

It's three weeks after Mike's funeral, the start of fall semester at Cornell.

Just another day, one more bone-rattling ride in the car with my mother. Abruptly, Mom hits the brakes and pulls over to the side of the road. My body lurches against the seat belt, sending lightning bolts through my ribs. *Stay calm.*

Mom leans her head on the steering wheel. "Madsy, help me, I'm lost."

"What's wrong, Mom? Are you okay?"

Her eyes are frightened. "Where are we, Mads? Where are we going?"

She's scaring me. I put my hand on her arm. "Mom. It's the end of August and we're headed to the Cornell Benefits Office. You remember, the insurance?"

"I knew that," she says, shaking her head and putting the car in drive. "I think I had a momentary blackout."

The stress we've been under is making her weird. This isn't the first time she's lost her mind for a few seconds.

The clerk at Day Hall tells me I'm not eligible for Cornell life insurance benefits. "You'll receive a formal letter from the insurance company, detailing their rationale," she says in her crisp, efficient voice.

I sink back in my wheelchair, my chest tightening against my tender bones.

"What do you mean 'not eligible'? We've been paying into this account since we first came to Cornell." I hear the shrill edge of panic in my voice. "Please could you call your supervisor?"

While we wait, I take my mother's hand, which is trembling. I'm trying to seem calm and in control, but how does one do that with the prospect of no money?

"A fatality due to a skydiving accident is specifically excluded from the policy," the supervisor explains. "It says so right here." He slides the offending document toward me, his finger jabbing the relevant clause. "You will, however, receive a one-time payout of $10,000, which is more than you paid in. You're just not eligible to receive the $250,000 that normally gets awarded. I'm sorry."

Mom looks stricken. "Oh God, Mads—"

"Don't worry, we'll manage. I'll figure something out—"

"It's not much, but there's always my pension," she says, which of course we can't use to pay the mortgage. It's a pittance, part of her legacy of moving from state to state with my father.

Everything's a battle. Physical therapy, getting benefits, steering the wheelchair so it doesn't crash into walls and small animals. I'm tired of fighting and have yet to broach the Computer Science Department.

The payroll lady tells me I'm due to receive a salary for three more months, until the grant expires in December. "Hopefully the PI—principal investigator—of your grant has already applied for a renewal," she says.

I don't tell her that the PI is at home on my mantelpiece, in a small bronze box.

My mom drives me to the computer science building, hauls my chair out of the trunk, belts me in, and says she'll get me when I text. It's my first day back at work. I need to reorient myself. I've been dreading this day but can't put things off any longer.

The cement at the bottom of the wheelchair ramp has severe winter-weather damage, which means no smooth ride to the entrance of the building. Nevertheless, I wave away a beefy guy who offers to carry me and my chair to my destination. With the forward motion in full throttle my chair lurches forward and careens over broken cement.

The elevator fails to respond when I press the fourth floor button. Instead, it stays mute on the ground, doors gaping wide; and there I sit like an idiot stuck in a wheelchair. As someone who's good at problem solving, I'm momentarily stumped. I know this elevator works—I've used it successfully for the past seven years.

I'm relieved when Dwayne Browning, one of my colleagues, steps into the elevator. "Hi, Madeline, welcome back," he says. He dangles a key fob in front of me and says, "New policy. Everyone in the building needs to use this to activate the elevator. They don't want riffraff wandering around the CS Department."

I smile weakly. "Well, there's a big security breach right there. Any number of strays could sneak in and hitch a ride on someone else's fob, like I'm doing."

"We're not supposed to allow that, but as the token Black professor in the department, I refuse to throw up obstacles to people who don't look like me."

Most people don't look like Dwayne. He's sharp and handsome in tan pants and a brown jacket. Dwayne, who got tenure last year, is soft spoken, very smooth, and doesn't broadcast his achievements. I don't know much else about him. He sure doesn't seem the type to provide encryption software to pornographers.

Why am I even thinking about that?

Aisha's office faces the elevator so she can keep an eye on the comings and goings in the department. She's quite a sight for anyone emerging onto the fourth floor, in a red and yellow Nigerian-print top. I admire people who look effortlessly stylish. Aisha adds a bit of class to the Computer Science Department.

When I approach the desk, she tells me she can't issue me an elevator fob without Judy's authorization. I don't believe her for a minute—she's laying down the new power dynamic between us. It's well known one shouldn't cross Aisha.

More shocks await me on my first day back. David Graham, the assistant professor who spoke at Mike's funeral, is sitting at Mike's desk in Mike's office. He has the grace to look embarrassed when he sees me. My wheelchair doesn't clear the doorframe and scrapes paint as I enter uninvited.

There's no trace of Mike here—his books are gone, his skydiving paperweight, his photo of me. There's an alien odor of male cologne.

"I'm sorry, Maggie—"

"It's time to learn my name's Madeline," I snap. "Where's Mike's stuff?"

"There's a box—I think they put it in your office—"

I execute a fast U-turn, unintentionally nicking a piece of the desk.

"Wait! Madeline—"

"What?" I turn to face him.

"We've reshuffled offices since Mike's…passing. Dwayne is in your old office—Judy said you'd be gone soon, and Dwayne has been trying for years to get an office with a window." He lowers his eyes. "You know how it is with offices—there's always competition—and to be honest, there was some resentment that Mike insisted on a window office for you as a condition of employment."

And I thought they gave it to me, you know, based on the quality of my research.

I resist the urge to bite his head off. I know from Mike that David is low in the department hierarchy and none of this is his fault. Besides, I must raise the level of my human interactions, now that I don't have Mike to speak up for me.

"Thank you, David, for the kind eulogy at Mike's funeral." I force myself to look at him from my chair. He's a sad sack who needs a haircut.

He seems relieved we've passed the awkwardness, and is happy to repeat the list of Mike's wonderful qualities—his generosity, his friendliness, his every attribute as a colleague that I don't have.

When I leave, I'm more careful steering through the doorframe.

He says, "I'm sorry, Madeline, no one let you know—about the offices."

I propel myself to my former office. The door is shut. I turn the doorknob then kick the door open with my unbroken leg.

Dwayne's arm is circling Aisha's waist. His head whips around and his hand comes off her left breast so fast I question my eyes. It seems just five minutes ago I saw her near the elevator. Didn't it occur to them I'd be headed this way?

"Madeline—you didn't knock—" Dwayne says, flustered.

"Oh, hi, Dwayne, Aisha. Sorry—last I knew, this was my office."

"Ah, my apologies, Madeline," Aisha says, her voice sorrowful. "I meant to tell you about the office situation earlier."

"I'm really sorry, Madeline," Dwayne says. "I should have said something in the elevator. I assumed you knew."

They'd never have done this to Mike.

I look around. There's a lovely photo of a young woman who's not Aisha on my desk, and a shelf full of computer science texts that don't belong to me.

"Where's my stuff?" I ask.

"I packed up your office and moved the boxes to your new space," Aisha says. The word "space" has an ominous ring to it. Have they put me in a hallway? Without glancing at Dwayne, Aisha sweeps out of the room—my beautiful ex-office with the panoramic view of Cornell—and says, "Follow me."

CHAPTER 7

It's not a hallway or a broom closet, but a real room without a window. If I were a monk in a monastery, I'd be happy with the privacy of this space, its ample bookshelves and old wooden desk. All it needs is a crucifix.

Aisha, true to her word, stacked my books—and Mike's—in alphabetical order and piled my boxes in a corner. "Let me know if you need anything," she says. "Meanwhile, I'll go see what I can do about that elevator fob for you." She's as cool as an iceberg and there's no threat whatsoever in her words, other than a subliminal something in the air that tells me the little incident with Dwayne never happened.

Mike once told me Aisha kept her private life to herself and probably scared men half to death. But Mike loved everyone. Who would have wanted to kill him?

I maneuver the wheelchair to my latest desk and contemplate the dismal scene—the buzzing fluorescent light, the dented boxes with my possessions, the detritus of my career. How have I let myself sink so low? I'm in the strange position of having a brain full of new ideas, while I myself am cast adrift, isolated, and invisible. The probability I'll be invited to talk about my work here, in this department, is practically nil. I'm not delusional—I have no one to blame but myself for sliding into irrelevancy.

They never asked for my input and I let it go.

Listlessly, I wheel myself to the corner to extricate Mike's box. But it's stuck, wedged underneath two of my boxes, unmovable from any angle of my chair. I loathe asking for help but could cause a box avalanche if I try to be a hero.

My wheelchair hums into the hallway and almost collides with Nigel Welbourne, who's emerging from his prime corner office.

"Whoa!" he cries, jumping back, causing coffee to splash from his cup. When he sees it's me, he steps up and squeezes my bad shoulder, letting his thumb brush my neck. "Maddie, Maddie, Maddie, *Wel*-come back! So sorry about Mike. Such rotten luck."

Nigel is the Carl Sagan of the Computer Science Department, a media darling, whose 2009 TV show *Security for Dummies*, based on his book of the same title, was a sensation ten years ago. Mike used to chuckle about Nigel and his tendency to be hands-on with young female fans.

"Don't move!" he commands, spinning around and going back into his office. He has the kind of plummy British voice that enthralls multitudes on *Masterpiece*, and I stay rooted to the spot. He emerges with a fat, hardcover book, which he plops onto my lap. A holographic robot on a computer screen adorns the cover. The book's title is *Pixelated Putty: The Art of Image Manipulation*. Nigel's name shines and sparkles above the title.

"This is going to be your new bible," he says. "Read it and weep."

"Thank you, Nigel—"

"I've signed the front page, and you can have this copy. I will be in your eternal debt if you write a five-star review—"

"Nigel, please could you carry a box for me—in my office..." I execute a perfect turn and, clutching his book, lead him into my new space.

"Well, this is a crappy room," he says cheerfully, as he places Mike's box on a chair. He taps his head. "Earth to Mars, Nigel—be humble—learn how the other half lives."

I too could take notes on his breezy confidence that bends the world to his will. Why aren't I striding the hallway with coffee steaming in my mug? Instead, I'm in a pokey room, adjusting to the dark. In Nigel's universe there are no obstacles. Mike once told me Nigel's contract at Cornell stipulated he have no teaching duties, no Ph.D. students, no service requirements, no annoying committees and obligations that other faculty members must perform. All they wanted from him was his presence to sprinkle fairy dust on the department.

He takes a seat at my desk and sips what's left of his coffee. "Too bad about the accident. I used to skydive, y'know, but gave it up. Too bloody hair raising."

I wish he'd leave so I can go through Mike's stuff, but don't have the wherewithal to tell him. So I sit and say nothing.

"Do you need help unpacking those boxes?" he says eventually, waving at the pile.

"No thanks, Nigel, I'm fine." But still he lingers.

"Do you know that my divorce became finalized last month?" He runs his hand through his brown hair. He's not bad looking if you like that pale English skin and jutting jaw.

"I'm sorry to hear it."

"I'm a lonely man. Perhaps when you feel up to it, Maddie, we can have dinner together."

"Mike's funeral was just a few weeks ago," I say mildly. "It will take a while."

He nods, and for a moment, seems like a sad, middle-aged man, not the lecherous rogue Mike has told me about. I take his offer at face value. He feels sorry for me. I look like shit. He's being kind.

"By the way, please call me Madeline," I say, my face burning.

"But that's so cold and formal. *Madeline*. It brings to mind French governesses with pointed umbrellas. Whereas 'Maddie' makes me think of warm fires and home cooking." I know I should banter and tell him he's put his finger on it exactly: I don't do fireplaces and home cooking. Instead, I say, "Does your revolutionary encryption method work with movies?"

"All the dirty pictures you want," he says.

I'm ready to collapse. Being back at work saps my energy. At home, I'm used to sliding onto my bed when the strain of sitting gets to be too much. The ache on my right side is a constant reminder, a throbbing that resonates from my shoulder, through my ribs, to my newly replaced knee and broken leg.

I've been disciplined with drug usage today and treat myself to just one painkiller before confronting the contents of Mike's box.

Inside, scattered about, are several scraps of notes and computer code scribbled on odd bits of paper. How can I bear it, his illegible scrawl, with the words *Bitmap? Too complicated? Ask Mads?* His favorite blue mug that went missing from the house a while ago, and a small, bent spoon. A video game, *League of Legends.* Did he really play at work? Further down is a new shirt and a pair of clean underwear. I hold his shorts up to my face, but there's nothing of Mike in their smell. Near the bottom of the box is an early framed photo of me that Mike kept on his desk. Carefree, smiling, showing dimples. I pause to look at this person who no longer exists. Underneath the photo is a glossy brochure with a rainbow-colored parachute.

A lacy black bra, coiled like a snake at the bottom of the box, is almost invisible. Huh? How did *that* get in there? I stare at it a few seconds, then, with the point of a pencil, lift it out gingerly and tip it onto the desk. Despite my instant aversion, I have the urge to feel the soft, filmy fabric between my finger and thumb. Where the hell did this come from?

Aisha packed the box. I could wheel myself to her office right now and demand answers. Did she lose a bra while packing? Was it in Mike's desk drawer? Which one? But a flush of shame comes over me. Does she think I wear this kind of Weimar Republic cabaret underwear? Is she entitled to know I don't?

What, exactly, does she know?

If Mike were here in this room, I could say, *Hey, Babe, what's the Victoria's Secret thing doing underneath the photo of me? Where are the matching black panties?* What a giggle we'd have over it. *April Fools!* he'd say, or *Got ya going there, Mads.*

I search my brain, trying to remember our lives during the weeks Before. All those nights he spent away from home. I never suspected him of being unfaithful, not for a minute. He loved me, didn't he? Even though he became distant toward the end.

Get a grip. A black bra in a work box doesn't signify an affair.

But now I want to ask him point blank, where were you all those nights? What happened to us, Mike?

Why must I be dealing with this in addition to everything else? In a fit of anger, I grab a pair of scissors off my desk, hack the offensive item in half, and throw the pieces away from me. One shiny boob lands on the desk, the other on the floor, tangled in the blades of the splayed-open scissors. Agatha Christie redux. With both hands I squeeze my chest, trying to contain the pain. Then I hug Mike's box against me and let the latest grief flow through.

Aisha, cool and statuesque, appears at my door. She's almost as tall as I was, with a close-cropped haircut and gold hoop earrings. "Madeline? Are you okay? Oh my gosh, girl, can I get you anything? Do you have a minute to see Judy? She's in her office and says now's a good time..."

I sit up straight, hand brush my hair, and recompose my face.

Of course I have a minute. An interminable number of minutes that stretch up to the sky.

CHAPTER 8

I maneuver my chair into the bathroom and catch sight of myself in the mirror. The band-aids and gauze are off my face, and the bruises faded into yellowish skin that has been indoors too long. My hair has grown back in spiky tufts that give me the look of a punk rocker. I start to pat it down, then realize I need all the cheeky attitude I can get.

The door to Judy's office is ajar, and I'm careful as I ease my way through it.

"Hello, Madeline, do come in," she says pleasantly, and stands up from her desk. "We're all devastated about Mike. This must be very difficult for you."

I wheel myself toward her, but she motions me to the couch. "Let's talk over here."

So it's not going to be a firing squad at the desk, but a fireside chat in the sitting room. Obediently, I hum along, then execute a good U-turn and park myself to face her. She kicks off her high heels and in a demure, fluid movement, tucks her legs underneath her. Even in this informal posture, she's intimidating and in control.

"I'm guessing this place—Cornell—holds painful memories and you'd like to leave as soon as possible," she says. "Perhaps I can help you."

Lowering the boom, just like that. "Help me how?"

"It's clear you were a wonderful assistant to Mike, and, according to him, a very competent programmer."

"He said that? *Competent?*"

"He was very complimentary about your abilities." Her voice has all the warmth of a steel blade. "I'm willing to write you an excellent letter of recommendation for whatever you want to do—high school teaching, community college..."

Each phrase is a blow to the gut.

"Judy, I have a Ph.D. from Caltech. I'm a computer scientist, a researcher. I'm not a high school teacher—"

"Here's the thing, Madeline." She shifts her position and chooses her words carefully. "Mike was the PI—principal investigator—of your McFall Grant..."

I know what a fucking PI is.

"...And that money technically belongs to Cornell—to us, the Computer Science Department. You *do* understand your position in the department was contingent on Mike's employment? And now that he's...no longer with us...we must move on." Her voice is pleasant and cajoling, but even I, with my social deficits, understand the subtext.

"I have another three months left in my contract, and another year's approval of grant money—" My voice is pathetic and defensive, but the sentence *does* come out in one coherent piece. I try to conceal the trembling in my hands by clasping my fingers tightly together on my lap. How could I possibly ever spy on her when I'm practically peeing in my pants just facing her? When did I become such a *wimp*?

Judy, on the other hand, is as relaxed as all hell on her white leather couch. "The new PI—Dwayne Browning, by the way—has his own research associate he'd like to fund, starting next semester. I'll be honest, Madeline, we need you to officially resign as soon as possible to enable a smooth transition. The McFall Foundation is on board—"

I wheel my chair away from her and her hateful words and find a pool of sunlight at the window. Her computer is open at her desk, which has stacks of folders and papers piled high on it. Having to deal with me is probably a nuisance. What important task did I interrupt?

From here there's an unobstructed view of her computer screen—no screen saver—and her desktop is visible for all to see. The screen is unlocked! She's not paranoid about intrusion and didn't shut her computer down before leading me to the couch. The sight of those unprotected icons passes though me like a shiver. I could unlock their secrets in a heartbeat.

How much time does she have for computer science with all this *stuff* on her desk? To provide state of the art encryption to a buyer means to be up to date on the latest research, the techie journals, the Google engineers and their bag of tricks. How could she possibly be a porn villain if she spends all her time on irritants like me?

I've always had this ability, compartmentalizing in the midst of bad news.

I wheel myself back to face Judy, who's studying her phone screen. Deep breath, like my therapist has shown me. "I've given some thought to what you said."

She raises her eyebrows and smiles with encouragement.

"I checked Mike's grant application at Day Hall this morning. It specifically mentions me by name as the research associate; so—legally—I can stay here until the grant runs out."

For the first time during our little chat, the pleasant façade of her face shifts. "That makes no difference to our situation here in the department. I'm under no obligation to renew your contract for next year."

"But I *am* entitled to three more months of an office at Cornell, a title of Research Associate in Computer Science, and the salary I've been receiving since the beginning of this year." I've rehearsed these words, but my nervousness and the effort of speaking with some kind of authority causes me to double over with pain.

"Madeline, slow down. Please compose yourself. Imagine what your life here will be like if you work under these circumstances."

"What circumstances?" Her utter contempt opens my eyes to what I've become. "I want to be part of the research in this department," I say. "To attend the computer science lunches every Wednesday like the postdocs and grad students do, and to take my turn—present a paper of my current work—"

"Oh, Madeline." She goes into sad mode, scrunching up her face with sympathy. "Do you think for a moment anyone here will take you seriously?"

Her words confirm I have nothing to lose. "They'll listen to me because I'm a freak show, someone who survived a skydiving accident against the odds. Some people are drawn to that. I'd like the chance to introduce my research—not Mike's, my own—I have some new ideas—"

"Why now? For all these years you've hidden away in your office, and suddenly, at this moment, your goal is to participate in the life of the department?"

Her barb hits home, and I ponder my reply. "I didn't want to get in the way of Mike's limelight," I say softly, realizing it's true. *I no longer have to worry about his sensitivities. His ego.*

She nods, seeing the truth of it. "If you leave now—clear out your office in the next week or so—I'm certainly willing to pay you a generous lump sum for helping us out. You could have a vacation while you plan the next phase of your life." Her tone is soft and seductive. She really wants me gone.

"No thank you, Judy. I've decided to stay until December."

CHAPTER 9

Despite a fitful night of skydiving nightmares—Mike, forever falling from my grasp—I haul myself out of bed early. My morning routine now features a roll onto the carpet for strengthening exercises, including leg lifts with both legs. I must force myself to do several repetitions, causing currents of pain.

When the bad foot is in the air, I examine it from several angles. With its long jagged toes and dough-colored hue, it's not an attractive sight.

"Let's practice walking on it," the physical therapist advised. Toggle your weight from left to right until you feel stable." *Stable?* Ha.

We're at the stage of trying crutches at home, but it's agony to walk on my injured leg. Thank God I have Mom to drive me places. *Pathetic.*

I arrive at work before eight and ride to the fourth floor on my new fob. Aisha is already at her desk, well-manicured fingernails clicking on her keyboard. "Bright and shiny, Madeline," she says without looking up.

In my office, I place a framed photo of Mike on my desk, and, with some slow, fearful moves on my legs, I maneuver an I BYTE poster onto the wall. I've splurged on a good lamp with several hinges and degrees of freedom, so every corner of my desk can be illuminated. Everything is ready. All that's left is to pry open my laptop and get my act together.

My work remains untouched since the accident. I unlock my screen and pass through various hoops to block hackers and trolls. You never know who's lurking, waiting to excavate your secrets.

It takes a load of threshold energy to get going. My brain has lost its muscle memory, much like my right leg. While I'm scouring my notes there's a tap at the door. I'm immediately wary of uninvited company and freeze, hoping the intruder will go away. After a more insistent knock, I clear my throat and say, "Come in."

The visitor is a computer science graduate student, Carol Bellamy, who's been given the task of organizing talks at the Wednesday lunches.

"You're a researcher here, right?" she says. "I'm sorry about Mike. Everyone liked him…"

"Can I help you?"

"Would you be willing to talk about your research tomorrow?" she says. "Pete—the postdoc—canceled on me and no one wants to speak on such short notice. Do you have something?"

I'm about to say no thank you, I'm still adjusting to my altered circumstances, when I remember my resolution to advocate for my work. Surely I can cobble together pieces of my latest research in a way that introduces me in a new light?

"I'll do it," I say. "How about 'Salt and Pepper in Encryption Trees'?"

"Excuse me?"

"The title of my talk. I have some new ideas for creating secure keys—passwords—to unlock files."

She looks startled, then pleased. "Wow—super—thank you!" She drops a notebook on my desk. "Please write your name for me, so if I make a poster, I don't screw up the spelling."

Gulp, a poster. So now there's a goal for tomorrow, an actual talk about my latest ideas. The thought terrifies me.

The secret of good encryption is to create keys that can't be broken, not even with the brute force of a computer. If the encryption key is weak, a smart hacker and reliable supercomputer can unlock the original file with just a small amount of competent coding. I know, because I've done it.

How Mike and I used to laugh at those TV crime shows in which the detective would push a button or two, and voilà! The evil-doer's file would fill the screen, decrypted and displayed for all to see.

In our latest project, Mike and I deepened our work with complicated encryption keys, adding "salt" and "pepper"—random strings of characters—to each key. No push of a button would open *these* files. I had a brainwave for storing the keys, a data structure of bushy trees, whose branches and leaves would hold the dark magic for decrypting the files.

To illuminate the data structure, I created an elegant diagram, a representation as beautiful as a Vermeer painting, whose light and shadows shimmered on the screen.

Mike's eyes had been wide in the reflected glow, and he burst out laughing.

"It's genius, Mads," he said. "We're going to be famous. There's nothing like it in the literature."

"Then code it up, my darling. Code it up." And he did, in a dazzling algorithm that maximized efficiency. What a team we were.

Here, alone in my office, I have a moral dilemma. Should I claim Mike's code as my own? The new ideas, the elegant diagram, and the algorithm all blossomed into being during the weeks before our fatal skydive. The work is recent, but Mike died before he could write it up.

The underlying idea of how to store the information trees is totally mine. Without it, there would be no code. I'm desperate to create my own little footprint in academia.

Looking up at the ceiling, I whisper, "Please, forgive me, Mike."

Slowly, inexorably, my work sucks me in. The time passes in a dream. I weave Mike's beautiful algorithm into the fabric of my talk and accept it as a blessing, his final gift. I experience peace the first time in weeks, the joy of returning to my orderly left-brain universe of interlocking parts.

When an unexpected glitch in the logic slows me down, I don't for a moment doubt my ability to fix it. In a state of flow, I can crack any code, unravel any knot, or solve any maze. It's always a matter of finding the answer buried deep in my knowledge or at the outer edges of my skill. It's not a boast. It's just the way it is.

Today, however, the bug persists. In a fit of fury, I slam my hand on the desk, grab my mouse, and unleash the debugger. I hate how rusty I am, how uncharacteristically slow.

A solution to the problem comes late in the afternoon, resonating with the constant ache in my body and releasing a flood of endorphins more powerful than any opioid.

The following day I'm psyched when I arrive at work. Despite some trepidation about speaking, I'm confident in the value and novelty of what I'll be presenting. What fun it'll be to blow everyone away and bask in their amazement when they see what a mere Senior Research Associate has accomplished, alone in her hidey hole.

The lunch is at noon, but I'll show up early to check the projector is working and my connector fits into whatever cables they have. Mike was always so cavalier about pesky tech details, but of course people flitted around him, making sure everything worked.

When I emerge from the dark hallway into the meeting room, a milk-white light is streaming through the windows. The brightness sparks the aura of a migraine, and my head starts to feel like an elastic band has stretched around my skull. Damn. Why today of all days?

Carol Bellamy, the graduate student who arranged my talk, apologizes profusely when she sees the setup for a normal-height person, not an invalid in a wheelchair. Yet again I must deal with the stand for my papers, and the mic, and the desk for my laptop.

The computer scientists trickle in slowly, and no one, other than Carol, pays any attention to me. They're all heading for the free lunch, a motley tray of cold cuts, soft buns, and pale fruit.

Judy walks in with a container of lunch, nods at me, and joins some faculty members at the back. I wonder what her reaction was when she saw I was the speaker.

When Nigel, the TV star, enters with a jaunty bounce, he sucks some of the air out of the room. Heads swivel to follow him as he moves to join Judy at the back, waving aloft a mug with the words "Kids Rock" in black letters.

Dwayne sits off to the side, chatting with some of the postdocs and grad students. He's a cool cat, relaxed and sexy, and, in my humble opinion, carries his sheen of intelligence very well. He hasn't cast one glance in my direction since that little scene with Aisha in my old office.

David Graham, the football player, is at the food table, holding up the line while he crafts a cold-cut masterpiece on a bun.

At last, it's time for my big moment. Carol introduces me as a senior researcher in the department, who has new work she'd like to share. The buzzing of conversation barely dies down. People are not exactly craning forward to hear about my research.

I have a pang of stage fright, my breath half-drawn, becoming something sharp and unexpressed in my chest. I clear my throat and plunge in. "Salt and pepper can and does grow on trees, especially in encryption and decryption algorithms." Damn! I should have greeted them first and said something nice about how happy I was to be here today and thank you everyone for your thoughts and sympathy.

Too late now. So I plow on.

I project a photo of myself, a serious, unsmiling picture taken by Mike while I was working at my desk. He has captured me perfectly, my hand thrust into my unruly brown hair, my total being caught up in the singular focus of solving a problem. Underneath the photo is an ENCRYPT button. I press the button and the photo dissolves into a galaxy of colored pixels unrecognizable as the image of a person.

There's a murmur I can't interpret and some laughter from the audience.

"Hey, abracadabra!" one of the grad students mutters loudly enough for me to hear. He looks like a weed, but is already one of the boys. Do they see where I'm heading?

"We all can do that, right?" I try to make eye contact with the students. "Computer Science 101. This is one of the standard encryption algorithms."

I now select a DECRYPT button, and there I am again, head bowed.

"I'm guessing all of us—well, most of us, anyway—can crack the decryption key, when we're looking at the original file." Some nervous laughter among the students. The abracadabra guy has a smirk on his face. Some people are tapping on their phones.

No one seems interested when I put up the latest research on encryption. Nothing new there. The ambient noise buzzes like an insect around me.

Is anyone listening? I can't tell. I don't have Mike's ability to hold people in the palm of my hand. *Come on, Mads, move it along, get to the good stuff,* Mike says in my ear.

My head throbs with a full-fledged migraine.

"I've devised a new encryption algorithm," I say, clearing my throat again. "It's practically impossible to break, even if you're looking at the original file. I've developed a unique way of storing salt and pepper strings in the keys."

I'm at the culmination of my talk and, with a flourish, display the figure at the heart of my idea. "The search trees are contained in a hash table—a specialized list of trees— and any collisions—um, duplicates—are handled with new branches."

I have beautified the picture with pale colors and elegant shadings using a new paint app.

My wheelchair hums as I wheel myself to the wall and reach up to dim the lights.

This is my moment of triumph.

Finally, I have their full attention, and heads lean forward to peer at my diagram, which—even if I say so myself—is a knockout of a data structure. I feel a surge of pride, like a mother whose offspring has turned out well.

The work speaks for itself, and I take a moment to bask in my glory. The room has gone completely quiet. *Stunned silence? Amazement? Awe?*

Dwayne raises his hand and stands when I acknowledge him. His face is serious, and he looks uncomfortable. "I'm sorry, Madeline, but none of this is new. That diagram is Mike's. And the whole salt and pepper idea? The hash table of trees? He showed it to me before he...passed. We spoke...a lot...about it—" He's embarrassed and looks away before sitting down.

That's impossible. We hadn't published yet.

I stare at Dwayne dumbly, disbelieving. Mike's idea? Not in his wildest dreams could Mike have come up with this. Dwayne's words slice through me, as realization dawns— *Mike stole my work.* He violated our sacred trust and showed people my data structure and diagram, representing them as his own. But most of all, he never told me how people reacted. He cut me out of the algorithm. He stole not only my work but my thunder.

His betrayal sucks the air from my lungs, and there isn't breath in my body to respond. The room is suddenly stifling despite the chug of the air conditioner. A flush of shame suffuses me. *Of course* they would think that Mike did it all. Why wouldn't they? I've kept myself out of circulation for seven years.

"Is it true?" Judy demands. "This is all Mike's work that you're presenting?" Her voice is imperious. "Don't you think you should have announced that upfront?"

"Over-the-top data structure," Nigel says. "But I must say, that's a jolly good drawing, Madeline."

Some of the postdocs and graduate students are having a joke at my expense; their wave of laughter floats across the room.

David Graham says nothing, but he's shaking his head and frowning. *Can it work?* Does he even understand the algorithm implicit in the diagram?

No one raises a hand to say, *Wow, that's amazing.* No one says, *Explain the trick.*

Something explodes in my head and I grab the live mic and bang on a table for silence. The noise ricochets off the ceiling.

Sparks fly out of me, a lightning storm. "This work is mine," I say, choking. "The idea, the diagram, the data structure. *All mine.*" I swipe the back of my hand across my face. "Mike helped with the coding. But the idea was mine."

Mine! The headache is running rampant.

Judy says, "It seems to me, Madeline, you should write this up as a paper—you know—like a final tribute to Mike.

It's completely understandable you'd want to show us what he was working on."

She sounds entirely reasonable, but it's a travesty. How smug and dismissive they are. Their contempt is everywhere.

Why would they believe me? I'm unattractive and inarticulate. I look small and weak in my wheelchair. And—it has to be said—I'm not a man. I look around at the audience and hear the booming bass and baritone of Computer Science. Carol Bellamy is the only female grad student in the department and of course she's the one saddled with organizing the lunch. I'm the spouse who couldn't apply for a real job. It was completely believable for everyone that a woman would shrink back in the shadows, being nothing more than Mike's research assistant. For a while it made sense to me. And what about Judy Holsinger, the attractive department chair? What did her male colleagues do to her? Ignore her work? Belittle it? Diminish her? At which stage of her career did she quit doing real computer science and go into admin? Was chairing the department the only way she could rule? How does she punish those who blocked her path?

As I sit in the wreckage of my career, certain truths about my life become clear. Computer science in academia is still a man's world. Men will judge my work. And men will control my professional destiny. No one in this room sees me as a computer scientist.

No one believes I have the brain power to create the scheme I presented. To them I'm just a girl.

My talk is over. Carol hastily swoops in to take the mic and thank me. While I dismantle my computer and gather my cables and notes, the wolf pack drifts back to their lunch.

Back in my office, I grab Mike's photo and throw it face down onto the lowest bookshelf. My wedding ring follows, a golden glint spinning on the frame with a small metallic clatter. For a few seconds I massage the indentation it leaves on my finger. Then I pull myself up from my wheelchair and, holding onto the ridge of my desk as if my life depended on it,

I walk haltingly around the table, allowing the full weight of my body and shitty existence onto my sore leg, leaning into the pain at last and letting it coalesce with all the other agonies, the migraine, Mike's betrayal, and the disillusionment of my marriage.

I will get my revenge...

I will call Joe Shelmann tonight.

CHAPTER 10

"Why so quiet, baby girl?" my mother says on the way home. "How was your talk—?"

"Please don't call me that."

I'm tired of being her passenger. I'm fed up with my mother's incessant scrutiny, which makes me feel guilty because she's basically put her life on hold to take care of me. I hate being accountable for every second of my existence.

She's probably had it up to her eyeballs with me too.

We say nothing the rest of the drive home, which is a long one on Brooktondale Road. Slowly, the bustling scene of students on campus gives way to the Ithaca I love: wide open fields and farmlands bursting with late summer flowers. Silos dot the landscape, with the occasional crumbling old barn and remnants of plows and burned-out tractors.

My house is an isolated old farmhouse on three acres of woodlands that Mike and I absolutely had to own as soon as we saw it. "Quaint old fixer-upper," was the description by the realtor, and also the reason we could afford it. Some of the fixing up has happened, but a lot of it hasn't. One of the house's big attractions was its spaciousness—lots of rooms with bathrooms, and an apartment-type setup on the other side, away from the main bedroom. "This is a place I can *breathe* in," Mike had said.

Mom and I clatter onto the jagged driveway with potholes gouged out by last winter's storms. This was supposed to be the summer Mike and I finally got the driveway paved.

Mom stands at the door of the car, brown hair incandescent in the rays of the setting sun. She looks like a Madonna. When she steps into the shadow to retrieve the wheelchair, the spell is broken, and I see up close how being my caregiver has taken its toll. Her face is grim and pinched as she gently reaches for me.

Instead of sliding into the chair, I put my arms around her neck and draw her cheek to my face. Her skin is soft. "I'm sorry, Mommy. You're a saint to put up with all this."

"Oh, Madsy," she says.

I've decided to try and wean myself from the wheelchair. It's time.

Supported by my mother, I walk haltingly to the front door. My physical therapist has told me not to favor my uninjured leg, but to walk straight and upright without a limp. This is not as easy as it sounds. I've been pampering the injured leg, elevating it on pillows, reluctant to put weight on it. My skydiving days are so far away.

Now the Earth is a wobbly planet that quivers under me as I try to plant my foot firmly. The sensation of my new knee is still strange, along with the pulsing of muscles and tendons surrounding it.

There's a divine fragrance in the house. My mother has baked my favorite dessert, an apple cake, which sits on the counter, glossy and glistening with glazed apples. We stop to admire it, and a lump the size of Ithaca sticks in my throat. I'm an imperfect daughter, for sure.

The decision to go undercover for Joe Shelmann weighs on my mind, and I must act before I lose my nerve. I say, "Mom, I have something to take care of. I'm going outside for a few minutes. I won't be long."

"Just a sec," my mother says, pulling on her sweater. "I'll come with you."

"Let me go alone. I want to think about stuff at work today."

She gets a firm line around her mouth, one I know well. "Why don't you tell me what happened while we're both outside? It'll be dark soon—"

"Mom! We can't live together if there has to be a debate every time I want to go out on my own. I'm a grown-up. I'm okay being outside in the dark."

She's stunned. Until today I've been docile, accepting her ministrations with grateful silence. Things have been more or less harmonious between us. She stares at me, hurt bafflement on her face. My mother and the apple cake, accusing me.

"Chill, Mom. Everything's good."

Before I've used up all my emotional energy, I push myself and my chair out the screen door, into the gathering dusk.

The view at the back of the house is what seduced Mike and me into giving up our savings. Trees lush with summer leaves, tinted purple by the setting sun. From the woods, a hum of insects and mosquitoes near the pond, proboscises out for blood.

I look back at the house, which is darker than the surroundings, as if its dark wood is absorbing the remaining light. The silhouette is stark, like the Bates Motel in *Psycho*. The kitchen curtain is pulled back. Mom watches me from the window.

My wheelchair rolls behind the trees then clatters over a knotty trail of roots and undergrowth. Other than the croak of frogs, there's no discernible sound, just silent tension, hissing and crackling in the branches.

Briefly, I wonder what I'm letting myself in for. I'm keyed up and anxious, a pulse beating in my neck. The shame and humiliation of today's debacle are still with me, and I'm spurred on by anger.

Joe Shelmann's number is programmed into the sleek black phone. I punch the call button. The ring tone is loud and clear like a cricket's chirp out here in the woods.

"Madeline. I've been waiting for your call." That same smooth drawl I remember.

"Tell me what to do."

He pauses so long I wonder if he's regretting his request.

"Before we discuss that, ma'am," he says, "it's my duty to warn you the assignment entails some risk."

"I'm a skydiver. I'm used to risk."

"This is different. For example, to protect yourself at work, you need to let it be known Mike didn't confide in you."

"That shouldn't be hard, because he didn't."

"Okay, I'm asking you to gather evidence, ma'am." He lets that sink in. "I don't know if the guy we're looking for gets his kicks from watching rape, or if he's just a greedy bastard enabling illegal porn. For simplicity, I'll refer to him as James—"

"James? So you've decided it's a he?"

"Listen up, Madeline. I don't know if James is operating from his work computer, but we can't rule it out. I'd like you to start by examining all the work computers—see if there's any activity outside academic norms."

I suppose I should be flattered, because he thinks I can do it—break into everyone's computer. There's a small matter of whether he'll bail me out if I'm arrested.

"Do you have search warrants?"

The delay in reply tells me all I want to know. He says, "Absolutely—but perhaps not in the conventional sense. We have a blanket warrant from a judge to conduct an investigation of the Computer Science Department. How we do it, exactly, is left to our discretion."

Pure baloney. But why lie? He seems genuine and intense.

He says, "I've concluded, Madeline, going in with guns blazing and impounding their computers will be a waste of fire power. Having you assess them from the inside is a better plan."

"What if I don't find anything relevant on their work computers?"

"Then, ma'am, we'll reassess where we're at." He says this quietly, dead serious.

"What kinds of evidence am I looking for? Names? Mailing lists? Porn movies? Encryption algorithms? Demands for payment? Blackmail? Bodies?"

I expect him to chuckle at my feeble attempt at humor. Instead, he says, "Good thinking, Madeline. All of the above. We're working on the assumption that more evidence will be revealed as you get close to the players."

"What does 'get close to' mean? Sleep with them? Is that my instruction?"

Now he does laugh, a long, low, drawly sound. "No, ma'am, we don't ask our informants to do that. All I'll say is play it by ear. I don't know what you'll be called on to do. Just stay alert at all times."

A sigh through the trees makes me shiver. The sun has gone.

"How will I report to you? Is there a post office box number? What if I need to send you a phone or a flash drive with potential evidence?"

"Don't mail anything. It involves third parties and creates a level of danger I'd rather not expose you to. Texting on the burner is okay."

"So how—?"

"For non-electronic evidence we'll do it the old-fashioned way, with a hidden dead-drop location at Cornell. I've already scoped one out."

Dead drop? I've seen enough spy thrillers to know it never ends well for the spy at the dead drop.

"Why can't we just meet in person—you know, like normal people—and have coffee off-campus, at a place like Collegetown Bagels?"

"Because I'm working a couple of other cases right now, and don't want to be seen in public."

So we arrange to meet tomorrow morning at Cornell, on a concealed path leading to Collegetown. From there, he can show me the dead drop. He instructs me to pretend not to know him when I spot him, just to follow him.

"Is it the same location Mike used?" I still can't picture Mike doing this work.

"No, ma'am. That wouldn't be wise."

"Will you tell me what Mike found during the time he worked for the FBI?"

"Not much I'm afraid. He'd only been at it a few weeks, and, to be honest, he had a problem hacking into his friends' computers."

It's pitch dark, time to go back inside. "Are we done?"

"Just a few pointers, ma'am, before we sign off. My main goal is to keep you safe while you assist our investigation."

"With all due respect, sir, if that was your main goal, we wouldn't be having this conversation."

"Touché, ma'am. Will you listen while I give you some advice? A few rules, if you will?"

"Go ahead. Be concise. I don't exactly have a pen and paper here."

"Number one rule: I don't exist. Don't ever mention me, not in any context."

"That won't be too difficult."

"Number two: If you need to talk to me, give two rings on the burner, wait five minutes, and then call. I will do the same. This should give us enough time to get some privacy."

I laugh at him. "This is so out there. What if I'm in danger? Is there a special word I should say when I call, like Geronimo?"

"Good thinking," he says. "If you're in danger, use your regular phone, not the burner. Pretend to call your mother. You may need to do that if you're in the company of a bad actor. Call me Mom in your address book. End the call with 'Love you.'"

"You can't be serious. What about my actual mother?"

"List her under her full name. If you're in danger, call Mom, and when I pick up, ask me how I'm doing and try to give me a clue as to your whereabouts."

Too bad my mother isn't standing next to me. She wouldn't believe any of this.

"Okay, those are the basic rules," Joe says. "Now I'll just give you some spy craft. Mostly common sense stuff, but I might as well say it."

Spy craft?

"It's important you don't blow your cover. Which means if you're caught in a place where you don't belong, have your story ready. They'll believe you. Everything you say will be taken at face value, so be prepared. Smile, stammer, and apologize. Men love to feel magnanimous and in control."

"Is that how you feel right now?" I can see him smiling on the other side of the line.

"If you do what I'm hoping, you're going to be searching various locations. Offices and such. Maybe even bedrooms."

"You're kidding, right?"

"Just make sure you don't disturb the places you search. Take a mental photo—or actual photo—before you start. You don't want to put someone's favorite paperweight back on the wrong pile."

"What if I don't find anything to put in the dead drop?"

"Then don't use it. And by the way, you only have until December break, so you'd better get going. Maybe ease up on your own research and try to find James."

"Okay, I'll do it." I try to sound confident, like I won't let him down.

"Watch your back and stay out of danger."

A knot tightens in my chest. "Well, that's kinda irrational, since I don't know who the threat is or where the danger is."

He gives another low chuckle. "Congratulations, Madeline, I like how your brain works. You're going to be great. I know your type—the brainy, over-achieving smart girl everyone underestimates. Especially men. No one will think you have the brains or the balls—excuse the expression, ma'am—to do this job, and they'll be wrong every time."

CHAPTER 11

I emerge from the trees, and in the sliver of moonlight see a shadow moving in the yard. I turn off my wheelchair and sit motionless. No one knows about the risky life I've just agreed to, yet the sight of an intruder lurking near my house unnerves me.

The light is dim, but he appears to be peering through the windows of dark rooms. Only the kitchen window is lit. Oh God, my mother will freak out if she sees him.

A nearby dog starts barking loudly, a sudden noise that sets my heart pounding. The intruder stops, steps away, then resumes his sinister reconnaissance.

I can't sit out here all night. Should I confront him? What if he punches me in the head? What if this giant—as I approach, I see he's a large man—pulls me out of the chair and stomps on my bad leg? What if...? Why am I overthinking? My mother's alone in the house.

Silently, like a leopard stalking prey, I manually wheel myself toward him. When I'm about ten feet away, I grab my large power flashlight from under my wheelchair, turn the chair on full throttle, and race toward him. Nothing else makes sense. I'd better get this right.

I squeeze my legs to the right and brace for pain. In the split second before the left side of the chair crashes into the back of his legs he swings around and his eyes open wide as I veer to the right and he thuds to the ground like a felled oak tree. Wincing through the pain of impact, I shine my flashlight into his eyes, and say, "Who the hell are you and what are you doing on my property?"

The kitchen door opens and my mother steps into the yard. "Madsy?"

"Stay back, Mom!"

"Who's out there?" she says, taking a step toward us.

The giant is blinded by the light. He lifts an arm to shade his eyes, but I hold the flashlight steady. He tries to hoist himself off the ground, but he's like a slab of beef, with a lot of weight to handle.

"Don't move. Not until you tell me why you're here."

A large dog appears in the yard and races toward me, barking its head off.

"Torvill, sit!" the giant commands. He has a beard and a foreign accent.

The dog drops down on the grass, but his ears are up and he's still menacing with a low growl. There's a cat in the mix, yowling, yellow-green eyes piercing in the light.

The man awkwardly rearranges himself into a sitting position. He seems to have been cushioned from the wheelchair blow. "So sorry to startle you. I'm Andri Eriksson, visiting scholar and writer—"

"What do you want?"

"I'm here about apartment for rent. I spoke with Mike Alvarez, this place is perfect for me and animals to run around, and today is arrival day."

"You can't live here," my mother says, approaching us. She's holding a rolling pin.

"Wait—Mike agreed to rent to you?" I remember now, we had an ad on craigslist. No one wanted the place because it was so far out in the country. But that was Before. I vaguely recall someone who called...

The dog is snarling again, and the giant scratches its head. "Yes, we agreed on phone. Also email."

"Why were you snooping around the house and looking in the windows?"

"Really very sorry to frighten you—I rang doorbell and no one answered."

"Do you have ID?" I ask.

He pats his plaid pockets and removes a small laminated card. "European driving license."

I snatch it, shine the flashlight in his face, then scrutinize the card. "Excuse me, but this isn't you." What the hell does he take me for, some kind of moron?

"It's younger, thinner me, when I didn't grow beard. Very sad, but it's me alright." The beard extends halfway up his face and obscures a good part of it. I check again and concede that his eyes and protruding ears do seem to match the photo.

"Where are you from?" His accent sounds Russian, but his name is Scandinavian.

He lifts the cat onto his lap and ruffles its ears. "Ukraine mostly. Swedish mother."

There's an unthreatening vibe coming off this strange man, who seems at peace with me crashing my wheelchair into him.

I make a decision. "Let's talk inside. You can bring the dog and cat into the kitchen."

"My luggage is in car parked in driveway," he says. "Is it safe? I can put it in house, yes?"

"I'm sorry—no. We don't know much about you."

"Visiting student for creative writing purposes in fall semester. Writer. You know, Scandinavian noir, very popular..."

When we move into the kitchen, Mom throws the rolling pin onto the counter. She is very agitated. "We can't have a strange man with animals staying in the house." She says it fiercely to me, as if he's an alien invader who cannot understand English.

"Very gentle creatures," he says, stroking the dog's fur. "This is Torvill—means wisdom in Swedish—half chocolate

Labrador—very mellow—and half Plott hound." Torvill has the same sad aura as his owner. He's quite a big dog. As he's being assessed, his brown tail wags from side to side, not a happy wag, a wistful one. He has large brown eyes that are strikingly human as they gaze reproachfully at my mother.

"Cat is Tosca," Andri says. "From opera. Diva—with caramel head and black stripes. Very beautiful and intelligent, but not good with self-control and food. Bit like me." He smiles ruefully.

"This is my mother, Janet Geiger," I say. "She's a retired English teacher."

He puts out a large hand, but my mother shrinks away from him. "Please, Mads, tell them to leave."

I wheel to her side and put my arm around her legs, my head against her thigh. "Mom. Give me a moment. Maybe I will."

The man stands awkwardly in the kitchen while his menagerie wanders about, sniffing the old wood floor and licking away crumbs. In the light, the man's nose appears out of alignment, as if it's been broken and badly put together.

"Mike is...deceased," I say.

I tell him about Before and After and he listens respectfully, then says he is now really embarrassed. He had no idea Mike was dead. "It explains why he didn't answer phone last week," he says. "I feel bad for you, Medeleen."

"Do you have any proof that Mike agreed to rent the apartment to you?" *Why didn't Mike tell me?*

"I have email with Mike and also letter."

He goes into his pocket again and produces a crumpled page that has the address of my house and detailed instructions for getting here. It has today's date as the arrival day and appears to be from Mike.

I shake my head. "It doesn't add up. Like, when did you come and look at the house?"

"No actual visit. I knew it was perfect from photos and said yes straight away."

"This is a crazy time for you to arrive. Why didn't you come during the day?"

"So sorry, big misjudgment of time. Too many restaurants prejudiced against dog and cat."

Despite the bumpiness of his accent, he's glib and has an answer for everything.

"You can't stay here tonight," I say. "We weren't expecting you. The apartment isn't ready, it hasn't been cleaned, there are no fresh linens on the bed. We would need time to think about the arrangements, meals, rent—"

"I have two months' rent right here. Three thousand dollars, we discussed, Mike and I." He pulls a fat envelope out of his pants, flips it open, and fans out the crisp one-hundred-dollar bills, like a criminal with a laundered stash. Mom and I stare at it. Monthly, it would cover the mortgage.

"Sorry about cash, like bank robber," he says, bashfully. "Very new in Ithaca and must get bank account."

"You know, you're going to have to excuse us, we haven't had dinner," my mother says. "I'm really nervous the cat and dog will ruin the furniture."

"Jenet, please don't worry. Torvill Eriksson knows all commands. If he climbs on furniture, you must say *Down*. And Tosca has light touch. No shedding, no scratching, perfect cat."

The three of them—dog, cat, intruder—stand there, three melancholy pairs of eyes with the same beseeching expression. They have the look of creatures who will be told to sleep in the car.

"Please, Medeleen—"

"Have you had dinner?" I ask.

"Yes, thank you, absolutely, finished with eating."

"Why don't you stay for a while and have some tea and cake?"

His eyes light up at the sight of the apple cake, so much so that my mother's face loses some of its animosity.

Afterward, I decide it's safe to leave him in the kitchen for a few minutes. My professional assessment (as a spy) is that he doesn't pose an immediate threat. Mom and I go to her bedroom to confer.

"I'm inclined to say yes," I say. "Mike made a very good deal with the rent. It would take some financial pressure off us. If it doesn't work out, we can give him the boot. Nothing's irrevocable."

"But what about those animals?"

"We can ask him to confine them to the apartment or outdoors."

The large cat, Tosca, shoots into the room and hops up onto my mother's favorite chair.

Mom lowers her voice, as if Tosca may listen and report back. "It's very risky," she says. "A large foreign man arrives at the house and tells you Mike arranged to rent to him. But don't you think it's odd that Mike didn't say anything to you and this weird man never came and looked at the place? You have no idea what he wants from us."

"He wants a quiet, decent place to stay. He's a writer. He wants a yard for his pets to run around in." I don't know why I'm pleading his case. Easing the stress of mortgage payments is irresistible. He's gentle with his animals.

Tosca is staring at us with those Halloween-yellow eyes, listening to every word.

"You don't know a thing about him," my mother whispers.

CHAPTER 12

With Andri wolfing down cake during dinner, my mother softens toward him. The bottom line is they get to stay, and I inform my new tenant that after one month, if everything's okay, we'll sign a longer lease.

I don't second-guess my decision. We need the money.

The apartment consists of a large bedroom and bathroom, a smaller sitting room, and a tiny kitchen with a microwave oven and fridge. When we bought the house, we assumed my mother would move into the apartment and we furnished it comfortably, with a queen-size bed, a plush couch, and a cherry-wood desk.

After the skydiving accident, when Mom actually did move into the house, she preferred the large spare bedroom close to mine, so she could be nearby for emergencies or bumps in the night. She's grown fond of this room, with its view of the woods, and wants to stay in it. She has everything she needs, including an attached bathroom and shower. I'm grateful now for the size of this old house.

I throw some fresh laundry and towels into Andri's arms and show him the ancient nook that contains a vacuum cleaner and other cleaning paraphernalia. Spiders have made a home for themselves on the walls. "You're on your own with this," I tell him. "The dust will probably kill you tonight if you don't give the bedroom a once-over."

Our arrangement, as advertised on craigslist, is we'll provide breakfast, but for lunch and dinner, he's on his own.

His happiness is all-encompassing. "A hundred thank yous, Medeleen, I will help, I promise. If you need fixing, I'm handy with hammer and nails."

Later, Andri traipses back and forth from his car, ferrying his belongings, which seem to consist mainly of equipment for his pets—beds, pillows, bowls, litterbox, and an assortment of toys. Even Torvill has perked up, running circles around Andri as he moves about.

Still later, the hoarse hum of the vacuum cleaner. Maybe we'll throw in lunch if he can be corralled to do the rest of the house.

It's a sobering thought. I've just allowed a stranger into my house, with no way of knowing who he is. He's clearly using his animals to weasel himself in, and I've obviously fallen for it. At the very least, I must check whether he's registered as a writing student at Cornell.

I'm bad at reading people. The only exception is my mother, for whom I can interpret every nuance and quiver. When she's lying, her right eye twitches slightly and her voice rises in a false attempt to sound innocent.

I've come up with a crude algorithm to assess the truthfulness of a person, using Mom for calibration. I assign a score from zero to five (where zero is true and five is a lie) for each of the following variables: face, voice, and body language. A total of fifteen would be a Pinocchio lie and zero would be Mother Teresa truth. Not foolproof.

The next morning at breakfast, I focus on Andri. He bangs in through the kitchen door after taking his animals for a run in the back.

"Very beautiful morning," he says. "Torvill wanted to eat ducks in pond."

Score ten. He's exaggerating. His face is eying me to see my reaction.

"Did you sleep well last night?" I ask.

He rubs his eyes, and says, "Torvill and Tosca very restless in night. I think they not used to house. Don't ask Torvill to ever be watchdog. He gets frightened and goes under bed." Torvill knows he's being discussed and hangs his chocolate-brown head in shame.

My mother is about to cook oatmeal and offers to make some for Andri. There's not much else for breakfast.

Andri says, "Yes, please, thank you, Jenet. I'm big lover of oatmeal."

Good. Below five. He likes it the way we have it, with milk and brown sugar. So far, he seems genuine, and I relax a bit.

"Where are you from?" Mom says.

He swallows, pours some milk, takes another spoonful, swallows, and puts his spoon down. "Born in Ukraine—Kyiv—then moved to Germany with family six years ago. Professor in European languages." His face has darkened.

Pure Pinocchio fifteen. Why would he lie about that? Maybe there's something painful in his past that he doesn't want to tell us. "Are you married?" I ask.

The spoon hangs in midair. "I got divorce last year," he says. "Very difficult. My wife liked Ukraine more than Germany and went back." He stares at his porridge.

My assessment is he's very unhappy about his wife. All scores plummeted to zero during the phrase "very difficult." However, his lying numbers soared to fifteen when he gave the reason. Maybe his wife was guilty of spousal abuse and nagged him about his weight. Perhaps on this our first morning he didn't want to share his private life.

After breakfast, I google Andri Eriksson. Why am I not surprised that I get no hits? Google asks me if I meant *Andre* Eriksson. Next, I visit Cornell's official website to check if he's really enrolled in a writing course at Cornell. What I get is a *yes*, a curt nod of confirmation. No details, no photo, no course info. Privacy laws forbid them.

While I'm at it, I google Joe Shelmann. An unusual name with only one hit, an elderly man who is definitely not my Joe. Perhaps the FBI shields agents from identification.

My right leg has become less sore, and rehab is going well, if you ignore that I shuffle about like I'm ninety. I decide to conceal my improving mobility from my Cornell colleagues and leave my newly acquired walker at home. It may come in handy if they think I'm still confined to a wheelchair.

Andri offers to drive me to work, but I decline. Mom knows my routine with the chair, and for now, I'll keep my distance.

When I arrive at work, Aisha is in her usual spot. My wheelchair hums to a stop at her desk, part of my new regimen of social accessibility.

Also, Joe's voice...*Let it be known Mike didn't confide in you...*

She stops typing. "How are you doing, Madeline?"

"It's hard. I miss Mike, even though you probably know we were...having trouble...in the last couple of months—"

"Yes, I kind of suspected..."

"We were barely talking," I whisper, and to my surprise, my eyes fill with tears. "But we were going to try and make things right with the skydiving date."

"I'm really sorry for your loss," she says. "Mike was a nice guy."

I give her a score of about five.

I shut myself in my office for a couple of hours, blessedly undisturbed by members of the Computer Science Department. Before eleven o'clock, I set off for my dead-drop assignation with Joe Shelmann. It's a raw September day, a flickering Ithaca sun weaving through the clouds. How strange I feel, slightly breathless. I'm really doing this.

Tower Road has a slight downslope, but by now I'm skillful at riding the wheelchair brakes. When I turn left onto Feeney Way, I surreptitiously check the people behind me. Am I being followed? I can't tell. There's a surge of people, any of whom could be watching me. When my chair rolls past the law school, I glance over my shoulder. The crowd has thinned, students, mostly, diffusing into the vast campus.

I park under an old oak tree, my eye on the spot across the road where Joe and I arranged to meet. Some of the passersby cast hooded glances at me, the woman in the wheelchair. I have no way of knowing if the coast is clear.

I almost fail to recognize Joe, with his back-to-front baseball cap, T-shirt, and blue jeans. He's walking briskly, swinging his arms with a carefree swagger. Without pausing or looking around, he turns onto the path we agreed on and disappears from sight. It's as if I saw him, blinked, and he was gone.

Slowly, uncertainly, I trundle across the road and follow him into a thicket of bushes and trees. It's a surprisingly beautiful area that smells of lilac and honeysuckle and has the splash of running water from the gorge. A hidden grotto. When I approach Joe, he's wearing a T-shirt that's famous in these parts: Ithaca is Gorges.

"How's the leg coming along?"

"I can walk without the wheelchair. I'm using the chair at work as part of my cover."

"That's well and good, but it makes you conspicuous, especially during the day. From now on, we'll use this place only after dark."

"We? It sounds like a tryst."

"No, ma'am. I meant each of us, when we come here separately." He looks at me a moment. "There's a danger of stumbling in the dark—you know, roots and bushes. Be sure to have your burner phone, and use the flashlight."

"How far away is the dead drop?" It's not an attractive landscape for navigating, day or night.

"Very near here." He points at a thick tree trunk ahead of us, whose branches are old and gnarly.

My chair bumps over the rough ground and we stop at the tree. The area is secluded.

Joe sits on a nearby rock and says, "Did anyone follow you?"

I laugh. "Probably."

He shakes his head, like I'm incorrigible. "I'm just sayin', when you're on the move, try and be aware of people behind you. Pause occasionally and listen. When you stop, do the footsteps behind you stop?"

"Joe, I'm not important enough to be followed."

He grimaces. "You have exactly the wrong attitude. You should act like you're being watched every minute—"

"Joe—stop! This is a group of nerdy programmers, not a bunch of Nazis."

"You have to take it seriously."

"Okay. Message received."

Joe stands, walks to my chair, and squeezes my shoulder affectionately. "Take risks if you must, but don't be reckless."

Is Andri a risk? He's paying the mortgage.

Joe is still holding my shoulder with his big, warm hand. "Point taken." I brush him off. What's up with him? I would never dream of squeezing *his* shoulder. Surely it's against cop protocol?

I'm getting a cramp in this position, my chair at an angle, wedged between a rock and a big root. "Okay, where are we headed?"

Joe says, "Park your wheelchair here, and I'll help you walk to the drop. There's a natural indentation behind the tree, which is perfect for what we need."

I'm not so thrilled to be dependent on his support, but there's no way my chair can wheel over the knotted roots.

He stands in front of me and holds out his arms. "Trust me. I won't let you fall."

But there's something demeaning about having him pull me up, so I don't reach out. Instead, I place my palms flat on the sides of the chair and lever myself up on my own, pushing heavily, and trusting the chair is wedged and will stay fixed on the ground. When I'm upright, I loop my left arm in his and say, "Okay, let's go."

Slowly, we make our way around the tree. To my relief, Joe's support is solid and muscular, his body comfortable to lean against.

Stones and shrubs carpet the area behind the tree. At the base of the trunk is a thorny bush that Joe picks up—literally—and tosses aside. Its spiky little branches lie tangled like a discarded bird's nest. Underneath is a hole about eighteen inches in diameter. The place is so well camouflaged I hope I find it when I come back.

Joe says, "I'd like you to try and kneel or squat so you can look carefully and try to put it together again."

Kneel or squat. He's so clueless.

"Why don't you move away and let me figure this out?"

"Yes, ma'am," he says, carefully unwinding himself.

First, I lean against the tree, my left side touching. Then, slowly, I inch down, aiming to get onto my haunches, healthy knee on the ground and right leg bent in front of me, skirting the hole. I'm good at spatial visualization of three-dimensional solids and lower myself with a final stable configuration of my body in mind. This way I can inspect the hole and maneuver its camouflage back into place.

The very instant I'm perfectly balanced, my head starts spinning and my stomach turns over and the ground seems to shift beneath me. Vertigo! "Ow!" I've misjudged the terrain. My right leg slips on some loose stones and my left leg—the so-called good one—buckles. I tumble forward causing the new knee to hit a rock and the good leg to land on a protruding root. All hell breaks loose in the pain centers of my brain as my right arm, trying to stop my fall, pitches into the hole.

"Madeline!" Joe springs forward to help lift me. "I'm so sorry. Are you okay?"

"Wait. Stay back!" I lie motionless for several seconds, taking inventory, letting the spin play out. *Breathe.* Everything is still attached. I shut my eyes and try to relax. The attack passes. The pain ebbs. Slowly, I maneuver my hand in the hole. It connects with something that isn't a rock or a root. It wasn't visible when we stood over the hole.

"Joe, come and take a look."

He peers into the part of the hole that I'm not occupying. "What—?"

"There's a cell phone in here."

CHAPTER 13

"Don't touch the phone!" Joe puts a restraining hand on my arm.

"Too late. My hand is resting on it." Carefully, I lift my arm out of the hole and arrange myself on terra firma. Joe sits cross-legged on the ground, riffles through his backpack, and removes a pair of thin gloves and a small tin container that looks like a shaving kit.

"How could you miss finding a phone in the dead drop?" I ask.

He reaches in, extracts the phone, places it on a cloth on the ground, and then uses a small brush to remove odd bits of soil and foliage. He stops and gazes at me with that slow, unfazed look, and says, "The last time I checked the hole, ma'am, the phone wasn't there." Score: fifteen. *Total liar.* He's making too much innocent eye contact. But what is he hiding?

"Who else used this dead drop? Did Mike ever use it?"

"No, ma'am. This was freshly dug for you."

"Joe, that's creepy. It doesn't make sense." I search his face, trying to read its bland expression without success.

But he's read mine. "It's possible Mike came here after he called me," he says slowly. "He knew our drop was compromised—long story—and we'd be moving to this tree."

"Hand me the phone so we can see who it belongs to and what's on it." I'm impatient with his dissembling.

"How will you do that? It's probably locked."

I shake my head and stare him down. "Wait—you've asked me to break into experts' computers, but you question if I can crack an obsolete iPhone 6?"

"Okay, mea culpa. Give me a moment to lift fingerprints."

He has a fingerprint kit! And in front of my eyes, Joe Shelmann becomes a wizard, deftly dipping his little brush in black powder, twirling the brush to remove excess, and twirling again over the phone. Several prints slowly bloom on the surface, as if by magic.

"Oh, baby, come to papa," he says softly.

Carefully, he lifts each print onto a piece of tape, then transfers it to an index card, which he labels before slipping it into a small sandwich bag.

"Now let's get some fingerprints from *you*." He opens what looks like a little stamp pad. "I need your prints so I can eliminate them."

Afterwards, he hands me small alcohol wipes that more or less remove the ink from my fingers.

"Okay, time to do your thing." He tosses the phone into my lap. The sudden movement spooks a squirrel that darts up the dead-drop tree.

"Do you mind helping me to my wheelchair first?" I say. "I'd prefer it if I didn't feel like we're playing woodland creatures in a preschool circle."

I allow him to grasp my hands and haul me up like a crane. I hate this but have no choice. He handles me like I'm fragile as he lets me down into the chair. I guess one spill for the day is about as much as I can take. When safely seated, I say, "Why must this hiding place be in such a difficult location? Why can't it be somewhere flat and normal like a post office box?"

"Because that involves other people and is less secure." He's reluctant to talk about it. For some reason, he's wedded to this location.

"Focus on the phone," he says. "Who does it belong to?"

"It's old technology, so no face recognition, which is good. Sometimes I find that hard to break." I power it on, relieved it still has some juice. "Look—" I hold it up for him to see. "Push-button unlocking, which is really so last century. With luck, the user was lazy like most people and didn't set up a password to get in."

I press the button, and sure enough, a familiar screen of icons appears. I'm in! "Not exactly rocket science," I say.

He grins, a spider web of lines at the corners of his eyes. "That's crazy. Now I won't get to see how good you are."

"In that case, power off your phone and hand it over." I reach toward him. "I'll leave it in the dead drop tomorrow with all your settings changed."

"No thanks, ma'am. I don't for a minute doubt your abilities. Now let's find out what's on this phone."

I tap the Settings icon and the name Mike Alvarez pops up.

For a moment, it doesn't register. Then it stops my heart. "Holy shit—Mike."

I've never seen this phone before. Mike's new Android phone was lost in the skydive. "This can't be my Mike."

"As I said, it's possible Mike came here after he called me." Joe's voice is curt.

"What are you saying—?"

"I'm not sure, Madeline. Have a look-see at what's on the phone."

His face is impassive. Something is missing. I peer at him, trying to decipher him like a code, the furrow on his forehead more pronounced than before, a bead of sweat on his eyebrow.

I tap Notes on the phone and find myself scrolling through a list of passwords as far as the eye can see. "This doesn't make sense. Half the people in the world are morons when it comes to security, but Mike wasn't one of them. He'd never keep his passwords on his phone."

"You're being harsh. It's convenient—"

"Except it's stupid. Should we look at his iCloud? Photos? What he sent to his girlfriends?" There's a catch in my throat, because I'm terrified about what I'll find, and why am I even looking at a phone with Mike's name on it? This all started out as a simple meeting for me to find the dead drop, and suddenly a dark pit has opened.

The browser shows a site called Chit Chat, and I find myself on some kind of online platform that says, *Welcome back, Mike. Press the button to continue.*

Joe moves beside me, resting his hand on the back of my chair. He's invading my space again with his looming physical presence, and in a gasp of suffocation, I jab at the Enter button and a young woman in a dainty bikini leans forward and shows me the top of her cleavage. *Hello, Mike. I'm Lolita. Wanna play a while, or go straight to the movies?* The text is in a bright yellow font, punctuated with smiley-face emoji.

"Oh God, give me some air." My stomach heaves.

"Take your time."

I have a bottle of water at the side of my chair and slug down a long, gasping drink. Mike is gone and I'd better pull myself together and grow a spine. The last thing I need is for Joe Shelmann to start patting me again, like *There, there.*

I type in the chat box, *What movies?*

You know—the usual. Girl-on-girl, man-on-man—

God. I stab at the first category. Don't ask me why. A site like this doesn't match with my Mike, nothing adds up and my analytical mind wants to know what the hell is going on.

Was this part of Joe's investigation? How did Mike find it?

Pale rays of sun quiver through the trees, the aura floating above my head.

"Be warned, Madeline," Joe says. "I've seen this type of thing before, and it can get ugly."

Lolita says, *Three hundred bucks, Mike, on your credit card, and I've sent you the link.* She drops her little top and cups her chest. *Have fun, baby.* She can't be more than eighteen years old.

The link is in Messages, and I click on it. A screen opens with a single flashing button: Play Movie. The programming setup is as familiar to me as my right hand.

"This button will generate a fresh password to decrypt the image. It's what I work on."

Joe says, "It looks like Mike was able to buy himself into the encrypted chat room. I think the phone holds his final message to me. Someone at Cornell must have—one way or another—led him to the site on the dark web. I guarantee you can't google it."

I hand the phone to Joe. "Okay, I've seen enough, thank you."

But he drops it back on my lap. "Look at what's behind the button."

The grainy film is in color, blurred images—the type that say *no consent.* My head spins with an aftershock of vertigo and I don't need to watch much to comprehend what Joe is investigating. I hit the Off button as the phone slides from my grasp and a branch cracks above my head and a hawk flaps through the trees.

Joe's voice is like an echo through the gorge "...sorry you had to watch that Madeline...but I wanted you to understand exactly what we're up against..."

CHAPTER 14

Joe has made me so paranoid that the first thing I do after lunch is shut the office door and sweep for hidden bugs. The small, windowless room is dark, giving me the shivers. I use a flashlight to scan the nooks and crannies, the shelves on the bookcases, the underside of the new lamp, the recesses of my printer, and the backs of my posters. Nothing.

Eventually, the only place that needs a look is the underside of my desk. After my morning tumble into the dead drop, I'm tentative about my injured leg, which throbs as I stand, leaning for support on the desk. I lower myself in slow motion, skinny flashlight in my teeth, and ease myself underneath. In the beam of light, there's nothing but dust. If I had asthma, I'd die here.

The jangle of my phone makes me drop my flashlight. Damn! It may be Mom.

There's a sharp rap on the door and I hold my breath. The door opens. Aisha enters the room and is confronted by the empty wheelchair and my phone ringing on the desk.

"Madeline?"

The flashlight has rolled away and I crawl out empty-handed on my belly, probably with spiders in my hair.

"Mother of Mercy, Madeline, what are you doing down there?"

"I lost a contact. But all's well. It was under the desk."

"You could've given me a call and I would've come right over." Her brow is furrowed, and her concern seems genuine.

"Yeah, I should have. It was annoying, and I made an impulsive move." I crawl out further. "This is embarrassing, but can you help pull me up?"

Her hands are dry and firm and in no time, I'm safely installed back in invalid territory.

After she's left, I realize she didn't tell me what she wanted. Also, the phone has gone quiet and there's no message. A moment of chaos, and now peace. This time I lock the door. The advantage of having a windowless office is you don't need to fear someone outside with a telephoto lens.

My immediate goal is to learn how to open locked doors without keys. The first hit on YouTube is an eye-opener, a video in which a man aims a Glock at a door and shoots the lock off. The gunshot rings out, and I hold my breath, waiting to see if anyone here has heard it. *Stupid!* Using Bluetooth and headphones, I cut the sound and continue scrolling. Eventually I find a video that explains in some detail how to use a small gadget that resembles a key with a thin rod, quite similar to what my mother has at home for opening sardine cans. I try to be analytic and visualize what, exactly, the rod is doing to gain entry. It's a bit like learning to play golf on YouTube.

I'll practice at home tonight. Does Andri keep his little apartment locked with the key I gave him? He doesn't strike me as the locked-door type. I wonder how my mother fared with all of them. Is Andri home yet? Did he leave Torvill and Tosca in the house? Were they respectful of Mom's boundaries?

After studying how to unlock doors, I get into the strange phone with Mike's name, which Joe has allowed me to borrow.

What was my husband trying to tell Joe with the pornography on his phone?

I banish the thought and go into analytical mode. Are the videos offered by Lolita saved? If not, there's no legitimate way I can break the encryption upfront. However, there obviously was a time the file was unencrypted, and if I can get hold of that, I can figure out the encryption algorithm. Its level of sophistication will tell me the caliber of the programmer who's hiding this stuff on the dark web. I'll figure it out eventually. It's a matter of when, not if.

Again, using Bluetooth, I transfer the contents of the phone to my MacBook Air. Now I can study the phone at home, at leisure, then throw the noxious thing back into the dead drop.

The rest of the afternoon passes in a surreal blur as I research and order spyware from Amazon. It's kind of fun contemplating nifty devices I'll place in strategic locations of the Computer Science Department. I can't shake the sense of imposter syndrome, how I'm sitting at my desk like a child, playing a game called "Spies."

The sardine key is exactly where I thought it would be, in my mother's gadget drawer. Mom has laid claim to the kitchen ever since she moved in permanently after the accident. I grab the key when she's not looking and put it in my jeans pocket.

Andri isn't home yet and Tosca the cat is sunning herself on my mother's windowsill.

"She likes this room," Mom says. "It's either my chair or the sill."

"Did you try shutting the door?"

Mom takes a sip of coffee. "Of course I did. She started yowling like a cat in heat and scratching the paint off the door."

In the haze of sunlight, the cat's ginger-black fur is thick and beautiful. Andri is right, she's a diva-deluxe cat and she knows it. "I don't have the energy to keep fighting," Mom says. "Thank God the dog respects boundaries."

Poor Torvill. Has he been locked in Andri's apartment?

"Mom, I'm going outside for a minute. I'll see you in the kitchen."

"Where are you—"

"See ya!" I say, rolling along the floor with my granny walker, trying to speed up without leaning too much. In my pocket are my house key and sardine opener. When I'm outside, I make sure the front door is locked and tentatively push the small metal tube into the lock. *Don't force it, feel the clicks of pushing aside the tumblers.*

There's resistance. I maneuver the tube to the side and hit an obstacle. No entry. It's frustrating—the instructor in the video made it look so effortless. How is it possible that someone who thinks she can crack any computer can't get past a simple lock? I start again. This time there's no resistance, the metal slides all the way in, right up to the bulge of the key, but the door remains stubbornly locked, and I'm standing here like an idiot with a sardine-can key.

"Did you lock yourself out of house, Medeleen?" Andri says, walking up the front path. "Here, use my key." I've been so intent on my task I didn't hear his car.

His appearance leads to a great barking and scratching on the other side of the front door.

Andri smiles like Santa Claus. "Torvill loves me, always happy when I come home. Here, let me open door."

I remove my makeshift key from the lock, and in a second or two, the door is open and Andri's dog is on the doorstep, going vertically bonkers, up and down, then jumping on Andri and slobbering all over him.

Andri stoops down and holds the big dog in a prolonged bear hug. When he stands, he hesitates, then pulls the door shut and locks it again. He moves Torvill gently and turns to me. "Let me show you, Medeleen, trick to opening door without key."

This is another one of those moments I must make a snap decision.

Silently, he takes the sardine key from my outstretched hand. He examines it closely, turning it over in his blunt fingers. "This is perfect tool." He slides it into the lock about half its length. "Trick is to go about one inch, jiggle up and down, go in further a little bit and then do side to side for final click." As he says the word "click," there's a click, and the door is open.

"Were you a burglar in your previous life?" I ask.

"Let's just say I have shady past," he says, eyes twinkling. He pushes open the door. "After you, Medeleen." Even Torvill inclines his head and steps aside to let the granny wheels through.

As we're about to sit down to dinner, right at the moment the timer pings that the rice is ready, Andri arrives in the kitchen bearing what looks like a week's supply of provisions. My mother has made enough beef stew to feed all of Brooktondale, so it seems mean-spirited not to invite our tenant to join us at the table.

"Jenet, can I keep some food in your fridge here?" Andri says. "Fridge in apartment is too small for growing boy like me." He pats his belly. "Good for snacks, but not real food."

I guess we'd imagined he'd eat out, but here he is, making us feel guilty at dinner time. "Sure, you can use the fridge," I say.

"Very many thank yous, Medeleen. Just one more request, please. Torvill has problem eating near Tosca's litterbox, even though cat very clean and fussy."

"Please—no litterboxes anywhere near us," Mom says.

Andri shakes his head. "Request not for cat, but for dog. Can Torvill have bowl here, in kitchen? He likes this room, good feng shui for dogs. Torvill is sensitive animal, no mess on floor ever."

Torvill, who's been standing at the stove, breathing the aroma of fragrant beef and wagging his tail, now turns baleful eyes on Mom, shrinking a bit under her stern gaze.

"I suppose," Mom says, "if we keep the bowl out of the way near the pantry." She points to a spot.

"You good woman, Jenet," Andri says. "Above rubies, yes?"

He makes no move to leave the kitchen. "And good cook too! Beef sure smells good." His round face is beaming.

"Would you like to join us for dinner tonight?" Mom asks.

After dinner, while I'm making tea, Andri says, "I see you very sad, Medeleen, missing husband, Mike, yes?" It's intrusive, but he's so somber and serious I can't take offence.

Mike stole my work. "Yes, I miss him."

"Tell me about Mike and accident. I know curiosity killed cat—"

"Nothing to tell. Mike crashed into a concrete building and died. I landed in a plowed field and lived. I had better luck than he did."

Mug in hand, I head to the sink. Eyes stinging.

I'm pleased Mom invited Andri to join us—it was the right thing to do—but Andri end-played her. He ambushed us right before dinner and pushed all of our buttons. Now we've created a precedent. His moves have been entirely transparent, and I don't want him to play us again.

Nor do I want to be interrogated about Mike during dinner.

It's awkward. Should I let it go? Where is Mike when I need him?

Mike is gone. And it can't be Mom, because she'd never push someone away from the table. It has to be me.

After doing the dishes, I'll reopen negotiations. He can join us for supper whenever he wants, provided he pays us a monthly stipend for food.

It's just a matter of getting the words out.

CHAPTER 15

I'm terrified to drive, which is irrational, because I've driven since I was fifteen. *Get in the damn car and put on the seatbelt,* I order myself. *Stop being pathetic.*

When I tentatively press on the gas pedal, pain knifes through the length of my leg. That's the price of freedom and liberating my long-suffering mother.

I spend an hour or so practicing on the back roads of Brooktondale, a bionic woman with metal pins and parts, getting used to the feel of her altered skeleton at the wheel. The pain diminishes.

The following evening after dinner, a late September night, I'm in my powder-blue Subaru Legacy, with my granny-wheels walker in the trunk, and my sardine key in my back pocket. The evening marks a milestone in my post-accident life.

The Brooktondale sky, untouched by the lights of the city, is a sight to behold, like diamonds on dark velvet. It seems to be a promise I can move on when all this is over.

Parking across from the computer science building is easy, but extricating myself from the car is another story. My injured leg is stiff and sore, unhappy after the long drive. I distract myself by thinking of the task ahead, and before too long, I'm rolling with my walker to the side door of the building.

My authorized key works perfectly, but then I must shove against the resistant door to get inside. Ouch! My pelvis has mostly healed but doesn't appreciate being smacked against heavy objects.

The foyer, devoid of people and daytime fluorescent lighting, has the look of a ghost city. I head to the elevator, fob ready, and in a moment, I'm juddering to the fourth floor.

Cornell conserves energy, which means dim lights in the computer science hallways. The place is strangely altered at night, deserted and cut off from daytime rhythms. The pale light throws shadows on the walls and helps me navigate to my current office without tripping over obstacles. I pause a moment, and play my phone light over the hallway ceiling. Not a camera in sight.

My nifty little gadget slips into the keyhole, and the door clicks open. Triumph of the sardine key!

Making my way down the hallway, I tackle each of the office doors. My success rate is good, about 70 percent. It's a revelation that my ungainly hands have some delicacy, able to tweak the little metal rod until it coaxes the locks to yield. I will, however, need to hone my skill.

With Joe's advice in my head, I make sure to relock all doors. I won't succeed as a spy if I leave a trail of unlocked doors.

Mike's old office has a plaque with the name David Graham. The unfamiliar nameplate gives me a surge of sadness. Our old turf. My makeshift key unlocks the door and in I go. How strange to be here at night, in the dark. I beam a flashlight around the room. A large-screen computer with mouse and mousepad are carelessly arrayed on the desk which is otherwise neat and orderly. No laptop—it's probably at home.

At the desk I jiggle the mouse to try and wake up the computer. There'll be nothing to do right now if it's powered down. But the screen blooms to life, showing a Microsoft interface. In an instant I've inserted a flash drive into a USB port and given an instruction to download the hard drive.

Why am I not surprised that David, not the sharpest tack in the toolbox, doesn't protect his computer from download?

While the process grinds along, I aim my flashlight at the walls, bookcase, lamps, and chairs, assessing places for surveillance equipment. The light picks up a small decal on the bookcase, which David must have overlooked, because it belonged to Mike—a logo for Skydive Finger Lakes. It jolts me into memories of our happy dives, and I stare at it a long while. This is why I'm here, really, to find out who killed Mike and stole away my life.

A sudden sound startles me, the jolting of the elevator as it comes to a stop on this floor. I glance at the computer screen—the download is almost done, the green line approaching completion. There are steps in the hallway, coming toward me. I can't wait for a perfect download and yank the drive out of the port and stuff it into my pocket as I hear a key at the door. As fast as I can, I race around the desk, leaning hard on the granny wheels, and sink to the floor. In my haste I knock the side of my walker, which topples over as David enters the room and hits the light switch.

"What the fuck—?"

This is what he sees: a woman clasping her knee and weeping. The pain and heartbreak are genuine, so the tears come easily.

This is what he does not see: the front of his computer.

"Madeline, what are you doing in my office?" The chill in his tone knocks me back a bit.

"I'm sorry, David," I gasp. "Tonight was a tough night for me, so I came to work."

"Why are you here?"

"It was impulsive. You know this was Mike's office—for years—I came in here to think about him—it was just sentimental—"

"How did you get in?" He's toned down the attack, but is still suspicious and unsympathetic.

"I have a key—from before—here…" I remove it from my pocket and hold it up to him. But something touches him at this moment, and he shakes his head.

"No—keep it, Madeline. I'm sorry I was so harsh. It was quite a shock suddenly seeing an intruder. I didn't realize it was you straight away."

"Please could you help me up?" I lift up both hands, beseeching. "I've got myself in a bit of a jam here." By now I'm hoping the computer screen has cooled and gone dark again.

He lopes toward me. He's a big guy. "I see you've graduated from your wheelchair."

"I'm trying this. Not sure I'm succeeding yet. It's slow going."

He reaches out toward me. There are reddish hairs on his thick arms. I grasp his hands and cry out as weight is transferred to my sore leg. The last shred of my dignity disappears when he abandons me against the wall and moves to retrieve my walker. He doesn't even glance at his computer.

Joe is right. I'm invisible. It wouldn't occur to him this weeping widow just invaded his hard drive.

"Do you mind if I take Mike's skydiving decal?" I say in a weak voice, pushing myself toward the bookcase.

He looks surprised, as if he hadn't noticed it. "Of course. Be my guest."

He heads to his desk and sees nothing amiss. He barely glances at his computer, but watches as I pull the decal from its corner of the shelf. There's something tiny stuck behind it that feels like a metal stud. I throw it all in my purse, which is in the basket of the walker.

My fingers felt something else on the shelf and I make a big show of rubbing away sticky residue from the decal. The tiny device goes into my pocket.

"All clean. Thanks, David, and I'm really sorry I startled you."

"No sweat, Madeline."

I trundle out and head to the elevator. It doesn't take a genius to know what I've removed from the office: an audio bug and a mini camera. Perhaps all my activities tonight have been observed. Joe was right. I'll need to be more careful.

Mike was being watched.

CHAPTER 16

From my car in the poorly lit parking lot, I call Joe on the burner. Two rings and hang up, as he instructed. Then an interminable five-minute wait while I contemplate the path forward.

"What's up, Madeline?" he asks, with none of the usual Good evenin', ma'am niceties. I guess it's Saturday night. Maybe he's on a hot date.

"Can you meet me at the dead drop tomorrow night?" I say. "We need to talk."

"Why can't we talk now?"

"It must be face-to-face. Right before seven-thirty?"

"Why not leave something for me in the dead drop?"

"Quit giving me flak, Joe," I say, and ring off.

When I get home—well after ten o'clock—my mom hurries into the kitchen in a state of agitation. "Where've you been, Mads?" She's shivering, pulling her sweater tightly around her.

"Let's go sit together," I say gently, steering her to her bedroom. When I flip the light switch, we find Tosca nestled deep into the pillows of the comfy armchair. She appears to be asleep.

We sit on the couch, side by side, thighs touching. "Mom, I went to work in my office at Cornell. Do you remember I told you before I left?"

She looks confused. "But how did you get there without me?"

"I took my car, Mommy. I can drive myself now and leave you in peace. We practiced together, remember?"

She shakes her head and tears roll down her face. "I forgot," she says. "I wanted to call you but couldn't find my phone."

"Hey, don't cry, Mom." I have my arm around her and squeeze her shoulders. "C'mon, the driving is good news. I'm getting better. And I'll find your phone in two seconds. Watch!"

I call her from my phone, and the shrill ring tone nearby comes from the cat. Tosca jolts awake, springs onto the floor, and darts out the door.

"Oh my God, the cat was sleeping on my phone," Mom says.

"Should I ask Andri to keep her out of our side of the house?"

My mom sighs. "No, don't bother, I've grown used to that cat. She doesn't disturb me, and she's a very pretty cat."

"Keep your phone in your pocket, Mom, and use Post-it notes to remind yourself of things you must remember."

She smiles, her beautiful face resurfacing. "I'm so proud of you, Maddie."

The following afternoon, when I enter the house after work, Torvill is resting peacefully on the couch in the living room. His head is on a couch cushion, which he has maneuvered into perfect position.

"Down, Torvill," I say.

He looks at me for several seconds before he descends—with great dignity—onto the wooden floor. His eyes don't leave me for a second. Reproach isn't the word.

"Hey, this isn't your room," I say defensively. "There's a lovely couch in your apartment. Go lie there."

"Sorry, Medeleen. Torvill not good in English," Andri says, entering the living room. He then lets loose a barrage of German, which somehow persuades the dog to follow him. Torvill, like Andri, is pushing buttons, and it's a matter of time before he shifts his entire base of operations to this part of the house. He's already started lapping food and water in the kitchen and panting expectantly at my mother to give him scraps. Andri has taken over a good part of the kitchen, loading our fridge with hearty supplies. He consumes a diet rich in fat, cheese, and sausages, and now he will enjoy Mom's cooking at dinner. I'm not a doctor but he's headed for trouble. He's very unconcerned about his weight. His face shone with joy and gratitude when I pulled him aside and offered him Mom's nightly cooking, for a fee.

Mom seems resigned to having Andri and his menagerie in the house. Despite her memory issues, she understands that with Andri's rent payments, we are now flush with cash. I haven't told her that next year I'll be out on my ear and need a new job.

Before I leave for my dead-drop meeting with Joe, I write a Post-it note: *Madeline is at Cornell* and press it to the back of Mom's hand. "Put this in a good place."

"Why can't you work at home?"

"Because I need the desktop computer in my office."

"But you don't, really," she says, in a moment of sharpness. "You could access it remotely from here. Even I know that. You've always been a computer whiz."

"Okay, Mom, you got me there. Truth is, I need some non-computer stuff from my office. I must be there for a couple of hours."

We're at the kitchen table; Torvill is lapping at his water bowl, and Andri has excused himself. Mom leans forward conspiratorially. "I know why you're going out." Her voice is soft. "You've been hyped up ever since you came home from work. You're meeting someone."

I stare at her. This is a different person from the befuddled one I comforted last night. "Can't get anything past you, can I, Momma? What if I confess I'm meeting someone in connection with work?"

"I knew it! I bet it's a guy." She sits back, triumphant. Poor Mike, his ashes barely cold.

"Gotta go." I kiss her forehead and finally escape.

It's a cool night, the middle of September, when the weather in Ithaca abruptly changes from summer to fall. For the first time I have on a light jacket, because we'll be outside.

The campus is surprisingly lively, and I have to park quite far away from the path. By the time I get there, it's a minute past 7:30, and Joe may already be waiting. The place we're meeting is, by design, not well lit, and to my annoyance, Joe has been so damn smart picking a concealed location that I can't find it. Shit. For someone who's supposed to have a brilliant mind, I somehow managed to not mark the spot.

Back and forth I go with the granny wheels, steering to where I think I should be, and tentatively pushing into the undergrowth. But all I encounter are thickets of brambles that lodge in my hair and scratch my face.

My heart is hammering when I finally shove my walker past the correct bush and find Joe leaning against a tree in his usual pose.

"Well, good evening, ma'am," he says. "Nice night for a stroll, I reckon."

"Sorry I'm late, Joe." I turn off my flashlight and activate the light on my walker.

"No lights." He waves at the source of the beam. "We're too near the road."

"Why don't I stand with my back to the road?" With my eyes accustomed to the dark, I don't need illumination and can see him just fine; but despite that, I turn on the pale light, because I want to see how he reacts to what I'm about to say.

I take my sweet time, fidgeting with the walker, trying to get comfortable, half-sitting on a middle rung. Because the ground is uneven, I must find an angle that wedges it and me into a stable position. My leg is throbbing. This is not ideal.

He makes no attempt to hide his irritation. "What was so important you had to see me tonight, in person, and couldn't tell me on your phone?"

He's being a jerk. Not even one comment congratulating me on graduating from the wheelchair. *Thanks, Joe, it feels great. I like being taller than men like you.*

Deep breath. "This conversation is necessary, Joe, because you've been lying to me. And *because*, Joe, what the hell is going on?"

CHAPTER 17

"Okay, you've got my attention, so why don't you tell me what's on your mind." He crosses his arms, still playing the cool guy, in his snug blue jeans and short leather jacket.

"I'm a problem solver, Joe, so here's a first grade logic puzzle."

He sighs ostentatiously. "Shoot."

"Question one: Who put Mike's phone in the dead drop? You and I, and possibly Mike—if I believe you—were the only ones who knew about the hole under the bush. I didn't do it. Therefore, Joe, it was either Mike or you."

"Bravo." He claps his hands slowly.

"Question two: When did Mike create those files on his so-called phone? It must have happened in the few months before he died—the chat room, the porn—as part of his undercover work for you."

"Go on." He has quit the sarcastic demeanor and is watching me intently.

"You may be interested to know I downloaded the contents of that phone to my hard drive. Bottom line: everything on the phone was created in the weeks *after* Mike's death."

Joe shifts his weight. "Doesn't make sense—"

"No, sir, it doesn't. Unless Mike, in some miracle of supernatural teleporting—"

"Okay, Madeline. I admit I'm the source of the phone. I used Mike's name. I buried the phone in the dead drop."

I didn't think he'd come clean so fast. It rattles me.

"Why, Joe? Why install stomach-churning porn on a phone with my dead husband's name? When he wasn't here to defend himself?" My voice cracks.

"Madeline—"

"I ran those encrypted files through an old algorithm of mine and regenerated the original files in two minutes. The encryption used was ancient history. If porn czars used that on today's social media platforms, the cops would break the code in minutes. So, I asked myself, why, why, why did Joe make this ridiculous fake phone?"

"Madeline, I can explain—" He moves toward me, and I put up both hands.

"Stay where you are. I'm not done." He goes back to his tree.

"Do you know when I became suspicious?" I say. "When you gave the phone to me instead of zipping it into an evidence bag and handing it over to Karla Mahoney, the detective investigating Mike's death. You, with your great magic show using the fingerprint kit. What kind of cop does that? I concluded the phone wasn't a serious piece of evidence because you didn't treat it as evidence."

For once, anger loosens my voice and makes me eloquent.

"I owe you an explanation, ma'am," he says.

"Damn right. Did you really think I was that stupid?"

"I underestimated you, Madeline—"

"I'm not done. Why? What was the big dramatic act with the phone about?"

He rubs his neck in what appears to be a rueful gesture. "I wanted you to *see*—not hear about—the kinds of abuse we're going after." This time he does move closer and touches my arm. "I'm really sorry, Madeline. I didn't want Mike's death to be your only motivation for helping me. I wanted you to see that...horror."

I shake his hand off. I'm so tired of being treated as less than an adult. "Why couldn't you just show me? Why the deceit?" I'm genuinely baffled.

"The subject matter is—difficult." He looks away. "I didn't want to sit beside you watching scenes of sexual torture...It would have been unseemly."

"*Unseemly?* You don't think what you did was unseemly? You could have given me the phone to look at in the privacy of my home, away from your sensitive presence."

"But then I couldn't be sure you'd give it the attention it needed—I'm sorry, that's the truth."

"What, poor naïve Madeline, too tender and innocent to take in the evil world of snuff pornography? Do you have any idea how insulting and condescending that is?"

"Please blame my Southern roots, ma'am, where women are put on pedestals and protected. I guess I looked for a more genteel way to show it to you."

In the dim light, something resembling remorse is on his face.

I nod. "Okay, it's weird, but I'll accept it. Still, I resent the time I wasted analyzing those files. You have to level with me, not throw red herrings, otherwise I can't work with you."

"Scout's honor, ma'am. I shouldn't have treated you like that or deceived you."

"Okay, in the light of our honest new relationship, built on trust, one last question."

He hesitates. "Shoot."

My right leg is stiff from sitting on the walker, and I shift position before choosing my words carefully. "Why should I believe anything you've told me? I have no evidence that Mike worked undercover for you. I think this whole business with Mike was a fabrication. An optical illusion. The fake phone, the fantastical tale at the funeral home, the myth of the other dead drop, the warnings of danger. I saw no evidence of a money infusion into our bank account. So here's my question: Was Mike really working for you?"

He stares at me a long time. "I did approach him, if that's what you mean. But he told me he liked his colleagues and didn't want to spy on them. He said he'd think about it, and after about two weeks, he declined. Said he wanted to spend more time on his research, that he had this fabulous new idea and didn't want distractions."

Then why was Mike away from home in the evenings? Was it really just a sleazy love affair?

"So you lied." I pull off my jacket and throw it into the basket of my walker. "Mike wasn't working for you at all."

The question was a shot in the dark, and my head is spinning from Joe's revelation.

"Please, Madeline, listen. It wasn't exactly a lie." Joe's voice is annoyingly unruffled, and I want to punch him in his self-assured, lying face.

He should be on his hands and knees begging me to keep working with him.

"A few days before he died, Mike called me on the burner phone I'd given him, and said he'd been looking into a couple of things. He thought he had something useful. Didn't want to talk about it on the phone. We arranged to meet at a pre-arranged location. But he didn't show."

I inhale and blow it out. "Mike would never spy on his friends. He was a nice, open guy. Creeping around wasn't his style."

"I reckoned, ma'am, that people wouldn't suspect him."

"Except, someone did," I say slowly. "There were eyes and ears on him—I found bugs in his office."

"You searched his old office?" He seems surprised, even though I've been doing exactly what he asked. "How did you handle the, uh, current occupant of the office?"

"I came at night when the place was deserted, broke into the office, swept it for bugs and downloaded the hard drive of his desktop computer."

He shakes his head and laughs. "I suppose you now have something to report back on this person?"

"Just that we can eliminate him—David Graham—from suspicion. There was nothing but sedate adult porn and godawful algorithms on his computer. And, as an aside, Mr. Shelmann, I went through all his porn movies and did not avert my gaze."

"Great going, Madeline," he says. "You have quite a talent for espionage."

"Tell me something, Joe—and remember, total honesty—have you been recording this meeting? Like maybe for your notes? Just to keep tabs on me?"

He's laughing again, a bit off balance. "Boy, you are something. What would you do if I said yes?"

"I would say, Joe, take out your phone, let's hear the quality of your recording."

"You're a strange one." He pulls his phone from his jacket pocket. "You already know what's on it. You really want me to press play?"

"Yes, I do."

He peers at his screen and taps it. His phone makes a shushing sound like the rustling of leaves. The wind whistling through the forest.

"What the heck is that?" he says. "It's dark, maybe I hit the wrong icon."

"Yeah, maybe. Let's hear it."

This time he really concentrates as he activates the audio. Again, there's nothing but static, a low hiss, and the vague muffled murmur of his voice in the background. Our conversation is lost.

He glares at me.

"Don't underestimate me again, Joe," I say.

CHAPTER 18

Joe's posture stiffens. "What's the deal with my phone, Madeline?" he demands.

"Your phone is fine. I zapped it with this." I pull up my jacket sleeve and display a chunky, Goth-like bangle on my arm.

"What the hell is that?"

The rough language is bracing. As long as I'm meek or subordinate, he plays the polite Southern gentleman.

"It's a bracelet of silence—emits ultrasonic signals, so when you try and play back your recording, all you get is white noise."

A dangerous energy crackles between us as he steps closer to see it in the dark. "May I?"

I hold up my arm like a sorcerer, watching the spiky metal bumps glint in the faint light. Joe takes my wrist carelessly, rotating the cyberpunk jewelry back and forth. I study it through his eyes. How well it sets off my long bony hand. His touch is disconcerting—electric—and jolts me from my complacent superiority.

I don't move a muscle. "Don't worry, I've deactivated it."

He drops my arm, but stays close. "This is unbelievable. How did you know I'd be recording you?"

"I didn't. I'm planning to use this in the computer science offices when I plant bugs." I smile in the darkness. "It was kind of a shot in the dark to test the bracelet on you before-hand. You should have asked my permission to record me."

A cool wind is blowing through, and he inclines his head as he zips up his jacket. He seems vulnerable at that moment, emitting a rare flash of self-awareness. He likes to be in control, and I've thrown him off track.

"Where does that gadget come from," he asks.

"Fellow grad students—computer scientists—quite a while ago. Mike wanted to use Alexa, which listens for words like "Alexa!" or "Hey, Siri," but also records everything else, so we invented these privacy gadgets I could wear when Alexa was on. At the time, I didn't realize I'd be aiming the bracelet at an actual person."

"What else should I know?"

My natural inclination is to be closemouthed about my secrets; but he's not the enemy. To be honest, it's fun to have the upper hand, and joust with him. I enjoy his droll humor and occasional lapses into quaint Southern gallantry.

But most of all, the mystery of Joe Shelmann intrigues me. He's very glib, and lies without blinking. And yet... he's intense and serious about our mission.

He appears more respectful now, but it could be a night-time delusion.

I say, "I'm wearing a jammer vest that will scramble pictures of me and blur my face, so no photos please."

He rolls his eyes, but he's finally smiling. "Are you for real?"

"How about you, Joe? Are you?"

I lift up my jacket and show him the chain-mail fabric. "It's called stealth-wear. Another invention from my student days."

He doesn't come and touch it, nor does he ask how it works. Instead he says, "You are one scary woman, Madeline. And I do apologize for not understanding that earlier."

I nod. There's work to do tonight, in the computer science building.

The foyer of Gates Hall is a deserted wasteland, eerie green lights blinking as I approach the elevator. The doors open with a ping, and Aisha steps out. She seems as disconcerted to see me as I am to see her. It's almost 9 PM.

"Madeline!" she says. "Coming to work at this hour?"

"Hi, Aisha. And it's late for *you* to be leaving work. Maybe we're both night owls."

"Not me," she says, forcing a laugh. "I had something I wanted done before tomorrow morning. I hate this place at night, it's like a morgue. Anyway, gotta go." And she's off with a breezy wave, her stylish red pumps clicking on the tiles.

It's disturbing she knows I'm here, but there's no undoing what's done. As far as my investigation is concerned, the clock is ticking. Not much more than two months to uncover the Cornell criminal, assuming there really is one.

There are three questions to answer before I leave Cornell. What happened to Mike? Is there a pornography enabler embedded in the department? Am I smart enough to find out?

So far I have a big fat zero. The bugs in David Graham's office turned out to be duds, no juice in them at all.

Tonight I'll try my luck in Judy's office.

The fourth floor is dark and forbidding in the dimly lit hallway. At the door of Judy's office, I shrink back into the shadows and listen for ambient sounds, before sliding my sardine key effortlessly into the keyhole. Quietly I wheel my walker into the room and lock the door behind me.

In the pale moonlight through the windows, the chairs look like sentinels at the desk. I park my walker in a far corner and drape it with a stealth-wear shawl to hide it. The awkward contraption, with its bulk and squeaks, is a giveaway. I should ditch the thing and practice walking without it, but I'm unsteady on my feet, the ground feeling soft and tilted.

I grope my way to Judy's desk and agitate the mouse of her computer. Unlike David Graham's setup, the screen remains dark. The computer is down and must be powered up. If Judy has security vulnerabilities, I'll find them. When light blooms on the screen, I must enter a password. Using my small flashlight, I examine the desk, casting about for a notebook or Post-it note that will reveal the key. Most people have an incredibly laissez-faire attitude toward security. A small shallow drawer near the top of the desk contains a page of notes and character strings. Passwords! I enter the shortest sequence of letters and digits, and, like magic, I'm in! Busy users are always impatient to get into to their computers. They also tend to use the same passwords over and over again.

This computer was easy to crack.

It's now a matter of inserting my gizmo and downloading the hard drive. As with David Graham's desktop, it's not much of a challenge. The familiar green progress bar appears on the screen, promising a smooth ride.

During the split second I congratulate myself on my brilliance, a key turns in the lock, and the door opens. Bright light floods the room. Henry, our janitor, enters with a cart of pails, mops, and cleansers. He stops dead when he sees me. "Hi, Madeline. I can come back later if you'd like."

Damn! I don't have my story ready, as Joe warned me to do, and now must think fast. Henry knows who belongs in which office. He's been around for years.

"Hello, Henry," I say, "could you give me five to ten minutes? I'll be done here soon—just reading something for Judy." It'll have to do. Act natural, like for all the world I belong in this room, on Judy's chair, working in the dark.

I'm flustered just thinking about it, and heat rises on my cheeks.

"Okay, I'll come back later," he says, sotto voce, pushing his cart out the door. "Lights on or off?"

God. "Off, please." *Stupid.* "I have a headache. Thanks." And again, I'm in the dark room, peering at the screen, with a surreal aura of after-light. My palms are sweating. When the download is complete, I pocket the precious flash drive and shut down the computer. Judy will find it as she left it.

There's one more task before I leave this office. Find a place to conceal a small recording device. The bug resembles a regular USB flash drive, and seeing it lying about in an office shouldn't arouse suspicion. But I plan to actually hide it and then grab it periodically. It's voice activated, battery powered, and ideal, because I can slot it into my computer and listen to conversations.

Judy's bookshelves are packed with computer science tomes she probably hasn't glanced at in years. I select a book that's obsolete and slip my small device in its spine. Perfect. She won't find it unless she goes searching.

Before too long, my wheels are back in the hallway.

There's a light on in my old office—Dwayne Browning's current office—and I assume Henry is in there, cleaning it. I decide to investigate. When I go by, however, instead of Henry, Dwayne is sitting at my old desk. Has he been there this whole time? There wasn't a light earlier, and I reckoned all offices were dark and empty.

A light bulb goes off in my head. Dwayne is the reason Aisha was here.

An outside observer would swear he's been hard at work for hours, head on his palm, mouse in his hand, eyes on his screen.

"Hey, Dwayne." I'm in the doorway, leaning on my walker.

"Madeline, come in!" He spins around to face me, but not before shutting down his computer and closing the lid. He's been working on a laptop.

It may not be a bad idea to case the joint. Something tells me Dwayne won't be as easy to crack as David and Judy.

I swivel from my walker and plop down into a soft chair. "Do you always shut down your computer when you have company?"

He's bemused. "You can call it programming while Black. My parents taught me to be paranoid, so I am."

"What's on your computer that you don't want people to see?" I sound like a jerk. No one gets near my computer either.

He looks long and hard at me, taking me in. Since that disastrous department lunch, I haven't been near him. He says, "I have some hot research going right now. Just imagine, if some dude with sticky fingers comes in here and downloads my files. Then presents my stuff at some public talk as his own work."

"Hey—"

"Now imagine I get pissed off, stand up and say, wait a minute, that's my work you're showing. Who they gonna believe, the White guy with a pedigree or the Black guy whose grandmother cleaned toilets?"

The irony is just too hard to take. "With all due respect, Dwayne, I don't need to imagine your scenario because it happened to me. Remember? At my lunchtime talk last week? Who did they believe did the work—the White guy with the pedigree or the girl in a wheelchair?"

He has the grace to look embarrassed. "Yeah, well—"

"You were very quick to accuse me of stealing Mike's work—"

"To be honest, I was so surprised when I saw Mike's diagram on the screen, I spoke up impulsively."

"That picture wasn't Mike's. It was mine."

I incline my head and examine his face. Handsome tan-brown skin without blemishes. Sensitive mouth. A hint of dimples when he smiles, which he's not doing now. He's being disingenuous. The damage to me is done.

"I'm sorry, Madeline," he says softly. "I should have spoken to you privately before making a public accusation. I had no way of knowing whether it was you or Mike who came up with the work."

I nod. There's no reply to that.

He adds, "Mike was so enthusiastic about his breakthrough data structure and his new ideas for encryption, I couldn't for a moment imagine the work wasn't his."

Time to change the topic. "By the way, I saw Aisha earlier, coming out the elevator."

"Oh, yeah?" He misses a beat or two, his face dejected. "I wish she'd have me. But there are always obstacles and conditions. I've been trying to persuade her for months."

I point to the young woman sitting on his desk in a silver frame. "Who's that?"

"My daughter. She's about to graduate from college." When he sees me staring, he says, "Yeah, I got into fatherhood at a young age."

No shit. He looks about thirty-five.

"Where's her mother?" I ask, embarrassed.

"Dead. Murder? Drug overdose? Suicide? It's all the same. Part of my life baggage."

His voice is so flat and unemotional it's chilling. I should be heading home—it's late. What am I doing here, broadcasting I'm snooping around? For someone supposed to be undercover, I've sure announced my presence. Aisha knows. Henry the janitor knows. David Graham knows. And now Dwayne Browning. There's no such thing as being under the radar anymore, not for me.

The shrill ringing of my phone makes me jump. "Excuse me, Dwayne, I must take this. It's my mother." There's no way I can heave myself out of my chair and run into the hallway, so I swipe Answer Phone, with Dwayne looking on.

"Mom?"

"Maddie, please come home," she half-whispers.

Torvill is barking in the background.

The phone shakes in my hand. "Mom, what's going on?" When she doesn't answer immediately, I fight to keep my voice calm. "Talk to me, Mom."

"Please help me Mads oh God there's someone outside looking in the window."

"Okay, I'm coming home now. Ask Andri to keep you company until I get there."

"I'm not leaving my room," she says. "I've locked the door."

CHAPTER 19

A steady drizzle and thick fog impede the drive home. This is a particular Ithaca-weather torment, mist rising off the road. Zero visibility. *Damn.* Cars approaching from the opposite direction look like ghost cars in a horror movie.

The stop-and-start driving causes my bionic leg to cramp, but I can't get out in the middle of the road and stretch. As the cars creep along, I try calling my mother, but she doesn't pick up, so I call Andri. I'm tossed into his voicemail, which crackles a message to me in German.

I curse and grind my teeth, but eventually pull into the garage next to Mom's car. I hurry through the mudroom door, past the dark living room and into the kitchen, where water is dripping through the ceiling, great fat drops plopping down next to Torvill's water bowl. Torvill thinks it's a game, and is barking at the falling water, jumping in the air to catch the drops in his mouth.

"Bad story with leaking ceiling, Medeleen," Andri says. "Probably damaged roof. I can check it out tomorrow."

"Andri, what's going on with my mom?"

He seems oblivious, entertaining his dog with a plastic bucket. "Jenet has Tosca, and bedroom door locked. She's not telling me the problem."

"Wait here, I'll be back—"

I hurry to the other side of the house and knock firmly on my mother's door. "Mom, open up."

"Are you alone?" she says softly, through the keyhole, startling me. It sounds like she's been sitting against the door, waiting.

"Yes. Let me in." I strain to hear her movements, masked by the rain pattering on the roof.

She opens the door about six inches, grabs my arm, pulls me in, and shuts the door. "Thank God, Mads. This is terrifying." The room is dark. Tosca is on Mom's bed, her eyes gleaming.

"I was getting ready for bed and saw a person at the window," Mom says, shivering. "He was watching me." I glance across at the opaque panes, the rain sluicing sideways. Mom is in a kind of twilight, seeing ghosts and mirages through the glass. It's not the first time this has happened. Last week she saw my father, calling to her across the divide.

"Were you in the dark?" I ask gently, flipping the light switch, and leading Mom to her couch.

"My lamp was on."

"Who would be outside on a night like this?"

The set of my mother's jaw is firm. "I know what I saw."

I wrap my arm around her and hug her close. "Hey, Momma, with the light on in your room, maybe you were seeing a reflection of yourself in the window."

She pushes me away. "Yes, and maybe he's still creeping around."

There's just one way to calm her down. "Put on your rain gear. We'll all go outside, Andri and Torvill too, and check the perimeter of the house."

"Just you and me," she says.

"No. Having a big man and his dog will add to our security." I actually hear myself saying that. *God.*

The granny wheels can't move through mud, so the walker must stay in the house. One of my hands must hold an umbrella, and one is for a flashlight. It's past time to wean myself from mechanical supports and mental wobbles and walk on my own. If for no other reason, to present a strong front for my mother.

In the kitchen, water is pouring through the ceiling, and Andri is placing towels from my linen closet on the floor. "Does Torvill have rain gear?" I ask. "We must all go out and check the exterior of the house."

To Andri's credit, he asks no questions. He takes one look at my mother in her rain hat and Wellington boots and disappears. I turn on all the outside lights and stand clinging to my quaking mom until Andri shows up draped in a voluminous black plastic tent. He has a poncho for Torvill, whose eyes are deep ponds of resignation.

"I'm scared," Mom says. "Someone is spying on us."

We're a strange procession, my mother and I, followed by Andri and his dog. Torvill is reluctant to set his paws into the mud—who can blame him?—but Andri has many treats up his sleeve and lures him out.

The suction of the wet grass is a drag on my legs, but my boots are solid on the ground. There's something bracing about the fresh autumn rain. My strength grows as I walk, slowly and carefully, the ache under control.

The back of the house is poorly lit, obscuring the rain and shadows of the trees.

I train my flashlight on the area outside the bedroom windows, where there's some shelter under the eaves. My goal is to point out to Mom that the ground is unbroken and the bushes undisturbed. "See, Mommy, nothing to worry about, you probably saw yourself in the glass..."

Torvill, who's been squelching along with us like a trouper, stops underneath Mom's window, growling, his head suddenly alert.

"Torvill can probably smell nice rabbit," Andri says.

I hand my umbrella to Mom and lean against the wall, crouching down and playing my light over the terrain. There are indentations, faint but unmistakable, maybe footprints, maybe not, already blurred around the edges, filling with water. Small bushes lining the wall have some stems broken, possibly by the punitive weather. But perhaps they've been trampled.

My mother sees it too. "So, Mads, I'm not senile yet."

I move to pat Torvill's wet head, and he licks my hand. "Good dog."

Just what we need, a Peeping Tom.

Andri digs around in his pocket and hands Torvill a bone-shaped cookie, which disappears with one snap.

Back in my mother's bedroom, I tell her not to worry, there wasn't any real evidence of an intruder.

"Someone is watching the house," she says.

"You should ask Andri for help if there's a problem when I'm not here. He's a good guy. He won't mind taking Torvill for a walk to check."

"I don't trust him."

"Why not? He's helpful."

Mom has her agitated and confused demeanor and looks away. "He's been snooping in the house."

I stare at her. Is this another hallucination? Medium score on the lying scale, but not Pinocchio either. "Snooping how?" My voice is neutral.

"Well, I know he doesn't belong on our side of the house, but this afternoon, I saw him—" Her look is vague and unfocused, the kind that often signals trouble. She waves her hand toward my bedroom and says, "He was coming out of your room."

"Mom, are you sure?"

"And he was in the living room earlier, going through the cabinets where you have your old CDs."

"Did you ask him what he was looking for?"

"He said he wanted the TV remote. The one for his TV set doesn't work."

"Did he try and hide that he was searching? Was he embarrassed?"

"No, he made small talk. Full of compliments about my cooking. Then he changed the subject and asked about Mike."

Can I believe her? "Why don't we give him the benefit of the doubt for the time being? He's offered to fix the roof, which is leaking buckets in the kitchen."

"He's a suspicious character, Mads. I've done some checking of my own."

"Mom, it's time for bed. We'll talk some more tomorrow, okay?"

"I went into *his* room," my relentless mother says. She lowers her voice, which is nevertheless triumphant. "And guess what I found."

"What?" I say, wearily.

"A gun," she whispers.

CHAPTER 20

The following Saturday, the first day of October, is a stunning Ithaca fall day, crisp and sunny, with raindrops from the previous night glinting on the grass. We're all out and about, my mother planting tulips and daffodils in the back garden, and Tosca nearby, stalking chipmunks. Andri has surprised me with his agility, scaling the long ladder, and hammering something on the roof. Torvill is going berserk at the foot of the ladder, because he wants to be on the roof with Andri, who leans over and shouts a long command in German. Defeated, Torvill sinks into the grass, lying spread-eagled on his stomach.

I'm installing a Ring camera outside Mom's bedroom, which will enable me to view video of anyone moving in the back yard. I've already placed one in the doorbell, providing a view of the front porch. The video transmitted by these little cameras is controlled by an app on my phone that has two-factor password authentication, so my spyware won't spy on me.

When Andri descends the ladder, it shakes against the wall. "Roof all patched up for now," he says proudly. Sweat is dripping down his face.

"Wow, thank you so much. Come and have a drink with me on the front porch."

I bring out lemon-lime iced drinks and watch him quaff his down—ice and all—in two great gulps. When his glass is safely on a side table, I say, "Andri, why do you have a gun in the house?"

He looks at me with wide-open eyes and mops his brow with a napkin. He's not defensive at all, and doesn't ask the obvious question, which is *how do I know?*

Instead, he says, "Gun is for murder mystery in novel. I'm studying old Glock from friend of mine. Come, I'll show you, Medeleen."

I haven't entered his apartment since he started living here. Cat and dog toys litter the floor, so reaching the couch is an obstacle course. The gun sits on his desk, under the lamp, a scene straight out of Agatha Christie. He grabs the gun and pulls up a chair.

"Whoa—" He could put me out of my misery right now.

"All okay, gun is empty," he says, opening the barrel. "This sliding mechanics is key to whole plot, but I'm not very good describing how it works, so must take gun apart."

I contemplate him and his gun. He's either very quick on his feet or very innocent. "Why were you in my bedroom last week?" Might as well get all the issues on the table.

He looks startled and unhappy, frowns, then nods his head, possibly concocting a lie. "Absolutely never in your bedroom, Medeleen, I swear on Torvill's head." Torvill gives me The Look that induces guilt in my heart. "But I did go in study to find stapler. So sorry to you and Jenet, I should have asked."

He was in my study.

A brief search of the study reveals nothing out of place. I settle in for an examination of Judy Holsinger's computer. It confirms exactly what I'd suspected: she's moved to the dark side—all administration all the time, and not a sign of computer science or programming anywhere to be found.

This is the place I should quit—ethically speaking—but I'm not a saint and dig into the file labeled Madeline Geiger. To my surprise, I've been a problem for years. There's a list of people bellyaching about my nice office, my university support, my failure to "fit in," and my lack of "productivity." The replies are all a variation on the same theme: "Mike is a great catch for Cornell, and if we want to retain him we must keep her happy." It hurts. A query to the Dean from Judy asks about the legality of firing me before December. The Dean advises caution, writing that Cornell is vulnerable in this litigious society. One puppet master after another, pulling the strings of my life.

Mike's folder is choc-a-bloc with glowing letters of recommendation supporting his tenure. The men—all men—rave about the originality of his work. *My work.* I understand, now, how thoroughly Mike sucked the academic marrow from my bones.

A salary letter from Judy announces Mike's 3.5 percent salary raise, the maximum allowed.

I move on to Nigel Welbourne, sneaking an irresistible, illicit peek at the so-called star of the Computer Science Department. Unsurprisingly, he's a hound dog, with a formal complaint from Carol Bellamy, the grad student who organized my talk. In it she claims he patted her butt and touched her breast at a colloquium. Nigel has responded to this accusation by denying it and writing he's never heard of Carol Bellamy.

Nigel is unhappy Judy asked him to serve on the Graduate Admissions Committee, reminding her of his "special status" in the department. Judy is unfazed by his claim and reminds him his special status would be useless if the harassment letter became public. There's also a salary letter from Judy approving Nigel's raise of 4 percent, above the maximum. In the letter Judy praises Nigel for the luster he imparts to the department.

In Dwayne Browning's file, there's a letter to Judy noting Nigel doesn't do his fair share of department service. Dwayne resents the unequal treatment of faculty members. "As a Black man, I've strived for equality all my life," he writes, "and I still haven't achieved it in this department." Nevertheless, his salary increase is 3.5 percent.

David Graham is coming up for his tenure review, and Judy has requested outside letters. He will not be getting a salary increase. His letter says, "Dave, I want to keep you here, but you'll need to broaden your research."

Unexpectedly, there is a folder for Aisha Robinson, in which she requests a pay raise based on the number of hours she works in the department. The raise has been denied, no reasons given. This is incomprehensible. Aisha works all the time. Up until now, I'd suspected Judy and Aisha were in each other's pockets, so the tidbit about Aisha's salary gives me pause. Perhaps Aisha's salary increase went to Nigel.

Judy is a fearless dictator.

Not a hint of a living, breathing person lurks on this computer, no warm and fuzzy images of Judy's life, no children, no adults, and certainly no pornography. Her browser history shows no secret fetishes, no whips and chains, and no dating sites. Judy's computer is a testament to her virtue at work.

I'll need to access her real computer, the one she uses at home.

The doorbell rings, followed by Torvill barking his head off. My mother gets the door, while I take the opportunity to check out my new Ring app, which controls the doorbell camera.

The video of the past five minutes is piercingly clear. Karla Mahoney, the homicide detective, walks toward the house, pausing, taking her time, and scoping out the landscape.

Hurriedly, I shut down my computer and lock it in my filing cabinet. My phone goes into my jeans pocket. It's possible

Andri was searching for nothing more than a stapler, but I'm taking no chances.

Detective Mahoney is dressed casually in smart denim pants and a blue sports jacket. She still has her jaunty top-knot and elegant glasses on a chain. Her face breaks into a warm smile when she sees me taking tentative steps toward her. "Lordy, Madeline! I wasn't sure I'd ever see you on your feet again. You being like this is good news. You doing okay?"

"Tell me the worst."

She sits on the couch and laces her fingers. "I'm still on Mike's homicide, but the case has gone cold."

"Cold?" I sit across from her and hug my arms.

"There's the same story from all the folks who knew Mike—his colleagues, the other skydivers—he was the super-smart guy everyone loved. No one saying a word against him. Also, we haven't located his phone—just not enough cop hours in the day."

"So all you have is the evidence of his broken chute?"

"You got it." She looks at me impassively.

Torvill pads into the room and lets out two short, sharp barks when he sees the detective, sitting in his favorite spot.

"What's up with you barking at brown people?" she says sternly. "You look in the mirror lately?"

He knows he's being rebuked and sits at her feet, where she scratches his head.

"There's one more avenue I'd like to explore in Mike's case," the detective says. "Your input. The remnants of your parachutes are in my car, and I also have Mike's computer, which we impounded from your mother the day after the accident. I'd like you to inspect the evidence and give me your thoughts."

Mom, who's been eavesdropping from the kitchen can't contain herself and bursts in. "Oh, Madeline, don't torture yourself with that. It's in the past. Detective, please let Madeline move on."

I go to give her a hug. "I have to see the evidence, Mom."

As we walk to the car, I say, "Detective Mahoney, isn't it against rules to take evidence out of police custody? Aren't you worried about corrupting it?"

"I *am* police custody, Madeline. After you've examined the evidence, I'll put it back in storage. Believe me, it's gone through forensics and every kind of inspection."

The remains of our parachutes are bulky, lying in a pile in the huge trunk of the state police SUV. Karla Mahoney hands me a pair of blue latex gloves and asks me to handle the chutes with care. "Go ahead, take a look."

Despite the mud and damage, the bright neon yellow of Mike's chute gleams on the dark carpet of the car. I want to wrap myself in the fabric and go back in time, but instead, I stroke the wreckage gingerly through the thin gloves. Sorrow rises in my throat. This is a part of me I've relinquished, and for all my brave plans, things will never go back to what they were.

Postponing this is not an option—I must confront the chute lines and knots that sabotaged Mike's dive. In the great tangled bundle of silky threads, my gentle exploration finds the two little bumps, barely visible at the base of the lines. The asymmetry can cause the canopy to spin, which is exactly what happened. The knots are tiny but unmistakable to a practiced eye. The skydiving inspector did well to find them hidden deep inside the wreckage.

"He was definitely murdered," I whisper, furiously blowing my nose. "These knots can't happen by accident." Is this what she wanted? My confirmation? A display of grief?

I force the pain to the back of my head and inspect the gear. Jamming the red and silver handles was a clumsy impediment that did its cruel work. I've seen enough and move to the side of the car.

"Who would know enough to sabotage the chute like this?" Karla Mahoney says.

"Anyone who's a skydiver. I could do it, for example."

She bangs the trunk shut and leans against the car, the two of us standing side by side in silence.

"Am I a suspect?"

"Not accusing you, Madeline."

"The wire jamming the handles was crude, like an amateur did it." Tears roll down my face. "And I'd never cause someone to endure such a horrible death."

She nods. "Just checking all the bases."

"Besides, I didn't have a motive to kill Mike."

Her face is impassive as she says, "But he did diminish you at work. He used your research to get ahead. I myself know how it feels to be invisible, where you gotta be twice as good as everyone else, twice as strong, twice as brave. People using your results to trample on you. I know the anger, Madeline. And I also know when the anger gets in your brain, you don't function on all cylinders."

"I didn't kill him."

"Did you know he was having an affair?"

Oh God. Her eyes are like lasers.

"I found out after the accident." I'm embarrassed and whisper, "How would you even know?"

"I didn't," she says, looking away. "I guessed. One of your colleagues voiced suspicion, and you just confirmed it."

"Who? Who told you that?" The heartbreak of Mike hits me at odd moments, always there below the surface. More tears pool in my eyes, an endless supply. People at work must be laughing at me, and it's like I'm back in high school.

Karla Mahoney puts a soft hand on my arm. "The person who said it is irrelevant, Madeline. I'm just keeping the facts straight."

She's not unsympathetic, just doing her job.

The slam of the trunk has lured Torvill out of the house, and he stands on the sidewalk watching us, his face neutral. He's not judging me. I've grown fond of him, our big brown dog, who carries himself with such dignity and grace. He has made peace with the detective, who kneels and ruffles his ears. He invites that kind of reaction. His sad eyes come to rest on me. Why is he melancholy? What is *his* excuse?

CHAPTER 21

When we're settled back in the living room, Karla Mahoney reaches into her large bag and hands me Mike's laptop. "Madeline, our tech guys have examined this, and need your help deciphering some files."

The love notes to his mistress?

The computer is warm and familiar, and despite everything, I hug it to my chest.

Detective Mahoney inclines her head and adds, "There's a bunch of computer code, and pages of unfamiliar symbols, maybe some encrypted files—"

"How did you get into Mike's computer, Detective?"

"You gave us Mike's password while you were in the hospital."

"I would never do that, no matter how much morphine they shot into me."

"You were very groggy, your mom helped us…"

Why is she lying? She seems like such a straight shooter.

"You didn't get into Mike's computer that way," I say, "because you needed his thumbprint."

"Or password," she says, gently. "I'm so sorry, Madeline. I understand this is painful."

Unbelievable. Why does everyone lie to spare my delicate feelings? "Tell me, Detective, how did you really get in?

Did you lift his thumbprint from his…frozen body…before his cremation?" *Oh, my poor Mike.*

"That wouldn't have worked," she says, matter-of-factly. "Only living fingers can activate a sensor." She pauses. "The truth is I impressed on your mother the need to get that password from you, and she did. It was soon after your accident—"

"That's obscene!" I cry, flicking away tears. Karla Mahoney can be a cold witch, like right now.

"I had no choice, Madeline," she says simply. "I needed access to the computer as part of the investigation."

I shut my eyes and picture her sweet-talking my grief-stricken mom into pressuring me while I was barely alive. *Unforgivable.*

Move on, it's done.

"How much encrypted stuff is on the computer?" I ask.

"A lot. And there were several folders we—our tech guys—couldn't even open." She seems relieved we're back on track.

"What makes you so sure I won't delete files that incriminate me? You know, like everything that confirms my motives." If I sound bitter, it's because I am.

She leans toward me. "My gut feeling tells me you're innocent and want to solve this case same as I do."

Tentatively, I open the lid of Mike's laptop, then think better of it and snap it shut. "May I keep this? It'll take time to crack it all." *To find everything.*

She changes position, crossing her legs. She meets my eyes, unsmiling. "I'm sorry, Madeline, I need to retain possession of the computer. It's evidence."

"You want me to examine it now? In front of you?"

She produces a flash drive, which she hands to me. "I'll wait while you copy the encrypted files," she says pleasantly. "Shouldn't be too long. Then I'll take the laptop and parachutes back to the evidence compound." When she sees the alarm on my face, she adds, "Take your time, Madeline, I'm not in a rush."

What she doesn't understand—or maybe she does and has her own ulterior motives—is I want to possess it all, the nooks and crannies of Mike's hard drive, the secret history of his browser, the files behind the files, as well as what he encrypted. I need his computer to solve the mystery of the man I was married to for ten years.

But downloading everything will take time, more time than Detective Mahoney seems willing to give me.

While I'm plotting my next move, a savory aroma of cheese and oregano wafts in from the kitchen, my mother's famous soufflé. We've invited Andri for lunch today, in lieu of payment for services on the roof.

I say, "While the folders are downloading, why don't you come in the kitchen and join us for lunch?"

Karla Mahoney is a tough old bird, unlikely to be swayed, but my mother's cooking smells are hard to resist. I suspect Karla lives on her own and isn't often treated to gourmet home cooking done by someone else.

Before too long, we are all at the table, knives and forks in hand.

The detective turns to me and says, "Good thinking, Madeline. This was a lovely idea."

She knows! The flash drive is in Mike's computer, downloading everything.

My mother blushes and glows from the compliments, but Andri is distracted by the detective's presence, uncharacteristically ignoring Torvill's nudges for treats under the table.

"What gives with computer in living room?" Andri asks.

"It's private," I say quickly. The less said about the computer the better.

"Mike's computer, yes?" Andri says, like he's obtuse, deaf, or challenged in English.

The detective rises in mid-bite. "It's probably done transferring files by now. Why don't I retrieve it and put it safely in my car?"

"Wait, Detective." I put a restraining hand on her arm. "Take your time and enjoy your lunch." I give my mother a meaningful glance, and she gets the message.

"Yes, please don't rush away, Detective. Madeline's right. Now would you like some tea and a lemon bar?"

Andri excuses himself from the table, and I know he's taking a trip to the computer. He can't help himself—he's transparent. I do the calculation: no harm done. All he will see is a growing green bar on the screen, showing files being downloaded. None of the computer's contents will be visible.

He's irritating me massively. My gratitude to him for repairing the roof extends only so far.

A toilet flushes down the hallway, followed by conspicuous splashes of handwashing noises. When Andri returns to his chair in the kitchen, he beams at me. "Computer all done copying," he says.

Detective Mahoney has not been deceived When she departs with Mike's computer, she asks for just one thing: the decrypted versions of all the encrypted files. "I'm not interested in Mike's personal emails," she says. "We've already been through those."

On Saturday night, I shut myself in my study to examine Mike's computer from the flash drive. I won't download the contents onto my desktop because I'm nervous of Andri's interest. He's an indecipherable character whose motives are nebulous.

A tour through Mike's emails is a revelation, the sheer number of invitations to talk about our work at prestigious institutions. I didn't know the half of it, how he enhanced his career using my work. My name isn't even mentioned in the invitations.

There are lots of demands from Judy. He's unfazed by her, more often than not writing, "Sorry, Judes, no can do." *Judes?*

Lots of back and forth between him and Aisha. "Hey, Aish," he writes. *Aish?*

Surprisingly intense guy-talk about video games. "No, Nige, terrible strategy." *Nige?*

Mike was just a friendly guy, I guess, with tons of affectionate messages to his colleagues. There's nothing edgy or astringent about him in these emails. How could I marry someone so different from myself? Perhaps I was attracted to the light.

There's nothing that could be construed as a love note. Perhaps those were reserved for his phone, the one lost in the accident.

I get up to stretch and take a break; and find Andri, Mom, Tosca, and Torvill riveted in front of the living room TV, watching Scandinavian noir, an Icelandic series called *Trapped*. As far as I can tell, it features a lot of ice and snow, and a detective called Andri, who looks just like our Andri. Mom pauses the show for a minute and follows me back to my study. She can't get over the physical resemblance. Apparently Andri was the one who suggested they watch the series, and since the fictional Andri has a lot of baggage in his past, Mom thinks it confirms her suspicions of our Andri, the one we have in the house.

She also concedes it's a very exciting show, and now she's sucked in, she'll probably watch the whole thing with him. "Not even that dog and cat can take their eyes off the screen," she says.

The critical moment has arrived: to tackle the encrypted files. Having no idea of what they contain raises bumps on my skin. *Was Mike hiding anything or just perfecting his coding techniques?*

I'm ambivalent about the task. On the one hand, it would be great if I could easily decrypt the files. On the other hand, Mike was trained by me, so if the decryption is easy, it'll mean I failed. A conundrum.

When I click on a file called Test 1, a sunburst of pixels fills the screen, a signature of an encrypted file. I run the file through the standard decryption methods, but the sunburst reappears. A data file has lists of possible passwords. Patiently I plow through them, deploying each one. No luck. *Good going, Mike.* I must dig deeper.

I walk to the window to think about the problem. It's dark outside, no moonlight. Mike's presence is in the room. *You always belittled me, Mads, now crack this if you dare.*

One after another, my decryption algorithms fail. Not even close.

The chase is on, my blood racing to meet the challenge. Moments like this give my life meaning, more than skydiving, more than sex, more than love itself.

It wasn't a level playing field when it came to hardcore programming. I always beat him. It drove him crazy. It was the only aspect of myself that walked on solid ground.

It's after midnight, and I've not yet cracked his code. I emerge from the study and lock the door. All is quiet. My mother's door is shut. There are no animal sounds. In my bedroom, I retrieve Nigel Welbourne's encryption book from my nightstand.

Nigel's book is good, better than I thought it would be. He has several suggestions for defeating the sunburst screen. Using his advice, I add a new variable to one of my algorithms, and to my surprise, the dazzling pixels are replaced by shadowy pictures, as yet unidentifiable. But progress is progress. A further refinement reveals a grainy scene of animals in a zoo-like setting. So this little movie was for practice, an encrypted video resistant to cracking. I'm impressed.

I try the new algorithm on Test 2, and have the same result, which is not exactly satisfactory. Grainy pictures of mundane scenes. People in the park. Boring.

I move to another folder and a new file. Untitled 1. A starburst appears, a kind of night sky. Running the video through the new improved decryption algorithm yields the identical starburst. No progress. So Mike has upgraded his encryption algorithm. When did he become so good at it?

I've reached the edges of Nigel's advice and still the file is stubbornly resistant to cracking. As the first pink streaks of dawn appear in the sky, I think hard about Mike and the limitations of his ability. He was always incapable of thinking outside the box, which means that whatever he used in his algorithm must be known to me. I just haven't found it yet.

It's not until the sun is peeking over the horizon that the answer occurs to me. He used my new data structure, the hash table of salt and pepper trees, in his encryption. Of course! This is why the file is resistant to decryption—I designed the algorithm that way. The pleasure and pain of realization strike me simultaneously and leave me dizzy. How could Mike hijack my work so brazenly?

The key to the solution is now clear, and the magic in my brain makes me light as air.

CHAPTER 22

I wake up at 1 PM, groggy from a fitful sleep. Everyone's at lunch, Andri chomping through a hamburger, Torvill crunching on kibble, and Tosca patting her mouth after dainty bites of chicken liver paté. When Torvill's paw strays tentatively to Tosca's dish, I expect her to bat him away, but instead she puts her paw over his and rests it there, in a rare moment of pure sweetness. Siblings.

My mother, who has an Ithaca-style salad sprinkled with bean sprouts, is in the midst of a heated discussion with Andri about last night's episode of *Trapped*.

"You can't blame the wife for leaving him," Mom says. "He's never home."

Andri wipes his mouth. "Being detective is tough life, Jenet, I know for sure."

She glares at him. "He ignores his children. How can you have sympathy for such a man?"

"But wife is very cruel to keep thin lover right in house, yes?"

"Her boyfriend cherishes her," Mom says, stabbing her salad.

My mother is looking very perky and sharp today, her wavy hair shining.

I pour a cup of coffee and slide into my chair at the table. The first sip is the best, and I close my eyes. I got so drunk on algorithms last night I feel as if I have a hangover.

"Glad you could join us," Mom says.

"I'm going to Cornell this afternoon. To use the supercomputer."

"Will your friend be there?" my mother asks.

"I don't have a friend, and the answer is no."

"Are you working on flash drive computer files, Medeleen?" Andri says.

This, more than the coffee, wakes me up. "Andri, that's completely private. You shouldn't know about it and you shouldn't ask."

He reacts the same way as his dog would, with remorseful eyes like saucers. "I am one big apology, Medeleen. I heard detective yesterday telling about Mike's computer, and saw you downloading files. I'm big lover of solving murder mysteries."

"Well, my life isn't your TV show." I stand up. "I've gotta go."

"Black coffee and no food is not a great way to start the day," Mom says.

"Get a life, Mom." I grab an apple and bang the door on my way out.

The university on a Sunday afternoon is deserted. My account on the supercomputer is accessed from my Cornell desktop. Now that I know which algorithm to use, I hope to decrypt Mike's files this afternoon.

I insert the flash drive into my computer.

While the program is running, I cross the hallway and have another crack at Nigel's office door. His lock gave me trouble the last time I tried—namely I couldn't get in—and it feels like unfinished business. To my annoyance, no amount of jiggling produces the familiar click.

I will have to give up on Nigel's office computer and devise another plan. Flattery. Step one is to open my laptop to a programming website and write a five-star review of Nigel's book. While it's uploading, there are footsteps in the hallway and the devil himself pops his handsome head around the door.

"What's a lovely young thing like you doing in a gloomy place like this on a nice fall afternoon?" He has on an open-necked shirt that reveals a sprinkling of brown curly hairs. Does he think he's exuding massive sex appeal?

Normally, I'd give a pest like him an aerosol blast of Raid, but instead I say, "I could ask the same of you, except I'd omit the words lovely and young."

"Oh, *well* said. I came to pick up a notebook from my office, then I'm off to watch the birds at Beebe Lake, and I don't mean the ones with feathers."

"May I see your office?" It pops out of my mouth because I want to see how he gets in.

"What on earth for?"

"Curiosity—you know, the inner sanctum of Cornell's big man on campus."

He has the grace to find that funny and laughs heartily. "In that case, be my guest. I can't guarantee everything's in pristine order, though."

I trail behind him like a lapdog, debasing myself because his lock has defeated me. Much as he gives me the creeps, I watch him intently at the door of his office.

He starts by taking out his phone and pushing buttons on an app that controls an alarm at the keyhole. Then he uses his regular office key to unlock the door. Just like that. So if someone manages to break into his office, Nigel will know about it from his alarm app.

"How does Henry get in to clean?" I ask.

"He doesn't. I clean it myself." Nigel seems bemused. "Why the interest? Tell me what you want to steal, and I'll give it to you."

It's my turn to chuckle.

His wall is covered with self-adulation. Nigel the Pied Piper, surrounded by adoring young girls. Serious Nigel receiving an award. Front and center, a picture of himself with Barack Obama, shaking his hand at the launch of his series, *Security for Dummies.*

"Oh, wow," I say. "I guess I should watch that."

"Don't bother, it's a piece of crap," he says cheerfully. "Completely obsolete by now."

"I read your book." I watch his reaction.

He looks surprised. "Really? And you understood it?"

I pause for a second or two. "I'll take that as a joke, but it'll cost you dinner at a fancy restaurant. We can discuss the book over cocktails and you can assess my comprehension." Anger always restores my gift of the gab.

His office has a small sitting nook with comfortable chairs and a coffee table. He takes a seat and gestures for me to sit opposite him. His scrutiny is frank, up and down, head to toes, his eyes lingering on my chest. I'm wearing my usual uniform, tight blue jeans, sneakers, and a skinny T-shirt. My charms consist of being tall, thin, and angular, more stick insect than ladybug.

"Yes to dinner," Nigel says, his hazel eyes calculating. "Did you know I'm a gourmet chef? No? Thought not. How about I whip up something spectacular at my house?"

"Name the day," I say.

In my office, the screen of my desktop flashes columns of numbers as the supercomputer grinds away. The windowless little room is oppressive, not conducive to happy thoughts. A dead spider on the industrial gray carpet has its legs woven into the fibers. How long has that been there?

It's already October and I'm mentally paralyzed as far as looking for a new job is concerned. Where will I go? Will something come up in Ithaca? How can I possibly leave my lovely old house? It's depressing to think about these things, so I banish them from my mind. A certain gloom and foreboding come over me during the wait to crack Mike's code.

What do I expect to find? Home movies?

After two hours the computer stops abruptly, lists of numbers frozen on the screen.

There's a single line of output: a long string of characters. So much of my time, energy and self-esteem, invested in such a fragile promise.

When I type an instruction to decrypt the file, it asks for a password. So far so good. Now that the moment of revelation is coming, I'm afraid of it. What if my calculations are wrong? Carefully, I copy the string of characters, paste it in, and hit Enter. For a few seconds the console goes black, and I fear I've blown it. Then the screen gradually lightens into soft gray. A tall boy, possibly a teenager, stands with his back to me. He is scantily clad. Slowly, he turns around, a gap-toothed grin on his face. Goosebumps creep up my arms.

"Hi, Maddie," he says out loud. "Wanna play?"

CHAPTER 23

I stare at the screen, and my stomach churns.

Mike? The pornography link at Cornell?

I shove the console away and rush to the bathroom to throw up my lunch. A brown-gray mush of apple and coffee sprays from my nose, hitting the rim of the bowl and dousing me with the stench.

Long afterward, I remain on the floor, hugging the cold porcelain, retching on empty.

The video with the young boy must have been Mike's practice movie, the debut of my data structure as encryption tool. Having the boy call me Maddie was a cynical twist of the knife, for Mike's benefit, not mine. This file was never meant for public consumption.

Back in my office, I squash my feelings of horror, straighten the screen, and decrypt every file on the memory stick, each one disgorging its own parade of horrors. The movies are packaged in virtually unbreakable shields of encryption. They're probably launched on the dark web by now, generating millions of dollars for shadowy pimps and players.

What was Mike's cut and where did it go?

By the time I shut down and lock my computer, it is well after six. I'm too beaten down to do battle with my mother, and don't trust myself to speak to her about any of this. I text that I can't make it home for dinner. *Don't wait up.*

Her response is almost instantaneous. *Enjoy, Mads. You deserve some fun.*

When I leave the building, the sun is sinking into rolling gray clouds. A fall chill is in the air, blowing through my thin denim jacket and weighing me down like a stone.

How could I not have known?

There were endless clues about his coldness—his dislike of kids and animals. Hints of his affairs too—his waning interest in sex and nights away from home. I had so many guilt feelings, rationalizations, excuses, more excuses, my mother saying Where is Mike? Always besotted with him. Always forgiving him.

How can I put him behind me now?

I blamed myself for his problems, because I taunted him about his academic shortcomings, punishing him for landing the job denied to me. I got even, and it cost me my marriage.

Even now I reproach myself for his theft of my work. What choice did I give him? To languish without inspiration at his time of tenure would have invited personal disaster. I hang my head as I walk blindly on the road to Collegetown. How clear it is now, we should have followed our own separate academic paths. I gave Mike no space to breathe, so he sucked in my ideas to survive.

But—oh God—the pornography? Where did that come from? Not from me. This part of his character is as alien to me as a UFO. The revelation knocks me apart like the skydiving crash, but this time I don't know how to pick myself up.

The exhilaration of last night, reveling in my own brilliance, is crushed like the remnants of my old knee.

It's dark and I'm in a familiar place, walking past the dead drop. The road has a downward slope. I've been so upset by the afternoon's discoveries I haven't noticed I've lost the shakiness of my gait. I'm striding without a limp or hitch, but with a certainty of step that leaves me breathless. The click in my bionic knee has been absorbed into my physiology, and it's like the metronome of my new life, signaling I'm regaining strength, the long slog of exercises and physical therapy finally paying dividends. It's strange how things sometimes work. I've lost my bearings but have regained my legs.

Walking past the ridiculous dead drop, I think of Joe. How can I let him know I've succeeded beyond his dreams, finding the Cornell connection and the encryption algorithm? The problem with telling Joe is I'm too embarrassed to meet him face-to-face, confessing how duped I've been.

The solution comes to me as I stand shivering on the road. The dead drop is there for a purpose, so I'll use it.

An hour later, I have a package for Joe with a complete report on how I determined that Mike was the Cornell perpetrator. All the damning evidence is compactly zipped up on a flash drive.

There's an identical flash drive for Detective Karla Mahoney, but no report about Joe's and my extracurricular activities.

The road is deserted. A flashlight helps me find the dead drop. There's a crackling in the branches, an owl or a bat, disturbed by my presence. The splash of the waterfall in the grotto has a damp coldness to it. It's about time I started dressing with some awareness of the changing weather.

The beam of my light picks up the spiky little bush that hides the spot, and I kneel down to toss it aside. Except it's attached to the ground and I'm at the wrong tree. Damn! This place is creepy at night.

Further into the woods, my light goes out, and darkness surrounds me. All I can make out are tangled tree limbs and black branches. It takes several seconds to locate my phone with its backup light.

In the distance, some animal screeches, except the sound is human. Students. Swimming in the creek beneath the waterfall. It's not allowed; there are warnings posted everywhere, but during the summertime, there are at least some morons who have to do it to complete their college experience. A few of them even survive.

Finally, I locate the right bush, toss it aside and drop the radioactive package into the hole. *Good riddance.*

On the road again, I text Joe. *Mission accomplished. I know who did it. Evidence in dead drop. Madeline.*

During the drive home, I think about my mother and her relationship with Mike. She saw something rotten in him right from the beginning. She begged me not to marry him, because he was "synthetic," not the real deal. She said, "There's a hole at his core. He's too full of himself. Emotionally stunted. This is a man who will take, take, take from you and not give anything back. Don't do it, Mads. You'll regret it."

But of course, that was exactly the wrong thing to say. Why would I ever listen to a tirade from my mother? I was in love.

The house is quiet and dark when I finally get home. Not a light to welcome me inside. Obviously, my mother thought I'd be out for the night.

I'm ravenous and go to the fridge to forage for leftovers. A container of spaghetti and meatballs triggers a rush of love and guilt. Mom always tucks something wonderful in the fridge for me.

I hope the loud whirr of the microwave doesn't wake them all up. When the pasta is steaming on my plate, there's a soft footfall, and Torvill pads into the kitchen, probably enticed by the divine aroma. He comes and sits beside me, looks up, sniffs my knee and lets out a soft little bark.

I feel his warmth on my leg, and offer him a meatball, which goes down the chute in one bite. Then I swallow a forkful and hold up another piece for him. He's patient and waits for each mouthful with panting anticipation. I'm down in the dumps tonight, and it cheers me up to share my late dinner with him.

The shrill ring of my burner phone startles both of us, sending Torvill into a sharp fit of barking. Then the phone goes quiet, just as Joe and I arranged. I must take the call outside.

My mother appears in the kitchen as I'm opening the door.

"Who's calling you at this hour? It's almost midnight."

"Mom, I have to take this call. I'll tell you about it tomorrow."

But she wouldn't be my mother if she let me go without a battle. "There's definitely someone watching the house. Don't go outside, Mads, it's dangerous." She pulls her robe tight around her and whispers, "Especially not at this time of night."

"I'll be fine, Mom. Please go back to sleep."

"Is it your friend?" she asks, anxiously. "Why didn't you stay out if he's going to bother us all? You know there's no shame in—"

"Gotta go, Mom. Don't let Torvill follow me."

His voice is urgent, crackling through the burner. "Madeline, I'm parked near your house. I need to see you."

I've moved beyond the trees, out of sight. "Have you picked up the package?"

"Yes. I want to discuss it."

"Joe, can we do this tomorrow? At Cornell."

"Let's meet now. I'm two minutes away. I can sneak around the back and stay hidden. Trust me, I know how to do this."

"That's insane. You can't come here. My mother is standing at the window looking out, my tenant is creeping around watching everything I do, and I think we have a prowler." The hysteria in my voice is pathetic.

But he's imperturbable. "Stay where you are, and I'll find you."

Big man coming, don't worry about a thing.

I sink to the ground and lean against a tree. This is exactly what I wanted to avoid. He'll ask directly, "How could you be so blind? Surely you had some clues?" And what is my defense? *I'm disabled that way. An idiot.*

I rehearse, say it out loud, and bat it around, "I've had enough. I quit."

He appears out of the trees and says, "You can't quit. You have to finish the job."

He's like a ghost, lit by the light of his phone. All I see are the creases of his face and the hollows of his eyes. He drops down beside me, too close, his leg brushing mine. I don't have the emotional energy to move away.

"Did you read my report? Did you see those...children?" *I don't want to do this anymore.*

He touches my arm. "Madeline, I'm so sorry."

And that's all it takes to release the day's horrors, which flood back over me. I let out a cry and start to shake with such wrenching sobs I can hardly breathe. Pain tears at my ribs, which are still tender and sore, but I can't stop. Hiccupping, howling, gasping, I let it all come out..

What he doesn't do is tell me *hush, it'll be okay*. Instead, he sits silently, waiting for it to play out.

So much for my goals of being strong and assertive in an ugly world.

"Why am I here?" I blow my nose.

He says, "It's probably not much consolation, Madeline, but I wanted to congratulate you. Not another soul on God's green earth would have had the brains or guts to figure this out. You've justified my faith in you, a hundred times over."

Despite my misery, I smile in the dark. I'm not *that* socially challenged I can't tell he wants something. He's so predictable it's ridiculous.

But so am I. Despite my desolation, his flattery is a tonic, like hot cider in my belly.

I turn to face him. "What was so important it couldn't wait until morning?"

He shifts his position. "I felt myself losing you, and while you were raw from the horror, I needed to impress on you the importance of staying the course."

"You could have told me tomorrow. What makes you think you can call me at all hours of the night?"

He sighs. "I'm sorry, I really am. We've just had another ping near Cornell, which means Mike had a collaborator in the department, or someone has taken over from him. There's a fresh surge of super-encrypted illegal porn on the dark web."

"Explain again why that involves me—specifically?"

"No one else can do the job."

"Oh, please—"

He gently shakes my shoulder, and his touch is urgent. "Are you listening, Madeline? You have to keep going, because Mike either had an accomplice or was set up."

CHAPTER 24

Monday morning starts badly when I can't find the flash drive for Karla Mahoney. All those decrypted pornography files from Mike's computer, lost or stolen. I thought I'd left the little memory stick in the kitchen, in a zippered compartment of my pocketbook, when I went outside to talk to Joe last night.

It's not a disaster, in the sense that I can create a new one from what I've saved, but it's a loose end, a moment of intolerable ineptitude.

Who could have taken it?

Mom was in the kitchen. She does a lot of things that drive me nuts, but invading my personal possessions isn't one of them.

Andri? He's my prime suspect, even though he was nowhere near the scene.

What about the intruder my mother keeps going on about? I installed the Ring outdoor cameras to humor Mom, and would love to be able to say I checked the videos front and back and they were clear. Her visions of faces at the window have unsettled me.

I tap the Ring app on my phone and examine last night's footage.

The nighttime visibility isn't great, and I peer at the screen. A hulking figure appears in the backyard. I stare at it, denying the reality. Replaying the video, I see him again—a man—walking in and out of camera range.

Did this stranger enter my house and search my purse? Did he take the flash drive but not the money? Did he follow me into the woods and witness my meeting with Joe? Who is he?

Andri is in the backyard romping with his animals.

"*Guten morgen*, Medeleen," he says, throwing out his arms, as Torvill races to catch a frisbee. "Crisp fall day is lovely, yes?"

The truth is, it's early October and threatening to snow. The cold aggravates my replaced knee.

"Sorry to spoil your morning, Andri, but I have disturbing news. Someone is creeping around this house at night."

His face sharpens, losing its friendly façade. "Then Jenet is right. Not losing marbles?"

So Mom has confided in him.

"I don't know who he's watching," I say. "It could be you."

He nods slowly, possibly agreeing with me. "We should catch man and ask. Maybe best case scenario is just creepy pervert."

If Andri were a normal person with nothing to hide, wouldn't he suggest I call the police?

Come to think of it, I know nothing about Andri, other than his amorphous writing course at Cornell. Mom says he goes in regularly for lectures. I should ask to read some writing samples...like, is he doing actual homework? But that's an investigation for another time.

To be honest, I myself would prefer to avoid the cops.

"Andri, maybe you could do some random patrols outside with your gun. Then we'd coax him to tell us what he wants."

I didn't intend to involve the gun, but now that I have, it sounds like a good plan.

It rattles Andri. "Medeleen, gun is empty, not for shooting people."

"Yes, I know, it's for your novel, but the guy spying on us doesn't know that."

"Show me spy cameras and video, so I see for myself." He's very much on high alert now, possibly alarmed. His request isn't unreasonable, given I've raised the stakes with the gun, so I give him a tour that includes the little Ring cameras and the grainy video of the intruder, recorded last night near my mother's window.

"Maybe I will load gun," he says.

When I step off the elevator at work, Aisha emerges from her office and says, "Happy Monday to you, Madeline, but" —and she lowers her voice— "Her Majesty wants to see you right away."

My heart falls all the way down to the toes of my sneakers.

Stalling for time, I say, "Oh? What about?" Is Aisha my ally? I have no idea.

She whisper-mouths at me, "I don't know what the story is, but I think she's ready to see you in an orange jumpsuit." *Shit.*

I put on my nice denim jacket and some lip gloss, then run a futile brush through my hair. Whatever the problem is, I refuse to look defeated.

The unpleasant news has put another crimp in my bad leg, and I lean to the left as I walk to Judy's office. Nevertheless, I rap briskly on the door, trying to sound like a person who's confident, with nothing to hide; namely, a person who has not hacked Judy's computer.

"Come in," says a voice that has nothing to hide either.

She's at her desk and doesn't rise to shake my hand, nor is there her usual enigmatic smile. I try to calibrate her and assess the damage. *Not good.*

Her cell phone rings and she turns away from me to take the call. On an impulse, I make a swift move to the bookshelves, limping through the pain, ostensibly to browse. In the periphery of my vision, I see she is still turned away from me. Like lightning, I grab my flash drive recording device from the spine of the old book where I hid it, and thrust it deep into my jeans pocket. *Focus. Don't lose this one too.*

I hang my head sideways, examining the book titles, while Judy takes her own sweet time. Her silence is aggressive, and my throat snaps shut.

"Why don't you have a seat," she says, eventually.

I take the chair, trying not to collapse into it, then face her and wait in silence.

"Please tell me, Madeline, why I shouldn't fire you right now and call Campus Police to accompany you off campus."

"What—?" I'm being fired?

She crosses her arms and gives me her laser-focused glare. "I have credible reports that you've been snooping around here, several nights, after hours."

"In my office—" Not enough breath to finish the sentence.

"David Graham reported that you broke into his office at night."

That rat fink. Why would he tell her?

"He has Mike's...old office. Did he tell you that when he came in, I was on the floor, grieving...for my dead husband?"

"And what about the night you broke into my office? Was that a grief-filled moment too?" *Bitch.*

Henry must have reported me.

I'm struggling to breathe. "I came...here...to use the computer science library—Nigel's book." I point to the bookshelf. "I knew you had a copy here—"

"How did you get in?" she says sharply.

"With...Mike's faculty key."

"And why were you sitting in the dark, like a common thief?"

I summon up the headache, which is pounding in my head right now. "I had a migraine." I hold my head in my hands now. "...using light from my phone...artificial light bothers me." *No faking, it's real.*

"Oh, please—" She opens her eyes wide at me with fake incredulity.

I force my vocal cords and brain synapses into alignment. "I didn't try and hide what I was doing—ask Henry—"

"You're quick with the excuses, Madeline, but from where I'm sitting, I think you've been, for whatever reason, spying on members of this department."

If shock registers on my face, it's because I'm horrified I've been so transparent. *Hopeless.* "That's ludicrous. After using Nigel's book, I went and chatted to Dwayne, who was also working late in his office. Wouldn't I just sneak out if I were spying?"

"Here's what I think. That you have no right to use Mike's faculty key—because you're not faculty—and should return it. That your explanations are bogus. That you've been searching for something in people's offices—maybe even trolling their research, looking for ideas—"

"That's outrageous. People come in here and use those books all the time." I gesture vaguely to the bookshelves.

"Not in the dark, at night."

"That's when I work, Judy...not a firing offense."

She hasn't lost that look of malevolence, freaking me out. "I don't know what game you're playing, but it's dangerous. Believe me, I can damage your academic future with a snap of my fingers."

Mike's dead presence suddenly appears—an unexpected churn in the air. *Don't look away, Mads. Be strong, stand up to her.*

It's a shock to remember something good.

I place my phone on her desk, breathe deeply, and say, "I'm recording this conversation, and, for the record, I disagree with your accusations and have noted your threats."

She presses a button on her desk and says, "Campus Security? This is Judy Holsinger from Gates—Computer Science—please could you send an officer to escort someone off campus." There's some buzzing from the other end, to which she replies, "Yes, thank you."

My muscles dissolving...

I stare at her. "I'll go quietly if you...write a note guaranteeing...my salary through December. Otherwise, I'll contact my lawyer and...sue for damages." Mike is still in the room, helping me with this one last thing. Leaving with my dignity intact.

Judy nods curtly and says, "Done." Then she's on her phone again. "Aisha, please help Madeline clean out her office—thanks."

Aisha is energetic and sympathetic as she helps me take down my books from the shelves. Her gold bangle flashes in the artificial light. "I'm so sorry, Madeline. Call me if you need anything. I mean it."

I'm quite numb and nod while I stumble around my office, submerging the jabs of pain, packing the odds and ends of my Cornell life.

Later, while carrying a box that includes, among other things, the framed photo of Mike, I encounter Nigel Welbourne in the hallway.

"Good God, Madeline, let me take that for you." Without shame, he peers into the box and riffles through my stuff. "I say, old girl, it looks like you're moving house." *Jerk.*

"Let's just say, I'm changing jobs."

"But what about our date tomorrow night?"

"Is it contingent on me working in this shithole department?"

"Oh, ho, ho, au contraire. You can tell me all about it, tomorrow."

Jerked around, ridiculed, everyone feeling free to unload on me.

I leave it all behind as we step into the elevator. Not even one backward glance after so many futile years.

CHAPTER 25

I'm too sad to go home. When my mother sees the boxes, she'll be relentless in her interrogation.

I call Joe on the burner. "We need to meet—not on campus." My voice is pinched, and I clear my throat. "Is now okay?"

Despite the pale sun, it's cold, and I'm shivering in the front seat of my car. It's a winter jacket day, but all I have is my thin denim. I start the car and punch on the heat.

He must hear something urgent in my voice, because he says, "Okay, I'm on my way to Robert Treman Park. Meet you in half an hour."

The drive is about six miles on Route 13, Ithaca's commercial strip of car dealerships and fast-food restaurants. The drive is pure aggravation, with stop-start traffic and idiotic drivers weaving in and out of lanes to overtake the clunkers.

In my rearview mirror, a small, darting gray car catches my eye. It was behind me earlier as I left campus, and it's still there, switching lanes to stay one or two cars back. It unnerves me, and I brake sharply to avoid hitting the car in front of me. I'm perspiring from the heat in my car and the tension in my back as I crane to see if that guy is still behind me. He is.

The Robert Treman State Park is a summer destination with waterfalls, streams, and lush foliage. We won't need to worry about being secluded. Yet I'm not the only car in the parking lot. I'm relieved when I finally pull in, and take a moment to recover from the harrowing drive. The gray car is nowhere in sight. I have no clue about Joe's ride. For all I know he has a Harley.

While I wait, I do some yoga breathing. Other cars trickle into the lot and dot themselves everywhere.

A gray car, similar to the one earlier, pulls in and parks a few spots away. The driver is not Joe and stays in his car. I shift in my seat and check my phone for messages. Nothing.

When Joe calls, I pick up immediately.

"I'll meet you on the main path to the falls," he says. "Keep going straight. I'll find you." And he hangs up. Not unfriendly, exactly, just efficient. I have no idea where he is right now. Perhaps he used an Uber.

The driver of the gray car has stepped out and is pacing as if waiting for someone. He doesn't look my way. I grab my phone, zoom in, and hurriedly take a few photos. My spying activities have made me nervous if anyone loiters near me. I don't think he saw me photographing him. But if he's an expert, of course he did.

Unfortunately, I'm not in a good position to take a photo of his license plate. I'm neither brave nor brazen enough to walk within five feet of a stranger and take a picture of his car.

Several minutes later, he hasn't budged. He's as still as a statue, which means there's no help for it, I must cross his line of sight. Without looking back, I hurry toward the park on shaky legs. *The Courageous Spy.* Soon I'm on a shady path with a steep rock face on one side, and trees and a fast-moving river on the other. The fall foliage is not at its peak, but the trees are beautiful, slightly glazed and golden. One day, if I think back on this interlude with Joe, I'll hear the splash of waterfalls and rustle of leaves, or the snap of branches in the sky.

I steal a glance over my shoulder, but the path is clear.

When I catch up with Joe, far along the trail, he's in his usual casual stance, leaning against the steep cliff. His face is as craggy as the rocks, and for a crazy moment he reminds me of Mike, the good looks and confident demeanor.

He's brought a small tarp with him, which he drapes on a stone bench that faces the falls. From his backpack he takes two small boxes of pizza and bottles of water, incongruous in this pristine setting.

"Lunch?" he says.

My spirits rise at the sight of food. The two Advil tablets I took for pain have been rattling around in an empty stomach, adding to my malaise.

What a sight we must be, sitting under a gorgeous bower of fall leaves, hair and faces getting sprayed by the mist, watching the cascade of white water, clutching our fast-food boxes.

"Joe, I'm being followed," I say, glancing back. "This guy was on my tail when I left Cornell."

"How sure are you?"

I'm relieved he doesn't laugh. "Not very. It could just be a coincidence that he was also headed to Treman."

He nods. "Stay on top of it."

He doesn't feel compelled to fill the silence, and for a while we sit mesmerized, watching the churning water.

Eventually, I say, "I was fired from Cornell today. For snooping. I'm not the genius spy you imagined."

He sits up straight. "What happened?"

The falls are noisy, and it's a challenge to shout above the roar. I brace myself and hope he doesn't berate me for not being careful enough and betraying the rules of spy craft.

Instead, he says, "It sounds as if we're okay. Judy doesn't know what you're searching for, which means your cover isn't blown and you can keep going." He takes a bite of pizza, and a shine of grease lines the top of his chin. *He's more concerned about his investigation than about me.*

"Joe, I've been fired. I can't keep spying if I'm not on location."

"Okay, let's review where we are. Tell me what you know so far."

"Nothing for sure, really, just what I've guessed. Mike had pornography on his computer, which was encrypted using my work. I'm pretty sure he wasn't running the whole show—"

My teeth are chattering. From our shady perch, the sun seems far away.

"To be honest, I didn't really know my husband. After he died, I found out he was having an affair." I look away. *The bottom is falling out.*

"Oh, Madeline, I'm so sorry." He moves closer to me.

Why did I tell him that? It has nothing to do with anything. "Let's change the subject. A few weeks ago, I hid a recording device in Judy's office. I managed to grab it earlier today and listened while driving here."

"Well that's pretty dang amazing," he says.

I feel flustered and try to cover it up by speaking quickly. "I didn't learn anything new about Judy. She's a world-class bitch, but I don't think she's the porn perp. She's not a programmer."

"Anything interesting I should know about her?"

"Not really. There was only one suspicious moment. Someone called her and she was furious. 'Didn't I tell you not to call me here? Ever?' And then she cut the person off. I reckon she was fielding a call from her ex, not one of the porn kings on her rolodex."

"You can make fun of it," Joe says, "but *someone* is enabling the distribution of the pornography. It may well be Judy."

"She sure is nasty enough."

"She's a question mark. Whether justified or not, she's taken the trouble to get you off campus. Would you be willing to keep investigating her? Possibly gain entry into her house?"

Did he just say that? I'm an amateur with no training, and yet he's willing to put me in danger.

I take a bite of lukewarm pizza. Thick gooey yellow cheese, onions, and mushrooms. My arteries are probably getting blocked as I chew and swallow. It's delicious.

"Remind me what you do, Joe? FBI? Master criminal?"

He wipes his mouth and glugs down some water. "It's really important that you keep going with this, Madeline. The pornography thing is personal. I've been on the case a long time." In his earnestness, he edges closer to me, and his knee brushes mine. "I care about your safety, and I care about you. I wouldn't ask if I didn't know you could do it."

Later I'll parse his body language and the words "I care about you." He knows exactly what he's doing—manipulating me, trying to get me to commit to the investigation. I'm proud of myself, being able to see through him. My people assessments have improved, maybe because Mike is no longer a buffer.

I move definitively away from Joe. "I'm not willing to investigate beyond our computer science floor." I realize the truth of it as I say it. "This creeping around in the dark has to end somewhere."

"Who's left on the computer science floor?"

"I've eliminated David Graham, the guy without tenure—not smart enough—and also Dwayne Browning—too upright. That leaves Nigel Welbourne."

There's a crunch of footsteps behind us and I turn around. The man from the gray car and a young woman are walking along the path, talking and laughing animatedly, like they're the only people in the world. As they pass our bench, the woman's eyes dart and catch mine—just a flicker—and that's all it takes for me to know for sure.

I lean toward Joe and whisper, "That's the man following me."

Joe says, "If he is watching you, he's very good. To me, he just looked like a guy on a date."

"Here's another piece of information. There's definitely someone watching my house. I saw him on an outside camera."

He inclines his head. "This could be good news. It means you're getting close. Someone is keeping tabs on you."

"Please forgive me, Joe, if I'm not feeling your excitement."

He's frowning, processing the information. "Call me if you see the watcher in real time—"

"And—what? You'll hurry to my house and tackle him to the ground?"

He chuckles, shaking his head like I'm just too much to take.

Men. The eternal riddle.

He says, "Madeline, you're doing great. What can you tell me about this Nigel character?"

So on we go. My chest tightens. How apt it is that dark clouds are gathering over the creek. Honestly, what did I expect from Joe? That he'd put his arm around me and say, "Okay, Madeline, you've done great, let's call it a day and quit. Let's do dinner next week." Of course not. He's obsessed with my mission, and if I'm roadkill in the end, so be it.

The main thing for my mental health is that I'm clear eyed about our relationship. There is no relationship. He wants just one thing from me.

So why am I continuing to endanger myself?

Those pornography files on Mike's computer click into focus, right now. *Wanna play?* They were just kids, really.

I'm not doing this for Joe. I'm doing it for myself.

I stiffen my spine and go back into spy mode, gathering my thoughts about Nigel Welbourne, the whole messy portrait of him.

"He's a celebrity hotshot professor. Despite that, he's very smart and inventive about security. He could write encryption and decryption algorithms in his sleep. He wrote a book on it. He's brilliant. He's also a jerk who sexually harasses female students." *There. Concise and professional. Done.*

Joe seems relieved that I've quit the Jittery Jane stuff—submerged the pain—and am back in harness. "Do you have a plan for finding out—about Nigel?" He pushes his blowing hair off his forehead. "I know it's tough for you, but we have to take this down, and fast."

Joe and his relentless need.

"I have a date with Nigel tomorrow. Dinner at his house. He's cooking for me."

I take another bite of cold pizza.

"Wow. Really?" He looks at me intently, with...what? Admiration? Relief? Love?

He's obviously counting on my self-esteem being tied up in solving the problem. And he's making the common mistake many men make.

They think you're doing it for them.

CHAPTER 26

I take a long, scenic route home from Treman, giving myself a view of Cayuga Lake at sunset, purple and gold shimmering on the water.

In my house, there's a cozy domestic scene in the living room. Andri and my mother are having cocktails, probably a Moscow Mule, since Andri loves his vodka and the drink is one of Mom's specialties, made with Ithaca ginger beer, lime, and grated ginger.

Tosca is sitting on Mom's lap, completely Zen about the cold drink resting on her fur. Torvill, as I suspected he would, has claimed the couch as his territory, and is stretched out on his side, his head on Andri's lap.

We're like a family in an American sitcom, with two widows—a beautiful mother and her awkward daughter—plus a strange Ukrainian tenant who has two telegenic pets. There's an endless musical chairs game with the imperious cat, who has identical feng shui requirements as the mother and competes for the same seats in the house. They've recently come to an accommodation. The mother sits on the chairs and the cat sits on the mother. As for the tenant's melancholy dog, who understands Ukrainian and German, he has insinuated himself into every part of the house.

I'm the interloper, restless and unmoored.

"What's with the box?" my mother says. "Are you moving out?"

"The box is coming in, not out," I say, retreating to the study, where I dump out the contents.

Mom, at the doorway, takes it all in. "Oh, Mads. What's going on?"

I open my mouth to tell her how Cornell wanted me out after Mike died, but my voice goes wobbly, and I end up with my arms around Mom, my face wordlessly on her shoulder, breathing in her fragrance of lime and fresh ginger.

She waits for me to get myself together, then says, "Did you and your friend have a breakup?"

The easiest route is to nod my head. This is pain she understands. She strokes my hair and says what all good mothers say, "You're so smart and beautiful, my darling Mads. Give it time. They'll be banging down the doors for you." She thinks that's my ultimate goal, to have men banging down the doors.

"I've also left Cornell," I add as if an afterthought. "I have severance pay until December."

After dinner, while I'm rearranging my study, I continue to think about the man at Treman. Was he really following me? And what about the prowler menacing my mother? It's now completely dark outside, a clear night. I check the video from my doorbell camera, and a figure on the lawn streaks by in real time. I blink and see an empty porch and vast darkness beyond. The software is set up to save the recordings on iCloud, so I rewind and replay in slow motion.

Someone is on my property. He's either cutting across the lawn, or going to the woods behind the house. But why? There's nothing here for miles around.

I turn off the lights in the living room and hallway and creep silently toward the kitchen. Torvill is napping peacefully on the couch, not even a growl out of him. He's hopeless.

Andri is drinking after-dinner tea with my mother. I join them at the table. Sliding into my chair, I say softly, "Mom, don't get alarmed, but there's someone on our grounds, at the back."

Mom's hands fly to her face. "What are we going to do, Mads?"

"Shh...you're going to sit here and keep the animals inside. Andri and I are going to catch him and see what he wants. Don't worry—"

"Of course I'll worry!" she snaps in a fierce whisper. "What if he harms you?"

"We'll take gun," Andri says.

She flings down her napkin and glares at him.

We hurry to Andri's side of the house, and without explanation or ceremony, he goes to his drawer, takes out the gun, and hands it to me. "You carry it. Gun loaded, so don't shoot me in back."

"Let's go out the front door," I whisper. "Quieter. We can creep around the back."

"Turn both phones to silent," he says.

How does he know I have more than one? This is not the time to ask, so I file it away as I pull them both out of my pockets and silence them.

It's a cloudless night, with clusters of icy stars and a slice of moon. Andri leads the way, treading softly in his rubber-soled sandals and socks. Before he rounds the corner, he motions me to stop and goes into a crouch, checking out the terrain. Something in his catlike stance tells me he's done this before, and if he's a real writer, then I'm a real spy.

In the faint moonlight, we see the prowler reaching up against the house and peering through my mother's window.

"I'll go around the house and distract him with the gun," I whisper. "Then you come from behind and take him down." Andri nods.

But as I hurry to the other side, my legs refuse to cooperate and I stumble, the gun flying out of my hand. The grass is soft, but I'm winded and can't move. Oh God, it's stage fright.

Stop it! Get up!

I retrieve the gun, touch two fingers to my wrist, and feel my pulse. It's racing. I take a deep breath and wait for it to settle. Andri must think I lost my way.

When I round the corner, I almost collide with the intruder, who is walking toward me.

"Stop!" I shout. "If you move, I'll shoot you." I point the gun straight at him, and he puts his arms up. "Don't shoot!" he yells.

My body is trembling with fright, but my arm is steady and the gun doesn't waver.

I can't see Andri and try to peer over the man's shoulder. That's all the encouragement he needs. He turns around and starts running toward the woods.

Andri comes out of the dark like a rugby player going in for the tackle. The prowler doesn't have a chance against his assailant's bulk and speed and crashes to the ground with a cry. While the man is momentarily stunned, Andri rolls him onto his stomach and sits on his thighs, straddling his body.

I watch in amazement as my mild-mannered tenant extracts a pair of handcuffs from his pocket and in one second flat has the prowler's hands cuffed behind his back.

"What are you doing in my yard?" I say to the prone man, whose face is turned away from me.

"I was taking a shortcut to Cemetery Road. Sorry for that. Now let me go."

"You're a liar," I say. "I know you've been looking in the windows, and tonight isn't the first time. What do you want?"

"I want my lawyer," he says, like we're at the police station.

"No lawyers to be seen." Andri takes out his phone and shines a light on the man's face. He jerks his head away.

"Who are you?" I ask. "What's your name?"

"Take off the cuffs and I'll tell you." His voice is rough, and there's a sour odor of sweat emanating from him. He gives the impression of someone my age, maybe older.

I pat down his pockets—no gun—and slide out his phone. It's locked. It asks for a password or thumbprint; so I take the man's callused hand and press his right thumb onto the screen. "Hey!"

The phone unlocks, and within a couple of moments I've gone to Settings and found a name.

"George Snyder." I show the screen to Andri.

"Who are you watching, George?" Andri says. "This lady over here, or me?"

I stare at Andri. Why would someone be following him?

"The mother," George says. "I'm watching the mother."

His words send ice down my spine. "You goddamn jerk! I should shoot your head off right now."

The man doesn't respond.

"Does house have basement?" Andri says. "Maybe overnight in cold basement can act as truth serum."

"We don't put people in the basement, Andri," I say, breathing heavily. "There's no heat."

The light goes on in the kitchen and my mother—backlit in her trim pantsuit—appears at the door with Torvill, who makes one of his happy barks and bounds toward Andri.

"Mom! Stay back!" I'm panicked by the thought that she'll be in this pervert's line of sight.

Mom has a flashlight and takes in the gun, handcuffs, and man on the ground. "Can someone please tell me—?"

"Jenet, this is George," Andri says, "and he will sleep in basement tonight."

Mom stares at him. "We don't have a bed down there."

"We don't need bed. We need rope, wire, and duct tape."

CHAPTER 27

I activate the flash on my phone, crouch in front of the man on the ground, and take a photo of his face. He squints and cries out. Then, with some difficulty, I stand and take a full body shot.

"Talk to me, George," I say. "Why are you spying on us?"

He says aggressively, "Screw you. I'm pleading the Fifth."

"No courts or justice system on property," Andri says. "Beautiful ladies here both very polite, but I'm old-school thug, and can sit on you while you rethink strategy."

I say, "Hold on a minute, Andri. I want to check something inside."

I hand over the gun and hurry to the study with Mom on my heels. "Mads—"

"Leave me for a minute, Mom."

She opens her mouth, then changes her mind and storms out of the room.

In a minute I've uploaded the photos from a minute ago and the earlier photo of the man trailing me at Treman. Placed side by side, the two images are easy to compare, inch by inch. The hairlines are the same—hair receding, high forehead—and also the noses. And, crucially, the ratios of skull height to neck length and skull height to body length. I home in on the faces, and everything tells me they belong to the same man.

The facial recognition app on my phone says the probability of these being the same person is 80 percent. With my own analysis, I put it at 90.

Back outside, silhouetted in the moonlight, Andri is hoisting the man to his feet. "Time for moving," he says.

"Okay," I nod. "We'll keep him here until he talks."

When we're at the kitchen door, he plants his feet and refuses to enter. This time I get a good look at him. He's muscular, in good shape, but his face is sallow. He has the look of a person who does weight training but stays unhealthy.

He's scowling now, twitching his head in a gesture of defiance.

Our tenant gives him a shove in the back and says, "Walk now or get thrown down basement stairs." To make his point, he puts the muzzle of the gun on the man's neck. I can feel it on my own neck, the hairs rising.

When we're in the hallway, Andri says to George, "If you must use bathroom, now is time to say."

"Yeah. I'll use the bathroom." His face lights up like we're offering an escape hatch.

"Come with me," Andri says roughly, then softly, to me, "I'll take him to apartment."

"What about my privacy?" the jerk says.

"Same privacy as for mother when you looked in window." Andri yanks at the handcuffs. "Let's go."

Mom—uncharacteristically—runs her hands through her perfect hair. "Dear God, Madeline, why can't we just call the cops?"

"Because they'll take him away and we won't know why he's spying on us."

She doesn't argue, which means she's really freaked out.

Eventually, she says, "Should I pack something for him to eat down there?"

"No, Mom." Gently, I put my arm around her shoulder. "We don't want him to be comfortable. We need him to talk."

There's a lot of scuffling, yelling, then flushing, before they reappear in the hallway. George's face is mottled with anger, his hands still cuffed behind his back.

The door to the basement is between the living room and Andri's apartment. Mike once used the downstairs area as his den, keeping tools and woodwork equipment in it. I haven't been down there in years. The door is wedged shut and needs a yank to pull it open. Luckily the light switch works, casting pale light on the old wooden stairs.

Andri shoves George's head down and says, "You go first. Gun pointed at head so no funny business."

This is not an attractive place. For one thing, it hasn't been cleaned in ages. Dried mud coats the stairs, and there's a moldy ooze from the cement walls. As we descend, there's a drip-dripping sound and also the occasional clank of the furnace.

The air is cold and dank.

The light on the stair is the only one that works, which means that the basement room itself is dimly lit and forbidding. George pulls back.

"Last chance, George," I say. "Tell me what's going on."

With a sudden sharp move, he turns around, heaving his shoulder against Andri's arm and dislodging the gun, which clatters down the staircase. In the same moment, he makes a dash upstairs, pushing his way past Andri and moving to shove me aside. In a reflexive reaction, I put out my left leg, tripping him on the stairs. He falls flat on his face in front of me, yelling in pain as he slides down feet first, his face hitting the steps on his way down. A trail of dust follows in his wake.

His fall is stopped by Andri, who grabs him by the shoulders and holds him in a bear hug, his powerful arms around George's chest. Both men heave and pant as Andri wrestles him down to the bottom of the steps and delivers a sickening punch to his gut.

George lets out a howl and drops to his knees, as Andri dives to retrieve the gun.

Using the wall to brace myself, I follow them down, holding my breath, struggling to inhale the thick, musty air.

Under the workbench is an old metal chair, whose coat of dust sends me into a fit of sneezing. "We'll use this," I say.

I prop the chair against a big pillar and attach it with a length of rope wound tightly around it. After some heavy lifting, Andri manages to maneuver George into the chair. I'll say this for him, he goes down fighting, struggling against the cuffs, and trying to kick our legs as we tie him up.

"Fuck!" he shouts, and the point of his shoe connects with my shin at the same time he head-butts me in the ribs that were once broken, and the pain makes me gasp and flail back. My hand glances off his face, greasing my fingers with a sticky ooze. I recoil in shock, inhaling the coppery stench of blood.

The light of my phone on his dazed face reveals a bloody mess. "What should we do?" *Tamp down the panic.*

"Nothing—we do nothing," Andri says. "Let him have hour or so to think about cooperation advantages."

It hurts to look at the swollen face, and I remind myself this guy is a jerk. Squatting down so my eyes are level with his, I plead with him. "Why don't you save yourself from being in this horrible room by just giving me some answers?"

He twists his mouth into a bizarre distortion, and I don't duck fast enough to evade the gob of spit that lands squarely in my right eye. In an instant, Andri is shoving me aside and punching George's head, which crashes against the pillar.

My stomach heaves.

With a smirk George turns to me and says, "Must be nice to have a fat goon to save your ass. Little pussy hiding behind the big guy."

Andri moves to smack him again, but I intercept him. With all the strength of my weight-trained, rehabilitated arm, I deliver an open-handed crack to George's bloody cheek, causing his head to bounce on its axis. "Give me the gun, Andri, and tie his legs to the chair with the wire and duct tape."

I swipe the disgusting mess off my eye, and with it, the layer of empathy that's been clouding my judgement.

This is the pervert who's been terrorizing my mother.

I move in close, point the gun at his head, and am rewarded with the first signs of respect, a cringing watchfulness in the prisoner's eyes and beads of perspiration on his upper lip.

"Let's try again," I say. "You're the guy who was following me at Treman today."

Through the sweat and gore, he looks startled. *Yes, it was him.*

But George goes sullen, and it's clear he's not yet given up the fight. I brace the gun with my other hand and aim it between his eyes.

What threat is hanging over his head, that he'd prefer this to just telling me?

Andri pushes the muzzle of the gun down. "Medeleen, be careful. Point at leg—"

"Don't worry, I know where to point."

In the diffuse, dusty light, I smell fear rising off our prisoner and see Andri backing away. He's clearly my ally in this drama, but—really—who is he?

At the edge of my vision, he produces some old wire that my mother found in our storage room. There's enough of it for two revolutions around George's legs. Andri pulls the wire tight and fortifies his handiwork with several go-arounds of duct tape. He works briskly and firmly, with an intimidating authority that tells me not only that George won't escape these bonds, but that he, Andri, is an expert at trussing up human packages.

Who the hell is he?

The reality of what we're doing in this awful basement fills me with disgust. How did the sinister man in the chair become my enemy? How did the menacing man tying him up become my friend?

I lay down the gun, take the duct tape from Andri, and hold it two inches from George's eyes. "This is for your mouth."

"No, no tape!" George rattles the chair as he struggles to move, but it's clear he doesn't have too many degrees of freedom.

I squat down again so we're eyeball to eyeball. He'll think before risking another wad of spit. "Here's something you should understand, George. You have frightened my mother, and I will keep you here until you tell me why you're spying on us."

He strains against his bonds. "You can't do this. It's illegal."

I tear off a strip of tape and the sound is like the stutter of a machine gun. In one swift movement I press the tape onto his gaping wound of a mouth.

When we get to the top of the stairs, Andri flips off the light switch, and shouts, "Goodbye, George. See you later."

But the man is finally beaten down, and there's nothing but silence.

"No, Andri." I flip the light back on. "We won't leave him in the dark until we've given him a chance to change his mind."

The session in the basement seems to have liberated me to speak, and before moving on I say, "You have as much to explain as he does. Sumo wrestling? Rugby tackles? Is this part of your training as a writer?"

He stops on the final step. "Shhh," he says, putting a finger to his lips. "Explaining later."

When we return to the living room, my mother's face is furrowed and anxious. "Did he tell you anything?"

It's like emerging from the underworld.

"No, Mom, not yet. We're hoping he'll change his mind."

My mother stares at me. "Mads, your hand—"

"It's nothing. Just a little accident. I'll wash it off." Blood, grime, bruises. All in a night's work.

Mom shivers and pulls her sweater tightly around her. "I heard terrible noises downstairs. What's going to happen, Mads? You can't keep him there all night."

"Jenet, come sit on couch," Andri pats the cushion next to him.

But he's underestimated my mother, who steps away from us and stands her ground. "No, Andri, you can't sweet-talk me into thinking it's okay for civilized people to do this."

For once I can't argue. But how to explain that this is part of finding out who's distributing illegal porn from Ithaca? I barely understand it myself.

She sees me wavering and presses on. "Mads, just remember—I also live in this house." Then she turns around and makes a dignified exit from the living room.

George Snyder's phone is a burner with exactly one contact, whose name is John Smith. He has an Ithaca area code. When I press the number, the call goes straight to voicemail. The familiar, generic voice says, *please leave a message at the tone*...I hang up.

Andri says, "Good going, Medeleen. Keep cards close to chest."

Next, I select Photos. It's not clear what's in there, but the first image freezes my blood: Joe Shelmann and me, leaning toward each other on a stone bench at Treman.

Joe is in danger.

Andri—staring at me—has a look of concern on his face. "Medeleen. What is it? What is on phone?"

A full-length shot of me walking to my car, my car's license plate, Mom and me at home, Mom and Andri, Torvill and Tosca, me and Nigel at Cornell, me and Aisha at her desk, me and Judy...

"A photo album of my life," I say. "We have to get him to talk."

"He's very low-level, third-rate amateur," Andri says. "Won't be hard making him sing like opera star."

"What if he just won't talk?" I'm in a state of suspended animation, trying to be rational.

"Leave him in basement another day and this time turn off light."

CHAPTER 28

It's almost 10 PM. I've had no luck googling George Snyder. Many hits, but none of them match our guy in the basement.

"Maybe underworld gangster with no profile," Andri says.

My mother reappears in the living room with her teacher face. "Is he still down there?"

"Hi, Jenet." Andri beams at her. "Yes, George in basement, deciding whether to spill beans about pervert activities."

Mom says, "I bet if we gave him a nice plate of savory scrambled eggs, it would loosen his tongue."

My mother's from another planet. What does she think we're running here—a luxury hotel?

I go and give her a hug. If nothing else, it relieves some of the tension in my neck. "Mom, thank you for offering, but—"

"You can't starve him. It's in the Geneva Convention."

Andri compounds the problem. "Medeleen, wait—food is good motivation for talking. Maybe we dangle scrambled eggs, yes?"

When Andri and I descend to the basement, we find George with his head slumped on his chest and his body limp in the chair. *Oh God, we've killed him.*

To my relief, he's breathing. I grab one end of the duct tape and pull it off.

He jerks in the chair and opens his eyes. "Fucking hell!"

Andri crouches down to face level. "How is state of mind, George? Ready to let cats out of bag?"

"Water," George says. He runs his tongue over his rough and reddened lips. I must push away the guilt and remind myself that this is the man who's been trailing me and ogling my mother.

I crouch down too. "I've seen the photos on your burner phone and want to know how you got that photo of me and my friend at Treman." Maybe he won't be able to resist the temptation to share how smart he is.

He shrugs his shoulders and smiles a horrible smile. "No sweat, lady. My girlfriend pointed her smartwatch at you when we walked past your bench."

Of course! And her glance at me to aim her camera tipped me off.

To reward him for the information, I unscrew the top off a new bottle of cold water. "Tip your head back. I'll help you drink this."

He doesn't ask for clarification but leans against his chair with his chin in the air, his mouth slackly open. My hands are shaky as I rest one hand on the pillar and with the other, tip the bottle slightly, so he doesn't choke. He takes the water greedily, getting into a slurping rhythm without spilling a drop. When the bottle is empty, he shuts his eyes and sighs.

"We are going to go upstairs," I say, "where you will tell me what's going on. If you don't, we'll have no choice but to bring you back to the basement for the night."

"Shit!" he says.

When we emerge into the light, my mother is waiting at the top of the stairs. Her hands fly to her face. "Madeline, what did you do to him?"

"We didn't do anything. He fell on the steps when he tried to escape."

She purses her lips and glares at all of us. "Bring him to the kitchen."

I don't want this scum in our kitchen, but I have to pick my battles with my mother. George reeks of skunk and stale sweat, and onward we go, into the pristine kitchen.

When George is seated at the table, Mom uses a facecloth steeped in hot water to wipe blood and grime off his face. He winces but doesn't protest. Blue bruises are flowering on his cheeks.

I take a seat opposite him. Andri sits at the end of the table, the gun dangling loosely between his knees. George's hands are still cuffed behind his back,

It's late, and I'm tired of these games. I push the Record button on my phone, smack it onto the table in front of him, and say, "Now tell me who you are and why you're following me."

Andri lifts the gun and points at the man's forehead. "Also name of employer, buddy."

"Andri, put the gun down," Mom says.

George gives Andri a look of pure hatred.

"If you cooperate, my kind mother will cook you some scrambled eggs, and we will negotiate your release," I say.

His face perks up, and he appears to struggle with some demons, before eventually saying, "Fucking-A." I give Mom the nod.

"Wait, Jenet." Andri raises his hand. "Don't start food until bird finished singing."

"There's a card in my jacket pocket," George says.

The thought of dipping my hand into this man's pocket—well, let's just say I hold my nose and do it fast. It's a business card of sorts. I place it on the table so Andri can see it too. It says *George Snyder. What do you need? I'll do it. Reasonable rates.*

"Sounds like thug for hire," Andri says.

It occurs to me that George's business isn't going anywhere without a website, and perhaps he's afraid of losing this gig. What I really should be thinking about is that someone is so anxious about my activities they're paying a person to spy on me.

"Who are you working for?" I ask, quietly. We're all subdued, a bit breathless, Andri at the edge of his seat.

He stares at me, this unwholesome man with the pale-yellow complexion and stubbly face. His shoulders droop. "Some guy contacted me a month ago—maybe a lawyer—left a note—offering me a job, following you and reporting back. They wanted everything—photos, people, places you went. They told me to call them if you went on campus—Cornell—any time, day or night."

His matter-of-fact telling chills my spine. "So you don't know anything about this person you're working for?"

He shifts uncomfortably. "I just do what I'm told, keep my mouth shut, and get paid."

My mother is staring at him with shocked incredulity, holding a spatula in the air, ready to swat him like a fly.

"How do you communicate with them?" I ask.

"I text on the burner phone."

"How do they pay you?" This is all beyond crazy.

"Cash transfer into my bank account. I don't ask for details. Just check my bank balance." He tosses his head as if to say he knows it's incredible, but that's the way it is.

"You weren't curious?" I say. "How do you know they're not planning to kidnap and murder me?"

"I don't ask for motives," George says, licking his lips. "I just check they're paying me. That's how my business model works."

"Why couldn't you tell me this? Avoid the drama in the basement?"

He squirms. "I didn't want to blow my cover and lose the gig."

"Not your lucky day, buddy," Andri says.

There's a creak in the roof and I shiver. This interrogation is surreal. "What about today, George? Those photos from Treman?"

"Gone already. I sent them a report that you were having lunch there with your boyfriend." A smirk on his face, his eyes on my mother.

Goose bumps rise on my arms. *We're in danger.*

Mom turns her prune-mouth toward George. "How much are they paying you?"

"Mom—"

"I want to know what my daughter's activities are worth to these people."

"Fifty dollars an hour," he says. He shrugs as if to say, yeah, it's not much, but times are hard.

"Does that count the hours you were watching me get ready for bed?" Mom snaps, shaking a fist at him. "I let you sit at my table because that's the civilized thing to do. But you're a weasel. What do you think your employer would do if they knew your business model included padding your bill by being a pervert at my window?"

My mother's vehemence startles him into silence.

We must get rid of him.

I say, "Okay, George, this is what'll happen. I'll keep your burner phone—"

"You can't do that—"

"Let me finish. You must go into quiet mode. If they contact you in some way, tell them you have nothing to report, that I've been at home, sick in bed. *Do not tell them about what happened tonight.* Make up some excuse, any-thing. Tell them you lost the burner, it must have fallen out your pocket."

He jerks his back and the handcuffs scrape the bars of the chair. I can only hope he gets the message: I'll let the Peeping Tom stuff go if he keeps his mouth shut.

With luck I've bought myself a week before his shadowy employer gets suspicious.

Andri says, "I think you know it's not good idea to tell anyone about Medeleen catching you snooping, yes?"

When George sends him a daggers glare, Andri adds, "Any monkey business, I'll find you, George, I promise."

Mom says, "Should I make him some eggs now?"

Andri gets up from the table. "Sorry, Jenet, mind is changed. Too late for dinner."

George sends a dark, aggrieved look to my poor mother. "You all *blackmailed* me." Like he's the victim here.

Undaunted, Mom goes to the fridge, grabs a cheese snack pack and soda, and bangs them down in front of George. She turns to glare at me. "Are we done?"

While Andri moves to unlock the handcuffs, George says to Mom, "You remind me of my mother. She died last year."

Mom's face relaxes, and for a moment she looks confused. "Yes, well—okay, then. But I want to warn you that my daughter, Madeline here is handy with a gun, and I can't be responsible for her actions if you trespass again."

Andri says, "Get lost, asshole. No one believes sob story."

George gives Andri the finger, and in a paralyzing moment I'm scared George will lunge at our big guy and punch his lights out. But George too has had enough and is ready to leave. In his haste, he knocks his chair over, kicks it aside, and without a backward glance, he slams out through the kitchen door and disappears into the cold night.

I go to my mother, wrap my arms around her, and pull her close. Her cheek is soft against mine.

"When you were a kid, you used to hug me like this whenever you wanted something," she says. "So tell me, Madsy, what do you need now?"

"Time, Mommy, that's what." I stroke her hair. "Eventually I'll tell you everything, including the story of my so-called boyfriend. But not now. It'll keep."

She nods and hugs me back. "I'm going to bed. I hope you know what you're doing, because that was one unhappy man who just left."

I resist the temptation to call Joe immediately and tell him his cover is blown. I don't want to see him tonight. My warning to him will have to wait until tomorrow. I have a more urgent matter to attend to, one that cannot be put off any longer, even though it's after eleven o'clock.

Andri has stood by silently, witnessing the scene between me and Mom. Afterwards, he says, "Interrogation like pro, Medeleen. You should be cop, yes?"

Focus. Breathe.

When my mother's door clicks shut, I say, "Andri, we need to talk."

"Uh-oh, I hear more interrogation sounds in voice."

The gun and handcuffs are gone. He's full of smiling benevolence. His dog is at his feet, and his cat is purring on his lap. *Resist this image.*

"Andri, it's time for you to tell me who you are and what you're doing in my house."

CHAPTER 29

It is almost midnight, no sounds in the room other than the faint creaking of the roof. Andri has gone silent too, and I gird myself for a tangle of half-truths.

Only one thing is clear in this whole mess. He hasn't been honest.

I know he's about to dissemble when he places his hands on his knees just so, in a way that his arms are perfectly parallel. He inhales and fills his cavernous chest with air. "I'm peaceful person, Medeleen. Writing course, mystery novel, divorced wife, all true." He smiles at me under his beard, lighting up his face.

This late at night, however, I'm immune to his charm. The experience with George has worn me out. "Andri, please don't tell me those handcuffs are part of your research. You know, like the gun. It's insulting."

"Ah, Medeleen, so many apologies. Real story is I'm crime detective with leave of absence to restore energy and faith in human race." He lets out a sigh that's half a groan. "Detective life all stress. Too many sleazebags. Bad guys threatening to shoot family. Wife always frightened, always shouting I must take safe job as insurance salesman—" He puts his head in his hands and rocks back and forth in some kind of anguish that is either genuine or an Academy Award performance.

"Oh, Andri—" I'm at a loss. Consoling people is not one of my strengths at the best of times.

"Wife got divorce from me," he says. "Flying to Sweden with new boyfriend. Everything gone. Tosca and Torvill only things left in house."

Torvill, hearing his name, perks up, jumps onto the couch, lets out some kind of sympathetic noise and slobbers over Andri's face.

"That's awful—losing everything. But you still haven't told me what you're doing in my house. I know you've been searching for something other than inner peace—in the living room, my bedroom, the study—my mother sometimes gets confused, but she's pretty shrewd, and she's probably 100 percent accurate when she describes the places you've been snooping."

"Is long and complicated, will take time—" He shakes his bushy head and lets out another sigh. I wait for him to get over the hump. I don't need to be a genius with people to see he's reluctant to come clean. I'm halfway nodding off to sleep when he says, "I'm investigator of juvenile abuse in Upstate New York. X-rated movies. When we find it on computer, we arrest owner, charge with trafficking, and put away in jail for long time."

Did I just dream that? I sit up and say sharply, "What does that have to do with me?"

"Michael Alvarez—husband—making inquiries about triple-X movies. Was he main perpetrator in Ithaca?"

Oh God. There's a sudden frost in the air, the furnace shutting down for the night.

I rub my eyes, which want to go to sleep. "You've got to be kidding—what kind of inquiries?"

"They not telling me this. When asking leave of absence in Upstate New York, my boss said go investigate Alvarez house and see if family involved in porno."

"What the—?"

"Boss said, maybe movies being produced in house. Look for kids and movie equipment on premises. Maybe stash of porn—"

I stare at him. "You think my mother and I make porn movies?"

For the first time he laughs, a real belly laugh. "No, Medeleen, of course not. When I meet you and Jenet, I know straight away this is police cuckoo-land." He taps the side of his head. "You and Jenet full of honor. And nice, too. But—big confession—house searched by me for evidence. For report back."

George Snyder and Andri Eriksson. Men relaying my activities to nebulous bosses. Who is Joe reporting to?

I have a flash of insight. "That letter you showed me was fake. You didn't really arrange with Mike to rent the apartment here, did you?"

His eyes open wide, the look of embarrassment clear. "No, sorry, Medeleen. Sometimes detective must be con man and actor. We knew about skydiving accident and death of Mike. Painful, yes?"

"You showed me an email from Mike!" I'm mortified by my gullibility. Stupid!

"I took chance," he says, sadly.

"What if I had checked?"

"I would have made big pretense of bafflement. That's where actor part comes in."

What an easy mark I was.

When I rest my forehead on my hand and try to process his deception, he says, "Abuse on web is terrible crime, using young victims—seen with own eyes. My need is to find thug helping system work."

I keep my face noncommittal, because I haven't forgiven him. He forges onward. "Please understand, Medeleen—forgetting porn situation—this house turned out totally perfect for me and pets." He leans toward me. "I needed peaceful place to repair damaged spirit and found new family."

He lifts his cat and places her on the carpet, comes to my chair, and crouches down on the floor. "You and Jenet very special for me, I think this you know." He places his large hand over his heart at the perfect angle.

"Nice acting."

When he looks crushed, I straighten my spine and fold my arms. "What evidence did you find here?" My tone is harsh.

"Flash drive with triple-X porn movies," he says. "From Mike's computer that Detective Karla asked you for."

The flash drive that went missing the night I met with Joe!

God, I'm hopeless. "How did you get your hands on that?"

"From purse when you went out late at night."

"How would you even know I had it?"

"Because, Medeleen, you at Cornell in afternoon to use supercomputer. You told Jenet at lunch time. I was at table. So when you came home late, flash drive must be in purse, for Karla." He pats his bulging stomach. "I may be big fat lug, but I'm good detective." His eyes swing sideways to gauge whether I'll forgive him. I'm not sure. I'm pretty damn irritated.

"Where does your money come from?" I blurt. I haven't forgotten that first night when he flashed $3,000—in cash— at us.

"Rich ex-wife with big guilty conscience."

Sounds fishy to me, but there's no question he's quick on his feet. One plausible explanation after another.

I'm about to give up on him and call it a night, when he says, "Medeleen, I think danger for you is very big. George on loose, criminal paying to track movements, kiddie porn on computer, skydiving sabotage, drive to Cornell for late-night activities."

"Andri, I'm handling it—"

"What are you doing? Who is man in picture at park?"

Who can I trust?

He reads my mind. "Do you trust this man? Is he boy-friend? What is story with calling on phone and meeting in woods at night? Why not come inside to meet mother? Detective nose on me very suspicious. Is he cop?"

There's a tightness in my chest, the old ache of broken bones. *Andri is watching everything I do.*

It's late and he's worn me down. I make a decision about Andri because he lives in my house and seems to be an ally.

"He's my spy handler," I say, quietly. "I'm undercover."

The softness has bled out of his face in the darkened room, and his crooked nose gives him a menace that he didn't have during the daytime light. He is hyper-alert.

"Who is this man, Medeleen?"

I hesitate, pull out George's phone, and call up the photo. "He is Joe Shelmann, FBI."

The whole story spills out, the funeral, the dead drop, the spying, the Computer Science Department, the main players. It's a relief to share this burden with him.

He rivets his glittering black eyes on me and absorbs every last detail, then inhales heavily, an audible rattle in the quiet room. "Medeleen, active child exploitation investigation is not existing in Ithaca. One hundred percent sure."

"Well you wouldn't know. Joe is also undercover."

"Not real agent to put inexperienced informant in such danger."

I push back. "There's no other way for Joe to get the information. He needs a computer science expert to secretly access suspects' computers."

"Man is unprofessional," Andri says, and the rough certainty of his voice scares me. Why would Joe be anyone other than who he says he is?

"Real cop wouldn't sit so nearby you. Is making sexual advances?"

This question shocks me on so many levels, I can barely find my voice to reply. "I'm a grownup, Andri. I can take care of myself. I like Joe Shelmann. Maybe I *want* to have a relationship with him."

Andri stands up abruptly. "Wait, don't move. Back in five minutes. Need for checking something."

I'm frozen in the chair. He's frightening me.

When he comes back into the living room, his face is very grave. He sits heavily on the couch. "News unhappy, sorry to say. I have good connections doing checking for me—"

"Oh God, Andri, I didn't give you permission to use Joe's name—"

"I need you understanding two facts, Medeleen. No local investigation and no FBI agent with name Joe Shelmann."

CHAPTER 30

Can Andri be trusted?

My mother would say yes, because he's endlessly kind. Kind to us and his animals. Generous in his praise and gratitude. He loves our house and its grounds. He adores watching Scandinavian crime thrillers on the big TV with her. He loves her cooking. Mom's voice is in my head, as if she were standing next to me: *He loves you too, Madeline. He tells me often, in so many ways. He loves how you do this and how you do that and how you do everything.*

So I decide to trust Andri, because continuing this risky enterprise on my own seems insurmountable. Trusting no one in the world can shrivel your soul.

Joe is another story. There's a brooding intensity and sadness about him that resonate with me no matter who he is. My attraction to him is confusing, so I'm avoiding him, for now. *If he's not an FBI agent, who is he?*

It's after midnight. The furnace is off, and the cold air seeps through the windows. I'm describing the Computer Science Department to Andri, speaking quietly, so Mom doesn't overhear.

"I have a date with Nigel Welbourne tomorrow. He's cooking dinner for me at his house."

"This is person who may be main porno trafficker in Upstate New York?"

I sigh. When he puts it like that, he makes me sound insane. "Yes, he's one of my suspects."

While he absorbs this, I say, "I need to finish the job."

"Why? Why can't professional—police—finish job?"

I stare at him. Does he really not comprehend that this is a personal challenge before I can move on? That Joe's search to find a porn enabler has evolved into my own quest? It's like proving an elusive theorem or getting a prickly algorithm to work. In my world, you don't quit until it's done.

I try to express all this to Andri, who nods, then says, "What is plan? To ask to this man's face about porn distribution?"

"No, of course not. During the evening I'll find his computer and download his hard drive."

When he shakes his great shaggy head, I say, "It's fine, Andri, I'm an old pro. I've done it more than once."

"This is big danger, Medeleen—"

"I'm going on a *date*, Andri, not a raid. He won't suspect a thing."

On Tuesday morning, the grass is crisp with frost. For the first time I wear cords instead of blue jeans. The cold weather creeps into my joints and repaired bones, an old and familiar pain. I bundle myself into a winter jacket and scarf, then go for a long walk along Brooktondale Road. In the spaciousness and solitude of farm country, the air's as fresh as whipped cream. Frost on the ground, yet the trees still have their golden leaves, the burning bushes flaming red. The landscape is strange today, like my life.

At breakfast I say to my mother, "I won't be home for dinner tonight. I have a date."

She puts down her spoon and smiles. I don't readily confide in her about my private life.

"He's a professor in the Computer Science Department. He's going to cook dinner, and we're going to discuss his book."

"Do you like him?" Mom says.

"No. You could call it a work date."

"So you won't be staying overnight?" She seems wistful.

"It depends how things develop. Don't wait up."

Andri, too, has paused, his oatmeal-laden spoon hovering over the bowl.

When Mom excuses herself to go out and check the garden, Andri says, "Free advice, Medeleen. Let me call FBI now to take over. This is bad date for you, not fun game with cat and mouse."

"I'll be fine, Andri—Nigel thinks I like him, and he's invited me out before. If I can't find his computer, at the very least I'll get a delicious dinner. He's a gourmet cook."

"Give me address of house, so I can be near if trouble."

"It may snow tonight—"

"Man from Ukraine and Scandinavia laughs at such snow."

"And woman from Ithaca laughs at your offer of protection."

In the early evening, Mom taps at my bedroom door to let me know the forecast isn't good. Snow flurries that will turn into real snow.

"I've been driving in snow for years. I'm fine. I have a good car, four-wheel drive."

"Do you need advice on what to wear?"

She riffles through my closet, her face increasingly grim as she comes to the end of my meager wardrobe. We go with my one good pair of warm, navy pants, and raise the level of shoes to dark sneakers. I select a plain, half-sleeve sweater, and Mom produces from her room a crushed velvet jacket—burgundy—that she bought at a vintage store. It actually looks pretty good on me. It will easily go under my lightweight winter coat.

I must at least look the part.

Snip snip snip, and some errant curls come off my head. Then a dab of lip gloss. Just about as sexy as I can be. I've read about women like me. I'm a honey trap.

"Drive carefully," Mom says when I leave.

Andri says nothing, but he gives me a dark and meaningful look.

The whole menagerie is there to see me off, Torvill sniffing around my shoes and Tosca, uncharacteristically, rubbing up against my ankle.

Nigel lives about half an hour away in a house on Cayuga Lake. This means a drive through Ithaca, then onto a dark, winding road along the lake. Not the best for driving in snow, but the clock is ticking on George the prowler's silence, so there's no turning back.

When I get onto Route 89, the lake road, a light snow has started to fall, obscuring visibility and sticking to my back window. I turn on the rear-window defroster, which heats the icy mess and opens a small window that reveals a car on my tail. I'm driving slowly, the key to staying alive in snow, and am irritated that the vehicle behind me is driving up my tailpipe. If I brake suddenly, he's going to bang into me. Math 101. I turn on my flashers and slow to a crawl. There's no shoulder for me to pull over and let the jerk pass, so I'll make him suffer instead. But he chooses to overtake me on a blind curve, and I almost skid into a ditch as I watch in horror. *Asshole.*

My car creeps along in dwindling visibility, until at last I'm pulling into Nigel's driveway. He gave me a very good marker, for which I'm grateful, a big sign with a yellow arrow, signaling a sudden bend in the road.

Small lights on the cobblestones lead to the front door. In the snow, the place has a Christmas feel to it. I walk carefully, clutching my purse, with its supply of flash drives for Nigel's computers, and a tote bag containing my indoor shoes and a small bottle of Kahlúa. This comes from my mother's lifelong admonition that you don't arrive empty handed at the house of someone who's cooking for you.

Nigel opens the door at the ring of the doorbell, which means he's been looking out for me. "Come into my parlor," he says, stepping aside to let me in, giving off a whiff of shampoo. He has spruced himself up for our date, his hair short and styled to look casual and wind tossed, his pale-blue shirt sleek with silver cufflinks.

When I step over his threshold, a pulse starts beating at my collarbone. Will I be able to speak to him without choking? *Of course you will. Go get what you came for.*

"Hey, Nigel," I say sweetly, thrusting my face forward for a peck on my cheek, while my boots track wet snow onto his gray wood floor.

As soon as he's relieved me of my coat, scarf, and gift, his hands are on me, stroking the burgundy velvet of my mother's jacket. "Oh my, you will outshine the wine."

An aroma of herbs wafts in the air, something delicious baking in the oven. If I weren't so keyed up, I'd be famished. *Relax. Play the part.*

Nigel leads me into a spectacular living room, a contemporary space that juts out over the lake. The design of this house is as different from mine as it possibly could be, no warm and lived-in rooms with slightly sagging couches. This place is all chrome, glass, and steel, as frosty as the weather outside.

"Nice pad," I say, clearing my throat. "Do I get a tour?"

There's no evidence of malfeasance. No pictures of nineteenth-century men in frockcoats, ogling young boys. No adorable Italian putti with wings and bows and arrows.

Instead, I find myself standing in front of a magnificent Escher print I haven't seen before, a tangle of ladders and colorful body parts in unlikely symmetry. It's mesmerizing. As far as I can make out, it has no evil connotations, just pure mathematical genius.

"Limited edition print," Nigel says, his hand on my velvet jacket again. "Blown-up version."

"Tour?" I say sweetly, squirming away from his touch.

"Of course. But first tell me what music you'd like to hear."

"Nothing loud. Classical or jazz." I wave my arm airily, to signify my sophistication.

"A girl who isn't opinionated about her music is not my type of woman," he says.

"That's a relief." I laugh at him. Pretentious prick. But he laughs right back like he thinks I'm joking.

"Alexa, play the Brahms Quintet," he commands. I did remember to wear my chunky bracelet, which is activated. Alexa won't be recording anything I say or do tonight.

Nigel leads me to his giant bedroom with its king-size bed and bland artwork on the walls. There's a fat book on the night table and a pair of skinny glasses. Any and all pornography is tucked away, out of sight. Except, perhaps, for a black-and-white photo of a young girl, her arms in the air and her face laughing at the sky.

"Who's that?" I ask. The picture is huge and has a prime spot on the wall facing his bed. The child is a charmer.

He takes a minute to examine it. "That's my favorite relative in the world, my sister's daughter, who's all grown up now, and, sad to say, still lives in England."

The bedroom lights are low, probably dimmed by Alexa to create a romantic glow. Will I sleep in this big bed to achieve my goal? I had thought the answer may be yes, but now I'm actually with Nigel in the flesh, the verdict is no. He thinks he's irresistible.

My original plan was to flirt with him, perhaps flutter an eyelash or two, but it's not in my nature. Instead, I'll switch to another technique: being in awe of the Big Man.

My eyes scan the room, and I peer into the en-suite bathroom. Marble and stone luxury, a giant bathtub in the middle, but no computers in sight. I exclaim and admire and poke my face into everything.

Back in the bedroom, I'm all wide eyes, tugging at the sliding door of his massive closet.

He's bemused. "Be my guest."

Nothing. Shoes and shirts. Belts and ties on racks. Smells like a department store. I don't touch anything, but do peer hard.

The study has a large, contemporary wood desk that holds a computer with a giant console. "This is where I play with pixels," he says.

"Oh, show me!" In order for me to download the hard drive easily, the computer must be warm, recently used, so I won't require a password unless he shuts it down.

"Absolutely," he says. "We'll do all that after dinner. My scheme is to seduce you with my cooking and then wow you with my brilliance."

"Let's do brilliance first." I inwardly laugh. *Men!* "Go on, turn it on. Show me something spectacular."

He looks at me quizzically. "Okay, let's go get drinks first."

The kitchen is all black granite and steel. Nigel checks on something in the oven, then steers me to a bar, sparkling with crystal and dark gold liquids. He stops abruptly, pretends to conduct the musicians during a violin crescendo of the quintet, then says, "What's your poison?"

I sit demurely on a black leather barstool and say, "Seltzer water and fresh lime, please. Tall glass. Lots of ice."

"Why don't I improve that for you. This is a drink that cries out for a splash of vodka and a dash of passion fruit liqueur."

"No to the vodka, but yes to the passion fruit." *Stay sober.*

He pours himself a Black Label Scotch over ice.

We carry our drinks and coasters to the study, where he activates the computer. On the wall is another Escher print. I study it, while listening to him type a long password. Are there security cameras? A quick scan of the room reveals nothing obvious.

Nigel and I clink glasses. "To our future relationship," he proclaims. I don't choke on my drink like an amateur. I sip it with cool nonchalance.

An image of Las Vegas blooms to life on Nigel's computer screen, bright lights sparkling in vivid technicolor.

"Nice," I say.

"I use that array of lights to encrypt images. Think of it as a four-dimensional lattice, like the theory of relativity." He looks at me with a probing look, possibly to assess my comprehension. "Each pixel has its unique location, color, and password. And I scramble the order, obviously. Almost impossible to decrypt." He's proud of himself and celebrates his little lecture with a slug of whiskey.

Why is he being so forthcoming about his work? In a moment, the answer comes to me. *He doesn't believe I'll understand a word of it.*

I take a few demure sips. "That sure is dazzling, Nigel, but it's inefficient. As a practical encryption method, it would never be viable."

He narrows his eyes. "You got it. That's where my brainwave comes in—a geometric scheme to make it viable. It's the *decryption* that isn't viable."

"You haven't gotten this to work yet, have you?" I say, slowly. "What you're describing is killer, though. It's beautiful. I love the image of each pixel as a miniature light bulb." His design is weird and original. Even though his algorithm is probably awful, his data structure gives me a stab of nostalgia. This is what I've missed most about Mike. The excitement of our collaboration.

Nigel is watching me intently, his face dark. He doesn't like having his balloon popped.

I nurse my drink—which is quite delicious—while playing through Nigel's idea in my head. It's completely different from my system of little trees, whose branches are very efficient pathways to traverse.

"Can your algorithm hold its own against quantum computers?" I ask, trying to probe for more weaknesses, like I used to do with Mike. "You know they're coming—"

"Crikey, Madeline." He stands up and drapes an arm around my shoulder. "It's time to go have dinner." In the hallway he forces a grin and says, "What fun to have a girl who talks my lingo." I don't rise to the bait. I'm nervous about what I must do before dinner.

When we're seated at the table, in front of the picture window, Nigel commands Alexa to dim the lights. In an instant we're in a romantic space, the fire crackling and the music softly playing.

"May I use the bathroom before we start?" I say. Oldest spy trick in the book, but as it happens, I really need to go.

"Be my guest." He gestures toward the hallway, then disappears into the kitchen.

My shoes are silent on the hardwood floor. A distant clank of dishes reassures me, and I slip into the study, which is somewhat illuminated by the hallway light. With shaky fingers I probe the side of the computer for a USB port, but perversely, the darn thing isn't where I expected it to be. The slot is on the other side. Roughly, I insert the flash drive. *Make this quick.*

I creep into the bathroom, flush the toilet, then hurry back to the study. Failure isn't an option. What's the point if I can't do this one simple thing?

I listen for footsteps in the hallway and hear reassuring noises from the kitchen.

In a few seconds I type the command to download Nigel's computer. But the familiar green bar doesn't appear. *The download is blocked!*

I slip back into the bathroom to have a quick pee. Now another flush, making the requisite bathroom noises.

When I emerge, Nigel is walking toward me. "Madeline? Everything okay?"

"Sorry, Nigel, I must fix something. I'll be with you in a minute."

"Fix what?" His face is bland.

"Female problems," I stammer like an idiot, my smooth, confident demeanor gone. *Go! Let me finish the job.*

My heart drums with relief when he heads back to the kitchen.

In the dark of his study, I wipe my sweaty palms on my pants, yank my flash drive out of his computer, then replace it with a spare that has a preprogrammed script to override the download blockage.

I speed-type some instructions and press return. I don't have the luxury to wait and see if my patch works, and in a minute I'm back in the living room, patting down my hair and girding myself to be sociable.

"Everything sorted?" he says, looking at me strangely.

I straighten my little jacket and say, "All good. Sorry… about that." Ugh. My voice is too high pitched, like a toy doll.

He moves to a window that faces the front of the house, pulls aside the curtain, and peers out. "Lots of bloody maniacs out on the roads tonight." At the window, all I see is a blur of headlights through the snow.

Nigel takes my arm and says, "Let's eat."

The table is set with a snow-white tablecloth and a small vase of roses. He's a scary man. Roses at this time of year means he can do anything he sets his mind to. He places in front of me an avocado half packed with some kind of lumpy seafood—lobster, shrimp, crabmeat—dressed with a pink sauce, and sprinkled with paprika.

It's a *Wow* moment.

He squeezes my velvet shoulder and admires his handiwork. "It's called Avocado Ritz. South African dish."

Sitting across from me, he watches as I take a bite. The combination of seafood and avocado is so exquisite I could almost forget why I'm here. I shut my eyes and savor the flavors. Hot paprika. Garlic.

"Nigel, you're a man of surprises. First a four-dimensional array of pixels. Now this."

"And you, Madeline, are a woman of mystery."

"Why don't you supervise students?" I blurt.

He takes a few bites, his face betraying nothing. "Because I've worked assiduously to be free of them. Not too long ago, I had many students, and they were an infinite sink of time, some of them as needy as children."

I scrape out the avocado and drop the empty shell of it on my plate.

"Why do you ask?" he says.

"Because Mike had eight students, and his load seemed unfair."

"Mike never learned how to play the game," he says.

"If everyone played the game, there'd be no one left to supervise students. Great hors d'oeuvre, by the way."

"But, Madeline, there'll always be suckers who do the so-called right thing. I depend on them." He grins, gets up abruptly, and places a cast-iron skillet on the stovetop. "Talking of playing games, watch this."

What ensues is a world-class performance with knives, a flamethrower and a deluge of red wine. The result is an entrée of tenderloin steak flambé, served with crisp, herb-seasoned potatoes, and roasted cauliflower.

"Notice how I fatten up my women," he says, placing a fragrant plate in front of me.

"As I've already said, I'm not one of your women."

"But of course you are. You're allowing me to cook for you."

"What do you do in your spare time? Or are you always working on your pixels?"

"Well, obviously, I like to cook—"

"You mean you cook like this, every day? For yourself?"

"Who said I was by myself?"

Dessert is a pear poached in port wine, with toasted pecans and French vanilla ice cream. As with everything that went before, this is divine.

It's probably halfway through downloading by now.

I make short work of the pear and say, "Nigel, this was magnificent. Thank you."

"It's quite something to watch you polish everything off, as if you haven't seen food in a week. Your mind seems miles away. Do you even know what it is you've eaten?"

"That's because everything was to die for."

"What will you do now?" he says, his face suddenly serious.

"Have a cup of tea or coffee, depending on what you offer."

He inclines his head. "I meant workwise—where will you go, since you're no longer at Cornell?"

"I'm not going anywhere for now. Maybe I'll be a programmer for hire."

"You could come and work as my assistant," he says. "I can tell you're one smart cookie."

"Or you could come and work as *my* assistant. You seem pretty smart yourself." I smile across the table.

"Tea or coffee?" he says.

"Tea please. Black and caffeinated, if you have it."

"I have everything." He moves to the kitchen counter, fussing with a teapot and fuzzy white tea cozy.

"You're funny, Madeline," he says. "Who knew?"

The download is probably complete.

"I need another break." I push my chair back and stand too quickly, light headed from more than a few sips of expensive red wine.

"Sit down," he says. His voice is not aggressive, but something in his tone makes me pause.

"Excuse me?" I sink back into the chair, and the room tilts.

A log falls in the grate, startling me, causing sparks to fly up in the fireplace. The Brahms Quintet ends, and all I can hear is the low crackle of fire. Through the window, the relentless snow.

Despite the warmth of the room, I shiver.

Nigel comes back to the table and sits down opposite me. His face has a mirthless smile, his eyes narrowed. "Okay, Madeline, the jig is up," he says. "It's time to tell me why you're downloading my hard drive."

CHAPTER 31

My palms are sweating, but I stay outwardly calm. I've become more practiced, more in control. Not blurting out the first thought in my head: *How do you know?*

He wasn't anywhere near the study.

I sit back and fold my arms, staring at him, eyeball to eyeball. I keep my mouth shut, waiting for him to make the next move.

"I have a Ring camera in the study," he says, grinning. Proud of himself, like he just won a pissing contest. "On the wall—the Escher that you looked at."

Did I really miss the wink of a camera lens when I studied the print?

"With everything going on in the picture—ladders going up to nowhere—that camera hides in plain sight." He watches for my reaction, so I keep my face bland, even though my heart is drumming. He's loving this.

He gets up and moves to the kitchen. "So I'll ask again. What are you searching for on my computer?"

I sigh, as if wrestling with myself. "Your research, Nigel. Mike stole my work and shared my ideas with his colleagues." I look across the table with wide and honest eyes.

But Nigel shakes his head dismissively. "Let me share something with you. Judy warned me you'd go after my computer." He pours the tea, the spout of the English teapot high in the air. "She said you'd downloaded her hard drive, and David's, and possibly Dwayne's, and she warned me to watch my back and my computer, because you'd be after me too. And here we are."

My neck is tense, and I must force myself into yoga breathing. I command my body to stop overreacting. *You can do this.*

"Mike betrayed me." My voice is steady and cold. "He presented my research as his work. I don't know how many of my ideas he shared with the department, so yes, I'm checking computers." His face is impassive. Fear and nervous energy spur me on. "Big powerful people—men mainly—would never admit to using my work, so I can't exactly come right out and ask them."

He returns to the table with our tea. Carefully, he sets down a steaming glass mug in front of me, with a slice of lemon on the side. The perfect symmetry of that lemon slice is chilling.

He takes his time arranging himself on the chair opposite me, and places both palms flat on the table. "I don't believe a word you're saying. Snooping around our offices at night? Invading people's privacy? For what? To check out their algorithms? I don't think so."

"Believe what you like. I lost my husband recently, so forgive me if I've become a bit paranoid."

He is adding a generous tot of Irish whiskey to his tea. "Want a drop?" he says.

I shake my head. It's the last thing I want.

"The reason I know your story is a pile of hooey is I *told* you about my research. You don't need to download my computer to find my current work. I've volunteered it. In fact, *Madeline*, I should be scared *you* will steal *my* ideas."

"That's ridiculous and you know it. A four-dimensional array traversal? Give me a break."

He glares at me, making a dismissive *tsk* in his throat.

"You're an enigma," he says. "I can't get a handle on you. Everyone else in the department is an open book—Judy, David, Dwayne—Mike even, when he was alive—apologies—but you? For years you've been an invisible mouse, and now you've roared back like a lion, claiming to be the source of all Mike's work. You're everywhere, creeping around the department, downloading computers left and right, standing like a demon in front of my office door, trying to crack the lock—yes, I've seen you—watching me like a hawk, following me into my office and throwing yourself at me, begging for a date. Who are you, Madeline Geiger, and what the hell do you want?"

Slowly, I exhale. I've underestimated him. "Oh, please. I'm a computer scientist, aiming to take ownership of my work, no more, no less."

"Bullshit," he says, with surprising vehemence. "There, are you satisfied? Rattling my cage until I fucking-well swear?"

Get over yourself.

He shuts his eyes, shudders, and drinks his tea. Part of his menace is the Shakespearean drama he thinks he's in. My body is bristling on high alert. *Who dies in the end?*

Andri was wrong. It *is* a cat and mouse game, and I'm the mouse.

I'm almost down to the dregs of my tea, sipping compulsively, when Nigel says, "You downloaded the wrong computer. That thing in the study is my plaything."

He claps his hands with one short crack and commands, "Alexa, unlock the safe!"

It startles me. "What if a burglar commands her to open the safe?"

"Don't insult me, Madeline. If it's not my voice, she loads my gun and shoots the burglar." I stare at him. He has the crazed look of Jack Nicholson in *The Shining*. He bursts out laughing and says, "Got you going there, huh? No worries. If it's not me, she ignores the command."

My mouth is dry. Whatever it is he's about to show me, I'm ready to go home.

"Okay, young lady, the game's afoot." He motions me to follow him into the living room, where he takes a small painting off the wall. A safe behind it swings open, revealing a sleek Dell laptop. "This is what you were looking for," he says. "The crown jewels." He places it in my arms. "My life and work. Pictures of my ex-wife. My latest algorithms. An outline of my next book. You don't need to crack my password; I'll enter it for you."

"What are you doing, Nigel?" The room is still lit for a romantic evening, with a white blur of snow through the picture window.

"I'm a man who makes women happy. I'm giving you what you came for."

"So what—you're going to let me take this home?"

"No, of course not. But you can search through it tomorrow. You're not going anywhere tonight—the house is snowbound."

I'm gripping his computer so hard my knuckles are white.

"You can't keep me here against my will." My voice is quiet, but my old rib injury is angry.

He shrugs his shoulders. "No matter what, you'd stay the night. Your car is buried under a foot of snow. There's a travel advisory, they're telling people to stay off the roads. It would be suicide for you to attempt to drive."

He claps his hands and says, "Alexa, lock the front door." A loud click echoes through the house, followed by an eerie silence. He probably sees a look of alarm on my face, because he adds hastily, "Calm down, Madeline, I do it every night. The house is now secure against prowlers and burglars."

"Nigel, this is nuts. If I stay overnight, I'll need privacy."

"Let me show you to the guest room. I omitted it on the tour." The tour, which is ancient history.

I follow him, my legs like water. Is he taking me to a basement dungeon?

A long staircase leads us down. "This house was built into the landscape," he says, as if we're touring a museum.

"The guest room leads out onto the lake shore, but of course you won't go out on such a night."

I expect a nasty basement like my own, but instead, I'm shown into a room that is surprisingly pleasant, with ivory walls and comfortable-looking furniture. A puffy gold comforter covers a queen-size bed. On the bed is a male fantasy of filmy black sleepwear. Not even on my honeymoon did I wear such garments.

I look away. A gust of air from the heating vent stirs the curtains, offering a glimpse of the swirling darkness.

"You planned this, didn't you?" I say, with a hair-raising pang of insight. "Everything down to Victoria's Secret."

"Let's put it this way—I had a feeling we'd have a sleepover. The weather forecast was dire. The bathroom is well stocked, by the way—toothbrush, robe, towels—whatever you need."

He is standing behind me, his breath warm on my neck. "Of course, if you'd prefer, you can spend the night upstairs, with me. This is what you offered, isn't it?" Then his arms are circling my waist, his overheated body pressed against me. "Mmm. You smell of English countryside, and all that pixel talk has turned me on."

Don't panic.

I shake him off and step away. "Don't touch me."

My purse is nearby on the bed. I do the calculation. With one lunge I can reach it, but I'm weak in the knees.

"What'll we do now, sweet Madeline?" he says.

"Nothing." I turn to face him, my elbows pressed into my side. "We'll do nothing."

He ignores me, walking toward me, his arms outstretched. "Come on, Maddie, be a sport, let me show you a good time."

I'm not as spry as I was Before, but in two quick, awkward strides I'm fumbling in my purse, grabbing my key ring with its small purple canister of pepper spray.

"Stop!" I've never used this thing before and I aim it at his face and scream, "One more step and you're blind!"

He flinches away from me, his mouth gaping. "Good God, Madeline, put that down." Raising his arms high, shielding his face. "No need to be hysterical."

I bite back my response, the spray locked and loaded, aimed at his eyes. I don't want to inflame him by pointing out what a walking, breathing cliché he is.

We stand like that, suspended in a kind of stalemate, before he says, "What will you do, all on your own down here?"

"Text my mother and let her know I won't be home tonight."

"Be my guest. I'm warning you, though, reception from this house is often blocked by bad weather." He laughs, his face ghastly in the artificial light. "But don't worry. She'll assume you're being a red-blooded woman and spending the night."

"Don't underestimate her. If she doesn't hear from me, she'll call the police and break down your door."

"On a night like this, I'm willing to take my chances."

"What's your plan, Nigel? I assume I'll be free to go tomorrow—?"

"You're free to go right now. Sleep in your car if that's what you'd prefer."

I nod curtly. Like it or not, I'm his guest.

He gestures at the bed, and I see the glint of a silver cuf-flink. "Sleep well."

At the door, he turns around. "Sure you won't change your mind? I do have talents that extend beyond coding and cooking."

I shake my head and gesture at the door with my spray canister. *Go already, asshole.*

He pulls the door behind him, and it clicks shut.

Barely breathing, I wait until his tread upstairs has faded, then try the doorknob.

The door is locked.

CHAPTER 32

That SOB has locked me in! I try to get his attention by slamming my hands on the door and screaming "Nigel!"

When I pull out my phone to call him, there's no reception. I grasp the handle of the sliding glass door, but it's locked. Of course it is. Alexa probably locked it too. I'm trapped.

Shallow breath, nose and mouth, in out, in out.

After a minute or two, I start to check the room for bugs. I've learned my lesson from the hidden camera in the study. There's nothing winking at me from the corners or ceiling. Nothing obvious on the lamp or furniture. A Stuart Davis print on the wall has an intricate geometric design in white, black, and red. Lightly, I run my hand over it. No bumps or suspicious topography.

He's watching me, I know it.

Think. Nigel is a joker who'd delight in finding an original way to spy on me. There's an innocuous-looking smoke detector on the ceiling. Of course! A perfect place to conceal a camera. Luckily, I'm tall and can reach it by standing on a chair. With the aid of some masking tape and note paper from my purse, I create a shield. If the hidden camera is here, it just went dark.

I check my phone again. He's right—it's blocked. I try to call my mother. No ring tone, just silence. I try Andri and get the same blank nothing. What about the burner phone? I haven't yet decided what to do about Joe, but in this situation I can't worry about the niceties. I press on his name. There's a light crackling of activity, but it's probably more wishful thinking than actual noise.

I sink into a comfortable armchair and analyze my situation. The indignity of it, besides anything else. To be honest, if I had caught someone invading *my* computer, I would have thrown them out of my house. At this moment I could be shivering on a snow-covered driveway, contemplating a hazardous drive home. Instead, I've been fed like a princess and dropped into a luxurious prison for the night.

How will I escape?

I won't forgive him for putting his hands and mouth on me without consent.

Shoving those thoughts aside, I think about his computer, the one from the safe. Why would he give me access? Only because it's the computer he wants me to see. What's on the computer in his study?

Making sense of the jumble of thoughts in my head is futile. I decide to call it a night and save my emotional energy for tomorrow.

The guest bathroom is pristine and more than adequate. I don't turn on the light, because I feel safer in the dark. After my teeth are brushed, and I've splashed myself here and there with soap and warm water, I sink into the fluffy towels, then throw on a fresh sweatshirt from the closet.

Afterwards, I consider hunkering down in the bathroom with the door bolted, but the lure of the bed is too much. I burrow in under the sheets and start worrying about my immediate future. What if Nigel comes back? The thought keeps me awake for what seems like several hours. Eventually I drift off, and my next conscious awareness is light streaming into the room.

I lie still for a moment, getting my bearings. It's eerily quiet, not a sound from upstairs. I'm at his mercy.

Pulling back the curtains reveals a dazzling vista of snow, lake, sun, and blue skies. A freak October storm has deposited over a foot of snow that will be half-melted by tonight.

I pad to the door and try the knob. It turns. I jump back. The thought of him down here, unlocking the door and silently watching me sleep, creeps me out. Perhaps he commanded Alexa, *Unlock the guest bedroom!*

Quietly, I push the door shut. There's no way to lock it from the inside. The bathroom, however, has a latch. I gather up my clothes—minus the velvet jacket—and head to the shower.

The corners, ceiling, pipes, shower head, attachments, and lights, seem to be free of hidden cameras. Failure to find spyware is probably a testament to my shortcomings as a spy, rather than a definitive statement about cameras. Nevertheless, I feel defiled after last night and want to shower. If Nigel is going to make a peep show of my skinny, wet body, so be it.

He's thought of everything. A bottle of Pretty Woman shampoo and matching conditioner stand in a wire shower tray, plus a new bar of perfumed French soap. With a kind of fatalism, I surrender myself to the hot needles of the shower, which is luxurious and a far cry from the rattling old sprinkler at my farmhouse in Brooktondale.

At about eight-thirty, I grab my belongings and ascend to the living room. He's wearing a ridiculous chef's apron and bustling about at the kitchen island. The sight of him makes me queasy. I drop my stuff near the dining room table, but cling to my purse.

"Top of the morning, Madeline!" he says jovially. "Hope you slept well. I have everything on order—eggs, bacon, waffles, pancakes, oatmeal—whatever your heart desires." *As if yesterday didn't happen.*

I take a step toward him. "You sound like a civilized person, and yet you locked me in my room last night. Aren't you afraid I'll file a complaint with the police?"

He puts down the coffee pot and stares at me. "Good God, Madeline, what on earth are you talking about?"

"I'm talking about being held against my will in your house, without any means of contacting the outside world. Why couldn't I just spend the night in your guest room, like a normal visitor?"

"God knows that whatever else you are, you're *not* a normal visitor. Breaking into people's offices and downloading their hard drives. You scare the bejesus out of me, to be honest; but just to clear the record, I didn't lock your door."

"Why do I scare you? What do you have to hide?" My brain is racing ahead of him, trying to solve the mystery of the door. It may be an Alexa malfunction. She treated the guest room door as an outside door and unlocked it this morning with the other outside doors.

Either that or he's lying.

He too is processing the problem. "Now that I think about it, I *should* have locked you in. What the hell do you want from me, Madeline?"

"My car," I say, slowly. "I want to go outside and see my car. And text my mother."

He looks at me for a good few seconds before saying, "Okay, no problem. Let's go see what the gods have wrought."

At the door, we put on boots and jackets. He looks like someone in a French farce, with his long apron and rugged boots.

"This is ridiculous, Nigel, I don't need a chaperone."

"Nevertheless, the front walk will be hazardous, even though I shoveled it at the crack of dawn." He smiles at me. "I would hate for you to take a spill on the stones."

So yes, he did unlock the outside doors.

He hooks his arm firmly through mine and tugs me onto the slippery walkway. Yet again I must shake him off. "Nigel, I can handle this."

We walk carefully in single file, him in front, into the bracing air of a gorgeous morning. No one observing us would suspect I'm a prisoner of the man ahead of me. The walkway is lined with decorative rocks. I could smash a rock on his head, claiming self-defense, but it's a fantasy I reject. So far, all I know for sure is he's a hound dog.

There's a drip-drip-dripping from the roof and colorful trees, autumn reclaiming its place.

My car is almost hidden on the driveway. The snow must be brushed off before it ices up, but my snow removal equipment is on the back seat. *Damn!*

"Wait here," Nigel says, "I'll get the brushes from my car in the garage." He disappears around the side of the house.

What a relief to see him go. I don't, however, jump into my car and make my escape. It's been a lot of trouble getting into his house and computers, so quitting now is not an option.

As soon as he disappears, I text Mom: *I'll be home for supper. All good.*

Then I text Andri: *If I'm not home by 4:30 call cops.* I forward him Nigel's address.

I don't contact Joe.

"So—breakfast?" Nigel says, when we're back inside. "Do you like French toast?" Snow glistens in his hair.

I do.

It seems ridiculous to accept breakfast from him, but I can't spend the day at his computer without eating. After last night's dinner, he surely won't poison me at breakfast.

Living dangerously is thrilling in a way, like skydiving. *Something* has to explain the risks I'm taking.

In the kitchen, Nigel is a magician, juggling implements and food with extravagant gestures. First he toasts a few slices of bread. Then he whisks some eggs with vanilla essence from Mexico.

"I opened this in your honor," he says, showing me the expensive-looking little bottle.

"Well, you shouldn't have. I won't taste the difference."

"Just wait." He melts an obscene gob of butter in a large skillet, dips the toast in egg mixture, and throws it onto the foaming butter. While it sizzles, he pours the remaining egg evenly over the slices, turns them, adds more butter as topping, and sprinkles all with cinnamon.

Everything he does is over the top.

He serves us each two slices, with fresh-squeezed orange juice.

It's to die for.

He's in an expansive mood, talking about his encryption book and the controversy it generated. He's been accused of aiding and abetting criminals with his encryption methods.

Is he goading me?

"So I've had to write responses to people, explaining that it's the joy of computer science—writing clever algorithms, solving problems, cracking codes—that motivates me."

I nod like a sage.

"I've been accused of being worse than the physicists who developed the atomic bomb," he says, stabbing his breakfast. "Can you imagine? And yet I know that those physicists—Oppenheimer and his crowd—did it because they could. Joy of physics and all that."

By now we're drinking coffee, which is also pretty damn good.

"Open your laptop and show me your work files," I say. "I've told you what I'm looking for."

He contemplates me for a few seconds, brings his laptop to the table, plugs in its power cord, and after a few brusque clicks, invites me to pull up a chair.

He doesn't relinquish the mouse.

"You're kidding me. You're really going to sit next to me?"

"Watching you examine my life will be a turn-on," he says. "I have nothing to hide." *Ugh.*

We start with the folder for his computer science book, the one I've already read. First proofs, preliminary notes, and computer programs. Despite his air of being a TV celebrity, he works like a demon.

"Open the Image file," I say. "I want to see your data structure."

He double-clicks. "I've been asked to do many things by various women, but never that. It's extraordinarily erotic."

Focus.

"Show me the outline of your second book."

He thinks about it. "Let's change seats—take the mouse."

"Why?" *Cringe.*

"I want to see what you click on, then watch you read my stuff. As I said, it'll turn me on."

My neck bristles. "Nigel, that's repulsive."

"Nothing's free, dear Madeline." He shifts his chair closer to mine. "I've given you my mouse. You can choose any files you fancy. Go on…"

So there it is, as Joe and I discussed many nights ago—the price of his information: some bizarre sexual fantasy in my airspace.

His second book is about decryption. Pros and cons of different data structures.

Where are the porn sites? I don't need a Ph.D. to know that if there were incriminating sites on this laptop, he wouldn't be sharing them.

His email is encrypted. When I try to read a message, I get a row of hieroglyphics, blocking the search. He's watching me, bemused.

"Why are your emails encrypted?" I ask.

"So people like you can't read them."

"If I pick one at random, will you decrypt it?"

"Do you really want to read my divorce settlement?" he says. "The bitter demands of my ex-wife and her nasty lawyer? Is this why you've wormed your way into my house?"

"No, that's not what I'm searching for. Pick any email and decrypt it."

"You choose and hit Shift-Control-F9."

So his decryption key is encrypted. Not much information there.

"Time for a bathroom break." I stand. *Will he accompany me?*

But he lets me go. "You know the way," he says, smirking.

Walking down the familiar hallway, I glance into the study. My flash drive is still in his computer! *By now, his hard drive is downloaded.* In all the drama, he must have forgotten to take it out. Except he wouldn't forget, because he's cleverer than that. If it's in the computer, he wants me to examine it. *Either way, I must take the bait.*

It's now or never. I go to the bathroom and check out the hallway. He's not there, but he may be watching the study through his Ring camera. There is, however, a way to elude detection. My Ring video at home has a limited range—it doesn't show the space above the floor. I'm guessing Nigel's video reveals nothing from the tabletop down.

There's no time to overthink it. In about three seconds I'm in through the study door and on the ground, crawling like a snake toward the computer. When I reach the table, I act like lightning, rising up to grab the flash drive, yank it out, and crawl on my belly out the room. With luck, if he's scrolling through his video, he won't see a hand that disappears in the blink of an eye.

I stuff the drive deep into my pants pocket, go and flush the toilet, and return to the living room table. He's at his computer, clicking away.

"I'm ready for your cloud storage," I say. "How do I access it?"

"Turn around, don't look, and I'll let you in." He's incorrigible.

He inclines his head for a few seconds, as if trying to decrypt me. "Why in God's name are you searching my cloud?"

"Show me photos of the department."

He grins, then unlocks the cloud. "Come back to the hot seat." Patting it.

What a creep.

I take a deep breath and open his world of photos. The young Nigel, who was spectacularly good looking. "Not a bad side of beef, huh?" He nudges my arm, and I flinch.

"Why so nervous? You should be leaping with joy that you have what you came for."

Please God don't let him fondle my hip with the flash drive.

"Hands off me, Nigel," I say, with an assertiveness I don't feel.

He grins again with that deranged look.

Compartmentalize. Concentrate.

Many photos of him with a beautiful young woman who could be his daughter. If it's his wife, I wonder what went wrong.

"Stupid cow," he says, reading my mind.

More recent photos appear. Nigel with other women, all petite with long blonde hair. I don't think I'm his type at all. He's rich and famous. Probably could have his pick.

There's a photo of the Computer Science Department. With a jolt I see Mike. Everyone's here, the whole gang. Where was I? No one invited me to the party. Even Aisha is in the picture.

Nigel has his arm around Judy. Mike has his arm around Aisha. David has his arm around Dwayne. They are all oh so buddy-buddy.

Album after album. All squeaky clean. Nigel looking older, resembling the man beside me. Distinguished. A more mature look.

Many, many files. Nothing suspicious.

I've seen enough.

He moves his chair back and says, "You've distracted me beyond reason. Now can you tell me what this is all about?"

I stand and stretch, looking at him frankly. He's such a strange combination of generosity and sleaziness. I haven't been the hottest date in the world, and he—perhaps— deserves some honesty. I surprise myself by saying, "I'll tell you, Nigel, but can't do it now."

He bangs his palms on the table, jarring his laptop. "You're kidding me."

"It's not something I can talk about. I'm sorry."

"Can you stay for lunch?"

"No, thank you, I'm going to drive home. Don't stop me. We're done."

"Tell me just one thing. Did you find what you were look- ing for?"

"Yes, thank you, I did."

He looks unsettled. I bet his other women don't elicit that look.

Despite his pomp and bravado, he's a lonely man. Under- neath the façade, he's a bit like me. He finds solace in his work.

But he's also an overbearing jerk who harasses women. Students, colleagues—anyone who will play along. And maybe those who won't. I don't want to speculate what would have happened in the absence of my pepper spray.

Here's what I might have said to him if I'd had the inclination:

This is what I'm doing here, Nigel. I've ascertained that above all, you're a Royal Asshole; but you're not the perpetrator I'm searching for. With all the work you do, you don't have time to sell encryption software to pornography vendors.

You wouldn't have believed me if I'd told you.

CHAPTER 33

I exit his driveway without a backward glance. *Good riddance.*

There are eyes on me everywhere, but who is my antagonist? Has George's employer hired someone else to follow me? Where's George, and what should we have done with him?

A car on my tail is making no effort to hide. No crossing the double-yellow line on a twisting road. Is this George's replacement? I speed up, flooring the accelerator, and he speeds up too. Eventually, the road straightens, and he overtakes me illegally with a great firing of cylinders. *Jerks everywhere.*

Time to change my train of thought. Who in the department needs extra money?

What about Judy? She's divorced, but she draws a big salary from Cornell. It's inconceivable she wants even more. But of course, using that criterion, I myself could be the prime suspect. Mom and I are a few rent payments away from poverty. Without Andri, we'd go under, something I'd rather not dwell on. I've been putting it off, the small problem of earning a living after the Cornell money runs out.

Driving through Ithaca, with an amorphous anxiety that's eating away at my determination to *get this job done*, I swerve and change course, heading toward Judy's house in

Cayuga Heights. It's lunchtime and Judy never leaves campus for lunch. I know where she lives from past department picnics on her sumptuous lawn. Housing prices are off the charts in this neck of the woods, the suburb with the mansions in walking distance of Cornell. After her divorce, Judy kept the house. Aisha shared a rumor she didn't get a great settlement. I remember Judy's husband, a brash veterinary surgeon who operated on race horses at the vet school. I have no idea where he ended up. After he disappeared from Judy's life, he disappeared from mine.

Without any kind of well-defined goal, I park on a parallel street, shed my winter jacket, and keep on the ribbed scarf knitted by my mother. The day is beautiful, and I slosh through the melting snow on the sidewalks. It feels good to be free, in the sense of not being locked up.

On Judy's property is a proliferation of signs telling me this house is protected by Sentry Alarms. There are signs at the entrance to the long driveway, and others popping up through the shrubbery leading to the front door. So there won't be another triumph of the sardine key, not here.

The house occupies about half an acre, a wooded lot with a bower of tall trees. I walk around the side, peering through windows that reveal a house that appears to be empty. The grounds are deserted.

Pressing myself against the brick exterior, I round the corner to the back of the house. There's a light on in a large window. I crouch low until I'm underneath it, then slowly lift my head to peer in. A woman with her back to me is peeling vegetables on an island. Probably a housekeeper. She freezes suddenly, as if some sixth sense alerts her. She spins around and walks to the sink as I drop out of sight. Did she see me? My heart pounds against the brick wall.

Since the woman is in the house, the burglar alarm is probably disarmed. Dare I come in on some pretext and slip into the study? Bad idea. Judy probably takes her laptop to work. The big question is how to access her home computer or laptop? Obviously I can't make a pass at Judy, trying to snag a romantic date.

The problem stays with me on the long drive to Brooktondale.

At home, there's a car I don't recognize in the driveway. I hurry inside to the sound of Torvill barking. Dwayne Browning is in the living room. He rises when I walk in but doesn't quite meet my eyes.

"Madeline, hey," he says. "Great to see you up and about."

Mom says, "Do you remember your friend, Dwayne? He's come for a visit." Her eyes are vague.

In two strides my arm is around her. "Mom. This is my colleague from Cornell, Dwayne."

"But you're not at Cornell anymore, are you Maddie?"

I sit beside her on the couch. "Hi, Dwayne, how're you doing?"

Dwayne sits. "I'm sorry, Madeline, about what happened. I didn't get to say goodbye. Is there someplace we could talk—?"

Mom stands. She's still sharp enough to recognize when her presence isn't wanted. "Andri's on the roof," she says. "We had a leak from the snowstorm last night. Dripping in a different place—this time over his bedroom. I'll go see how he's doing." She's wearing her slippers and a thin sweater, and heads to the front door.

"Mom, it's cold outside. You need your boots and jacket to go out into the garden." I cast a look at Dwayne, who nods.

"I'll be fine," Mom says, disappearing in the direction of her room. "Bye, Dwayne, nice to see you again."

My mother freaks me out in this state, as does the roof. And my mind is focused on Judy, so I'm quite curt with Dwayne. "You could have called me. Aisha would have given you my number. You didn't have to drive all the way to Brooktondale to tell me you're sorry."

His eyes widen. I was more abrupt than necessary.

"Forgive me, Dwayne—that was rude." I put my face in my hands and rub my eyes. "Can we start again? Thank you for your condolences. Judy fired me and didn't exactly have a farewell party to celebrate my time at Cornell." I sound bitter. I don't care. The past twenty-four hours have been harrowing, and my social graces, such as they are, have deteriorated. Still, I don't say what I'm thinking, which is, *what do you want?*

"Did you get into my computer?" Dwayne says, meeting my eyes then looking down.

Oh, hell. My reputation has spread.

"Why?" There's no apology in my voice. "Is there anything you'd like to explain?"

"Mike and I were collaborating in secret," he says. "For security, we kept the files on my computer, not his. I'm sorry, Madeline, he didn't want you to know. He was going to tell you when he got preliminary results from his code."

Another betrayal from Mike.

"You were using my research, without including me."

"I didn't know it was yours. Honestly—Mike approached me—I had no reason to disbelieve him."

"What else did you collaborate on?" *Porn videos?*

The furrows on his brow deepen. To his credit, he seems genuinely remorseful. "Encrypting private data. Spreadsheets, bank accounts, financial transactions—"

"Mike worked on that?" It's news to me. It's exactly what purveyors of porn would need. Is Dwayne involved? Is he the Cornell link I've been searching for? If he were, why would he volunteer such information? *Why is he here?*

"Do you have Mike's computer?" he says. "I'd like to check how far he got with his algorithms for our joint project."

Did I miss those algorithms?

"I'm so sorry." With an innocent look, I meet his eyes. "Mike's computer is being held by the police as evidence."

Dismay and frustration on Dwayne's face. Torvill barking his head off in the kitchen. Andri banging the screen door, stomping snow of his boots. He comes into the living room beaming at me. "Medeleen, thank you to gods, you're safe!"

Dwayne stands in confusion, Mom does something she's never done before—trails mud and snow into the living room.

The sharp ringing of my phone echoes in the room. Two long rings and then silence from my burner.

Joe.

CHAPTER 34

I can't take Joe's callback—there's too much turmoil in my living room.

Andri walks up to Dwayne, hand outstretched. "Hi, I'm lodger in this house. Andri Eriksson." Meanwhile, Torvill is barking at Dwayne, who is sitting in his favorite spot on the couch. "Down, Torvill Eriksson!" Andri commands, letting loose a string of German, which sounds to me like *Shut the fuck up.*

Andri can be an intimidating presence to those who don't know him, and when Torvill sinks to the ground, his head between his paws, Dwayne shrinks back into the cushions.

"Do you have a copy of Mike's programming files?" he says faintly.

"Dwayne, you'll probably need to work on something else—those programs are my ideas. Or email me what you're working on."

Tosca meanders into the middle of this scene and jumps onto Mom's lap. Andri appears to notice Mom in her chair with her boots and outdoor jacket. He strides to the chair and lifts his cat high in the air, saying, "How is my beautiful diva today?" He jiggles her and envelops her in a hug that sets her off yowling in outrage. "Come, Jenet," Andri says. "Let's get rid of boots and hat and leave stupid cat alone." Gently he places the ruffled cat on the floor and eases Mom out of the chair, walking her to the kitchen with his arm around her shoulders.

"Sorry, Dwayne. Things are a bit crazy today. Tell me about the Computer Science Department. How's it going? Does everyone miss me? Ha—joke."

He smiles thinly. "I kinda miss you, Madeline. I have a new research assistant, who has moved into your office—your small office—she's new, just started—"

He looks down, embarrassed. It was no secret he wanted me out so he could take over Mike's grant.

"How's Aisha? Any success on the romantic front?"

He stares at Torvill, who's still on the floor. "We're on again, off again. The usual story—she won't commit, she's always busy, always says she has stuff to do instead of saying yes. Sometimes I think she just doesn't like me."

"I bet you're wrong. Aisha has a mind of her own. She wouldn't give you the time of day if she didn't like you. But don't take my word for it, I—of all people—am not qualified to give you relationship advice."

My burner phone rings again.

"Sorry, I have to take this privately." I stand. "Nice to see you, Dwayne—please see yourself out."

Watching from the window, I wait for him to leave, then rush to my bedroom and lock the door. It's not until I've locked myself in the bathroom that I pause.

If I trust Andri, then Joe has lied to me. So why am I rushing to return his call?

The answer is, I have unfinished business with Joe.

He picks up immediately. "Madeline! Where've you been?" *Like he owns me.*

"I can't talk now. We need to meet tonight. My backyard, in the woods, 9 PM."

"Why not the dead drop?" No warmth in his voice at all, but it could just be a buzz of tension, communicated through the phone.

"There are issues at home." My breath catches. "I want to be able to slip out for just a while. Meet at the usual place. Be careful. Drive on back roads and don't come anywhere near the front of my house. Use a flashlight and don't fall into the pond."

There's a long enough silence that I think I've lost him. "Joe?"

"Is the porn guy Nigel Welbourne?" he says, softly.

"See you tonight, Joe." Equally quietly. "Watch your back."

Mom's brooding silence during dinner worries me, the fact she doesn't press me for details about my date with the professor. Her eyes are listless and darting, watching the animals chow down dinner, then swiveling to me and Andri. I'm afraid she's forgotten I spent the night with a man.

Out of nowhere, she hugs her arms and says, "The Peeping Tom—George—is back. I saw him last night at Andri's bedroom window."

There's a lot to process in this sentence. "Oh God, Mom, are you sure?"

She folds her arms. "Take it or leave it."

"Okay...I'll install another Ring camera," I say, turning to Andri. "This time, if we catch him, we'll call the police."

Andri is antsy—fidgeting with his cutlery—making no effort to be his usual genial self. "Things not safe for you, Medeleen. And also not Jenet, walking around house watching windows."

Mom pouts and looks away from us.

Andri is more worried about me and wants to debrief me about Nigel. I'm close-mouthed, unwilling to leave my mother on her own. Supper is last night's leftovers, which I heat in the microwave and dump onto plates. The broccoli is overcooked, a pale olive green, instead of the light, crunchy perfection we're used to.

Torvill is unhappy because Andri hasn't added grated cheese to his kibble, a treat that usually happens in a ceremony of great love. Tosca growls when Torvill wanders over to inspect her bowl, and she bats him away. We're all on edge.

Even the weather has turned, and the gorgeous sunny day has become a night of light drizzle, the cold rain pattering on the window. Ithaca weather is volatile and can change in an instant.

At ten minutes before nine, I find Mom in her room and tell her I'm going outside for a walk. "It's stuffy in here."

Mom chooses this moment to be lucid, and says, "Why go outside in this miserable weather?" She and Tosca both look at me with piercing eyes.

"I'll take my jacket and umbrella." Dutiful, like a fifteen-year-old.

She's right about one thing. The weather is lousy. A wind has arisen, blowing the rain sideways and stinging my face. The snow has mostly melted, and my boots squelch through the mush on the lawn. The only light is from my mother's window, where she is silhouetted against it. She probably can't see me. There's no moon out tonight. Just the gray blackness of the rolling clouds.

I navigate through the trees and winding path like an old pro—these woods are familiar. The hood of my jacket covers my hair, more or less. I hang my umbrella on a low-lying branch and shine my phone light through the tangle of wood bark and soggy leaves. Despite the cold, there's heat in my face as I search for him.

"I don't use an umbrella either, ma'am." He's behind a tree, watching me. "You're a creature of nature, just like me."

I gasp with relief and fright, then he's in my space, his arms around me, his wet face against mine. "Lordy, Madeline, I worried about you."

I pocket my phone and hug him back. He's warm and solid, sliding his hand under my jacket and stroking my back.

"You're in danger, Joe," I say in his ear. "Your cover is blown."

"What?" He pulls away. "How do you know?"

George Snyder's burner is in my pocket. Raindrops run down the furrows of Joe's brow as I tell him about George and his sojourn in the basement, glossing over details—it's an embarrassment to me now.

"Why didn't you call me?" Joe says.

"Because there were other people involved." *And you didn't care enough about my safety. And I still don't know if I can trust you.*

I tell him that George's shadowy employer now has George's photo album of my life. The picture of Joe and me at Treman Park is as clear as daylight. The two of us, knee to knee on a stone bench eating pizza.

"Jesus Christ," my genteel so-called Southern handler says. His face is grim. He shakes his head and whistles. "Unbelievable." After a pause, he adds, "I'll have to go to ground for a while." He takes my hand in both of his own. "You know how much this investigation means to me. Be careful."

His first concession I may be in trouble.

"I have less than a week to sort things out," I say. "The perpetrator probably isn't Nigel."

He squeezes my hand. "Maybe I don't want to hear it, but what happened with Nigel?"

I tell Joe in plain language with no euphemisms, including the parts about the sexual advances I endured to procure the crucial information.

At the mention of pepper spray, Joe starts to laugh, a low rumble lost in the distant thunder. "Sounds like you're more than capable of taking care of yourself."

Now's my chance to contradict him and say that I dread the threat of violence and danger. That it's past time for him, Joe, to call off the whole operation, with no shame on my part.

That being subjected to the sleaziness of Nigel was a path too far. But as I stand in the woods in the circle of Joe's force field, I know I'll finish the job. Do I really want to go back to the peace and quiet of pure research, without resolving the issue at hand? Pushing my academic credentials in front of men who don't want to see them? Despite my initial resistance to Joe's lunatic mission of spying, I feel a perverse sense of loss at the thought of quitting without getting the answer.

"So what's next?" Joe says. "Judy?"

This question must wait, because I have unfinished business. "My tenant, Andri Eriksson, is also a detective. He helped me capture George."

"What's that got to do with anything?" Suddenly he's alert to the implications.

"There is no FBI agent by the name of Joe Shelmann." I put my hand on his arm—hating this—and my voice is subdued. "And there's no FBI porn investigation in Ithaca. Who are you, Joe?"

He steps away. In the dark, his eyes are fierce. "You *told* this person my *name*?"

"My run-in with George the prowler was harrowing. Andri helped me. But when we grabbed George's phone, we both saw that photo of you."

"I'm undercover, you know that," he says curtly. "My name for this mission is Joe Shelmann. You shouldn't have mentioned it."

The Southern drawl has disappeared.

His demeanor rates a big fat fifteen on my scale. "So you've been lying to me again?" *Someone is lying, either Joe or Andri.*

Joe's breath is ragged as he moves away from me, with a muddy *squelch* of boots in the clearing.

I'm so deeply focused on Joe and his uneasiness that I don't hear the rustling through the woods until it's almost upon me. My mother bursts into our space, her head uncovered, her jacket open, and says, "Maddie, here you are! Is this your boyfriend? The professor you were with last night?" She walks to Joe, who freezes in place.

Peering up at him, her flashlight shining in his face, she says in her most ingratiating tone, "Hi, I'm Maddie's mother, Janet. Why don't you come inside and have tea with us, so I can get to know you?"

"Mom!" I put my arm on her back. "You're right. Let's go in the house."

It's only then I hear the frantic barking of a dog nearby. Torvill! And Andri shouting, "Jenet! Jenet!" Then they're all over us, Torvill as frenzied as he's ever been, jumping on Mom, his muddy paws scraping down the front of her wet clothing and Andri running into our space, flooding it with industrial-level light, and Mom's scarf in his hands, and Andri taking Mom in his arms, "Thank Father in heaven," and Joe—or whoever he is—nowhere in sight, gone, like a mirage into the woods.

CHAPTER 35

It won't be easy, this family discussion. It's after eleven o'clock, and we're gathered in the living room, clean and dry, sipping hot cocoa provided by my mother, who has morphed back into her old self.

Be conciliatory.

"Mom, it's not safe for you to wander out into the woods at night. If—"

"But it's okay for *you* to wander out?" she says sharply. "Is there an over-sixty rule?"

"You were acting like a crazy person. No umbrella, jacket open—"

"And you? Meeting your boyfriend in the woods? It was pouring rain and no umbrella either, so now you have an over-sixty rule for umbrellas too?"

Her logic is impeccable—I can't argue with her. Even her speech is relatively sophisticated—despite the dementia—remnants of her days as an eloquent English teacher.

She turns a laser gaze on Andri. "As for you siccing your dog on me—I warned Madeline we shouldn't let animals in the house. Torvill—attacking me like a pit bull—ruining my clothes—I'm lucky he didn't bite my neck off ."

It's a step too far. Torvill, who's been sitting on the carpet, his doleful eyes following us like a tennis match, stands and

221

fixes his Look on Mom until she lowers her eyes and says, "I'm sorry. I shouldn't have said that."

Andri pats his knee and Torvill leaps onto Andri's lap, curling into a fetal ball. "I am big apology, Jenet. So frightened when you disappeared. I gave command for Torvill to be real dog and find you. He was so happy with success." Andri scratches his maligned dog's head.

"You can't have it both ways," I say to Mom. "You can't demand to be treated like a normal adult, when you keep telling me that Daddy appears at your window."

"I know Daddy's dead," she says. "But sometimes he visits me in my mind and tells me to let it go when you lie to me, which you do all the time."

She leans forward. "Do you think I'm stupid? That I don't know you're involved in something dangerous that may kill you?"

The currents in the room shift. I'm aware of Andri and his high-alert look, his air of danger. The gears grind in my head, trying to figure out the next lie I'll tell to reassure her.

"Mom—"

"I know George Snyder wasn't a random Peeping Tom. You would have called the police and been done with it. I know he's dangerous, and now he's back, watching Andri."

My chair creaks as I gulp some cocoa. I can't meet her eyes right now, because earlier today I dismissed her warning as dementia. Mom is right—I've been distracted and reckless.

"Andri, why don't you go outside now and check out the perimeter." I'm belatedly alarmed. "Take your gun and attack dog."

Nothing is resolved. My mother says goodnight with her mouth set in a grim line, and she rebuffs my attempt to mollify her with a hug.

Sleep is elusive—three hours at most, waking at every groan of the roof in the wind, and the footfalls of animals in the house. They're not sleeping either. Is George really back?

As soon as the first pink streaks of dawn filter through my curtains, I climb out of bed, shower, grab a banana, and set out on a long walk. The freezing air has sprinkled frost on the lawn, but also clears my brain. I have a germ of an idea for solving the Judy problem, and the first step is to call Aisha, now, before she gets to work.

"Madeline, hi," she says, her voice warm and husky. "How're you doing?"

"Aisha, I've kind of been banished—as you know, I guess—can you meet me for lunch in Collegetown?"

"What, today?"

"Yes," I say softly. "At The Fountain, that little place..."

"I know where The Fountain is, I've been there." She pauses a while, probably deciding about the wisdom of meeting a persona non grata. "Okay. How about noon?"

"Perfect." I exhale. "Please don't tell anyone you're meeting me, or where you're going for lunch." What I don't say is *Especially not Judy.*

"Well that sounds ominous. Can you give me a hint?"

"Not now," I whisper. "All will become clear when I see you." I'm outside on the porch, and since I've become a spy, the house has ears.

The thought of the meeting makes me anxious. My plan is feeble, not exactly John le Carré. I'm banking on Aisha's compassion for me and her dissatisfaction with Judy, her bitterness at not getting a salary raise.

About twenty minutes before noon, I park on a side street, a good walk from the restaurant. The wind is like ice on my neck, and I flip the hood of my jacket over my head. On

College Avenue, the main drag, I pull the jacket flaps close around my face. My senses are on high alert, and my neck prickles with the uneasy sense of possibly being watched. I'm no longer a neophyte, striding along at a happy pace, oblivious to people who lurk in the shadows.

Near the end of the block, I hover briefly outside a bookstore, whose glass windows reflect the people behind me. Collegetown is a hub of activity, with students in pairs or small groups passing in both directions. Snatches of conversation and laughter trail behind them, peppered with occasional raucous shouts. As far as I can tell, no one has ducked into a store entrance behind me, no one has halted their stride in my wake.

On Dryden Road, where the crowds are thinner, I pull my jacket tightly around me and hold the sides of the hood over my face. Who am I kidding with this cloak and dagger stuff? Anyone who's concentrating can identify me because of my height.

The Fountain is on a cul-de-sac without much foot traffic. It's an informal restaurant with wooden tables and chairs organized haphazardly in the space, the waiters and waitresses clattering on the pinewood floors, students mingling and shouting.

It's a place people can talk without being overheard.

A large blackboard displays the quintessential Ithaca menu, wholesome items like an avocado and bean sprout omelet, or a vegan broth bowl with quinoa and black beans.

I'm lucky to grab a corner seat and sit with my back to the wall. Aisha is punctual, of course she is, smiling as she joins me at the table. Her clothing, as usual, transcends the weather, a woolen poncho in rustic fall colors.

"You look terrific, Madeline," she says. "Winter agrees with you." My cheeks must be ruddy from the walk.

Aisha looks like she always does. Mysterious. Regal. Dark-brown eyes, set wide apart. Those eyes are frank and questioning at this moment. She likes to be the one in control.

"I need a huge favor," I say, scanning the room to see if anyone is tuned into us.

"You seem awfully nervous, Madeline," she says pleasantly. "What's on your mind."

"I need to download Judy's laptop and can't do it without your help," I say in one gulp.

She bursts out laughing, a low elegant guffaw. "That's all? Praise the Lord. And I thought it would be something difficult."

"Hear me out." I lean toward her. "I'm starting to apply for jobs, and Judy has crucial information about me."

"Ask her for it," she says crisply. "Legally, she's bound to give you your personal data."

"Aisha, I've been banished from the Computer Science Department, and if I call her, she'll hang up."

"Do you want me to get the contents of your file? I'd be cool with that."

"I need more." My fists clench under the table.

"So...what? You're planning to steal her laptop for a while, to answer your questions?"

She orders tomato soup and gluten-free bread, and I go with the avocado omelet. "One check," I say to the waitress. "My treat."

Then the forced smile comes off my face.

"Aisha, I'm not going to play games with you. You know I've been looking at other people's computers. The reason is some of them are using my work. Mike stole my research, and some of his colleagues took my results. They think the ideas are Mike's."

She's listening intently, shaking her head. "That's really out there, Madeline."

It all spills out—the disastrous talk to the department and the vilification from department members. "I can't go to each guy and ask directly, 'Are you using my work?' But I think you'll see my quandary—how can I get a job without original research?"

"I'm sorry, Madeline, that's the pits," she says. "But I don't see how Judy's computer can help you out with that."

This is a delicate moment. "I need to see the file she's keeping on me and also her emails. I think Mike was having an affair with her."

Her eyes widen. "Really? I doubt that. I, of all people, would have known."

Is she lying? I can't read her.

Our food arrives. The waitress sets down a yellow omelet glistening with grease, and my stomach recoils. Aisha watches me with undisguised interest while she sips her carrot juice. I place a mini-bite of lunch in my mouth and by sheer force of will push down the bile inside.

With my cutlery arranged on the table and my palms on the cool wood, I look into those deep, dark eyes. "Please, Aisha. Will you do this for me?"

My request hangs in the air while we eat in silence. Loud conversations buzz around us. A scan of the room says no one is interested in a pair of older girls tucking in.

Aisha dabs her mouth delicately with her napkin, then says, "Whatever your motives are, don't do it, Madeline. It's dangerous."

"You are the only one I can ask." I lower my voice. "I don't trust anyone else."

She, too, speaks softly. "If you cross her, Judy can be trouble. Whatever you're looking for, she'll hurt you—really hurt you—if she finds out."

The threat in her voice is real, but I'm out of options. "Will you do it?" I whisper. Arrgghh, this is pathetic. A real spy would disable an alarm somewhere, grab the computer, and shimmy down the drainpipe.

She folds her arms and sits back, staring at the wall behind me.

"There's nothing in it for me. I'm sorry." Finally, a deep frown creases her forehead. "I truly sympathize with you,

Madeline, I think you've been harshly treated; but if I get caught, I'll lose my job."

It's hopeless. Judy is the culmination of my search, but I can't break into her house while she's there, nor can I slip into her office at Cornell. Aisha is my only pathway.

"What would you say if I told you I was an FBI informant searching for evidence of criminal activity involving snuff pornography? Teenagers." Bam. There it is, on the table, all in one breath. My final card. The truth.

She stretches her neck forward. "Sweet Jesus, Madeline, you really are desperate to read those emails."

I laugh uneasily and crease my eyes in an effort to make them twinkle. How did Mike do it? If ever there was a time to use his lessons about body language, eye contact, and boot licking, this is it. I lean across and place my hand on hers. "Please, Aisha, will you do it for me?" *Ugh.*

We sit in silence, our hands joined for a long minute. Sweating like a pig, I tell myself to calm the fuck down, that I'm interacting like a normal person. Not as bad as I used to be, *but I'd rather be creeping around a dark office or in a forest in Transylvania or the bottom of Fall Creek and—I can't read her. Is she doing long division in her head or deciding to snitch to Judy or figuring out how to call the cops or take advantage of my request or just get up and yell for help or push away from the table and ditch me or go back to her porn collaboration with Judy—*

"Suppose I say yes?" she says, slowly. "What exactly is it you want me to do?"

CHAPTER 36

Another night of fitful sleep brings a familiar sense of foreboding.

What if Aisha goes straight to Judy, exposing my request, relaying my offhand comment about searching for enablers of porn? *God.* There could be cops on my doorstep before the sun is up.

What makes me think I can trust Aisha?

When I pull back the shutters, dull light trickles into the room.

At breakfast, Torvill and Tosca are deep in their food bowls. Torvill's tail is wagging energetically, like Andri sprinkled magic on his kibble this morning. It warms my heart to know the animals are happy in my house.

Andri beams at his pets, but his face darkens when I sit across from him with my banana and bowl of cornflakes.

"I'm investigating Judy," I say. "She's my last suspect. If the perpetrator is in the Computer Science Department, by process of elimination, she has to be the one."

"Maybe it's chase of wild goose. Let me be backup for safety." He puts his large hand on my skinny arm. "I know you brave but sometimes reckless. Please think of mother."

So now there are two people in the house telling me what to do.

On cue, Mom wanders into the kitchen in her robe, an ominous sign. She usually appears at breakfast immaculately dressed. "Why aren't you out walking with Mike?" she says pleasantly. "You love your walks."

Oh please, not this.

"Come sit, Mom." Gently, I lead her to a chair. "Would you like me to cut up some fruit for you?"

"Well, that would be lovely. What's the occasion? Is it my birthday?"

Her hair is mussed, framing her face with a bird's nest of feathery waves. Even in this state she's beautiful. It's futile to get a formal diagnosis of her cognitive impairment, because Mom is with me for the long haul, irrespective of labels.

Seeing her like this, however, completely lost, causes a knot of dread to tighten in my throat. Will I be able to take care of her?

Eventually I escape to my study to examine the contents of Nigel Welbourne's computer—the other one, his 'plaything,' the one he ostensibly didn't want me to see.

The flash drive opens a world of lights, image after image of combinations of color and sparkle. Did he program these amazing graphics? His algorithms are as good as the hype, his versatility impressive. His love for graphics shines through.

We're both solitary in our work.

In another time and place, it would have been fun to collaborate with him. Our programming sensibilities are different, and yet our interests meld well. We could write some stunning academic papers together.

His folder of video games contains, to my surprise, a huge number of games. He wasn't kidding when he said he played on his computer. He's a forty-five-year-old kid. What is it with guys and their video games? I've never been a video-game girl. The cartoon violence and misogyny in the online community is a total turn-off.

The first game in the folder has no title, just Video 1. The setting is a fantasy urban landscape, with signs and portents signaling buildings that can be entered. I create an avatar for myself, a warrior, and my character icon pops up on the screen with enough realism to raise a prickle on my neck. Suddenly, I'm intrigued, but when I try to find a button to start the game, there isn't one. Maybe the game is in development. Nigel is creating his own video game!

My phone vibrates with a text from Aisha: *It's done. Judy's hard drive.*

Within five minutes I'm on my way to Cornell. Andri is home with Mom and will keep an eye on her. She's still in a faraway universe, undisturbed by reality.

The flash drive is in the dead drop, under the bush, as arranged with Aisha. "There's a good place to leave it," I told her. "Far from Judy and computer science." Joe would have a fit if he knew, but who's going to tell him, and why should I care?

Next stop is Olin Library across campus. A light drizzle has come out of nowhere and the raindrops are cold on my skin. I turn my face to the sky and hope this little soaking isn't in vain.

Inside the dry warmth of the library, I slide into a computer carrel and glance around to see if anyone is interested in me. Yes, someone is. A young guy at a nearby table is gazing at me intently. If he's Judy's spy, he's not very subtle. Maybe he's just giving me the eye.

The library's electronic card catalogue has several entries for Judy Holsinger. The first hit is in *Scientific American*, an article she wrote when she was just sixteen, on computer guessing games for kids. She was a programming whiz kid, fast tracked to MIT, and hired by Cornell in 1998, during their affirmative action push. I'm particularly interested in the papers she wrote at this time. Who were her collaborators? Anyone I know?

But there were no collaborators. Just ground-breaking research. Mathematical analyses of algorithms. Spreadsheets and artificial intelligence. An outside-the-box algorithm to create decryption passwords. It's all there. She was an exceptional computer scientist. And yet the Judy of today is keeping track of salaries and supplies, doling out service assignments to department members, and dealing with hiring and firing renegades like me. Why?

How many years did it take her to become disillusioned? How many lesser lights—men in the department—were promoted ahead of her? At which stage did she accept the Faustian bargain to perform the shit work in the department in return for absolute power?

When did she decide to go to the dark side, making money in porn encryption? How did Mike get roped in?

It's time to study Judy's computer. The plain white envelope from Aisha contains a flash drive. Also a small piece of paper with a typed string of characters: Judy's password.

Every fiber of my brain says this is where Judy is keeping track of sales. How is she concealing the data? This is my area of expertise. If the information is here, I'll find it.

The personality that comes through is the velvet-gloved bitch I know so well. A scan of her messages, however, doesn't produce anything that says *Porno Queen*. There are no communications with members of the Computer Science Department. Nothing that mentions Mike. No mysterious, encrypted files.

Judy's bank account is hard to crack. There are, however, emails galore that suggest she's a concierge customer, which means huge deposits of cash. Not from her job as department chair, that's for sure.

There are multiple spreadsheets, with cryptic lists of dates, numbers, and large dollar amounts. No names. Does she contact her customers by phone? This could be it!

The data, however, are opaque. No identifying marks on the transactions. *It's not evidence. You can't prove a negative.*

With a jolt I realize my investigation is over. No exciting revelations. No smoking gun. Somewhere in there, just beyond my grasp, are interlocking pieces of a puzzle. Perhaps I'll copy the spreadsheets and hand them over to Joe. It's his problem now, not mine. I've gone as far as I can. It's time for me to figure out what's next in my life.

My phone lights up and buzzes on the desk. Detective Karla Mahoney.

Time to pack up my computer and head outside. It's a relief to leave the blowing heat of the library. That same young guy who was watching me earlier follows me out and parks himself against a tree, from which he can feast his eyes on me, his view unobstructed. There's a certain kind of nerdy guy that finds me irresistible. I smile and wave, but he shrinks into the shadows. I shrug it off. He's allowed to stand under a tree.

Don't be paranoid.

"Madeline?" Detective Karla Mahoney says in her low voice. "Is this a good time to come to your house?"

"Hi, Detective," I say. "What's up?"

"There's a development. We've found Mike's cell phone."

CHAPTER 37

The doorbell rings. Mom beats me to the door and says to Karla Mahoney, "Hello. Are you the dog groomer?"

"Mrs. Geiger, I'm Detective Mahoney—"

"Of course! I'm so sorry." Mom shakes her head. "I remember you now."

"Hi, Madeline." The detective steps inside, giving Mom's arm a squeeze. "Is there a private place to talk?"

"Don't leave the living room on my account," Mom says. "I'll join Andri in the garden. He's playing chump ball with the animals."

"Okay, you got me there, Mrs. Geiger. What's chump ball?"

"Andri our tenant throws a ball, the dog and cat go crazy and run around the yard, but no one fetches the ball. Then, when they come back to him, he throws another ball."

Mom is going off her rocker. She's having a *really* bad day today. She sees my face and says, "If you don't believe me, go outside and look at the backyard. It's littered with tennis balls."

Karla, in a forest-green pantsuit, moves briskly to her favorite armchair while I crash down nearby onto the couch and stretch my legs out. The detective is all business and takes a Ziploc bag containing Mike's phone from her pocket.

Unlike Mike, his phone has survived the fall, and looks like any other used iPhone. I recoil from it. It's a little snake, coiled in the baggie, waiting to strike with its fangs.

"Where did you find it?" *It doesn't matter.*

"In an area not too far from the parachutes. Our guys missed it the first time." Karla removes it from the bag and places it next to me on the couch.

"We can't get in," she says. "I recharged it and our tech guys worked on it for a few hours but were stymied."

"What about fingerprints? How do you know it wasn't in the wrong hands?"

"Madeline, please trust me to do my job. The only prints we found were Mike's. All I need now is access."

Her harsh tone riles me up, and a pulse starts beating in my neck.

"Detective Mahoney, how does this work? Did you get a subpoena to get into Mike's phone?"

Love notes, sexting, photos, my husband's secret life.

She pauses, then chooses her words carefully. "Yes, I have a warrant to examine all of Mike's personal effects. The problem is that Apple refuses to give police direct access to their devices."

"So you want me to break into Mike's phone."

"You've been incredibly helpful before. I was hoping you'd help me now. I would bet, honey, you want to see this case solved as much as I do."

"May I keep Mike's phone after you've examined it?"

"I'm sorry, Madeline—you know I can't do that. It's part of the evidence."

Panic rises inside me. Fear of what I'll find. "Can I look at it ahead of time, before you take it away."

"Madeline, please—" She puts a restraining hand on my arm. "I do need your help, and of course I won't snatch the phone away." Her hand with its cool grip stays firmly on my arm. Her voice is as smooth as syrup. "Why don't we sit here and examine it together?"

The phone has been handled a lot and is grubby in my hand. Can't postpone this any longer. *Suck it up, Madeline.*

There was a time I knew Mike's passcode, but he probably changed it. Sure enough, when I push the old buttons, the phone gives a little shudder and refuses to let me in. It'll have to be a hack.

It's now four o'clock, the light already slipping away outside. I press the Siri button and command the phone to set the alarm for 4:01 PM. Then I place it on the side table, sit back, and wait.

Detective Mahoney's eyebrows rise toward her hairline as she looks from me to the phone. "Madeline?"

"A trick I learned from a Cornell student," I say.

The shrill ring of the alarm jangles my nerves. It's the jarring personal ringtone Mike programmed on his phone, which used to wake us up every morning.

I let out an involuntary cry as I grab the phone and press several buttons simultaneously, bringing back all the pain of losing him, holding down those buttons for dear life. The noise stops and Mike's icons pop up on the screen and I'm in. We're in.

Karla Mahoney gawps at me.

"Thank you, Madeline," she says faintly.

But she gets right back to the task at hand. "Let's examine his most recent texts. Why don't you open his messages?"

The last exchange before he died was with Judy Holsinger.

Mike: *Hey juju, same time and place tonight?*

Judy: *Be careful, babe.*

"I think she was his mistress," I say, sadly. No sense in hiding it.

"Scroll through the texts." She squeezes my arm sympathetically, and sighs.

Screen after screen of texting with Judy. A shitload of texts.

> Mike: May come late, Judes. Stay hot and
> wet for me, OK?

I squeeze myself together and bear down, a voyeur, swiping through my dead husband's sordid affair. It makes me nauseous.

It's a humbling exercise to scroll through messages between Mike and his mistress. Where was I when he tapped them out? In the same room, gazing at him with adoration? It's really hard to put distance and perspective between my brain and my fingertips, and I struggle to hold the phone steady.

We come upon a pair of texts, written a week before Mike died.

Wordlessly, I hold the phone close to Karla's face and point. She adjusts her glasses.

> Mike: Hey Juju, about an hour to Ovid, OK?
>
> Judy: See you at noon. 🖤🖤🖤

She had the gall to send hearts to my husband. *How dare she?*

"Here's your evidence," I say roughly, thrusting the phone at her. "Judy killed Mike."

Karla frowns with momentary puzzlement, so I spell it out. "They were driving to the skydiving drop zone in Ovid. So she knew where to find his parachute."

Light bulbs go off in her eyes. "Ah. Well done."

A memory surfaces, and I say, "Judy used to skydive with her husband before their divorce. She knew enough to make those knots in the chute lines that killed Mike."

Pure hatred drives my hand over the screen, scrolling through all the texts. *Focus.* Pretend Karla Mahoney isn't sitting next to me, breathing down my T-shirt.

Torvill wanders into the room, surveys the possibilities, then drops down near the detective. "Hello, crazy dawg," she says, scratching his ears.

The floor creaks with the unmistakable sound of Andri hovering nearby.

On Mike's phone: Aisha, Judy, Dwayne, David, Nigel, all part of Mike's messaging system. Meeting after meeting. Phone calls to and from Nigel, to and from Dwayne and Judy. Did he discuss my work with all of them? Times and places. Lots of slots for Judy, opportunities to help herself to my husband. *Poor unsuspecting Maddie.* Did they discuss porn encryption, or was it all fucking, all the time?

I should ask her.

How in God's name did Judy rope him into the porn thing? *Would she tell me if I asked?*

Why did Judy kill him? *Ask her!*

Karla is in the dark about the pornography side of things, because it would complicate matters.

Judy killed Mike. That's all she needs to know.

I have to get to Judy before Karla does.

CHAPTER 38

When Karla leaves, it's early evening and pitch-black outside. I follow her out, breathing in a blast of ice.

"When will you contact...Judy?" My voice hisses with venom, just at the thought of that brazen slut who sexted with Mike. How dare she? *Snuff her out.*

In the flare of her Maglite, Karla gives me a side-eye. "I'm on top of it, Madeline, I'll speak with her sooner rather than later." Then she softens a bit and says, "Hang in there—I'll keep you updated."

She won't visit Judy before tomorrow morning—Saturday—which means I must get to her tonight. *How?*

Back on my porch, a twig snaps nearby, which sends a flicker up the back of my neck, a feeling of being watched. But when I creep around the house, there isn't a human soul around, just woodland animals disturbing the bushes. I shiver and move back inside to the warmth and aroma of dinner.

My mother's cooking seems unaffected by her dementia, and my stomach rumbles for the beef stew bubbling in the pot. Torvill is panting and begging at the stove, and Mom says, "Down, Torvill! When we have dinner, I'll add some to your bowl." He droops his tail and bats his head against her leg but seems to accept the verdict.

Andri is in his apartment, working at his desk. When he sees me, he swings around and says, "Tough day, Medeleen?" Is my face really that transparent?

"I have to go see that woman—*Judy*—tonight, and don't know how to get to her."

"What is goal?"

Uninvited, I sink down on his couch. "I hate her. She had an affair with Mike. She killed him—"

"So what is plan? To take gun and shoot her? Here." He pulls open a drawer, grabs the gun, and drops it on the desk.

I stare at both Andri and his gun. This is not helpful.

He gets up, moves to sit next to me, and puts his hand on my shoulder. "I also had marriage pain, Medeleen, with unfaithful wife, but is not good to be obsessing. Affair is past tense."

His arm is solidly comforting. "I need to confront her face-to-face—about Mike, and his death, and the pornography, and how she got him into it, but I'm out of ideas. I can't just break into her house."

"So you thinking Judy and Mike porno partners?" His demeanor is suddenly serious and thoughtful.

But I'm impatient. "Tell me how to get to her."

He sighs. "In old cop days, sometimes talking was what got into house. No burglar keys. No glass breaking and snooping in dark. Just one big acting job for convincing criminal to opening door. Call Judy on phone and make excuse for seeing her. Not hard, Medeleen, just use brain." He taps his head.

God, he's telling me to talk my way into her house. My worst nightmare. What if she says *No, I have nothing to say to you?*

But of course he's right. I must call that bitch and convince her to see me tonight. Anxiety rises in my ribcage, a rush of heart pounding like I've had too much coffee.

Hard as I try to tamp down this reaction—a lifelong thing—the caffeinated feeling stays with me during dinner, my swallowing too slow, the food lingering in my gullet, above my heart.

"What's wrong, Madsy?" Mom says. "Why aren't you eating? Too much salt?"

"Stew is from heaven, Jenet," Andri says. "Medeleen must go out soon and brain is full."

"It has to be tonight. It's urgent." I want Judy to deny it to my face. Her affair with Mike. Her illegal pornography. *Her awfulness.*

"I won't ask if it's dangerous," Mom says. "I already know…" Her face is sad and resigned.

Andri gets up to help himself to seconds, and on the way, he stops to hug my mother. "Jenet, tonight we watch *The Bridge.* Nice juicy murder mystery in Sweden and Denmark."

In my bedroom, I shut the door. *Do this.* My phone has four bars. Nothing to stop me from calling but the throbbing in my head.

There are seven rings. Please send it to voicemail. Let me off the hook.

"Judy Holsinger," she says, the voice I know and detest.

"I read your paper on alternating decryption strings—from 1980—it's brilliant—" It comes out as a super blurt in a rush of too much adrenaline.

"Who is this? Madeline?" I'm not one of her contacts.

"Yes—I couldn't find the follow-up paper—your idea—"

Gibbering like an incoherent idiot. *Slow down! Collect your thoughts and modulate your voice. Say hi to the witch who stole Mike. Worm your way in.* It's not Mike's voice in my head. It's my own. Once and for all, I *will* get this untrammeled blurting under control.

"Hi, Judy?—I'm sorry—I've had time to think about things—how I left Cornell on a bad note—can I come and see you? Now?" I cross my fingers and bite my tongue. The sweet, conciliatory voice belongs to a stranger.

"What's wrong, Madeline?" she says, cutting through my blathering.

"I'd like to speak to you in person." My grip on the phone tightens, like if I let up for a minute, the call will drop.

I expect her to hang up or say goodbye; but instead, she says, "Why don't you make an appointment with Aisha for next week? My calendar is fairly clear." She sounds completely reasonable—agreeing to see me again.

"It has to be now." My voice is low and urgent. "I have new information about the computers—Mike—everything that happened." I whisper, *Please...*

A long silence ensues, and I picture her face, that look of steel, the calculating tilt of her head, trying to guess what this pesky caller wants, weighing what's in it for her...

"Come around to the back door and ring the doorbell," she says. "I'll expect you in the next hour." *Yes!*

It's a victory. I half-run through the house on my rejiggered leg, my ribs whole again, my body powered by relief, and throw my arms around my mother. I kiss her head and breathe in her hair. "Stay strong. I'll be back soon."

"Be careful, my Madsy, I'm going to need you." Mom is transferring power to me, and it wrenches my heart.

"Don't worry, Mom, I'll be fine."

Andri beams at me. "You found key to door."

"You're a genius," I say.

This is the snapshot of them that will always stay with me. Mom, somewhat addled but smiling. Andri, with a grin as broad as he is, his arm encircling her waist. And his animals going bonkers, running in happy circles around them.

A small light outside marks Judy's house; the rest is blackness. No cheerful little amber lantern above the front door saying *Welcome.* The bushes are probably crawling with hidden cameras, uploading images of me and my car straight to the cloud, following my progress to the back door, with special filters that allow night vision. I'm a pale green alien stumbling on dark terrain toward civilization.

My suspicions about surveillance are confirmed as soon as Judy opens the door to me, even before I've pressed the doorbell. *She's hypervigilant because she's in a dangerous business.*

"Sorry to bring you through the back," she says pleasantly, "but this is an easier entrance." *Yeah, and I'm from Jupiter.*

There's a fragrance of eau de cologne, as I follow her through a kitchen in which copper pots and pans glint from a wooden beam. An enormous stove with six burners sits like a squat monster in the corner.

In the living room, music is playing: Schubert's "Death and the Maiden," with its intense, dark phrasing. Odd pieces of functional furniture dot the room, creating an unwelcoming space with no harmony, as if the furnishings were an afterthought.

Despite the rugs thrown about on the wood floors, it's cold in this room.

"Would you like something to drink?" Judy says pleasantly. "Water, wine, cocoa? I even have apple cider from the orchard."

"Apple cider would be great, thank you."

When she disappears into the kitchen, I survey the walls, which are mostly bare, except for one wall that draws me close.

A naked little boy, a snowy white prince with wheat-gold hair, stretches out on a chair and has the sweet spot on Judy's wall. The photographer is Robert Mapplethorpe, who set off thunderstorms with his art. A tiny girl runs away from the camera, her body luminous. Sally Mann's children are here too, in all their innocence. Another girl is seated in a position that reveals her underwear: *Thérèse Dreaming* by Balthus. Print after print, a gallery to inspire prurient thoughts in pedophiles and makers of illegal pornography.

The photos are beautiful. Some might say *damning.*

Judy follows my gaze as she hands me a tall glass of cider, and says, "This collection was one of the sticking points in my divorce. I chose these photos—limited editions, they weren't widely available—and he wanted them."

"But you won in the end." I grasp the icy glass, shivering.

"I would have given up this house to keep them," she says bitterly, crossing her legs under her on the couch. "As it is, they cost me a lot."

That probably explains the furnishings. He got it all. *She needs the money.*

With her comfortable-looking sweatpants and face without makeup, Judy looks like a humanoid in the barely lit room, a computer-generated version of Judy.

I sit across from her in an uncomfortable, hard leather chair. "So you're into young children."

She stares at me, surprised. "Please don't tell me you're one of those philistines who thinks these works of great art are obscene."

"No. I think child pornography is obscene." *Ugh. I sound like a jerk.*

Her reaction is one of outrage. "What's your problem, Madeline? Why are you here?" Her imperious job voice, like she's still my boss. I crumble in front of that voice, my throat constricts. With Judy, I've never been able to establish my identity as anything other than a subordinate, the same shy neophyte I was in my earliest days at Cornell. I place my drink on a small side table, and then don't know where to put my hands.

Thoughts spin in my head, then tumble out. "You must call off George, your attack dog. Tell him to stop snooping around my house. I'll tell you for free everything that you're paying him to find out."

I wait for her to protest or accuse me of being insane. Instead, she leans toward me with menace in her narrowed eyes.

"George is my protection," she says, "against people like you."

I absorb the blow as the room vibrates with the discordant passion of the strings.

Eventually, I find my voice. "So you admit it? You've been spying on me."

She untucks her legs and sits forward, hands on knees. "George keeps me up to date on all the threats against me. You probably have no idea what it's like for a woman in a position of power, who receives constant threats from physically large but mentally small men." Her eyes are fixed on me. "You, Madeline, are one of the more interesting threats I'm dealing with."

Is this really how it ends? In this room? "So you *are* the Cornell link—"

The expression on her face is pure malice. "Your clueless brain probably has no idea why I let you into my house tonight. Did you really think I'm so gullible I'd be swayed by some contrived flattery of obscure work I did more than twenty years ago?"

"How did you persuade Mike to go along with your illegal software scheme?" This is the crux of it: their collaboration.

She stares at me intently, possibly trying to fathom my motives.

Nor does she immediately deny it. She's doing that Judy thing, absorbing the facts at hand and trying to divine the subtext. Her head is inclined, her brow furrowed, the dusky bare walls in the room leaning in toward her.

"Be careful, Madeline," she says softly, her voice sinister. "These accusations could get you in real trouble."

"So you're denying it?"

"I don't need to justify anything I do to you."

"And I suppose you didn't have an affair with Mike." This bursts from my mouth because it's right under my skin and I'm desperate to pierce her armor of control and superiority.

She has the grace, finally, to lower her eyes. When she looks up, she says, "I loved Mike. He was wonderful. You didn't appreciate what you had."

How dare she? Her self-satisfied complacency pries open the vise on my vocal cords. "Don't call that love! It was an affair! You were *fucking* my husband."

"Be an adult, Madeline," she says contemptuously.

"If you loved him so much, why did you kill him?" My voice is ice and fire. I'm so angry with her that my body can't control my fury. It spews out of me, water springing from my eyes, muscles pulling me out of my chair, propelling me toward the couch, grasping to wipe out that self-satisfied smugness. She recoils in horror as I slap her face with all my strength, spoiling for a fight, wanting to tear her eyes out, yank her hair, pay her back for ruining my life and taking my beautiful husband from me.

But something of civilization holds me back—my mother's sad eyes?—and I turn abruptly, gasping for breath, not allowing tears, not breaking down, just silent and seething in my accusations, while she absorbs the shocks. Some cider has splashed onto her pants leg.

"Of course I didn't kill him," she says softly. "I loved him."

Her fake declarations of love for my husband enrage me further, releasing the pent-up thoughts in my brain, causing the words to spill out on top of each other.

I turn to face her again. "You drove to Ovid with Mike, the skydiving drop zone, where he showed you his parachute. Did you go back to sabotage it? Was he threatening to end the porn thing you had going?"

She finally looks startled, like I've broken through the veneer of calm that makes her so formidable. "What are you talking about? I never drove to Ovid with Mike."

She doesn't know the cops found Mike's phone! She thinks it's her word against mine.

She also doesn't know my phone is recording everything.

She's frowning, but her expression softens. "Mike was a lovely man. He's the last person I'd kill."

I'm ready to go back and claw her face, when something in me realizes I believe her—maybe she *did* love him. At his funeral, she seemed broken up and red eyed. I'd assumed it was a big act, but now I'm not so sure.

It takes me a long minute to absorb the implications.

A sharp wind outside shakes the panes and whistles
faintly through the window. The house is like a refrigerator,
but at this fraught moment, the cold sharpens my mind.

I've been operating under the wrong hypothesis.

Those knots in the parachute were meant for me.

CHAPTER 39

She tried to murder me.

The realization pins me to my chair.

"Mike and I used…each other's parachutes." My voice is strained. "Randomly. We were the same size."

Her face, like a mask, gives nothing away, her expression as blank and empty as the walls and as cold as the rhythm thrumming from the stereo speakers. Despite the modern touches, this house is old like mine, with frigid air squeezing through the cracks. We're in some kind of clichéd stalemate—the injured wife facing the unrepentant mistress.

She's looking at me, too, her face impassive. "He was ending it," she says. "Our relationship."

"Your relationship—?" I say stupidly, goosebumps rising.

"He was going back to you." She says it quietly, eyes flickering with anger, and for a fleeting moment, she looks her age.

Mike offering me the skydive as a new start.

"So you tried to sabotage my parachute, the one Mike ended up using." She doesn't acknowledge it—or deny it—but her motive shines clearly in my mind, and that piece of the puzzle drops into its slot. The murder had nothing to do with pornography and everything to do with lust for my husband. Unless, of course, Mike threatened to drop out of their business partnership too.

In either case, she must have been mad with grief when she realized she had killed him. The daily sight of me getting stronger must have driven her out of her mind. No wonder she was so hateful toward me—I was living proof of her incompetence.

"I too have a theory," she says, watching me. "*You* murdered Mike. No one had greater access or control of the parachutes—"

"How dare you—" The accusation is so brazen I can barely find words to respond. "Why? Why would I kill him?"

She shrugs, her eyes never leaving mine. "You were jealous of him—his success, his good looks, his elevated position in the department—all things you didn't have. And the supreme reason—he was cheating on you."

Her accusation is a ploy to throw me off balance. Somehow, understanding that gives me strength. "What about the illegal pornography? And how did you blackmail Mike to go along with it?"

"Aisha warned me you may ask about that. It's time to set you straight about a few things."

Aisha?

Her legs come out from under her, and she assumes her straight-backed Judy posture, the kind she had when she fired me. Formal. Threatening.

"Number one, do you really believe that Aisha, who has been with me for thirteen years, would go behind my back and download my personal laptop?"

She's spitting out the words, an ugly twist to her mouth. "Are you really so inept, you thought Aisha would put her job on the line for you?"

My body starts to tingle, a strange neuropathy in my hands and feet. Not for a moment did my brilliant brain imagine that Aisha would betray me. In the Collegetown restaurant she was so sympathetic, so open to helping me.

Does Aisha know about the pornography?

"If Aisha told you, how come I got to see your computer?" My voice sounds like it's traveling through molasses.

"I wanted to find out what you were up to. And here we are."

"So you deleted the pornography. That's why I couldn't find it." I push myself up off my chair. "It's time for me to leave."

"Oh, don't go yet," she says. "I'm not done."

"You can't prevent me from leaving." Though how I'll actually drive is another story. The walls are closing in, and I grasp the arms of the chair to stay upright. Vertigo, my chair spinning on its axis. I sink down again, my head between my knees.

Judy's voice floats toward me. "Would you like some water?"

"No, I'm fine." I don't feel fine. Has she drugged me? The cider had a strong flavor, sure to disguise any additives. And I've quaffed down a full glass. My head weighs a thousand tons.

"We're problem solvers, we computer scientists." Her voice comes from far away. "So I set myself the interesting task of breaking the Madeline code."

It takes a Herculean effort to lift my head, which seems unstable on my neck. This strange weakness has attacked me more than once since the accident. Judy's face is serene, showing no ill effects from the drink. *I should have taken the one made for her.*

She says, "For several years you were the meek little wife, and then, after Mike dies—"

"After you kill him."

"After his death, you're in my face, demanding an office, threatening to sue Cornell, giving a talk using Mike's encryption work—"

"What did you put in my drink?" Finally, I'm able to meet her eyes.

"Some hard apple cider, that's all," she says calmly. "It does have a buzz, doesn't it?"

It's like she's dropped Benadryl into my cider. How will I get out of here? I've shown my hand and am at her mercy.

She's unconcerned about me, warming up to her litany. "Suddenly you've become super visible, showing up at meetings, spying on the CS Department, breaking into our offices, downloading computers, committing God-knows-what cybercrimes, maybe installing spyware on our computers—"

"No...no spyware, no viruses, no installations—" My tongue has fur on it. I straighten my neck. "No cybercrimes—"

"Invading people's privacy is a crime. Helping yourself to our personal info—passwords, emails, computer algorithms, private documents—all of that is a crime."

"You had me followed by your goon."

"I wanted to find out who you were passing information to. That required surveillance, yes."

"So you hired a two-bit criminal who doubled as a Peeping Tom at night."

"George has worked for me before—my divorce, for example. He may be rough around the edges, but he always gives me valuable information. Like the foreign national—Ukrainian—who moved into your house, just before you started your surreptitious spying activities."

It takes more than a few seconds to figure out who she's talking about. Andri! She makes him sound like an international gangster.

Through the fog, it's a struggle to come to physical and mental equilibrium so my brain can absorb the threat I presented to Judy. No one has ever noticed me, let alone been threatened by me. I've never been assertive enough to be on anyone's radar. This alternative narrative of me is fascinating, an alter ego, the kind of weighty persona I now crave. Except I'm trapped in one of her living room chairs.

She continues. "Things escalate when the foreigner attacks George, and the two of you torture him and keep him locked in a filthy basement."

She pauses a moment to inspect me. "Does this ring a bell, Madeline? Am I describing it accurately?" Her voice is chilling.

My head is aching. "You left out the part where George watched my mother undress for bed. That's why my tenant captured him."

"Your tenant is a thug," she says. "Be assured George is now monitoring him too."

Andri, who is with my mother on the couch, the animals spread around them.

Are they safe?

"Do you know that this so-called nice man was on the run from his country, for government interference? That he got involved in trafficking children?"

"He was a detective—"

"Are you aware he stole millions from the trafficking ring? That he left behind a wife?"

"She left him!"

"That's a detail," she says, drily.

She's agreed to see me tonight to get me out of the way. George is in my house.

"I need to leave." But my head continues to spin.

She rises from the couch and moves toward me so slowly it would be funny if it weren't so sinister. "Let me help you lie down, Madeline, to shake off the effects of the cider. I should have warned you it was potent."

As my body slides off the chair, she moves in close, easing me down flat on one of the rugs. There's a fragrance of rose water and sweat.

"I must call my mother," I say. "Mom hasn't been well—"

"Oh, sure, go ahead." Languidly, she moves back to her perch on the couch, watching me.

Rolling onto my elbows, I pull out my phone, hit Favorites, and dial Mom. My first use of Joe's escape hatch. *Please God, let him pick up.*

A deep voice says, "Hi, Madeline, where are you?"

"Remember, I told you? I'm in Cayuga Heights. I'll be home soon. Love you."

"Love you, too." The voice is soft, as the phone clicks off.

I shut my eyes. "My mom has dementia."

"Sorry to hear it," Judy says, in a flat voice. She pauses for a couple of seconds. "You're so naïve that I wonder if you have any idea about the man you've been reporting to."

"What are you talking about?"

"You know quite well—the man you met at Treman Park? The assignations behind your house? Meetings at Cornell?"

She's been keeping tabs on Joe.

"Aisha told me you imagined yourself an informant for the FBI—some story—but it seemed clear this was your "handler," the person directing you to break into all our computers."

Maintaining my dignity is a challenge. Sensing a flush of alarm on my cheeks, I lie still with my mouth shut.

She sits on a foot stool and peers down at me. "Do you think you're the only one who can hack databases? And facial recognition software? I wrote the book on facial recognition. It took me exactly two minutes to track down this man you've been working for."

She's still an expert programmer.

It clicks into place. She hasn't quit competing with academic men—she's taken her skills to a different arena. The admin stuff at Cornell is just a cover. She's the one doing encryption/decryption coding for illegal porn sites, and she somehow roped Mike into her racket. Had he decided to quit?

How long will it take for Joe to get here? Is this how my quest ends—being saved by a man?

"How did he get you on board?" Judy says. "This handler of yours."

Silence is the name of the game. I'm not about to betray Joe to Judy.

"That photo George took was very helpful," Judy says, "the one at Treman."

Where is Joe?

She stands, and with lithe grace moves to a small desk, from which she extracts some papers. "Take a look at these." She drops the loose pages onto my upper body, a smirk on her face.

I shrink back from the papers, which will surely hurt me. Nevertheless, with some effort, I pull myself into a sitting position, leaning against the chair.

"Go ahead," she says softly. "Take a look."

Clasping my knees together and hugging my arms, I lower my eyes to the first page. A newspaper article, xeroxed, with a photo of Joe—a younger version of Joe—his arm around a dark-haired woman with anguish on her face. Words and phrases flash before my eyes—dead child...body found...tip line...boy recognized in porn movie...encryption hinders cops...no arrests.

"This man is from Ohio," Judy says. "Did you know that?" Her voice is muted in the background of my thoughts. "He obviously got to you under false pretenses, as did your foreign tenant. And somehow these men are using you to infiltrate the Computer Science Department at Cornell."

The music has stopped, and the wind is gusting outside, causing a creaking and scratching above us, as if the tall trees are bending their branches and scraping the roof.

I've lost track of the time.

A beep on Judy's phone causes her to grab it and jump up from her stool. "What the—?" *Can Judy see Joe outside?*

The idea of Joe at Judy's mercy sends me into a sweat. Up until now, I've been the center of my own drama, giving no thought to Joe and the danger he may face. A sudden noise startles me, a distant crash and tinkle of shattering glass, like a broken tree branch smashed into the house.

Judy's hands fly to her neck. She hurries from the room with a quick glance back at me. "Wait here."

A rush of adrenaline lets me drag myself up onto two legs. Steadying myself against the wall, I somehow make it to the closet in the foyer and clutch at my coat. The hanger clatters to the floor and I stumble against the door as it opens, letting in an icy blast, and pitching me forward against Joe, who catches me as I go down.

"Let's get outta here," he says. "Run now, talk later."

CHAPTER 40

Under cover of darkness in the garden, he half-carries me to my car. Even in my dazed state, I'm scared someone will intercept us.

"How did you get here?" He never seems to drive, always showing up in places, leaning against trees in the forest, like a woodland troll.

He pulls open the passenger door and sets me down gently. "Okay, let's go!"

There's no sign of lurking danger, and the car hums to life. Buckling myself in, I lean my head back and shut my eyes. The world is going haywire.

He presses down on the gas and revs off the scale as the car roars down the winding Cayuga Heights Road. "Slow down, they trap in this village," I say, alarmed. "The cops sit in the bushes with the deer and jump out when you approach." No chuckle from him. He's as tense as a tripwire.

Within five minutes, he makes a screeching turn onto the Cornell campus, which adjoins Cayuga Heights. There's a dark, deserted parking lot behind one of the physics buildings, where he pulls in and cuts the engine.

"Whoa!" We bump to a stop.

"What happened tonight?" he says. "Are you okay?" He's all hyped up.

"She spiked my drink. That's why I called you to come get me. Thank God you did. She was about to roll me up in the rug and throw me into the lake."

Still no smile from him. "Did you nail her down? Is she the one?"

"*Hello*, Joe. Can I have a minute to breathe?"

He shifts closer to me and takes my hand. Unexpectedly, he raises it to his cheek, and the feel of his skin is surprisingly soft. "Tell me." In the close confines of the Subaru, the smell of his sweat is faint and alive.

"She's the one," I say.

We sit without speaking while he absorbs this. There's a vibration of the car in the wind and the throb of a nearby generator.

"Judy had an affair with Mike," I say, "and roped him into the online pornography business. When he threatened to end their relationship, she murdered him—probably trying to kill me."

"Wow. What evidence of the porn thing do you have? And why Judy?"

"Well, for starters, she has a perfect base of operations at Cornell, with data on everyone and access to any type of computer. She has file after file of spreadsheets and transactions, with unique passwords for each entry. She's a master administrator. She has a wall covered with children in suggestive poses. For sure, she's capable of murder. She's also an outstanding hacker. She identified you and my tenant from photos, and then broke into some obscure databases, which means she has the programming chops to create encryption-decryption code. Unfortunately, she was warned by Aisha I'd be examining her computer, which gave her time to wipe away any smoking gun."

"This is a weak case," Joe says.

"I'm not done." I lean toward him. "She has a mansion in Cayuga Heights, on half an acre of wooded property, some of the most expensive real estate in Ithaca. The taxes alone are enormous. She has a full-time housekeeper and gardener. She gets nothing from her ex-husband. Where's the money coming from?"

Joe is still not satisfied. His skepticism's so tangible I can reach out and feel it.

"There's something else." I place my palm on his forehead, which is dry and cool. "Stop frowning and listen."

He takes my hand, holds it to his mouth, and kisses my palm. "Tell me." *God.*

"That lowlife George I told you about, the guy following us at Treman? He's Judy's thug. She hired him for 'protection,' but she had him keep tabs on me twenty-four seven. She wanted to find out what I knew and who I was contacting. No one pays for that kind of surveillance unless you have serious business to protect."

He nods slowly, weighing the accumulation of evidence. Eventually, he says, "You've done a great job, Madeline. This is impressive." He squeezes my hand. It's like a punctuation mark—I'm done. How he uses the information is his business, not mine.

"Are you going to move back to Ohio?" I don't want him to go.

Scared to hear the answer, already missing him.

My fingertips touch his cheek. "Joe, I know the story about your son. I'm so sorry. Can you tell me how I became involved?"

He rolls down the window, letting in a rush of freezing air and blowing leaves. We sit like that, shivering for so long that I reckon he doesn't want to talk about it.

Eventually he closes the window and turns up the heating fan in the car. "I caused my son's death," he says. "I've been doing penance ever since."

"No, don't say that." I take his hand. Both of us are sitting without gloves, and touching him is like joining two icicles that stick together and melt in the heat.

He's facing me, his eyes glistening. "I was a full-time cop, an absentee father, and my twelve-year-old kid got involved online with a chat room of predators."

How does one respond to something like that?

"Where was his mother?" I say.

The air in the car is oppressive. The rattling hum of the heating fan.

Joe says, "Neither my wife nor I were home the night our boy went out to meet someone. We never saw him again."

"God, that's awful. Did they ever find your son's murderer?" I whisper. It's an indelicate question. The last thing I want is to hurt Joe—I want to hug him and be kind; I want to take him home with me and undress him and put him in my bed; but I also want to find out what led him to me from Ohio.

"No arrests were made," he says.

"What did you do?"

When he doesn't reply, I assume it's too painful. Then I surprise myself with a sudden insight. *His marriage didn't survive.*

"Your wife left you, didn't she?"

He sighs, one long shuddering exhalation. "You could say that. She killed herself." His voice cracks.

I squeeze his hand again, because I'm helpless in the face of such awful loss. But my brain forges ahead. *Joe has involved me in his tragedy.*

He turns to me and says bitterly, "My wife left me money, so I quit my job to go after the enablers who keep encryption up to date for porn makers. Without that software, the cops could easily shut down illegal pornography."

"What do you do when you find the enablers?"

"I neutralize them," Joe says, so matter-of-factly that prickles rise under my skin. "You kill them?"

Did he murder Mike? It's unbearable to look at him. I hold my breath.

But he says, "No, ma'am, I don't kill them. I threaten them with loss of their reputations. Many of them are so-called respectable people, but in reality they're just scumbags."

He's trembling, tapping the steering wheel.

Judy's a malevolent, evil bitch. I hope he makes her pay.

"Tell me how I came into this story."

"The only thing you need to know, Madeline, is I think you're amazing." He puts his hand over his heart. "I mean it. You and your funky gadgets, your zapper bracelet, your sardine key, your Ring cameras, your bravery—"

"Stop! You're a bullshit artist."

"And you're so beautiful."

He clicks off his seatbelt and leans across, puts his arm around my neck, and draws me toward him. When he kisses my mouth, I melt into the taste and smell of him and bury my hands in his windblown hair. I'm impossibly drawn to him, with his aura of tragedy and mystery. He's revived my interest in life, and I put all that into kissing him back.

He pulls away. "I'm damaged goods, Mads."

"How did you find me?" My voice comes out breathless, like I've emerged from a dive in deep water.

He straightens himself and goes back to his side.

"My colleague in the FBI said there had been juvenile porn activity near Ithaca, but they couldn't pinpoint it. He reckoned that the source was Cornell University, the Computer Science Department—"

"Why contact me? I was a minor player in that department, barely visible—"

"Mike called the police regarding his suspicions, but died before sharing them."

"So Mike spoke to you?—"

"Not to me personally. I read about your accident in a newspaper—you know it made national news—the death of your husband, a brilliant computer scientist at Cornell, and the terrible injuries of his widow, also a computer scientist in the department."

The physical pain in my ribs flares up again. "You lied to me."

"I needed to find out, Madeline, if Mike shared his suspicions with you. Then I got the idea to enlist you—your computer skills—to investigate the department."

"Why couldn't you just tell me the truth? You know—*ask* me to do it."

"Because you'd have refused. Using an FBI badge seemed a more convincing way to get your attention."

"Wait—your FBI badge was fake?" I hug myself and lean away from him. "What does an FBI badge sell for these days?"

He lowers his head. "I'm sorry."

What kind of spy can't figure out that her handler is a scam artist? *A really stupid one.*

"So the spy stuff was bogus?"

"I figured you'd be attracted to the excitement of a spying scenario—the dead drop, late-night meetings, burner phone, all the trappings, living on the edge."

How well he played me. He must have been a great cop.

"And Mike being your informant was pure fiction?" The answer is already clear.

He slumps. "Not completely. He *did* have information. But I admit I used that line to try and persuade you."

"What about all that bullshit with Mike's phone, and his burner—"

"I wanted it all to seem more authentic to you." He puts his hand on my arm. "Mads, now that I know you, I'm not proud of myself—the way I deceived you."

I shake him off, focusing on the whole picture. His deception is becoming uglier every second. "So the story that Mike contacted you personally the week before he died was also a fabrication."

"I'm so sorry, Madeline. At the time, I thought it would be another incentive for you, if you thought you were also searching for Mike's killer."

I shrink from him. "That's so Godawful cynical and cruel. Approaching me on the day of my husband's cremation. Did you give one thought to my feelings? That you'd be inflicting more pain on me?"

"I shouldn't have done it, Mads. I've become obsessed with finding these criminals. It clouded my judgment."

Grief and sadness, always under my skin, rise to the surface again.

What am I doing with this man?

"Take me home, Joe," I say.

During the long drive to my house, I unspool the movie of Joe Shelmann backwards, to that first day of "Pardon me ma'am" and "If you please" and how he looked at me at the funeral. His craggy face, handsome if you squinted right, sexy with the dark glasses, but cold and remote in the shadows of night.

The craziness and romance of the spy paraphernalia, how he assessed me and sucked me into his shadowy obsession. His disarming drawl and faint praise. His so-called admiration.

A sideways glance at his profile tells me nothing, though his hands are gripping the wheel and his back is not relaxed against the seat. Somehow, this interlude with him tonight has cleared my head. And yet...*I'll miss the bastard.*

About a mile from the house my phone pierces the silence in the car and I grab it. *Mom!*

The only time my mother calls me this late is when there's a problem. I force down the panic and say, "Hey, Mom, what's up?"

"Come home, Maddie...No, God..." Torvill in the background, barking his lungs out.

"Mom! Sit down and tell me what's happening. I'll be home in one minute." I turn to Joe. "Speed up—" He asks no questions and steps down so hard we're almost in takeoff.

But the call has been dropped or abandoned.

"My mom's in trouble." I jab at the button to call her back, but she doesn't pick up. Nothing. Voicemail. *Christ!*

We almost miss the driveway, because the light at the entrance, always a beacon in the dark, is out. Joe banks sharp left and—too late—I recognize the crunch of glass under the tires. Our beautiful crystal orb, that Mike and I lovingly installed many years ago, has been smashed off its post.

"There's an intruder," I say. "The garage door will alert them, but I have to go in."

"I'll come in with you," Joe says. "Be careful, Mads."

When he parks, I cringe for a moment in the darkness, reluctant to leave the safe cocoon of the car. We emerge to the sound of Torvill's hysterical barking and my mother screaming. I rush in through the mudroom door—grabbing the fire extinguisher—through the living room, and into the kitchen, where the noise is coming from.

My brain refuses to process the image in front of me. It can't be happening. Andri is lying flat on his back on the floor, his eyes glazed, blood pooling around his neck. Torvill is nudging Andri's head with his snout. Tosca is batting his face and mewling like a baby. The acrid smell of gunsmoke fills the kitchen.

And my mother, screaming and screaming, is pointing a gun at Andri's chest.

CHAPTER 41

I rush toward Mom, and Joe says, "Wait!"

Something in his voice makes me freeze. He approaches my mother cautiously, gently putting his arm around her and lowering the arm pointing the gun. "The danger is over, Ms. Geiger. May I take the gun?"

A paper towel and Ziploc bag have materialized in his hands, and after a minute he is kneeling next to Andri with a finger on the blood-free side of his neck. Torvill growls and barks at him, a sad, soft sound.

"I'm so sorry," Joe says to me and Mom. "I'll call 911." He has morphed into a real cop, taking photos of the scene on his phone, crouching, avoiding the blood, and luring the animals away from the body. It's as if I'm seeing Joe for the first time, a more authentic version.

Andri gone! It's a crushing weight in my chest, the air too thin to breathe. I can't bring myself to look at him again. What did he do to provoke Mom to shoot him? She loved him.

I lead my sobbing, heartbroken mother into the living room and dial Karla's number, the private one she gave me to call in an emergency. *Drop everything and speed to Brooktondale*, I want to tell her, because it's an unbearable thought to have some random law enforcement officer interrogate

Mom, who is rocking back and forth on the couch, keening, her eyes shut and tears on her cheeks.

"Detective Mahoney, there's been a terrible accident—shooting—a body in my kitchen—my tenant, you've met him—he's been killed—"

"Are you in danger, Madeline?" she says, firmly and quietly.

"I don't think so." My voice is weak. "There's a cop in my house—a friend—an ex-cop—"

"May I speak to him?"

"Yes—wait, no. We have the body and the gun and the shooter. But we don't know what happened. Please come *now.*" My heart is hammering and I'm barely coherent. The reality is settling in. *Mom shot our beloved Andri, and he's dead.*

I can't explain death to Torvill, who's trying to nudge Andri awake. Tosca has disappeared. I send Joe to search for her and hear him calling her name, but he comes back shaking his head.

My mother won't tell me what happened. "Is Andri dead?" she asks, over and over again.

The Ring video feed, for the time I was away, shows the hulking figure of George Snyder outside the house. His image is replaced by nothingness, and I interpolate the information to mean he invaded our home. It must have been some kind of surprise attack on Andri, who was nimble and strong enough to throw George in the air with his pinkie.

Our big man about the house. *Nevermore...*

Karla will need to know everything so she understands the danger we're in.

In record time, a blaring siren announces her arrival. My call must have pulled her from her bed, because she blows through the door in a fleece tracksuit and sneakers, with her hair unbound, flowing wild and free, humanizing her in a way. A pang of gratitude, almost love, surges through me. She didn't have to come.

Wordlessly, I hug her, resting my face on her fleecy shoulder, while Joe hovers nearby.

"Joe is a friend of mine," I say. Deferentially, he hands her the bag with the gun.

"I'll text you the photos I took of the crime scene," he says, already swiping on his phone. *Really?* Is he trying to incriminate Mom? My heart hardens.

Karla has activated a homicide team, and before long, strange men are bringing icy blasts into the house.

A burly officer emerges from the kitchen carrying Torvill, who is barking plaintively and whose limbs and paws hang listlessly. He seems to have shrunk in size, a piece of him shriveled up and still in the kitchen with Andri.

"Who's in charge of the dog, ma'am?" he says. "Are you the next of kin?"

I hold out my arms. "Yes." But Torvill doesn't want me. He barks until I let him down, and hurries back to the kitchen, leaving bloody paw prints on the carpet.

Joe stands, saying, "I'll take him for a walk." *Good idea.*

"I'll need a statement from you, sir," the officer says.

Karla has her arm around my mother. "Hello, Janet. Do you remember me? Detective Mahoney from the State Police."

"Yes," Mom says, dabbing at her eyes with a tissue. "Karla."

"Can you tell me what happened here tonight?"

"There was a home invasion," I say, before Mom can reply. "I can identify—"

"Please, Madeline," Karla says sharply. "I'd like to hear it from your mother."

"We heard...a noise...in the kitchen," Mom says, "and Andri" —her voice catches— "Andri...went to investigate. He yelled—it was terrible—" and she breaks down crying again.

"What did you do?" Karla says, cool and sympathetic at the same time.

Mom turns to me, weeping as she speaks. "It was George, Madsy, and he had a knife, and he was stabbing Andri, and Andri fell against the counter and there was blood—all over everything—and George was going to kill him, and I knew Andri had a gun in his desk. and I ran and grabbed it." She is crying again.

"I just wanted to threaten him," she says, "because he would have killed Andri."

"Go on," Karla says.

"I pointed the gun at him—I was shaking so bad—I've never used a gun—and screamed at him to stop, and he came at me with his knife and knocked my arm as I shot him, except the bullet went into Andri, and George ran out the kitchen—"

"Oh God, George is going to come back for me." A clamp tightens around my throat.

Mom aims a hostile glare at me through her tears. "I knew you should never have locked him in the basement. If you'd listened to me, we'd still have Andri."

"Who's George?" Karla says. When she sees me hesitating and inwardly debating, she pushes her hair back, gathers it up with the *snap!* of a rubber band, and says firmly, "Madeline, honey, I know it's late, but now I'm here, you need to come clean with me. The sooner I know what we're dealing with, the sooner we can clear your mom."

"She doesn't have to be *cleared*. It's an obvious case of self-defense. Go and find the stab wounds on Andri to confirm it."

"Tell me about George," Karla says. "We need to put out an alert to pick him up."

My resistance is low, and I tell her everything. "After Mike's funeral, I was approached by a man with a fake FBI badge, who convinced me to spy on the Computer Science Department at Cornell under false pretenses."

"Go on." Her face barely twitches.

"He encouraged me to break into the offices of all the faculty members and download the hard drives of their computers. He told me he had search warrants, and if I was caught or arrested, he would vouch for me with his credentials."

"That's probably when you should have contacted me," Karla says.

"I believed his bullshit that he was undercover, and I was a secret informant and was going to be a heroic spy who would identify the person supplying state-of-the-art encryption software to illegal pornographers." I put my head in my hands and listen to myself. Even to *my* ears I sound delusional.

Karla adjusts her glasses and stares at me over the rims. "That porn on the flash drive—?"

"Yes, that's one of the things I learned about my dead husband. I'm not proud of it—that I didn't somehow guess."

"Did you succeed in finding the perpetrator you were searching for?" She's leaning forward, giving serious weight to my story. She's not laughing at me at all, which is somehow, through my grief, a huge relief.

"I've identified that person," I say, and proceed to explain how I know it's Judy. Everything spills out, the Peeping Tom stuff, the basement episode, and Judy's admission that George was her employee.

Even for Karla, the coolest person on the planet, this is a road too far. "Whoa, slow down, Madeline. Holding someone against their will is a crime. Kidnapping. And impersonating an FBI agent is a federal offense. I'll have to open investigations into all of this."

"Judy roped Mike into her illegal schemes," I say. "That explains the porn on Mike's computer."

"What happened to your handler?" Karla says.

At that moment, there's a scuffling at the front door, and the unmistakable sound of Torvill—my dog—barking furiously. In the middle of all this turmoil, Torvill and Joe are back.

I make another fateful decision: to protect Joe's identity—for now. Despite everything, I'm sad for him, for his lost son and wife, and his futile quest. What he chooses to tell Karla later is his business.

"I'm through with my handler. I'm moving on."

The stab wounds in Andri's back and shoulder corroborate my mother's story. The burly officer in charge sets up an office in my study and takes statements from me, Mom, and Joe. Like it or not, Joe is involved. What name he'll give, and how he'll describe his relationship to our family, are not my problems.

When Andri's body is eventually removed, Torvill tries to leave with him, barking furiously at the men who are wheeling out the stretcher. I run to him, crouch down, and hug his big furry body, trying to encompass all of him, shielding him from the horror that has engulfed us all. Amazingly, he yields for a moment, and I cling to his neck as we cry together for our lost Andri. Then he pulls free and stands at the door, perhaps waiting for Andri to come home again.

It's well after midnight, time for bed. I stagger about in a blur of events swirling around me. An officer says they'll protect our house until they find George. Karla asks me for the photos of George taken on the day we captured him. Joe, who's been sitting in the background, eventually leaves with Karla, hitching a ride. He touches my arm before he leaves.

Finally, it's just Mom and me in the living room. Without Andri's larger than life presence, the house is like a mausoleum. I bring Mom a tranquilizer and a glass of water, and she obediently swallows them. It breaks my heart.

"We must find Tosca," I say. "She's been missing for a while."

"She'll be in Andri's apartment," Mom says. "Let's get her."

We creep under Karla's yellow tape—she's already ransacked Andri's room and carted off a box of his papers—and pause for a minute, already missing him. The search for Tosca is surprisingly short. A faint noise emanates from under Andri's bed, where Tosca is lying on her side, crying piteously. To reach her, I must crawl under the bed myself, on my stomach. It seems outrageous to pull her toward me, so I maneuver myself on the dusty floor until I'm behind her and parallel to her body, so I can put an arm around her before trying to extract her.

"Madsy?" Mom calls out. I've disappeared from her view.

I stroke the cat's warm fur, but she yowls and wriggles free.

She wants to grieve on her own.

CHAPTER 42

Andri has written me a letter, which drops from the void like a blast from the underworld. Karla is the messenger, visiting me in mid-afternoon, two weeks after Andri's death. "This was among his papers," she says, standing on my welcome mat, stomping wet leaves off her boots. "I took the liberty of reading it." She's unapologetic. "We're trying to find out who he was, and as part of our investigation, we went through his effects."

Torvill is at the door, panting, waiting for Andri to return. Karla scratches his head. "Poor sad dawg," she says.

After the Ithaca ritual of coat, hat, scarf, Karla is finally in the warmth of the living room. She rubs her elegant hands together. "Blocks of ice," she says. "I'm too thin for this weather."

I sit facing her in a nearby chair, waiting patiently for her to come to room temperature.

Eventually, she speaks. "An update. First and most important—we've arrested George Snyder."

"Oh, thank God," Mom says. "I had nightmares about that man."

"How did you find him?" I'd been sure he'd be on the other side of the country by now.

Karla shakes her head, precipitating a shower of wet weather from her topknot. "George Snyder is his real name, and he has, believe it or not, a rap sheet and a home address in Ithaca. We picked him up at his house. By the way, his fingerprints were on the knife, which we found in your yard."

"Did he say anything? Like, why he did it?"

She taps her fingers on the arms of her chair. "I can tell you he said what they all say—he didn't mean to kill the big guy, just rough him up a bit." She gives me her stern, disapproving look. "His lawyer is making loud noises about what went down in your basement."

"He menaced us on my property. Andri tried to persuade him to tell us why."

"That's what cops are for," Karla says.

"What about Judy?" I'm still on edge from my visit to Judy's house.

Karla shifts in her seat. "Yes...Judy." Something in her demeanor alarms me.

"She admitted to sleeping with your man, but not to killing him. No fiddling with the parachutes, no animosity toward you, nothing. She had a lawyer present, who kept putting his big hand over her mouth and saying, 'My client is guilty of adultery and nothing else.'"

Judy will wriggle off the hook. "What did she say when you confronted her with the evidence on Mike's phone?"

My tone is sharp, and Karla hesitates a beat. "She said she went to the drop zone in Ovid, and Mike showed her around. And yes, she handled his kit and may have left a fingerprint or two, but her motives were pure. No killing on her mind."

"What about her motive to kill *me?* Did you ask about that?"

Karla gives a low chuckle. "Madeline, in the interest of truth telling, I'll confess, she laughed and said, 'Madeline was a nonentity in my calculations, Detective. I would not have wasted bandwidth on her.'"

That's me, alright. The person no one wasted bandwidth on.

"Did you ask about all those encrypted spreadsheets on her computer? The huge amounts of money? The pornography?"

Karla, again, chooses her words carefully. "Bottom line, Madeline—she's an efficient administrator. Her lawyer was sweating meatballs every time she opened her mouth, but to be honest, she managed just fine without him. I didn't have enough evidence to hold her."

"But she was having an affair with my husband!" I cry.

"Oh, Madsy," Mom says.

"We'd fill up the jails, Madeline..." Karla says sadly. "Folks just aren't monogamous. That's the truth."

So that's it. They've found George, who'll implicate me, and they'll give up on Judy, who's involved in pornography and tried to murder me. I feel empty and betrayed.

"Take a look at the letter from Andri," Karla says, "then we'll talk some more."

Mom says, "I want to see it too."

So I read it aloud, hearing Andri's unique, lost voice. Mom, who's been in mourning all this time, has a tissue ready. To be honest, I'm wrung out from grief—Mom, the animals, and me, all in a suffering contest.

My Dear Medeleen,

If you are reading letter, I am no longer in land of living. Maybe in warmer place now, but with angels.

I want to tell you I have been fugitive in your house, "hiding out from enemies," as Americans say. I am guessing enemy found me and shot head off. I was high-up investigator in Ukraine, for trafficking of teenage children on international market. Big appetite for kiddie porn and young slaves in Europe, big money business, big thugs killing investigators, big bribes of cops to shut eyes at borders. Big decision from me to arrest big shot in government after watching kids in porno movie. Now fatwa on my head like Salman Rushdie.

Wife scared of death threats but also convenient excuse to run off with oligarch Swedish lover, leaving money and animals and big danger for my life. Long story coming to America and dodging criminals.

You and Jenet and house—perfect hideout for me in Ithaca. Don't be sad. You gave big fat lug happiest days of life, and special place in heart for Jenet and Ukrainian stew and watching dark Scandinavian TV.

Worldly goods of Andri Eriksson go to you and Jenet and Cayuga Dog Rescue. All money and papers in strong box in Tompkins County Bank in Ithaca. Lawyer in Ithaca, Jessica Seymour, has will. No mortgage trouble to keep house for Torvill and Tosca forever.

Medeleen, animals will be very sad. Please give love and food and nice bed until happy again.

Medeleen, you are brilliant spy. You will catch Ithaca porn perp. I thank you from grave for finishing last personal goal of Andri Eriksson.

Jenet, you are perfect woman of my soul.

Goodbye from heart.
Andri.

P.S. Real name was Ostap Kolisnyk.

Mom started sobbing at the Ukrainian stew, and I'm barely holding it together, when Karla says, "Did you and Janet know you were the beneficiaries of Andri's will?"

My brain goes into overdrive. "Are you suggesting I instructed my mother to find a chance to shoot him dead? Or that my mom took the initiative on her own?" I want to tear her throat out.

"Tell me, honey, do you have any idea of how much you'll be inheriting?" Karla says coldly.

"Millions," Mom pipes up through the sniffling. "Literally millions. He told me last week."

"Oh, for heaven's sakes, Mom, don't you have any sense of self-preservation at all? She's trying to find out if you had a motive for killing Andri and you've just provided one. Congratulations."

"Madeline, put a cork in it," Mom says. She turns to Karla. "We loved him, Detective." She dabs her eyes. "His death is a late-life tragedy for me personally. I don't care how much money he had, it won't bring him back."

Karla nods and starts to say something else. While we're all sitting in silence, Tosca comes into the room on snowflake feet. She's emerged from under the bed!

"I lured her out with Fancy Feast Ocean Fish and Salmon," Mom says. "Come here, darling, Momma's waiting." She pats her lap, and Tosca, who is newly slender from loss of appetite, jumps onto Mom's lap and snuggles in.

There's a jarring ring on my phone while I'm sipping a glass of white wine and helping Mom with dinner. She usually trusts me with the rice because there's a clear algorithm for cooking it.

Joe Shelmann, calling on the burner, telling me to find a private space and call him back.

I could power off the phone and throw it someplace in my closet or bury it in the garbage and move on with my life.

But somehow the adrenaline is pumping and I'm grabbing my coat and heading to the door.

But then I rethink. Why freeze my ass off every time he calls?

"I'll be a minute, Mom." I flop onto the couch in the living room.

"Madeline, how are you?" he says smoothly, like in a normal conversation.

"Make it fast, Joe. We're about to have dinner." It's not a lie.

"I've decided to stay in Ithaca," he says, as if I'm panting to hear his plans.

"Why? I thought you didn't want to blow your cover."

There's a pause. He's probably running his hands through his hair. "I'd like to see you again. Start fresh with our relationship." *What relationship?*

There was a time I would have been thrilled to receive this call, but I've grown wise to him and his lies.

Mom, who's probably been eavesdropping with every fiber of her ears, comes into the living room and mouths at me, "Invite Joe for dinner sometime." Of course she knows who I'm talking to. She's been tuned into Joe from the beginning.

"What's the purpose of this call, exactly?" I say to the phone.

A silence at the other end tells me he's probably fabricating something new.

"I got a call today from my contact in the FBI," he says. "There's been more…activity…a whole new batch of videos on the dark web. Fresh children on tap. Brand new encryption keeping out the cops. And the link" —his voice cracks— "is right here in beautiful Ithaca."

CHAPTER 43

He thinks he's left me salivating with a tantalizing morsel that'll galvanize me into action, but this time I'm not going to bite. There's more pornography in the world than I could ever make a dent in. I've done my bit. He has the name of the perpetrator. It's over.

Joe is bad news. He's never going to let go of his obsession. Ever since he showed up at Mike's funeral, he's distorted my sense of time and purpose. Why would I ever again want my life to be spliced into another man's self-centered existence?

On Saturday morning, with my new backbone in place, I decide, finally, to clean out Mike's side of the closet. His boxes of magazines and piles of clothes, which have sat there for months, half-hidden.

After breakfast, I come upon Torvill, lying on my bed. He's given up on Andri's apartment and has been exploring other options, sniffing his way through each room of the house. Tosca won't let him muscle in on Mom's territory—Mom has always been hers. Poor Torvill. He's lost his daddy, and now he's stuck with me.

Sitting on the bed, I massage his side. "Hey, Torvill Eriksson." My voice is a pale imitation of Andri's booming foreign voice. If only I could say something loud and jolly in German, but instead I rest my head on his fur and listen to his heart.

How soft and fragile it sounds. The good news is he allows me to do it. Nor does he run away when I move to the closet.

There's a distance now between me and the skydiving accident, so I'm okay with sorting through Mike's things. When I pull out the first box, Mike shocks me by appearing in my mind, so fresh and vivid I can smell him. Where did this wholesome vision come from, his wide, quick smile beaming to me from space?

That pornography on his computer was so uncharacteristic.

Slowly, painfully, I examine his assortment of papers, trying to keep my distance. The pages of rules for video games, with stapled sheets about power levels and portals. A vaguely familiar map of a fantasy world, with multiple diagrams and arrows. Do all these games look the same, or is it just me? A jumble of comic books, *Superman, Iron Man, Captain Marvel,* with their skewed realities. Scribbled, impromptu algorithms on scraps of paper, piles and piles of them, all annotated and lovingly preserved in this box. *Mike's life of the mind.*

I straighten everything and shove the box back into the closet. Somehow this was the essence of my romance with Mike, and I can't bring myself to discard any piece of it.

The clothes are another story, headed for the Salvation Army charities without a second glance. My heart is steeled as I seal the box. No burying my face in his shirts and underwear. That part of him is gone for good.

Did Andri see all this stuff when he searched my room? I'll never know.

It's time to walk and clear my head.

Torvill has been trained to frolic in Scandinavian snow, so one thing we have in common is the joy of walking in cold weather. "Come on, boy, let's go!" I say, with my fake doggie voice, getting the leash, and putting on my jacket. He swivels his head and eyes me sideways, without bestirring himself. His sluggish body needs a tug from the bed to get him on the move.

There's snow on the lawn, but no new snowfall, which means we can walk on the plowed road without slipping and sliding. Our pace increases, and we lift our faces to the wind, breathing deeply until we can no longer taste the sadness in the house. Torvill's snout points upward for the first time in this terrible month. All that sky and road, stretching to infinity, is like a benediction.

Afterwards, when we're back at home, Torvill collapses onto my bed again, exhausted.

"You should hold him on your lap," my mother advises. "Stroke him, give him love."

But he doesn't want love, he wants Andri. Nor does he want to sit on my bony lap when he can lie on the couch. He ignores me most of the time, but when he does glance my way, his large brown eyes are no longer melancholy. They're baleful, full of accusation, because I'm somehow withholding the thing he wants most in the world.

After lunch, I try to escape this gloomy atmosphere by getting back into my computer science research. Something Nigel showed me on his game computer has triggered a spark of an idea. His lightbulb data structure is exquisite, but processing each bulb in such a huge array would take forever. It's one thing to admire the aesthetics, but another to create useful software. I mull it over. It would be great to give it a go, but obviously I can't steal his work.

How will I get back into academia?

There's another pathway open to me, learning how to hack into apps by embedding invisible strings in the code. These would lie dormant up until the moment of activation, then—pow! If my program worked, it would expose vulnerabilities in the app's code. Of course there's no malice in my thinking, just intellectual curiosity. How does one hack without detection, then unleash it as needed?

I download a random app onto my phone and fire a rocket or two into the code. Nothing stops me from accessing the source and modifying the program that runs the app.

It's shocking how easily the app's defenses can be penetrated. After an hour or two of diabolical fun, I dream of marketing myself as The Happy Hacker.

My recurring nightmare. I'm floating in the air on a cloudless day. Mike is in the distance, a tiny dot with a dab of bright yellow. When he gets near, I struggle to reach him and startle awake. The fantasy is so vivid, it continues. He is with me in the room.

Someone is in this room—I can hear him breathing.

Motionless, my chest hammering.

I see him now, his impenetrable eyes glinting in the moonlight. How long has he been standing there watching me?

Lying still, hardly daring to breathe. Don't break the spell.

He moves closer, sniffing softly, barely brushing my neck. He places a paw on my cheek, and when my breath stops, the paw moves across my shoulder, like a caress, then lands gently in the center of my chest, where it rises and falls with my breath. Is he feeling my heart or checking out the topography? So alien compared to the mountain that was Andri.

Be still.

After a while he climbs onto the bed and lies down beside me. How can I sleep with a dog on my bed? I've never slept with an animal anywhere near me, but don't have the heart to shoo him away.

The next morning, the dog apparition has gone. Was it a dream? Mom is in the kitchen and our pets are at their food bowls in the pantry. No happy barks for me, but it's Torvill's first time back at his bowl. I kneel behind our animal family and do a double hug, one in each arm. Tosca bats me away and Torvill squirms out of my grasp; but I'm so relieved to see them eating again, I don't take it personally.

After breakfast, I log into the Cornell website and click on the Computer Science Department. A sudden urge to see what those jokers are up to. Judy, of course, has revoked my faculty ID, but after a minute, I've overridden her. There's an announcement: a combination colloquium/fall celebration party on Monday at four o'clock. Nigel is speaking about his lightbulb algorithm for encryption and decryption.

I wonder how he solved the problem of efficiency. An insane idea hits me—why not show up and find out? What's the worst that can happen? They could arrest me (they won't). They could ask me to leave (they may). Judy could have a fit (anyone's guess). Nigel would love to have me there—it would stroke his ego. And what about the others— David and Dwayne—who never had the grace to say goodbye and wish me well? And Aisha? Would she be able to face me? My presence would probably make them all nervous as hell, and in a strange way, that appeals to me.

A little poke in the eye.

After all I've been through, they don't frighten me at all.

CHAPTER 44

The colloquium is in the very same room where I had my humiliation. It's as if it happened yesterday. The same table piled with cheese and cheap wine, the flickering fluorescent lights, and a clique of loud-mouthed grad students doing their version of macho in the nerd universe.

Dwayne Browning is in his regular seat by the window, talking earnestly—too earnestly, too cozily—to a young woman who looks like Miss Vietnam. She's a real eye-catcher. Is she Dwayne's research assistant, the one who has my old office? Has she taken Aisha's place in Dwayne's affections?

Aisha, the Queen of Cool, is dressed like Cleopatra this afternoon, while she replenishes the cheese platter and decorates the table with tiny skeletons. Her betrayal is fresh in my mind. *Snake.*

Judy, near the back, is sipping white wine, rolling it languidly in the glass, as she surveys the scene. It burns me up she's so untroubled by her crimes, so untouched by law enforcement. Is she contemplating a new batch of pornographic movies? Will she ever be caught? What about Mike's murder? *Bitch.*

Nigel, ever the showman, is throwing his weight around at the front, directing his computer be set up just so, and the wide overhead screen be lit from the bottom, and the rolling white board be positioned in front at a slight angle. He's directing his minions like some foreign auteur, getting ready for a film shoot. *Jerk.*

I've dressed for the occasion, wearing a new pair of skin-tight red cords, a form-fitting black woolen turtleneck, and black leather jacket. Dangling silver earrings in the shape of Möbius strips adorn my ears. If things get boring, I can take one off and study its twisty topology. My appearance has been meticulously planned, down to the red shoelaces of my black sneakers so the Computer Science Department doesn't have any illusions about whether I've thrived since leaving Cornell.

At the entrance, rays from the setting sun bathe me in golden light. I hesitate a moment, marveling that this room, these people, were once part of my life.

My entrance causes a stir—even the students stop their chatter. Everyone cringes away from me as if I'm bearing some medieval plague, which is a ridiculous thought. *Stop it!* The reality is probably more mundane, with no one noticing me or giving a damn. As I scan the audience for a vacant seat, Nigel, up front, gives me a breezy wave, which—perversely— makes me happy.

The room is buzzing, because Nigel is such a big attraction. There's a seat in the center, and I hurriedly squeeze myself past strangers. It's almost time. I arrange my bony frame in the uncomfortable metal chair and am ready to watch Nigel strut his stuff.

If I believe, however, I'll enjoy the talk unmolested, I have another think coming. Judy, her mouth set in a thin line, is bearing down on me. "Madeline, may I speak to you?" she says, imperiously, standing in the aisle of my row, like she's commanding an errant schoolgirl.

But I'm not her pupil and don't have to follow her commands.

Raising my voice over the heads of people in my row, I say, "I'm sorry. Can it wait? I don't want to miss the start of the talk."

She turns and calls out to Nigel, saying, "Please forgive me, Professor Welbourne. I need to take care of something before we begin."

But Nigel isn't one of her serfs either and approaches the end of my row. "What's the problem, Judy?" he says, obviously irritated he's being delayed—and upstaged.

"This is not a public talk, Nigel," Judy says, annoyed. "It's open to the Cornell community, but not to outsiders." She raises her voice. "Please leave right now, Madeline."

Nigel raises his voice too. "You can't ask her to leave because she's my guest. I invited her."

Say what? Both Judy and I are stunned into silence. Nigel will probably catch hell afterwards. As for me, I cross my arms, place a slender ankle onto my bionic knee, and try to assume the attitude of an invited guest.

Nigel has prepared a luminous magic show to wow his audience. From the instant the room goes dark, the twinkling lights of his data structure fill the big screen and spill over onto the second screen. A musical accompaniment underscores the various states of the little bulbs, from bright white to yellow to all colors of the rainbow, each representing different attributes of a pixel. Trills of a harp, as each light is switched off, represent the encryption process, while a rumble of drums signals the end, when all is dark and the data is hidden from view. A slow clap in the audience swells to raucous applause.

"Billions and billions of pixels," Nigel intones, channeling Carl Sagan. "How do we retrieve them?"

What we do to decrypt, apparently, is reverse the process, the lights on both screens taking on a ghostly blue hue, before the harp music twinkles them back to brilliant life.

But he hasn't solved the problem. Accessing each and every pixel takes far too long to be viable; so even though this is a gorgeous piece of theater and stunning data structure, it's not even remotely successful as a piece of decryption software. I anticipated he'd surprise me with some kind of Dragon Variation of a chess move, riding a bishop to victory; but instead, he's presented a mediocre computer science algorithm, that any B-plus graduate student could have come up with.

Asking questions is a waste of time. Those in the know can surely see this for what it is. But there they are, the grad students, bowing and scraping and licking Nigel's boots, throwing all sorts of inane questions at him that he handles with flair.

Mouth tightly shut, I refuse to be part of the circus. Instead, I prepare to make a fast exit and slink out unnoticed. Sitting in the middle of a row, however, is awkward, forcing me to wait until some of the crowd has thinned.

Nigel catches me at the door, literally hanging on to my arm. "Wait. Don't go."

I shake him off. "Nice show, Nigel."

"You didn't fall for any of it, did you?" he says, with an uncharacteristically hangdog face.

"The decryption harp music was good, but it went on too long," I say, tactfully.

"Sad but true. That traversal is a bear." He motions toward the food table. "Join me in a glass of execrable wine?"

"Why should I join you in anything? You locked me in a room of your house, remember?"

He looks down at his shoes, an uncharacteristic gesture. "I owe you an apology, Madeline—I have *truly* regretted you were locked in." He gives me his best cow eyes. "I swear on my niece's head that the locked door was unintentional—an Alexa malfunction—and I *beg* of you to forgive me."

After a few moments of contemplation, I pick a pinot grigio. Nigel pours himself a generous amount of something red, relief on his face. There are eyes on my back, and I turn to see Judy staring at us with what I charitably interpret as loathing.

"How would you like to write a paper with me?" Nigel says.

Really? It may give me the lift I need to jump start my academic career. *But Nigel? Christ.*

"What kind of paper? I don't do *Popular Mechanics* or *Computer Science for Dummies.*"

He chuckles. "This is why I can't get you out of my skin, Madeline. Exactly this."

There are metal chairs against the wall, and he joins me. It's already pitch dark outside, and I worry about my mother. There's a Post-it note on the back of her phone, reminding her I'm at Cornell.

My blood is warmed by the wine, which is surprisingly fruity and good. "Sure, I'll work with you," I say, "but I have three conditions." *As of two seconds ago.*

"Okay, shoot. I'm all ears." He takes a long, smooth shot of wine.

If he had said "I don't do conditions," I would have blown him a kiss and said bye-bye. Instead, I say, "Okay, number one. My name goes first on the paper, as lead author. Second, we post the paper on the regular academic computer science forum. And finally, when I'm ready to apply for an academic job, you will write me a strong letter of recommendation that cites this paper we're going to write and some of my other publications."

I listen to myself in amazement. Who *is* this person?

Nigel seems surprised, too, and doesn't respond immediately. "That's all you want, huh? What if I refuse?"

"Then you can solve your own pixel traversal problem."

His hazel eyes gleam in the fluorescent light. "In that case, I have some conditions of my own," he says.

CHAPTER 45

For an absurd, obscene moment, I'm afraid he's going to ask me to sleep with him. What he says is, "First and foremost, we must work in my study at home, where I have spectacular high-res graphics and a speedy Wi-Fi connection. Everything is set up there—two desktop computers, special routers, storage—"

"What's the second condition?"

He gives a brittle laugh. "What's your rush?"

"I'm the queen of efficiency, remember?"

"Well, alright. I want you to work with me on the video game I'm developing. Also at my house. What says you, huh?" The plummy accent. The charm.

"I say no. I hate video games, especially shoot-em-ups and phallic power plays."

He shakes his head. "The one I'm working on now is a cerebral game. You'll love it, I promise." Underneath his languid tone, his voice seems strained.

"Fine," I say. "We'll give it a go. Do you want to put it all in writing, or should I?"

"Why can't we just shake on it?" He seems genuinely surprised.

"Because I've been screwed on things I just shook on."

We agree to start on his pixel algorithm tomorrow and see how it goes.

When I enter my house through the garage, Torvill is at the mudroom door. He doesn't bark with joy to see me, nor does he jump on me and slobber over my face. But he does lift his snout toward me and allows me to scratch his head behind his ears. The mudroom floor needs a mop, but I sit on it and open my arms wide. He doesn't fling himself into my embrace. He hangs back, then steps gingerly onto my lap. I wrap him in a soft hug. We sit there for a while, head to head, reminiscing about Andri, until Mom comes looking for me because she heard the car.

At dinner I say, "Do you remember that computer science professor who cooked dinner for me? The night of that huge snowstorm?"

"Nigel," she says. "I didn't think you liked him."

The things she remembers.

"I don't much like him. But he's an important professor and he's asked me to write a paper with him."

"What's the point if you don't like him?" Mom says.

"I'm not always shopping around for a new husband, Mom," I say, irritated.

"Who said anything about a husband?" she says.

The next morning is crisp and sunny when I set out to Nigel's house, contract in hand. Such a different feeling from the snowy night when I last crossed his doorstep. This time my goal is single-minded and upfront: to earn some street cred in the city of computer science.

After I've maneuvered my car into Nigel's narrow drive-way, I check my supplies—Alexa protection, two phones, pepper spray, flash drives, an apple with a sharp paring knife, and a bottle of water.

He has a casual look today, with a beige fisherman sweater and slightly rumpled hair that's not unattractive.

The last time I was in his study, my heart was in my throat. This time, when he leads me inside, I say, "Get a pen. Let's sign and seal this." I drop the contract onto the table.

"You're so—venal—and delectably cold-blooded." He produces a silver Parker and a flourishing signature. I wave away his pen and sign on my side with my own chic little BIC.

"Now show me your algorithm—the plain code with no frills and graphics," I say.

Instead of rushing to his computer to do my bidding, he stands and monitors me while I unload my computer and find a convenient plug for the power cord.

"Did you wonder, yesterday, about my vertiginous plunge in self-belief?"

"Your what?" I'm ready to go and he's talking in riddles.

"This." He gestures in my direction. "Inviting you to write papers with me."

"Um, Nigel, are you telling me I should be flattered, or that you've lost your mind?"

"Not sure," he says. "But be assured I'm delighted to add your brain power to my program."

I tap the contract. "*Our* program, Nigel." What an odd bird he is.

"Do you want to drink to it? I have some great vino."

"At ten in the morning? Are you serious? Drinking while programming?"

"I enjoy getting a rise out of you," he says.

His data structure is beautiful but inflexible, laying down roadblocks in accessing the pixels. I have several suggestions for pulling the structure apart, unwinding the elements into a linked list, like a string of colored lights that can be wrapped around a Christmas tree. This would preserve the data and speed up the processing.

If I expect him to fall all over me with gratitude, he sets me straight pretty quickly. He's in love with his Las Vegas array and doesn't want to alter it. But he does move closer to inspect the data structure I've sketched out.

My suggestion is to keep the array and store the features of each pixel in a data tree. He's intrigued, but not convinced.

In a computerized image, any given pixel is similar in color and texture to its surroundings. One of my brain waves is to create neighborhoods of like pixels, little circles that can be processed as one data point. This will speed up access by a lot. Not great, he says, but a start.

He puts on thin, rimless glasses and peers at my notepad, while I scribble some rudimentary pseudocode to see how this will pan out. He has some terrific ideas for refinement, and by lunchtime we have a whirlwind of code that we unleash on his program. Finally, we're ready to test that it all works with his graphics. It doesn't. There are two screens full of error messages.

I dig in and start fixing the bugs, one by one. Nigel perks up, and after a while, he's trilling with happiness. "You're a wonder, Madeline."

"I haven't debugged it yet."

He offers to make lunch, omelette au fromage, but I decline. "I don't break for lunch when there's something to be debugged," I say, without looking up. "You go ahead. I'll munch on an apple here and think about the code."

"That's not normal behavior," Nigel says. "The world won't end if we debug it after lunch."

He disappears for some indeterminate time and reappears with steaming mugs of coffee and flaky croissants for both of us, which I nibble on intermittently.

Late in the afternoon, the program finally generates output, but we are left with the mother of all bugs, a logic glitch in which the code runs and the lights flash, but the decrypted image doesn't appear. *Damn!*

It's just a matter of time—I trust myself—but it'll have to wait until tomorrow. I promised my mother I'd be home for dinner.

I don't want to leave. A magnetic force field pulls me back—the way he watches me play with raw code and the challenge and excitement of the chase. He's fun to work with, as I knew he would be, capable of the same deep focus and intensity. It's impossible to extricate myself in this state—high and turned on and remembering the familiar feeling with Mike, falling in love with him as we pooled our brainpower.

There's a period during debugging that I forgive Nigel.

While I'm puttering about, gathering my papers, he pulls me toward him and kisses my mouth. It's a moment to say, "No thanks, Nigel, gotta go," but some primal impulse draws me closer to him, and I kiss him back, because his touch is firm and delicious and I'm thirty years old and don't need permission or romance or love stories or fairy tales, just this one moment of pure lust.

I drop everything and allow myself to be pulled into his bedroom and onto that great big shiny bed.

Not a shard of love or tenderness passes between us, just his taut demanding body, his intense face, and some kind of exorcism at the end.

"That was something," he says, afterwards, somewhat breathless. "What in God's name was in your head?"

Not you, Nigel, just your colored lights and miniature comets swirling through space, faster and faster, rocking the universe...

"I've debugged the problem," I say.

After I've patted down my hair and am headed out the door, he says, "Before you go, take a peek at the video game we'll be working on. Don't forget, it's part of our contract."

"Why can't it wait until tomorrow?"

He pecks my cheek. "Because I want you to be excited about coming back."

Interesting—he doesn't think his personal sexual allure will be sufficient enticement.

He's gotten me at a mellow moment, and I grin. "Sure, why not? Just a quick look."

He takes my hand and leads me back to the study.

Just a few clicks and I'm gazing at an alien, fantasy landscape. As yet, it's unpeopled by characters, quite different from his original game on my flash drive. Nevertheless, it's very familiar, because I've seen this very vista not too long ago.

I search my brain.

The wasteland is exquisitely rendered in subtle sepia colorings, Nigel at his absolute best. He's a master of graphics, a modern-day Picasso on the computer.

"Not bad, huh?" he says. He wants a great big wet kiss of admiration from me, and because my mood is indulgent, I give it to him.

"You're a graphics god."

He strokes my back, reveling in the praise.

Something clicks in my head, and I look more closely at the screen. The perfect symmetry of castles and steeples in the distance, the Escher-like swoop of hills and valleys, and the mouth of Hades stamped with ancient lettering across the River Styx.

I remember now where I saw this identical picture. In my closet, shoved into a dark corner, packed away in Mike's box.

CHAPTER 46

"So he's not so bad after all," Mom says at dinner.

My best defense is to say not one word.

"You've lost your lean and hungry look." She tenderly places slices of sirloin in front of me, with potatoes and asparagus.

Torvill comes sniffing at my chair and I slip him some steak under the table. No one could accuse him of having a lean and hungry look.

After dinner I escape to my bedroom and haul out Mike's box again. The rules of the video game are easy to find, and this time I pay attention.

There's no question Mike has a black-and-white version of Nigel's game. Stapled together is a thick sheaf of pages, strategies for playing. Why are these in Mike's box?

The game is called Utopia, and it is set in the city of Uteland, which is peopled with ute-warriors and ute-peons. The coin of the realm are ute-coins, which the players will use to enter the medieval fortress called Utopia. What is the ultimate goal? It's not explicitly spelled out.

The game has every video-game cliché I loathe—treasure hunts, swords, alchemy, spells, villains, underground lairs, and portals. Ute-peons can gain powers and become ute-warriors. Utes can perish in a moat or languish in a dungeon. They can burn in Hades. They can acquire evil capabilities that vaporize them. But they could also win loot boxes brimming with golden ute-coins. It's complicated.

The game happens in real time, with role-playing characters who are robots or real people playing online. When a character logs off, they retain their powers and money.

This is about as far as I read in Mike's notes. The game is crushingly boring. I'm much more intrigued by the fact that Mike played such intense games with Nigel, and I didn't know about it.

An examination of Mike's texts, downloaded on my computer, shows his texting history loaded with video-game chats between him and Nigel.

Special game tonight? Nigel asks.

Sure, why not? Mike replies.

Note to self: What's a special game?

The next morning the lawn is crackling with frost.

Mom is bustling in the kitchen, feeding Tosca and Torvill. While I'm placing some Post-it reminders on the fridge for her, she says, "So you're going back to him today." It's not a question.

"What are you talking about?"

"You've raised the level," she says. "Usually you lounge about the house in sweatpants."

Have I really gone from being a brainy spy in jeans and T-shirt to a honeypot in sexy threads? Where's the serious, invisible woman who used to hack into computers?

Maybe she's evolved and doesn't want to be that woman.

Ithaca weather at the end of October can be a smorgasbord of snow, sleet, freezing rain, and wind. Mom has knitted a wonderful winter doggie coat for Torvill, which Andri would probably have sneered at. When Torvill and I go walking, he slides and slithers on the black ice of the driveway, emitting a mild bark of protest. The Yaktrax on my sneakers grip the ice and keep me upright, but I'm still mastering the art of a new pooper-scooper, which is a challenge on the ice.

If ever there was a day for staying home, this is it. I tell myself I'm really curious about the video game story and can't postpone knowing for another day. But the truth is that the thought of working closely with Nigel makes me hug myself with anticipation, warmth flooding me to the core.

When it's time to say goodbye, I give my family big hugs, which make them all squirm away from me. Mom, in particular, is rolling her eyes, which means, thank God, she is lucid.

The long drive to Nigel's house is a nightmare of poor visibility and slippery roads. Of all the bad driving conditions, freezing rain is the worst. To keep my windshield from becoming an opaque crust of ice, the front fan must be turned to maximum hot power, blasting me with noise and broiling my head. Other nutcases out on the roads are slip-sliding all over the place, and I'm just as scared of them as of the weather.

When my Subaru finally sloshes into Nigel's driveway, I'm a pile of nerves and sweat, and must rest my head on the steering wheel to regain my equilibrium.

He's heard my car and eventually comes looking for me, rapping on the window and rousing me from my reveries. He's wearing a ridiculous woolen hat with a pom-pom on top, a deranged Santa peering at me through the scrim of sleet.

He half-drags me from the car and envelops me in a bear hug. "Let's get you warmed up," he says, leading me through the garage and into his mudroom to shed my boots and various layers. He looks at me appraisingly.

"You're gorgeous. Let's get into bed and stay there all day."

"Show me your video game and make me some coffee." I push him away.

It's on the tip of my tongue to call him a ute-peon, which is pronounced "yute-peon," when something holds me back. He hasn't yet shared with me the rules of the game, and it suddenly doesn't seem wise to reveal to him what I know.

When we're ready to go with the video game, Nigel puts me in the hot seat, facing his divinely big console, and pulls up a chair next to me. This way we can both work off this screen while he ostensibly gives me game instructions.

"Let's create your character," he says. "You'll be blown away by the graphics." *He's right. I've seen them on his hard drive.*

I name my character Lina and specify my avatar requirements—tall and skinny, with dark, curly hair. My starting status is a ute-peon, because I have no power. I am, however, given an allocation of one ute-coin, which can buy me an additional physical quality, like arm strength or flexibility, and one mental attribute like wisdom, humor, cunning, and so on. Swiftness and brain power are the features I pick, because what do I know?

When I click Create, a lifelike version of myself pops into the landscape and starts jogging along a road. Lina looks up, catches my eye, and waves as she runs past. She's so real she unsettles me.

"Isn't she something?" Nigel says. "Hyper-realistic pixel art, Dazzle-4-D."

"I'm impressed." I turn to face Nigel. "What do you need me for? I could never create people who look this great. It is *so* not my thing."

"Wait until we have more interacting players. The action slows down to a crawl. I need your efficiency expertise."

He throws two simple gamepad controllers onto the table and says, "Okay, let's play and see how long you survive."

Nigel's avatar is equally uncanny in its realism. A younger, more chiseled version of himself with more hair. His opening choices are physical strength and cunning, and within two seconds he has grabbed Lina, thrown her into the moat, and assumed her powers. Game over. Checkmated in two moves, before I've even figured out which end of the gamepad is up.

"Bummer," I say, ruefully. "Tell me the strategy."

"For one thing, don't stand and wait for me to rush you…"

He shows me some moves, like ducking into an underground maze, getting a key from under a mat, kicking in a door, grabbing a player's ute-pouch of coins, strong-arming and beating up on enemies.

Then he sets me loose to play against a couple of robot humanoids, and by the time I get the hang of it, I'm running circles around the robots, ducking and weaving, and kicking them to Hades. I cling to my brainpower, and in addition, acquire the robots' loot and their spell-casting powers.

But Nigel is right. The reason they were so easy to catch is obvious. They were moving like tortoises.

"Brava!" Nigel says. "Now try another game with me. Don't forget, I still have the powers from before."

I think he expects Lina to run away from him as soon as he hits go, but I've anticipated his thinking, and run directly toward him and head-butt him in the balls. If his code is any good this will slow him down. Sure enough, he doubles over. In the seconds that he's incapacitated, I steal his ute-pouch and move to pick his pockets and—

He disappears! Then he reappears in front of a portal on a hill, punching a keypad—and is gone. Through the door, lost in a maze of turrets and probably out a back entrance somewhere.

"Hey, no fair!" I scream in the heat of it. When he sneaks up behind me, I don't anticipate him. He throws a sack over Lina's head, and it's lights out for my character.

Damn!

"Did Mike ever beat you?" I ask.

A cloud passes over his face so quickly I think I imagined it. "Mike? I never played with Mike. The game is in development. I haven't even beta tested it."

Such a simple question, and yet he's lying. *Why?*

"How did you get the password to that portal?" I ask.

"I stole it from a robot in a previous game. Neat, huh?"

"Yeah, I was jealous of that skill." *He cheated. It wasn't in the rules.*

I turn to face him. "What's behind those magical little portals."

He brushes a curl off my forehead. "Spells, powers, the usual. Promotion to ute-warrior."

"What if they're already a ute-warrior? No, stop it! I really want to know." His hand has become a happy wanderer and I smack it away.

"There are gradations of warriors, with some massively nasty weapons." He draws out the word "nahs-ty."

"It's a boring game, Nige."

He looks at me, and his face has a wicked grin. "You've hardly plumbed the depths, my dear."

"You need more than good-looking characters."

"Let's go in the other room," he murmurs, tugging me toward him, touching the soft knots of my spine. "Whisper in my ear what else the game needs."

It's chilly in his room, with icy rain pattering on the window. We climb under the covers onto his cool sheets, where I shiver at his touch and the memory of the moat.

Afterward, when my blood is still racing, I relax on the pillow, buzzing with the video game. "Tell me about the castle you escaped into—Utopia." I run my finger over the soft flesh on the inside of his arm.

"Anyone who gets in is rewarded with flashing lights and fireworks, gongs, music—"

"Bor-ing."

He smiles. "What do you want me to tell you? That when players enter the portal, they'll win a million dollars?"

I prop myself on my elbows. "Sure. Some kind of jackpot. The way you describe it now, it's really lame."

"If you're so smart, maybe you could suggest better ideas."

I lie back and stare at the ceiling. A gray water stain has some seepage. Shutting my eyes, I try to unravel the mystery of this game. So much energy spent to achieve so little. Adult characters running around and doing adolescent things so they can get into a cheesy castle with flashing lights. *What's the point?*

He says he only started it a couple of months ago. *But Mike had detailed notes.*

A shadow passes through the room, the branches of a tree near the window obscuring the gray light.

"You're like a block of ice," he says. "I see goosebumps."

A line from Mike's notes comes into my head. *One ute-coin is about $100.*

Real money, yet no evidence of it today.

Lazily, carefully, I say, "What's the deal with ute-coins? Do players have to pay to play? Is there a bank?"

"Not yet there isn't." *Another lie.*

Mike's notes are black and white, and I trust them 100 percent. My brain cells are racing at ninety miles an hour, way ahead of me, trying to figure it out.

"Can the characters in the game communicate with each other?" I ask.

"Sure they can, but they have to buy that skill. It's expensive."

It's all a code. The clues are everywhere, tucked into the fantasy landscape. Even the smallest detail is waiting to flare into significance. All I must do is move outside the frame, gather the pieces, rearrange them, and create a narrative that solves the problem. My superpower.

"Can kids play the game? I think it would be a great game for teenagers."

He pauses for about five beats, watching me. "Sure, why not? A character creates their own avatar. I even have a name for a kid. A ute." He pronounces it "yute," As Mike described.

One ute costs ten ute-coins. Mike's notes, still in my head. One thousand dollars.

Nigel reaches across to me and starts tracing circles around my nipples. "So sweet…little raspberries…in such a pretty package. So full of questions, aren't you?"

"I'm intrigued…about…your game." The words are forced.

Everything is snapping into place. Different levels of purchase. Many portals. Keeping track of transactions, hiding in plain sight. Secret rewards behind closed doors. *Children for sale.*

Darkness settles on me slowly, as the true nature of the game unfolds in my mind.

Why has he roped me in when he knows what I've been searching for?

Pure hubris, and because it's a game. He's toying with me. That's what he's been doing all along, salivating, daring me to come get him, flirting with danger.

He didn't for a moment imagine I'd figure it out. Without Mike's papers I wouldn't have. I would have taken the game at face value. But now it's clear he communicates with his customers by speaking in ciphers to characters in the game. Their payments are disguised as ute currency.

A child pornography business masquerading as a simple video game for teenagers, its true nature undetectable to any outside investigator.

My body recoils the more I understand, here in this murky room, with ice skittering across the window, and me in bed with a pedophile.

All along, it's been my girly body that turned him on. Shame burns in my stomach.

I can hardly bear to look at him, and try to shield myself from the horror by turning away and curling up. But even as I do that, the dangers associated with this moment are uppermost in my mind.

He mustn't suspect I know what's behind the portals in Utopia.

CHAPTER 47

Full comprehension of how he operates his evil business dawns on me while I'm naked in his bed. I put on a happy face and touch his cheek with trembling fingers. This is the ultimate compartmentalization, not moving a false muscle, because he's cunning, and will pick it up in an instant.

Bile rises in the back of my throat as I concentrate on how to get out of this house—today—without arousing his suspicion. First, I loosen my muscles, then let my bones dissolve into his pillows.

He has underestimated me.

Lunch is scrambled eggs. My demeanor is all sweetness and light. I smile up at him while he sprinkles herbs on my plate.

"Not your usual appetite, Maddie," he says. *Ugh.*

"Look outside at the weather, Nigel. I'm going to make an early start home."

"Meet again tomorrow?" he says.

I pretend to consider it. "How about Monday? I want a few days to think about the game without you breathing down my neck."

"Ah, but it's a lovely neck," he says, putting his face on me and nuzzling. *Don't flinch.*

Edging toward the door, I sense his eyes on my back. Casually, I put on my coat and scarf.

Outside, the air is fresh and unsullied. I sigh with relief to be free of him, even though there's a wintry mix and travelers' advisory. A glittering shell of ice encases my car, and it takes several jabs at the windshield to open a small window of visibility.

Nigel blows frosty kisses from the driveway, and with trepidation, I ease my car onto the icy road. The temperature is on the cusp of freezing, sending down big wet snowflakes that clump around the edges of the windshield, causing the wipers to groan and scrape against the glass.

As cars inch along the road, I think about the facts—the data points. It's crucial not to let down my emotional guard, because if I do, I'll go under.

Nigel and Mike were involved in some enterprise that included pornography with minors. Mike never told me. They communicated through the Utopia video game, using passwords to enter the various portals. Their business dealings and secret activities took place behind closed doors of the game. Nigel needed Mike for his coding abilities.

Interpolating between data points, I surmise that customers used the game to place orders and buy—*Oh fuck!*

The tires are skidding on a patch of ice, and when I try to steer into the skid, it's too late and the car slides to the left, crosses the divider, misses an oncoming truck, pitches into a deep ditch, rolls over once, and lands on its side. I hang suspended in my seat belt. *Shit.*

In the great scheme of accidents, it was a gentle landing. Despite being roughly banged about, I'm fine. *Ridiculous.* I boast to people about my brilliant winter driving, and here I am, upside down like a fucking moron.

My backpack on the front seat is in reach, and I grab my phone. The AAA number is programmed in, and when I call and give them my location, they tell me I'm about twentieth in line. "Keep your engine running with the heat on," they advise. "We'll get to you eventually."

I call my mother. She's worried about me because of the weather. "Are you having fun?" she says. "Where are you?"

"In a place I don't want to discuss right now. But I'll see you for dinner."

"Use protection, Mads," she says.

Yoga in my position is impossible, but some shallow breathing brings me back to equilibrium. My seat belt chafes against me, and my bad knee aches, but my free-floating head is clear.

I understand with 100 percent certainty that Mike was supplying Nigel with state-of-the-art software—my work!—to enable porn production on the dark web. My husband played the video game, that's how they communicated. His motive is beyond me.

Another chilling insight strikes me: Nigel knew I was searching for the perpetrator, so he lured me in. He's playing games with me—literally—titillating himself by daring me to figure it all out. He doesn't believe for a minute I can do it.

Arrogant bastard.

What a fool I've been. So flattered by his attention. I think I'm cool and clever, but he played me like a violin. Nevertheless, the one thing going for me right now is his hubris. When I come for him a second time, he'll continue to underestimate me, which will help find proof of his guilt. Somehow, I must convince him to let me play that video game on my own, without him looking over my shoulder.

Slowly, suspended in a surreal winter landscape, shuffling puzzle pieces in my head, I start to plot my revenge against an antagonist who has upended my life since the day of the funeral. There's no Mike to finish off the code, no Andri for big-man support, and no Joe waiting in the wings to save a girl in danger. Just me and my brain versus a villain who duped me so completely.

The car heater is drying out the air, causing my eyes to sting. Just when this cramped position becomes unbearable, the blessed orange lights of the tow truck glow through the ice. There must be a cop car accompanying it, flashing its lights, blocking a lane of traffic, and placing flares on the road. Two men alight from the truck and walk carefully toward me. The road is a skating rink.

"Looks like you got lucky, miss," the big beefy guy who's built like Andri says. "You and your car both."

I endure the indignity of being extracted and placed in their truck while they manage to attach a giant hook to the car and haul it out of the ditch. "Not a scratch on her," the guy says. "Must be beginner's luck." I don't ask him what the hell he means.

The cop requires my driver's license and insurance card and takes his sweet time examining them. Then he subjects me to a lecture about winter driving and getting the car out of a skid.

* * *

"He's not the one for me," I tell Mom at dinner. "Just not my type. When I'm finished with the paper we're writing, I'm through with him."

She has a wistful look. "Sorry it isn't working out. You were so happy this morning. What happened?"

"The handsome man turned into a frog, and the princess had to move on."

* * *

After dinner, I warm my hands in front of the rickety space heater in my bedroom. An intermittent drizzle blows across the window panes, rattling the frames. I ponder what to do next about Nigel. Now that I'm in the comfort of my house, my courage is ebbing away.

He's ruthless and won't think twice about harming me.

I could contact Karla and relay my suspicions to her. This man is a criminal who enables illegal porn on the web— young teenagers, torture, you name it.

Or I could call Joe and hand it off to him. I've done exactly what you wanted; I've found the Cornell link. It's your call. I'm done.

There's no dishonor in quitting now.

Nigel's gloating face, however, taunts me. The night he locked me in his guest room. His patronizing glee in deceiving me now.

Nothing will bring me greater pleasure than taking him down myself.

During the next several days, I formulate a plan whose execution depends on hacking into Nigel's personal information. It seems like years ago since that fancy dinner when I sneaked off with a copy of his hard drive. Combing through his files, I see that he doesn't use a password manager, so it's easy to find what I need.

Next comes something I swore I'd never do. I download the Alexa app onto my phone. Just seeing that icon winking at me makes me queasy, but it must be done. I log on with Nigel's account. The saccharine voice says "Hello Nigel, Welcome." So far so good. I answer back.

On Saturday he texts me.

> Let me cook for you tonight and sleep over?

I wait for a couple of hours before replying.

> Sorry, no can do. Let's stick to Monday.

His response is immediate.

> Horny thinking about it. You?

I text him a link.

> Check this out. Starlight 3D Solutions. Latest animation graphics. It will turn you on because it's not as good as yours. LOL♥

Saturday is a relatively balmy day, with a bright blue sky and pale sun. In the afternoon, Torvill, Mom, and I bundle up and go for a long walk. Mom is going through a good patch, and when we pause to allow Torvill to sniff the grass, I say, "Mom, I want to come clean about some of the stuff I've been doing—"

"Your spy work," she says. "Undercover. Working for Joe."

I'm so shocked that I jerk the leash, just about strangling my dog.

Mom says, "Andri kept me posted. He thought I should know."

I put my arm around her. "I never guessed. You're good at keeping secrets." She's pleased. Sadly, she may not remember this conversation.

After dinner, Nigel sends me another text.

> Hey Maddie you're right. Starlight software sucks.

He has clicked on the link, falling for the oldest trick in the book: letting me into his computer.

Now I own him.

CHAPTER 48

Halloween Monday dawns sunny and cold, causing the cracked ice on the lawn to glitter.

My mood, however, doesn't match the brightness of the day, an anxiety that chips away at my confidence. This is it for my spy story, my Hail Mary pass. If I succeed, it's all over for Nigel. If I fail—well, that's for another day. The closest thing to a backup plan is the flurry of Post-it notes for my mother, telling her to contact Karla with Nigel's address if I'm not home by suppertime.

"Be careful, Mads," she pleads tearfully, as I pull on my coat. During our goodbye hug, I cling to her a while, because she hasn't begged me not to go.

The roads are clear and the drive to Nigel's house takes just thirty minutes.

When Nigel lets me in, it's the same old handsome Nigel, with his brown eyes crinkling at the corners and his casual jaunty air. But everything about him is sinister now, and I shudder at how thoroughly I misread him. There are kisses to be endured, as well as fondling, and even my head resting on his shoulder after dispensing with my heavy winter gear.

"Bedroom?" he murmurs.

"The study," I murmur back.

He offers me Nespresso coffee, which I politely refuse, holding up my water bottle and taking a slug.

He squeezes in next to me in front of the big screen. "Okay, let's go."

"Not this morning. Let me learn this game a bit before we play."

"Oh, but wait—"

"No ifs and buts, Nigel. You had too much of an advantage last week. I'd like to have a fighting chance—"

"Okay, you little devil, I'll watch you during this exercise in futility." He insinuates his hand under my woolen sweater and places his hot palm flat on my belly. *Relax. Let him do it.*

"Go sit on the other side of the table, Nigel. You're distracting me."

"Spoilsport."

Finally, he and his laptop move about six feet away, probably far enough so he won't see what I'm doing. *Dear God.* How long he'll stay there is anyone's guess. The clock is ticking.

First, I explore the locked doors, depositing ute-coins into various slots to gain entry. Nothing but garbage in the minor portals, singing gnomes and evil wizards.

"Boo!" Nigel says. He has sneaked up behind me!

My heart stops and I jab the wrong button, allowing a robot to vaporize me.

"You'll never beat me at this game if you jump out of your skin every time there's a surprise," he says. "Happy Halloween, Mad-e-*leen*."

Focus. "Are the scenarios behind the portals randomly generated? Or must I memorize which doors are bad news?"

"Random. Not only that—inside the different setups, there are random variations."

He puts his hands on my shoulders and lets them wander down.

"Go away." My voice is light and playful, as he slinks back to his laptop *Creep*.

Before I move to check out the *real* game, the world beneath the colorful veneer, I mute the sound. Call it an over-abundance of caution, but imagine the effect of clanking chains or high-pitched screams ringing out across the room.

Surreptitiously, I refer to my phone, which contains all of Mike's notes, with special passwords to every entrance.

My hand is shaking as I type Mike's key to enter Hades. This is the crucial moment. Is Nigel who I think he is?

Behind the entrance is a gloomy tunnel of opaque shadows, leading into a pit of S&M fantasy, naked men and black-corseted women with whips, chains, and handcuffs. *This is it! The stuff of the dark web.*

I peer closely to ascertain whether these people in leather harnesses and nipple rings are real, or figments of Nigel's coding genius. *It doesn't matter. I'm in.*

A glance at Nigel says he's engrossed in his screen.

Mike's password to the bank leads to an eerie window with bars, and a teller selling ute-coins for real dollars. So this is where Nigel collects the loot, actual payment, in hard, cold currency. I steal another peek across the table and am disconcerted to catch his eye. He jumps up and says, "Let's see how you're making out," and comes toward me. Quick as lightning, I cancel the Mute button, click out of the bank, and shove my phone under my backside. When Nigel examines my screen, Lina, my avatar, is walking on the main street, giving me a thumbs up.

"I'm learning...the terrain." Does he notice the tremor in my voice?

"Fancy another go with me?" he says, with a leer.

"Show me how you got into Utopia in the last game."

He pulls up a chair and moves so close he's practically on my lap. "There's a power you can get that buys you a password—"

"I don't want another power. Just give me the password and let me see what's behind the door." Playfully, I elbow him in the ribs. My heart is thudding.

He thinks about it, then writes down a pathetic puffball combination of letters and numerals, nothing resembling the killer password in Mike's notes. Keeping a bland face, I type in his weak key to the portal. The door swings wide, taking me into a festive room with popped corks, balloons, and a familiar billboard of different-colored lights.

"Fantastic, huh?" he says, banging his chest like Tarzan.

"Yeah, nice graphics. But not exactly mind blowing. It needs *something...*"

"I'll think about it," he says, going back to his laptop.

There's not much time left. Again, I hit the Mute button. Beneath the table I retrieve my phone and gain entry to a garden of frolicking, scantily-clad children, a pedophile's paradise. Another building is a sex store, probably where Nigel conducts illegal sales of software, and buries the records of all customers among the dildos and massage creams.

Finally, I type in Mike's long, complicated password to Utopia, the castle on the hill. My stomach clenches as the screen goes black. Slowly, a nubile young girl becomes visible. She leans toward me.

I don't need the sound on to read her lips. "Hi, Lina, wanna play?"

I've seen this scenario before. *Oh, Mike.*

Nigel is studiously watching his computer screen.

My hand trembles, typing *yes*. The girl leads me to a chat room of preteens.

All the evidence is in front of me. My search ends here.

I restore the sound and hit Quit on the gamepad.

"Seen enough, Madeline?" Nigel says. "Did you find what you were searching for?"

Something in his voice stops me cold. His hooded eyes have narrowed.

In that instant, I know he has a replica of my screen on his laptop and has been watching me all along. Still toying with me.

A shudder passes through my body, an uncontrollable shaking. "I apologize for maligning your game, Nigel." *Phlegm in my throat.* "It's much more—interesting—than I imagined."

"Did you really think I'd allow you to destroy it? Everything I've built?" His face is bloodless. "For a smart girl, you've sure made a lot of bad decisions."

"How...did you get...Mike...to go along with this?"

"Yeah, Mike." He sighs ostentatiously. "I imagine you got the passwords from him, stupid bugger."

Goosebumps, crawling out of my skin.

"Don't fret too much about your precious Mike. He thought he was getting into a legitimate software business. You know, selling great encryption algorithms to reputable dealers."

"But why didn't he tell me?" I barely whisper.

"Oh, Maddie, poor innocent Maddie." His look is one of malice. "The oldest story in the book. He needed *moolah*, dahl-ing, and not for you." *Judy?*

He must see the shock on my face because he explains. "Your beloved husband had an expensive mistress."

That's why our bank account was empty when he died.

Nigel leans back languidly. "So no, you were not in the loop. Mike and I communicated through the video game, for security, which was a brilliant scheme, even if I say so—"

"*Why*, Nigel? You've got so much money? Why are you doing this?"

"*Because*, Maddie, my ex-wife cleaned me out. She suspected...everything...and basically blackmailed me. She's still blackmailing me—"

"Why *Mike*?" I ask. "Why did you have to involve Mike?"

"Because to go into business selling software, you need *great* software. Mike had brilliant ideas for financial privacy and terrific encryption/decryption code—"

"*My* code!" I cry. "You were selling *my* work to pornographers."

He studies me for a moment or two. "Yes," he says, slowly, "I believe I was."

"What went wrong with your scheme?" Something thuds at the window. Chunks of ice falling off the roof.

"Mike became curious about my insistence on security—to the point of obsessiveness—and he somehow figured out how to get into the 'deep state' of the game, as I refer to it. Maybe I became careless. So he managed to download some of the—how should I put it—verboten—videos onto his computer."

"Did he even know what he was downloading?" I whisper. "Stupid, stupid fool—"

"You killed him." It's clear as day. Joe inadvertently got it right. Mike was murdered for what he knew.

Poor Mike, with his sunny face and innocent nature. He was no match for Nigel, who gobbled him up for breakfast. And now, how clear it is, he was no match for Judy either. Mike needed both of them for advancement in the department. How easily they manipulated him. *How callously they took him away from me.*

I mourn my loss anew, tears spilling down my cheeks.

"Too late to cry now, Maddie. Obviously, I have to hold onto you for a while—same reason I couldn't let Mike go. Such a shame. What beautiful music we were making together."

When he takes my hand, I offer no resistance. Down the staircase we go, back to that infamous guest room. His playfulness and humor are gone, replaced by a threat of violence. All the way down, I'm docile, my legs weak, tears flowing freely. Nigel appears to be unmoved. Something has closed in his expression, like a door shutting. His grip on my arm is fierce.

"What do you want from me?" I ask, meekly.

He stops abruptly on the stair, yanking me to a standstill. "How about some honesty, Madeline? So far, you've rewarded my hospitality with nothing but subterfuge. Perhaps after a few days of pondering your lies, you'll come around to my way of seeing things. Show some gratitude. Think about Utopia and the rewards we could reap—together."

Is he offering me a partnership? He's insane.

At the door to the guestroom, I say, "Wait. Not yet." I blow my nose.

He pauses again, keeping an iron grip on me. "What do you have in mind now, little girl? Another bouncy in the bedroom?"

No, you jerk. I'd fuck Satan first.

"Can you ask Alexa to play Beethoven's Ninth Symphony," I say, in a pathetic, small voice.

He looks at me in astonishment, loosening his hold on my arm.

I've learned enough in the past six months to know that men fall for this ploy every time. It can't fail. The pitiful sound of a female who needs help from a man. One hundred percent.

A smile comes over his face. "Oh, that's perfect. After all this, why not? 'Ode to Joy.'"

He lets go of me, claps his hands, and in a loud tenor voice, commands, "Alexa, play Beethoven's Ninth!"

While he inclines his head and listens for the haunting opening strains, I move behind him, stealthy as a fox, and shove him with all my physical strength into the small room. He stumbles and pitches forward at the same time I pull the door shut. He lets out a roar, and I scream as loudly as I can, "Alexa, lock the guest room door!"

There's a momentary silence followed by the click of a lock.

He's my prisoner.

And there's no music playing, except in my head.

Nigel pulls at the doorknob and shouts, "Alexa, unlock the bloody guest room door!"

"It won't work, Nigel," I call out to him, "I've hacked your Alexa account."

"You've what?" There's a pause of incredulity. "You cahn't be serious."

I lean against the door, breathing heavily. "I downloaded your account information, and this past weekend added myself as a user to your Alexa. I taught her my voice and this morning deleted your profile as a user."

"That's impossible," he says, eventually. "The master code is at Amazon.com. There's no way you could change that code."

"You let me in, Nigel," I say triumphantly. "You clicked on the software link I sent you. The malware I embedded went straight to Amazon.com and injected a line of code into your Alexa account. Just one teeny weeny string. That's all it took. Afterwards, it was easy. I removed your 'lock door' command and added it to *my* set of commands.

"You are goddamn kidding me," he yells through the door.

"Everything got activated when you commanded Alexa to play Beethoven's Ninth," I shout back. "I knew you wouldn't say no to that."

"Where the fuck did you learn how to do it?" he says. He wants to sound pissed off, but admiration in his voice leaks through the door.

"Mike loved Alexa and learned all the ins and outs. We used to play with Alexa together, figuring out her weaknesses."

There's a long silence.

"Madsy?" he says. He must be standing up against the door because his voice is suddenly intimate and close. "Remember what I said? We could be a great team, you and I. With our combined skills we could go places. Forget about today and let's start over. We're good together. Think about it before you do something you'll regret."

"You're a lowlife, Nigel. You're going down for what you did to Mike, and what you're doing in Utopia. I'm going upstairs."

"Wait, Madeline!"

I won't make the same mistake again. No more heroics in anyone's basement.

I dial 911.

At the top of the stairs, so much adrenaline is pumping, I'm tempted to tell the dispatcher I have a homicidal maniac under lock and key in his own guest room, that there's illegal pornography on his computer, that he murdered my husband, and is threatening to kill me too. I resist the urge. The first question he asks is, "Where are you, ma'am?" Nigel's address is right at my fingertips.

"Please come quickly. There's a man here threatening me. He's dangerous."

They'll send officers straight away, he says, and I should sit tight and not provoke the man further. I do not parse that. They have a tough job.

As backup, I call Karla Mahoney's police station and leave a message with her sergeant. "Mike Alvarez's killer is Nigel Welbourne. He's confessed. I've made a citizen's arrest in his house. Detective Mahoney should call when she has a moment."

My whole body is still shaking when I hear a terrible splintering of glass, like a car crashing through a picture window. It takes a few seconds to register that he's picked up a heavy object and smashed his way out of the guest room— the big reinforced plate-glass window on the lake front. He's coming to get me—probably sprinting around the house at this moment, heading for the front door.

Think!

Panicked, I yell out, "Alexa, lock all outside doors!"

I run into the living room and look around wildly for a place to hide. But there isn't one, not in this open space. Where can I get a weapon? One of his cooking knives? There's a poker near the fireplace and I grab it. What a cliché, a young woman in mortal danger, wielding a poker. *God.* If he comes anywhere near me, I'll smash his head like a pumpkin.

He's at the door, rattling the doorknob, and my heart stops beating. No more playing at spies. This is for real.

There's nowhere to go, and he is hammering what sounds like an axe against the door, slamming the wood until it splinters through.

What a brave heroine I am, screaming with terror, swinging the poker down in an accelerating arc, striking the hand that comes through the door and fumbles for the lock, smashing his wrist and hearing his screams and the shriek of police sirens approaching the house.

CHAPTER 49

One week later, in early November, my mother and I meet Karla at her headquarters in Marathon, New York, not far from Ovid, where I first met her so many months ago.

She examines us through her glasses and says, "Madeline, honey, I hope you and Janet are doing okay."

"We're fine," Mom says, unexpectedly. She is quieter these days, not unaware that her memory is seeping away, and she's more and more dependent on me.

"Janet, you should know you've been cleared of all charges in the death of Ostap Kolisnyk—"

"That's Andri, Mom—"

"The shooting, as far as you're concerned, was ruled an accident." Karla reaches across her desk and puts her hand on Mom's. Tears are welling up in Mom's eyes. She's still not able to talk about Andri without crying.

"Your Andri—Kolisnyk—was quite a character." Karla squeezes Mom's hand. "He worked in Ukraine, helping oligarchs hide their assets and their mistresses. But he drew the line at crimes against kids."

"He wouldn't harm a fly," Mom says, blowing her nose.

A look passes between me and Karla, who says, "Kolisnyk's motives in your house were unclear. He appears to have been hiding from the Ukrainian authorities, but he was also an undercover agent with Interpol, working to shut down an international pornography ring. The Americans got him out of Ukraine and recruited him. Apparently, he escaped with millions from those wealthy Ukrainians."

So Mom and I will be living high on the hog with Andri's tainted money. I'm fine with that.

Andri would have been so interested in Nigel's video game. We'll never know for sure what Andri's story was, but in our family, he became a benign presence that we grew to love.

Karla says, "Congratulations, Madeline—you seem to have single-handedly figured out how to access a major juvenile pornography ring." Mom stares at me, confused.

"So the passwords worked," I say. "How did you identify the players?"

The detective smiles. "I didn't do any of it. I handed your evidence and phone recordings to the FBI, who have an ongoing investigation in New York State. Once the agents had your special passwords, they could track down all the players. Those FBI guys were blown away by that video game. And by your unorthodox investigation. They'll be contacting you soon about the details of how you broke the case—"

"She broke it by meeting strange men in the woods behind our house," Mom says. "After midnight." She's pissed off because she's forgotten everything I told her.

Karla picks up the prickly vibes and says hastily, "I got myself a warrant to search Nigel Welbourne's house and found evidence to support your theory that he murdered Mike."

"His confession to me? On my phone?"

"Well, that too." She leans forward. "We searched Welbourne's bedroom and found piles of notes and articles about skydiving mishaps. These included magazines in which he'd circled the exact same knots found in Mike's chute." *Oh, what an incredible spy I was, managing to search his computers, but not his bedroom.*

"But Nigel isn't a skydiver! It's impossible that he found Mike's chute at night and inserted those knots."

"Too true, Madeline, those were my thoughts exactly. But it all made sense—Mike's involvement—the motive—so I followed up. The manager of the drop zone recognized a photo of him."

A shivery moment. Mike told everyone about our proposed skydiving trip.

"The manager particularly remembered this guy with a British accent," Karla says. "He told 'em he was interested in joining the place and wanted to see how the kits were stored,"

"Is this the older professor you were sleeping with?" Mom says.

"We've arrested him," Karla says nimbly, "on suspicion of murder and dealing in illegal pornography. I'm sure there'll be further charges as the FBI completes its investigation."

***

A week later I call Judy and invite her to have dinner with me at the Heights Café, a restaurant not far from her house. "My treat," I say, before she can hang up. "I owe you some explanations."

She hesitates, then says, "Fine. Why not? Tonight. Seven thirty and I'll pay for my own dinner, thank you."

Perhaps she has good reason to be aggrieved, but she *did* steal my husband and treat me like shit at Cornell.

Judy is punctual—of course she is—and we greet each other like robots, stiff and straight-backed. Later, sipping white wine, in the soft light of the restaurant, I'm taken aback to see how attractive she is.

No more game playing for me. I apologize immediately for breaking into offices at Cornell and for accusing her of tampering with our parachutes. Her exterior cracks a moment—she's surprised by my candor—and I relax, no longer intimidated. I don't need her for career advancement.

I tell her about Joe—his ruse, his supposed warrant to search the department's computers, and my certainty that she, Judy, was the villain.

"Your spreadsheets and numbers showed me what I wanted to see, namely evidence of many sales of illicit software." I smile and shake my head, acknowledging how warped my brain became. "Your only crime was you were too organized and efficient, too good at your job."

For a moment, a glimpse of humanity breaks through on her enigmatic face, and she smiles back, tilting her head. "Well, I have a confession to make too," she says. "I knew you were doing weird stuff in the department, so I called on George Snyder to keep tabs on you. I warned him on pain of firing to keep my identity secret. Unfortunately, he became fixated on your mother, and I really regret the grief he caused you."

The conversation is distasteful; she doesn't like apologizing, but it's a clearing of the air. We're never going to be best friends, but I feel much better about taking the initiative to speak to her.

My vertigo at Judy's house remains a mystery. It was probably triggered by standing up too fast, or too much adrenaline, which has happened to me before. Unpleasant, but not sinister. Judy assures me that my reaction to the hard apple cider was mystifying to her. We leave it at that and order rich desserts.

Judy is still absorbing the shock waves of Nigel's arrest. The explanation of how I brought him down is enough to make her choke on her chocolate mousse.

"I hacked his Alexa code," I say, "and locked him in his own guest room."

She puts down her fork and regards me with renewed interest. "How did you access his account?"

"I downloaded the hard drive of his computer."

Something in her shifts, a slight perturbation of the air.

Judy has worshipped with the others at the shrine of Nigel for a long time, and now the department has lost its star. I bet she'll take more than a few moments to examine why she didn't suspect him.

She eats her dessert in silence, then meets my eyes.

"So the work you presented to the department really *was* yours, not Mike's." It's not a question, just an acknowledgment.

I accept it gracefully and nod without a word.

"Mike was involved in Nigel's shady business—supplying software," I say. I hadn't planned on mentioning Mike, but in this interlude of truth telling, it seems right.

Her face registers shock. "Mike—?"

"So he didn't tell you either." The revelation is bizarrely comforting.

A waiter brings coffee, and we spend a few minutes in silent communion, thinking about Mike, who was beautiful but weak, and lost to both of us.

It's all in the past. She loved him too.

When we say our brief goodbyes, shaking hands like old business associates, everything I found hard to take about Judy has softened.

I'm liberated from her at last.

After dinner, I'm a bit light headed, and decide to come to equilibrium before driving home. Did Judy slip something into my wine? Will she follow me?

Stop this. Of course Judy didn't. And *of course* she won't. The investigation is over.

As I pull out of the parking lot, I activate Bluetooth and call Joe. Like it or not, I've become intertwined with his long and lonely quest to avenge his family. I haven't spoken to him in weeks, but now feel an obligation to share with him the final pieces of the puzzle.

For the first time, I use the contacts of my real phone, not the burner, calling the number now listed under "Joe," not "Mom."

I let the phone ring, rather than hanging up and calling back later. It feels weird to have a so-called normal phone call with Joe. Why isn't he picking up?

"Madeline?" His voice sounds far away, puzzled, and sleepy. Either he was fast asleep or the connection is bad. This is the guy who used to meet me after midnight. It's barely ten thirty.

"Joe, can you meet me—?"

"When? Now?" His voice cracks a bit on the "Now." I picture his sleepy head, his deep blue eyes, and mussed hair.

"No—tomorrow—at my house, after two o'clock? I have an update for you."

"Can I take you out to lunch?" he says. Suddenly he's in full voice, transmitting loud and clear. I've woken him up.

"No, thanks. I have lots to tell you and would rather do it on my home turf."

"Can you give me a hint?"

I switch my headlights to bright, carefully navigating a dark patch of rural countryside. This is where deer run out of the shadows, their eyes red as they thud against metal and glass. I'm watching the road when I say, "You probably know by now the porn link at Cornell turned out to be Nigel, not Judy. He's going down."

"Christ, Madeline. Why didn't you call as soon as you knew?"

Because my life isn't ruled by you anymore.

"I'm letting you know now." I terminate the call.

The Wednesday of our meeting in mid-November is cold, gray, and windy, with brown, curled-up leaves swirling in the air. When a car crunches on the driveway, I stand at the living-room window and watch Joe heading to our front door. Never before has he arrived like a regular person, visible and solid.

Torvill runs to the door when the doorbell rings, panting with anticipation. In his doggy head he still waits for Daddy Andri, to show up. Instead, Joe blows into the house, a leaf or two in his hair, and squats down to fondle Torvill's ears. "Do you remember me, Torvill Eriksson? Yes, you do, yes, you do." And my fickle dog rolls over onto his back.

The living room is warm, a fake gas fire in the grate. Mom's in her favorite chair with Tosca on her lap. They're inseparable.

"Joe, this is my mother, Janet Geiger."

Mom gently puts the cat down, stands in front of Joe, and extends her hand. "You're one of Madsy's friends." She examines him. "You're the one who never came into the house. So...welcome."

He takes her hand. "I didn't know Madeline had such an elegant and beautiful mother."

"This one's a keeper," Mom says to me. She offers to make coffee and disappears into the kitchen.

In two strides he's up against me, encircling me, pinning my arms to my sides and kissing my cheek. "I've missed you, Madeline."

How easily I could forgive him and succumb to his familiar fragrance of pine trees and wood smoke. His grief and intensity always resonated with me. How close I came to falling in love with him. *How many times has he done this before? Who else fell for his charms?* He used me, exploited me, exposed me to danger, and, most of all, lied to me on day one, day two, day three...

They all lied to me. Mike, Andri, Joe, and Nigel.

My history with men is studded with deception. Perhaps, if it's truth I crave, I should listen to myself.

Torvill muscles in between Joe and me and gives a small woof.

"Listen to my dog and go sit down," I say. "Let me tell you how I figured out it was Nigel."

My anger at Joe has evaporated, leaving behind nothing but vague regret.

Reluctantly, he pulls away from me and sits on the edge of a chair in his characteristic pose, the way he sat on tree stumps and rocks, hands dangling between his legs. Without embellishment, I tell him about the video game, Mike's passwords, Alexa, and Beethoven's Ninth. He shakes his head at all of it, saying, "You're unbelievable."

"Mike was innocent. He didn't know he was helping a pornographer."

Mom brings a sublime coffee aroma into the room, a tray of steaming mugs. Then, beaming at us, she settles back down with her beloved cat.

"Hi," she says to Joe. "Do I know you?"

He looks at me quizzically, and I give him a slight shake of my head. *Let it go.*

I say, "I'm leaving Ithaca in April. I've taken a job in Boston at a startup doing cybersecurity—"

"Whoa," he says. "Just like that?"

"They hired me—at an obscene salary—soon after I applied. So you corrupted me, Joe. I'm going back to being a spy."

"No kidding..." He becomes pensive, and we chill in the cozy room for a while, listening to the crackling of the fire.

"Are your pets going with you to Boston?"

It takes a second to deconstruct his thought processes. "Of course! The whole family is coming, my mom too. I've put the house on the market."

"You'll probably get a nice chunk of change for this big old house. Those woods."

"The actual house is falling apart. If you go outside and take a look, you'll notice how the gutters are sagging and the window frames are crumbling. You've never seen it during the day."

Joe swivels around, taking in the wooden beams above the living room. "You love this house."

"I don't love it," Mom says. "Too far from town."

"It was *our* house, Mike's and mine..." I pause, remembering.

Darling Mike, who betrayed me in so many ways.

"I was happy to live a secluded life with him in the country, but now...it's lonely out here...we should be in a neighborhood where Mom and I can make friends."

He absorbs this and nods slowly. "I'll miss you, Madeline, that's for sure." His tone is wistful.

I'll miss him too. Definitely won't forget him. "What will you do now?" *Find another sucker like me?*

He smiles ruefully, embarrassed. "I'm volunteering for community service—ready to give up life on the run, the vigilante life..."

His admission shocks me, but I'm not surprised. Joe is a good guy at heart.

"Did you turn yourself in?" I ask.

"Your Detective Karla Mahoney and I have an—understanding—she won't file charges." Of course, the fake badge! She must have figured out it was Joe as soon as she heard my story.

He says, "When all this is over, I'm going back to being a cop."

"That's great news." I'm happy for him and have a small surge of joy on his behalf. I hope it's true. I have no way of knowing.

He runs his hand through his hair and catches my mother's eye. "Maybe I'll apply for a job in Boston..."

I've become a legend at Skydive Finger Lakes: the woman who survived a parachute disaster.

Oh, how I've missed my carefree flying days, the rush of wind and sky, the final downward floating, like a princess under a bright canopy.

My personal skydiving trainer, Annalise, palpates my arms and legs like we're at a cattle auction. "Muscles like marshmallows," she says. "But don't worry, you're young and strong. We'll rebuild from scratch. You'll be landing on those legs in no time."

When I tell her I've been rebuilding for months at physical therapy, she's not impressed. "PT is for children," she scoffs.

Physical training isn't the issue. The big question everyone is asking of course is will I have what it takes to jump from the plane? I've had skydiving nightmares for months. *What if my parachute doesn't open?*

Friends have offered to jump with me in tandem, hooked to their harness like a neophyte; but I'd die before I'd do that. It would be an admission of failure, an embarrassment. Jumping under someone else's steam is *not* who I am. My body is a battlefield of ridges and valleys and dented hardware—the body of a woman who defied gravity and survived. It's the body of a warrior who decrypted an alien world and triumphed against a bully.

I'm the fearless spy who took down a pornography ring.

Of course I'll jump.

ACKNOWLEDGEMENTS

So many people helped in the creation of *A Reluctant Spy*.

First and foremost, Todd Supple, skydiving consultant extraordinaire, who generously volunteered his time, expertise, and personal anecdotes for use in the book.

Thanks also to my wonderful editors, who made unique contributions at various stages along the way: Lauren Baratz-Logsted, Rob Costello, Sara J. Henry, Ann Kelly, Allison Maretti, and Elizabeth White.

There's a special place in heaven for my beta readers, who gave me detailed and bracingly honest feedback: Felicia Ansty, Sharon Durr, Dominique Moore, and Tamara Watson.

I have heartfelt gratitude for the many readers and critiquers of this novel: Nick Barner, Deb Begley, Sheila Bloch, Mary Bowes, Steve Browne, Pat Carlson, Curtis Chin, Pat Civale, Lisa David, Julie Dawning, Gaby Guardado, Pat Holmes, Emily Johnson, Janis Kelly, Hiromi Komiya, Edy Krauss, Chris Kowalchuk, Martha Lasley, Gabi Lorino-Tyner, William Loving, Jen Mann, Susan Mattern, Jesse McBride, Paul McEuen, Kevin McMahon, June Meyer, Axel Milens, Nicky Morris, Linda Myers, Colleen Radus, BJ Rae, Helen Rivers, Linda Rose, Lynn Rosenberg, Ellen Ryan, Cody Sisco, Don Small, Teddy

Swanson, Susan Wiser, Doris Wright, and Aryn Youngless.

Thanks also to the Bookies book club for reading an early version of the book and providing invaluable feedback.

I have a special thank-you for Holly Adams, the wonderful narrator of the audiobook, whose energetic, multi-voice reading brought my characters to vibrant life.

Many people have given my writing a boost in so many ways. Thank you Carol Amato, Dee Buckingham, Mary Helen Cathles, Kathy Dewart, Karen Dionne, Ruth Fisher, David Flaccus, Trisha Flaccus, Kim Gottlieb-Walker, Kathy Henion, Lisa King, Aimee Lehmann, Alan Lightman, Ellie O'Connor, and Nancy Ridenour.

There's a warm spot in my heart for the Bridge Club of Ithaca, whose members have nurtured me and supported my writing career for many years. Love you all!

And what can I say about my sister, Brenda Cooper, whose fate in life was to endure my fiction writing, book after outlandish book. I've grown to love the Brenda Gnome, who constantly perches on my shoulder, casting a sardonic but loving eye as I write. That's the shtick, Brenda: I followed your advice and became a writer.

Love and thank you to the lights of my life, Saul Teukolsky, Rachel Teukolsky, Lauren Teukolsky, Caleb Stapleton, Josh Adams, Noah Adams, and Jacob Adams. With special mention to Gordy Stapleton and the Clydester.

My husband, Saul, gets the last word. He is, in all things, my beloved partner in crime.

ABOUT THE AUTHOR

Roselyn Teukolsky was born in Johannesburg, South Africa, where she graduated from the University of the Witwatersrand with a B.Sc. in Math and Chemistry. She immigrated to the US when she was 23 and graduated from Cornell University with an M.S. in Mathematics Education. She taught Math and Computer Science for many years, mostly at Ithaca High School in Upstate New York.

She is the author of the Barron's review book for AP Computer Science, which is currently in its 12th edition, and also *How to Play Bridge with Your Spouse ... and Survive* (Master Point Press).

Roselyn retired from teaching in 2009. Since then she has worked full time as a writer of crime fiction. She lives in Pasadena, California with her husband, Saul Teukolsky. *A Reluctant Spy* is her debut novel.